# The Hunters Club

Alis Hawkins is a founding member of Welsh crime writers' collective, Crime Cymru, and a member of the Society of Authors and the Crime Writers' Association. Two of her four Teifi Valley Coroner novels have been shortlisted for the CWA's prestigious Historical Dagger award. She lives on the Welsh border in the Forest of Dean with her partner, and makes regular forays to west Wales and Oxford.

# Also by Alis Hawkins

## The Teifi Valley Coroner Series

*None So Blind*
*In Two Minds*
*Those Who Know*
*Not One Of Us*

## The Oxford Mysteries

*A Bitter Remedy*
*The Skeleton Army*
*The Hunters Club*

# THE HUNTERS CLUB

## ALIS HAWKINS

CANELO CRIME

First published in the United Kingdom in 2025 by

Canelo Crime, an imprint of
Canelo Digital Publishing Limited,
20 Vauxhall Bridge Road,
London SW1V 2SA
United Kingdom

A Penguin Random House Company
The authorised representative in the EEA is Dorling Kindersley Verlag GmbH. Arnulfstr. 124, 80636 Munich, Germany

Copyright © Alis Hawkins 2025

The moral right of Alis Hawkins to be identified as the creator of this work has been asserted in accordance with the Copyright, Designs and Patents Act, 1988.
All rights reserved. No part of this publication may be reproduced or transmitted in any form or by any means, electronic or mechanical, including photocopy, recording, or any information storage and retrieval system, without permission in writing from the publisher.
No part of this book may be used or reproduced in any manner for the purpose of training artificial intelligence technologies or systems. In accordance with Article 4(3) of the DSM Directive 2019/790, Canelo expressly reserves this work from the text and data mining exception.

A CIP catalogue record for this book is available from the British Library.

Print ISBN 978 1 80436 685 1
Ebook ISBN 978 1 80436 688 2

This book is a work of fiction. Names, characters, businesses, organizations, places and events are either the product of the author's imagination or are used fictitiously. Any resemblance to actual persons, living or dead, events or locales is entirely coincidental.

Cover design by Sarah Whittaker

Cover images © *A View of the Conduit (a), part of Carfax Church (b), the Piazza called the Butter Market (c), the Town Hall (d), the west Front of Christ Church College (e), &c. in the University of* OXFORD from the British Library King's Topographical Collection via Flickr

Printed and bound in Great Britain by Clays Ltd, Elcograf S.p.A.

Look for more great books at
www.canelo.co | www.dk.com

*In memory of my Mum, Elizabeth Hawkins.*

*You were one in a million, Mum.*

*Part 1*

## Chapter 1

*Non*

For the umpteenth time in the last five minutes, I peered around the corner from my hidden vantage point towards Oxford Castle. I was damp from the early morning mist and fed up with waiting. It was after seven o'clock; why weren't the prison's gates open?

I stared at the Castle walls and wondered what first impression they made on people coming up from the railway station into Oxford. They weren't exactly Matthew Arnold's dreaming spires. Nobody dreamed of the Castle – not unless they were having a nightmare. It had been a prison for more than two hundred years, and it showed. Even if you'd painted those pitiless walls sky blue and hung flowers from the huge, iron-banded gates, they'd still have looked unwelcoming. It would've been like putting a wedding dress on a bull.

Through the mist, I could see somebody standing less than a hundred yards away, right opposite the prison gates.

Felicia Skene.

My job would have been far easier if Miss Skene hadn't been there, but to be honest there'd been precious little chance of her staying away. She'd be waiting for the same person I'd come to see.

I wondered if the prison looked as intimidating to Miss Skene as it did to me. Probably not. She was in and out of those gates like clockwork.

I shivered and stifled a cough. The river mist had caught the coal smoke from the city's chimneys and turned it into something that was a taste on your tongue and a scratch in your throat. And there wasn't much hope of it clearing in the next few hours. The sun was just about up, but it was stuck behind clouds that were still full of dust from Krakatoa.

Felicia Skene didn't look as if the cold or the mist bothered her. She stood tall and upright, wrapped in the kind of woollen cloak that had gone out of fashion before I was born, and her small-brimmed hat was there for warmth not decorative value. Still, I was the last person to criticise what anybody wore.

The little dog that had been lying at her feet suddenly sprang up. Miss Skene didn't move from her position but something in her posture changed, and I followed her gaze across the road. The prison gates were opening, and people started stumbling out – people who hadn't been able to pay a fine or, if the magistrates had been particularly bad-tempered, hadn't been given the option.

I counted only seven men alongside the young woman I was there to see. Evidently quite a few of the usual disorderly drunks, brawlers, wife beaters and prostitutes had stumped up the shillings they needed to pay for their misdemeanours instead of putting themselves through days of pointless hard labour.

The men all gave Miss Skene a nod or a tip of the cap as they walked past her – probably straight to the nearest pub. But as soon as the young woman saw her standing there, she stopped in her tracks. Then something unexpected happened. I'd expected her to ignore Miss Skene or shrug her off as she walked by, but she didn't. She just broke down. Even from where I was standing, I could see her shoulders shaking as she sobbed.

Felicia Skene stepped forward and embraced her and the girl just sobbed harder.

I sighed. I was going to have to wait my turn.

I pulled back into Bulwarks Lane and skipped up the steps. I knew where Felicia Skene lived. I'd just have to possess my soul in patience until she was finished with Miss Sarah Critchley.

I wanted to talk to that young woman about the encounter with an undergraduate that had landed her in Oxford Prison.

## Chapter 2

### *Basil*

I was still eating breakfast when I heard the characteristic footsteps of the messenger's boy on my staircase. His tendency to take the stairs an exuberant two at a time had been trained out of him in the four years and more that he'd worked for the college, and now he trotted lightly up the stairs, like a marionette dancing on a puppeteer's strings. I waited, hoping he'd pass my door and continue up the stairs. Instead, a confident knock sounded.

Setting my coffee down, I opened the door and was greeted with a bright morning smile and the young man's increasingly smart appearance. He'd recently celebrated his eighteenth birthday and had been furnished with a new suit of clothes. After a seemingly interminable probationary period, the college messenger now allowed him to venture outside the walls of Jesus, so it was essential that he represent the college in a well-dressed and respectable manner.

'Morning, Mr Rice. Note just arrived for you,' he said, handing it to me by one pristine corner. 'Shall I wait?'

'Yes, please, Fred.'

There was no envelope. The note was simply folded and addressed to 'Mr B. Rice, Jesus College'.

*Magdalen College*
*Friday 18th Oct*

*Dear Rice*
   *Apologies for trespassing on your time when you're no doubt still getting to grips with new men at this point*

*in term, but might I beg the favour of a few moments of your time this morning in my rooms at Magdalen?*

*Yours, etc.*

*W. Kaye, Senior Proctor*

It was typical of Kaye to have included his title. Not because he wished to vaunt his authority, quite the reverse; Kaye was the kind of man who never assumed that one would remember his position.

'No reply, Fred,' I told the boy and watched him skip down the staircase with the ease of a well-heeled undergraduate.

My curiosity aroused as to what the Senior Proctor could want from me, I finished my breakfast, donned cap and gown and sallied forth to find out.

—

Magdalen College was less than ten minutes' walk from Jesus and as I ducked into the porter's lodge, I glanced along the road to the east where work to widen and improve Magdalen Bridge had been in progress for months. I wondered whether the disruption affected the peace of the college.

I might have discussed the matter with Kaye but when I was shown to his first-floor rooms, the Senior Proctor lost no time in idle chit-chat.

'Thank you for coming so promptly, Rice. I hope not to trespass on your time too egregiously.'

The Senior Proctor and I were more or less contemporaries. Kaye, having taken his degree a couple of years before me would now be thirty-seven or -eight but with his thin, greying hair he looked several years older. He was a theologian and, in an academic tradition now honoured more in the breach than the observance, he'd taken holy orders.

I sat, as invited, in a comfortable wing-backed chair which commanded a view of substantial lawns. Sitting outside the city walls, Magdalen enjoyed extensive grounds and had a spacious grandeur that my own college, nestled in the crowded heart of the medieval city, could never aspire to. Jesus College's very modest Principal's garden looked like a pauper's portion when compared with the deer park which Magdalen's head of house had at his disposal.

'I'm afraid I've asked you here to discuss a rather ticklish subject,' Kaye said, wordlessly offering me a glass of sherry, which I declined in the same manner. Any sensitive subject required a clear head and the Senior Proctor's obvious embarrassment was a trifle alarming. Was *I* the ticklish subject under discussion here?

I cleared my throat, trying to quell my unease. 'I assume that, since you invited me here *ex officio*, as it were, this is a proctorial matter?' Though the proctors' role as overseers of undergraduate discipline didn't extend to college fellows, a well-disposed proctor might choose to approach a colleague confidentially if he'd heard rumours to his discredit. I took great pains to prevent such rumours, but the possibility of their arising had lodged a constant fear somewhere between my shoulder blades, as if I might be shot in the back without warning.

Kaye sat down, heavily. He'd followed my lead in forgoing a glass of sherry, but his expression suggested that he might have done better to pour himself one. He was finding it difficult to meet my eye and his fingers drummed on the arms of his chair.

'Perhaps it might be best if I start with why I wished to speak to you, particularly, Rice.'

I waited with mounting alarm, uncrossing my legs when I became aware that my raised foot was twitching rapidly in time with my racing heart. 'Please do,' I managed.

'You've been of service to the University on a couple of recent occasions when certain individuals found themselves in –' Kaye hesitated slightly – '*disconcerting* circumstances.'

I gazed at him. Disconcerting wasn't the word I would have chosen to refer to murder, nor to riotous behaviour and blackmail, but I let his description slide with some relief. It seemed that I had not, after all, been summoned because of rumours about my sexual proclivities.

'I hesitate to intrude on your time and goodwill once more, but the Junior Proctor and I find ourselves in need of your insight.' He paused, blinking and meeting my eye fleetingly.

'If this involves criminal activity of some kind, Senior Proctor, then I'm not sure—'

'That's just it, you see, Rice. We're not sure any criminality has taken place. Not per se. To come to the point,' he said, his voice becoming louder, as if broaching the subject required actual muscular effort, 'very early this morning, when I returned to college after patrolling the city, I found one of our young men sitting on the pavement outside the gate, insensible.' He stopped, abruptly.

I waited. A drunken undergraduate was hardly unusual, though few chose to display their inebriation outside their college gates.

Kaye blinked rapidly. 'He'd been bound hand and foot, gagged and had a hood or bag of some kind placed over his head.'

He produced something from his pocket and handed it to me.

'This was pinned to the hood.'

I found myself looking at a printed invitation card. On one side, the simple message read,

**Supper**

**Trinity College**

**7 p.m. Tuesday, 9th October**

On the other there was a single word: **VENATORES**. Above it stood an emblem: a silhouetted lion with one forepaw raised, the base of a winged V resting lightly on its back.

'It seems,' Kaye said, 'to be intended as some species of calling card.'

I stared at the invitation, a frisson of unease raising the hairs on the nape of my neck. *Venatores*: the Latin word for hunters.

## Chapter 3

*Non*

I stood on the corner of New Inn Hall Street East and stared across at the second little house. Inside Miss Skene would be offering comfort – and probably breakfast – to Sarah Critchley.

Basil Rice – whose college was a quick two minutes' walk from where I stood – had once told me that, in the eighteenth century, New Inn Hall Street had been known as the Street of the Seven Deadly Sins. Knowing the kind of people who went in and out of Miss Skene's house, that seemed entirely appropriate.

While I waited for Sarah Critchley to emerge, I let my mind dwell on Basil. Since I'd been tutoring at Somerville Hall and writing for various newspapers and periodicals, I hadn't had time for the Welsh lessons I'd been giving him, so he and I didn't see as much of each other as we'd used to. Now, I relied on him coming to dinner once a week to keep in touch. My landlady and cousin, Lily Maddox, was very fond of Basil and she thought it did him good to escape from the exclusively male environment of his college. 'Those dons live like monks,' she'd say; 'I don't know how they think they're going to prepare boys for life when they know so little about it themselves.'

She was right. Basil was unmarried and he lived in college with all the other celibates, but that didn't stop him thinking he had the right to advise me on how to run my life. I was still furious from some unsolicited advice he'd given me the previous Friday.

I was just getting cross again at the thought of some of the things he'd said when the door to Miss Skene's house opened.

I skipped over the road. 'Miss Critchley?'

She pulled her threadbare green coat a bit more tightly around her, as if it would protect her from me. 'Who wants to know?'

'My name is Non Vaughan. Well, Rhiannon, really—'

'Miss Vaughan? I was on my way to leave you a note at the *Mercury* offices!' Sarah Critchley whipped an envelope out of her coat pocket and held it out to me.

'Miss Skene said I should write to you.'

'Did she indeed?' It was a surprise to me that Felicia Skene knew I existed.

I opened the envelope and unfolded the small sheet of writing paper.

> Dear Miss Vaughan
> I would be very glad if you would call on me today at my home to discuss my recent imprisonment by the Vice Chancellor. I believe my treatment may be of some interest to you.
> Yours very sincerely,
> Sarah Critchley (Miss)

I could see she'd written the note herself. The handwriting was nicely legible, and the spelling was good, but you could tell it hadn't been written by a regular writer. There was something about the way the letters were formed that made you think of a tongue sticking out of the corner of a mouth. Where I came from, there was a word for that kind of effort. A Welsh word: *panso*. Concentrating hard to do your best.

An address had been written at the bottom of the letter, telling me what I already knew. Sarah Critchley lived less than five minutes' walk from my own lodgings in Jericho. I'd probably never have heard about what had happened to her otherwise. But, luckily for me, our maid-of-all-work, Edie, was a mine of local gossip and, according to her, Sarah being thrown into prison 'for no good reason' was the talk of the parish. If half of what Edie'd told me about what had happened to Sarah was true, a miscarriage of justice had taken place. In fact, there had been no justice at all.

'Seeing as Miss Skene recommended me,' I said, 'perhaps we should discuss matters with her?' And, before Sarah could answer, I knocked on the door.

When the maid answered and saw me standing there, she gave a twisted smile, as if she'd lost a bet but admired the skill of the winner. 'You'd better come in. She's expecting you.'

Without further explanation, she turned back into the house and opened the door to Miss Skene's little parlour.

'Miss Vaughan. As you predicted,' she announced as if she was speaking to a friend, not a mistress. 'And Miss Critchley's back with her.'

The room was small and the addition of Sarah and me made it feel crowded, even with the maid standing outside in the passage. The chairs facing the hearth knocked arms with each other and there was a little table under the window with a small vase with three chrysanthemums in it, one yellow, one red and one orange. I wondered if one of Miss Skene's visitors had leaned over somebody's garden wall and picked them to give her.

Even though the room was south-facing, the gloom of the day and the narrowness of the street made it murky enough to need a lamp. The decoration didn't help. The walls were lined with bookshelves and heavy-framed paintings of landscapes.

Miss Skene stood up as we came in. The fact that she hadn't left the parlour to get on with her work as soon as the door closed on Sarah Critchley backed up the servant's story about my being expected. Felicia Skene was famous for never sitting still. When she wasn't at the prison or the women's refuge or in the houses of the great and the good petitioning them for something, she was writing articles and books. And letters. According to Basil she wrote to everybody from ex-convicts to the Prime Minister.

'Miss Vaughan.' She inclined her head in an old-fashioned kind of courtesy.

I was surprised to hear Miss Skene's faint accent. She was so much a part of Oxford life that I'd forgotten she was Scottish.

The maid or housekeeper or whatever she was was still hovering in the doorway. 'Make another pot of tea, shall I?'

'That would be very kind, Jane, thank you. Now, ladies,' Miss Skene looked from me to Sarah, 'do sit down.'

Sarah took the chair opposite her at the little table and, at Miss Skene's suggestion, I turned one of the armchairs around to face them.

'Jane said you were expecting me, Miss Skene?'

Despite being a lady in her sixties, Felicia Skene grinned like a schoolgirl who's just played a trick on her friends. 'Yes, indeed. I was quite certain you would take an interest in Sarah's case, and I happened to catch a glimpse of you over the road.'

I glanced at the window. She'd have had a perfect view of me standing on the corner.

'Your hair and the fact that you go hatless make you quite distinctive.'

The grin I gave Miss Skene was different from the one she'd given me; less delight, more embarrassment. 'I'll have to take pains to be less conspicuous.'

'I fear that ship has sailed, Miss Vaughan. You're becoming well known in Oxford – the *Mercury*'s lady reporter, often seen cycling around the city on a tandem tricycle which, rumour has it, you won in a bet? Those things are quite enough to make you notable, even to people who don't know that you're also a tutor at Somerville and a contributor to the *Pall Mall Gazette*.'

Felicia Skene had made it her business to find out about me. Why?

She answered the question without me asking it. 'Never fear, my dear, I've not been spying on you. We simply have acquaintances in common.'

I wanted to ask who those acquaintances were, but that was a question for another time.

'Miss Critchley says that you suggested she should write to me?'

'I did indeed. Knowing your relationship with the London press, I felt sure that Sarah's case would be of great interest to you.'

Sarah Critchley made a small sound of distress and Miss Skene turned to her. I remembered how she'd embraced the girl when she'd started to sob outside the prison. If Felicia Skene hadn't been who she was, it would have been an extraordinary sight – an upper-class lady embracing a convict. But Felicia Skene was a most unusual person.

I followed her gaze. Underneath Sarah Critchley's red eyes and tear-stained face, she was a striking young woman with something about her that made you look twice. A tilt of the head that told you she might not be educated or well off, but she wasn't somebody to be overlooked.

'Miss Critchley,' I said, 'would you mind telling me how you came to be in prison? All I know is Jericho gossip.'

And you couldn't write gossip in the papers. At least not in the *Oxford Mercury*.

Sarah turned from me to Miss Skene, looking for reassurance.

'You said you wanted to do something, my dear,' the older woman said, gently. 'Something to clear your name? I believe Miss Vaughan may be able to help.'

Sarah Critchley swallowed. She'd been going to deliver her note to me via the *Mercury*'s offices on the High Street, so she'd have had time to think about what she was going to say when we met. Now, unexpectedly confronted with me, she wasn't prepared.

But with the best part of two years' working for the *Mercury* under my belt, I knew how to get information out of people pretty efficiently. 'You were arrested by one of the proctors on Cornmarket Street, is that right?' I asked. 'When you were talking to an undergraduate?'

'Yes, *talking*,' she said bitterly. 'A little chat. He started it – the student. He was very polite – "excuse me, miss", like that – wanting to know if I could tell him where to buy some pretty ribbons for his little sister. He'd seen the ribbons on my hat. That was his excuse, anyway.'

'Excuse?' I knew what she meant; I just wanted her to tell me.

'Course it was,' she said, scornfully. 'I knew that as soon as he didn't just take himself off when I'd told him what he wanted to know. "Badcock's on Queen Street", I told him. That's where he'd get the best ribbons for his money. "And I should know", I told him. "I work there." I was going home for my tea, and I wasn't best pleased to be stopped, if I'm honest. But you don't want to be uncivil, do you? And I thought it would be all right because—'

She stopped as the door opened and Jane brought the tea in. The three of us watched, silently, as she laid clean cups out. Jane probably knew everything that went on under Miss Skene's roof – it was a very small house – but it was one thing to know she was probably eavesdropping and another thing to actually speak in front of her.

'So,' I said once she'd gone, 'if this student didn't thank you politely and leave you in peace after you'd told him where to get his ribbons, what did he do?'

'Started asking me about myself. Did Badcock's treat me well, did they pay me a decent wage – that kind of chit-chat.' She paused. 'Well, he didn't look like a masher, one of those flashy dressers who fancy themselves with the girls. He seemed honest. Bit shy, to be truthful. And I'd seen him about. Didn't see any harm in exchanging a few polite words. They don't get to talk to girls much, do they, the students?

Don't see a female from one month's end to the next in those colleges of theirs.'

That was true enough. Dons might be allowed to marry now – and most of the younger ones did – but their wives and sisters lived at a safe distance on St Giles or in the modern suburbs up the Banbury and Woodstock roads. Heaven forbid that they should be seen in the cloistered quads.

'Well, he'd just worked up the courage to ask me if he could walk me home – which I wouldn't've let him do – when three men come out of the passageway that leads to the Clarrie Tap.' Sarah was agitated now. 'The one in the cap and gown – I suppose he was the proctor – grabs young feller-me-lad and says, "Name and college, sir. Name and college." And the other two – the bulldogs – grab me, one on each arm, like I'm a criminal. And the proctor tells them, "Lock her up. The VC can see her tomorrow." And off they drag me. Cried out something pitiful, I did. Asked the lad to explain, but he didn't say anything!'

Her accent and grammar had slipped in her distress. Badcock's wouldn't have approved. They liked their shop girls to be nicely spoken.

'Didn't anybody try and help you?' I asked.

'Couple of lads I know saw what was happenin' and tried to pull 'em off me. But one of the bulldogs told 'em it was University business and if they didn't want throwing into the cells with me, they'd better be on their way.' She looked at me. Her hackles were up just talking about what had happened and I could imagine her raising Cain when they'd dragged her off.

'Well,' she went on, 'we all know what the proctors and their bulldogs are like – do as they please, don't they, and nobody can stop 'em. So Frank and Alfie – that's the lads who tried to help, Frank Dodds and Alfie Smart from down in Blackfriars where me and Mum used to live – they left me to it. Don't exactly blame 'em,' she muttered, 'but I do wish they'd knocked the proctor and his bulldogs down, then I could've run off.'

'So the proctor's officers – the bulldogs – they took you off to the cells under the Clarendon Building?' I asked.

'Yes. I kept trying to tell them we'd only been having a chat about ribbons, but they wouldn't have it.' She accepted the cup of tea Felicia Skene held out to her with a bob of the head and a 'thank you, Miss Skene'.

'I heard they made a fuss about you taking hold of the undergraduate's arm,' I said. 'Is that right?' I needed to be sure of the facts if I was going to write this up.

'I never did!' she exploded. Tea sloshed into her saucer. 'They kept saying that, but I never did lay hold of him. All I did was put my hand to him like this—' She rested her hand lightly on my forearm. 'Just for a second, much as to say, "Oh, bless your kind heart", when he asked me if he could walk me home – just like I might have done with Frank or Alfie. I wasn't going to *let* him. I *wasn't*, Miss Vaughan! We all know better than that. You're not safe if they see you walking with one of the students of an evening.'

'But that one touch of his arm was enough?' I said, taking a sip of my tea.

'Well, they went on and on about it, so I suppose it must've been. They said I'd been "detaining" him. But they was too far away to hear what we were saying so how could they *know* what I was doing?'

'So you had an unpleasant night in the cells under the Clarendon Building?'

'I did. Nearly froze to death. And then they dragged me upstairs the following morning and the Vice Chancellor came and listened to the proctor and sent me to prison for a week! He didn't even listen to a word I said. The proctor said I'd been *detaining* the student and flirting with him and that I was no better than I ought to be. And it's not true! None of it.'

'Didn't Reverend Jowett want to hear your side of things?' I asked.

'Who's Reverend Jowett?'

'The Vice Chancellor.'

'That's not what his name was,' Sarah said, quite sure of her facts. 'I can't remember what it was, but it was something ordinary. I'd've remembered Jowett.'

Somebody must have been deputising for the Vice Chancellor. I wasn't familiar enough with the Vice Chancellor's court to know whether that was normal, but I was pretty sure Benjamin Jowett wouldn't have packed Sarah off to jail.

'Well, whoever this was, didn't he ask you for your version of events?' I asked.

'He asked me how I come to be talking to the boy,' Sarah said, 'so I told him, just like I've just told you. And d'you know what he said? He said I'd encouraged that boy to loiter because I had *immoral intentions*. Immoral intentions? I was just being polite!'

'Why did he think you had immoral intentions?' I asked. I knew that was the phrase the proctors used when they thought undergraduates had it in mind to seduce a girl, so they must have suspected Sarah Critchley of wanting to take this student for a quick tumble and a few shillings.

'I don't know! All I know is, he said he'd seen me on Cornmarket Street before. Said I *paraded about* most evenings. I don't *parade about* – I walk home!'

I didn't want to admit it, but perhaps the proctor had a point. 'Why do you walk home up Cornmarket Street?' I asked. 'From Badcock's, wouldn't you be quicker walking up New Inn Hall Street to George Street and on to Walton Street?'

'I do that as a rule, but that evening I was going to the Covered Market to see what meat Rowes were selling off cheap at the end of the day. There's only me and Mum – we have to make ends meet on two women's wages. And now Badcock's won't have me back.'

Suddenly she started to cry, covering her face with her hands.

'My dear,' Miss Skene said softly, 'do you not remember? I've found a new job for you at Hyde's. They'll be expecting you tomorrow.'

Half the working women in Oxford seemed to work for Hyde's or Lucas's, the two big garment manufacturers. It wasn't as good a job as working at Badcock's drapers, but at least it was paid employment. Most girls who spent time in the prison had no choice but to go on the streets when they came out. But if Felicia Skene spoke for you, you'd be given at least half a second chance.

'Did you tell the Vice Chancellor's deputy that you had to go and buy meat?' I asked when Sarah'd calmed down again.

'Yes, and d'you know what he said?' She wiped her eyes with the backs of her hands. 'He just asked the proctor whether I'd had any meat *about my person* when I was taken up! But you know where the Clarrie Tap is, Miss Vaughan – down the alleyway by the side of the Clarence Hotel. I hadn't got as far as Market Street yet!'

Whoever'd been standing in for the Vice Chancellor would have no experience of shopping for food. He wouldn't have a clue where Rowes the butcher's was, or how you'd get to it from Badcock's.

'D'you know what he told me when he told the bulldogs to take me to the prison?' Sarah asked. 'He said he had a duty to protect his undergraduates from being corrupted.' She stared at me. '*Girls* corrupting *men*? If that's what he thinks happens, then he lives in a different world from the one I live in.'

I nodded. But the truth was, he did live in a different world. The University and the city might be cheek by jowl geographically, but they were like oil and water; their natures were very different and they didn't mix. At least, not if the University could help it.

'And when you wrote me that letter,' I asked, 'what did you want me to do?'

Sarah Critchley didn't hesitate. 'I want you to help me get my good name back! Without my reputation, there's no future for me.'

## Chapter 4

*Basil*

I stared at the Senior Proctor, the image he'd conjured up clear in my mind's eye. The unfortunate undergraduate with his hands and feet bound, the hood over his head hiding his attackers from him.

'We'd have considered it a harmless student prank,' Kaye continued, 'young men ragging on a friend…'

'Were it not for…?' I prompted.

He gave a restrained sigh. 'Were it not for the fact that he's the third undergraduate to be found bound, gagged and hooded since the beginning of term. All left outside their colleges. All discovered by myself, the Junior Proctor or the pro-proctors.'

The Michaelmas term was barely ten days old; I'd hardly mastered all our new undergraduates' names, but somebody had already taken it upon themselves to intervene very particularly in the lives of these three young men. What, if anything, were we to infer from that?

'Are they all known to each other?' I asked.

'Apparently not, and they're all from different colleges. But they do have this in common: none of them offered any suggestion as to who might have been responsible.'

'I assume you interviewed the Magdalen man personally?'

'I did. He professed complete ignorance as to who might have been responsible or what their motive might be.'

'And do you believe him?'

Kaye gave me what Non's landlady, Lily Maddox, would have called an 'old-fashioned' look. 'What I believe is beside the point, Rice. The fact is, this kind of thing is injurious to the University's good name. If we're not careful it'll end up in the press.'

'Or, worse, a student will suffer real harm.'

'Yes, of course, that's also a concern,' Kaye said. 'All the victims had some species of cloth stuffed into their mouths before the gag was tied – suffocation was a very real possibility. Whatever this is, it has to be stopped.'

With a sinking heart, I waited for him to explain the role he saw for me in all this.

'Are you quite sure you won't take a glass of sherry, Rice?'

'It's a little early for me, thank you.'

'Then a cup of coffee? The scout who serves the fellows on this staircase has a spirit burner and he makes a very creditable pot.'

I wondered how soon all senior members of the University would adopt this habit of using the undergraduates' term for servants who attended their rooms. 'Scout' seemed so dismissive, but perhaps I was being old-fashioned. Be that as it may, Kaye seemed awfully keen to offer me hospitality so, just to oblige him, I agreed, and he left the room to arrange matters.

Once the door had closed behind him, I crossed to the window. The morning mist was still drifting in opalescent wisps from the Cherwell which I could just make out beyond the trees, and the last green leaves of summer lingered on the boughs that fringed the lawns.

As I gazed over this pleasant prospect, I wondered whether the Vice Chancellor had suggested that Kaye might ask for my advice. I had, unintentionally, gained something of a reputation amongst senior figures as someone who could prevent embarrassment to the University by uncovering the truth behind disturbing events. However, unless Jowett had been uncharacteristically indiscreet, the Senior Proctor would not be aware that I owed much of my success to Non Vaughan's unorthodox and uncompromising investigative methods.

Apart from the view, Kaye's room was not unlike my own. Book-lined, slightly austere in the way that spaces designed exclusively for the use of men tend to be, but comfortable. However, unlike my own rooms, which I'd been slowly modernising ever since I'd been made a fellow, Kaye's walls looked as if they hadn't been painted in a generation. Perhaps he felt that having a preference for the decoration of one's personal surroundings was mere vanity.

I resumed my seat just before he returned.

'Coffee will be here directly,' he said. If his excursion to procure coffee had been intended to settle his mind as to what he wished to say, it had proved ineffective; his difficulty meeting my eye persisted and his discomfort revived my earlier fears. Did he suspect that these young men had been attacked because they shared my proclivities? Could he be nerving himself to ask for information he imagined I might have?

If so, my best bet was robust obliviousness. 'Kaye,' I said, briskly, 'I'm flattered that you would take me into your confidence concerning these attacks on our young men, but I'm not entirely sure how you think I might be able to help.'

The look he gave me now was devoid of embarrassment. In fact he appeared genuinely surprised. 'My dear fellow, you're far too modest. If there's a senior man in the University who can help us get to the bottom of what's going on here, it's you. You're well respected, but at the same time you're prepared to adopt, shall we say, unconventional means to do what's necessary.'

I found this characterisation slightly alarming; I didn't recognise myself as the defier of convention he described.

'I may have been useful on one or two occasions,' I allowed, 'but this concerns the undergrads – I'd have to speak to them, and they won't be aware of me at all—'

'Not aware of the man who saved a Corpus student from almost certain death? My dear Rice, you must know that your reputation precedes you with the young men who attend your lectures?'

Mentally I squirmed in embarrassment.

'Things are rarely as simple as they seem in third-hand gossip,' I said, 'or even, regrettably, as simple as newspaper reports would suggest. I was, in fact, not the prime mover in the rescue to which you refer.' I didn't dare mention Non's name. If the Senior Proctor already feared that the press would get wind of these events, then mentioning the *Mercury*'s female reporter would give him an apoplexy.

'Be that as it may, Rice, neither I nor their college authorities have managed to extract any useful information from these young men about the attacks to which they were subjected, and we *must* understand what is going on here if we're to prevent future outrages. You sit outside the normal disciplinary apparatus. The young chaps might be more forthcoming with you.'

I looked him squarely in the eye. 'To be frank, Kaye, I consider that most unlikely.' It was better not to collude with him in the fantasy he appeared to be confecting: Basil Rice, omni-competent hero, saviour of the University.

'Nevertheless, may I beg of you to try? I'd be most grateful. As would the Vice Chancellor.'

So I was right. I was here at Jowett's suggestion.

Which really left me no choice.

## Chapter 5

*Non*

After speaking to Miss Skene and Sarah Critchley, I found myself in a quandary. Reporting Sarah's story to expose the powers and prejudices of the proctors was one thing; helping her clear her name was something else altogether. I needed time to think, so instead of going home, I walked down the High Street to the coffee house on the corner of Queen's Lane.

The undergraduates at the nearby colleges – St Edmund Hall, Queen's, Magdalen and University College – thought of the coffee house as their own personal territory and that meant trouble when anybody who wasn't wearing a gown walked in. I always had to take a deep breath before opening the door, but it had to be done. They could keep their colleges as little male bastions if they liked, but I wasn't going to let them have the rest of Oxford as well, and certainly not the place where they brewed the best pot of coffee in the city.

Most of the female students at Somerville and Lady Margaret Hall didn't venture out into town much unless they were going to a lecture in one of the colleges with a chaperone. But the 'home students' – young women who were living at home or in lodgings while they were studying under the AEW, officially known as the Association for Promoting the Higher Education of Women in Oxford – weren't limited by rules about going out in groups or with a chaperone. And anyway, I wasn't a student any more.

The chatter in the coffee house stopped as I walked in, and hostile eyes stared at me. But if the gownsmen thought they could intimidate me, they had another think coming. I'd worked on a coal smack in Cardigan Bay, and the male species didn't get more rough and ready than a sailor on the coastal runs.

'At ease, gentlemen,' I said, 'female coming aboard.'

'So we see,' a voice called out. 'But nobody gave you permission, did they?'

'Good job I don't need your permission, then, isn't it?' I nodded at the waiter, who was trying not to grin. It wasn't often he saw college men being put in their place.

'You're not welcome here,' another brave boy joined in.

I glared at him. 'I don't suppose your college fellows would be particularly impressed by your lack of civility. I should remind University College men that Mr Bright was one of the first heads of house to allow women into his college for lectures. Or perhaps you've forgotten that?'

James Bright's undergraduates looked about as happy to be reminded about women coming into their college as my father's sailors had been to see me on board ship. And they were going to be just as disappointed at the amount of notice I took of their opposition.

While my coffee was being made, I sat down at a small table in the corner next to the window, where other women going past could see me sitting alone in a coffee house.

The undergraduates were still staring at me and making audible comments. I ignored them, took my shorthand notebook out of my satchel and started to write down everything Sarah Critchley'd told me. Right from a child I'd had an almost perfect memory for things that interested me, and years of studying had honed that skill to a fine edge. I didn't very often have to consult notes I'd made but making them seemed to fix things more firmly in my mind.

Sarah's story of arrest and imprisonment was far from unique. And that was why, from the moment Edie'd told me what had happened, I'd been determined to bring Sarah's treatment to the world's notice. Or the newspaper-reading public's notice, at any rate. Lower-class girls were constantly being harassed by the proctors and their bulldogs, and occasionally a young woman would be carted off to the cells under the Clarendon Building to be packed off to prison the following morning by the Vice Chancellor's court.

But the Vice Chancellor's court wasn't a court as the rest of the world understood the word. There was no counsel for the defence, and whatever the accused girl might say, she was always given the blame for whatever the proctor suspected had been going on, never the undergraduate she'd been caught with. There was always the presumption that if a gentleman gave his word, then it was the truth, no matter how unlikely it was.

Never mind that the young women concerned had committed no actual crime – off to prison they went. Of course, soliciting was illegal, but all Sarah Critchley'd done was to put her hand on a boy's arm, momentarily, and that had been enough for the proctor waiting in that alleyway. He'd seen her 'detaining' him and he'd pounced.

It was intimidation, pure and simple. The young women of Oxford were being warned in the harshest possible terms to stay away from undergraduates.

'D'you know what I think?' Sarah'd asked before we'd left Miss Skene's parlour. 'I think that if I'd sobbed and wrung my hands and said I was very sorry and I didn't ought to have done it, he'd have let me go. But I wouldn't. I stood there and told him to his face that I'd done nothing wrong. "I spoke to a student", I told him. "That's not a crime. A cat may look at a king and I should be allowed to speak to somebody if they speak to me first."'

She'd glared at me then, as if I was a stand-in for the University and all its works. 'Didn't like that, did he? Thought I was getting above myself. That's why he sent me down to the Castle.'

I sat in the window of the coffee house, thinking about that. Would Sarah Critchley have been sent to jail – the Castle, as Oxford people called it – if Benjamin Jowett had been presiding over the Vice Chancellor's court?

I knew Jowett slightly. I'd eaten at his table, and I knew he wasn't a woman-hater. Quite the reverse; he liked women. Even women with opinions. He'd been a friend of the late George Eliot – or to give her her proper name, Mrs Cross – and there was a rumour that he'd asked Florence Nightingale to marry him once upon a time. But it hadn't been him sitting in judgement at the Vice Chancellor's court on the morning Sarah was brought in. And, in the minds of most of Jowett's fellow academics, shop girls refusing to show proper contrition for trying to corrupt the morals of undergraduates was not to be tolerated.

Miss Skene had been relieved when she'd realised that it hadn't been Jowett who'd sent Sarah to jail. 'Reverend Jowett came to see me when he was made Vice Chancellor,' she'd said, 'to ask for my advice on the problem of young men seeking out girls for immoral purposes. I told him that he mustn't tolerate any suggestion that "boys will be boys". I suggested that, instead of hounding girls, the proctors should detain the young men who approach them. He agreed, but perhaps he has found himself unable to persuade the proctors to the same point of view.'

I wasn't surprised that Jowett had asked for Miss Skene's opinion. She knew what she was talking about when it came to the lower classes of Oxford and their intentions. She was a prison visitor and a constant rescuer of women from their circumstances. Every woman who was released from Oxford Prison found Felicia Skene waiting for her to offer help. But just because Jowett valued her advice, that didn't mean the proctors would, and they were the ones patrolling the streets.

As soon as she'd heard what had happened to Sarah, Felicia Skene had known I'd want to write about it. Not for the *Mercury* – the editor wouldn't go near that kind of story – but for the *Pall Mall Gazette* in London. It was just the kind of issue its editor, William Stead, liked to bring to light. A story like this could spark a campaign against the Vice Chancellors' courts in Oxford and Cambridge. And, writing anonymously, I could say what I liked, not what men thought it was appropriate for a woman to say.

'*Whatever William Stead encourages you to do, you want to think before you write this story, my girl.*'

A second female voice speaking Welsh inside the Queen's Lane coffee house. But nobody could hear her except me. The voice belonged to my twin sister, Angharad – Hara. She'd died when we were six years old but that had never stopped her putting her tuppence-worth in.

'*Think?*' I asked without making a sound or moving my lips. '*About what, exactly?*'

'*About what people have been saying to you. About recruiting supporters.*'

She was talking about my ambition to edit my own paper. A newspaper that was supportive of women and their ambitions but not specifically *for* women. A paper for all liberal, open-minded people. And, as astonishing as it might be, I'd been encouraged to think of such a thing by the University's Savilian Professor of Mathematics. He and his sister, Miss Eleanor Smith, a founder member of the AEW, had introduced me to some influential and wealthy people who might consider funding a newspaper like that. But their response had been disappointingly cautious.

Before they'd consider investing, they'd suggested that I should try to place the kind of stories I wanted to publish in a few liberal newspapers and periodicals first, to gauge the reading public's reaction. In other words, to see how many letters came in supporting my point of view.

'You can't blame them,' Hara said in her reasonable voice. 'They'd be putting their names as well as their money behind you.'

I knew that perfectly well. And anyway, she'd said the same thing a dozen times before. But having to bide my time and keep proving myself over and over again to editors who looked on me as an interesting novelty – not just female and an academic at Oxford but *Welsh, my dear* – was frustrating. Still, Stead was different. He seemed to think we were cut from the same cloth.

'Look,' Hara persisted, '*Miss Skene is very well respected in Oxford, but she's not as well known as she should be elsewhere. If you wrote a piece about her first, and then, in a subsequent article, you mentioned her meeting Sarah from the prison, people might take more notice.*'

I sighed. It was a good idea, but what Hara was suggesting wouldn't have the immediate impact that I'd been looking for. I'd been going to start my article with: *This morning I witnessed the release from prison of a woman who'd committed no crime. Who, in point of fact, had been accused of no crime…*

But maybe my sister was right. If readers of the Pall Mall Gazette – modern, forward-thinking people – knew that a good Christian woman, who went to church every day and wrote devotional books, supported Sarah, they might be more inclined to take the unfair treatment of lower-class girls in Oxford seriously. It was too easy for middle-class people to dismiss the young women who were arrested by the proctors as having questionable morals.

Right. I'd strike while the iron was hot and go back to Felicia Skene's house. I had a feeling that Sarah's story was the one that might finally persuade potential supporters to invest in a new paper, and Miss Skene had willingly involved herself in it when she told Sarah to write to me. She was fair game.

## Chapter 6

*Basil*

If he'd had his way, the Senior Proctor would have introduced me immediately to the Magdalen undergraduate who'd been found trussed up outside the college gates that morning, but I had a lecture to deliver at Jesus in an hour followed by a Board of Guardians meeting at the workhouse, so I'd suggested that he send the boy to me the following day. Perhaps twenty-four hours to reflect might bring him to his senses and persuade him that being more forthcoming about his ordeal would be the wiser course.

Before leaving Magdalen, however, I'd asked Kaye for further details of exactly where and when all the young men who'd been attacked had been discovered.

Kaye himself had discovered the Magdalen undergraduate when he returned to college in the early hours after his patrol; and it appeared that the Junior Proctor, Waddesworth, had discovered the previous victim outside the gates of his own college, Queen's, at a similar hour. Both young men would, therefore, have been very visible on the High Street. The first victim, however, had been found by one of the pro-proctors outside New College's gate, hidden away in one of the ancient, medieval lanes of the city.

So now, instead of walking straight back to college along the High, I cut up Queen's Lane. As I made my way towards New College, I reflected on the fact that the young men had been displayed outside their college gates at a time when they were most likely to be found by the University's disciplinary officers.

'Do you think,' I'd asked Kaye, 'that, in presenting you with your own curfew-breaking undergraduates at Magdalen and Queen's, somebody might be trying to encourage you and the Junior Proctor to be more vigilant? Forgive me if that sounds critical,' I added hastily as a frown gathered on his brow, 'it's not meant in that spirit.'

'Encourage us to be more vigilant? You think somebody's suggesting that if we don't catch curfew-breakers, they will? Is that what you mean?'

Evidently the Senior Proctor hadn't anticipated my investigation being in any way critical of him or the University. 'It's possible,' I said, sticking to my guns.

Walking past St Edmund Hall, I glanced into the churchyard of St Peter-in-the-East. It was a welcome splash of green in a lane which was, otherwise, relentlessly enclosed by towering walls. I stopped and looked over the gate, cogitating.

If my reputation amongst the students was genuinely as Kaye had represented it, then my asking questions and making enquiries might alarm whoever was responsible for these attacks sufficiently to make them desist. I profoundly hoped so. Though my fear that Kaye might suspect the hooded men of illegal sexual acts had arisen from a perpetual low hum of apprehension on my own behalf rather than from any actual evidence in the case, now that the notion had taken root, I found I could not easily dislodge it.

Shivering in the misty chill, I set off once more, rounding the sharp corner at the end of the churchyard and making my way along the lane between Queen's and New College.

The fact that the three hooded undergraduates had been bound and dumped in exactly the same way suggested some connection between them, despite their protestations to the contrary. What that connection might be, however, was unclear. The initial victim had been found late on the first Tuesday night of term, the second the following Sunday, and the Magdalen student a week to the day since the first attack. Was there any significance in two of the victims having been found late on Tuesday night? Looking up at the high walls of Queen's on my left and, opposite, the misleadingly named New College, I wondered how many undergraduates had been the victims of violence in this narrow lane. Even today it was provided with very few street lamps, and, in the Stygian gloom of previous centuries, gownsmen would have been easy prey unless they banded together for protection.

In front of me, a shaft of autumn sun slanted through the mist, gilding the finials of the towers and gables of All Souls College, but I quickly passed out of the brief brightness into deep shadow as the lane dog-legged towards New College. Making my way towards the point where an upper room in the New College Warden's Lodgings passed over the lane to provide a link with the garden on the other side, I saw two gownsmen standing in the shadow of the bridging storey, apparently deep in conversation. Their posture – heads inclined towards each other – suggested a degree of intimacy. Without thinking, I slowed my pace.

Hearing my footsteps, the young men straightened up and one shoved the other into motion, hastening them both away. Memories of my own undergraduate days tumbled helter-skelter into my mind, each as vivid as if it had happened yesterday.

Discretion, however, had dictated that most of the events playing themselves out so graphically before my mind's eye had taken place not in the lanes of Oxford but in London. The clubs I had frequented with a small group of similarly inclined friends would have appalled the upright morals of the University proctors, and being discovered there would have seen us sent down with immediate effect, our reputations in irreparable tatters.

I swallowed and walked on. I'd been thirteen years old when the death penalty had been abolished for acts of sodomy. However, the passing of a law consigning medieval penalties to history didn't mean that the average middle-class Englishman was any less repulsed by thoughts of what men like me did in private. If my proclivities were to be discovered by my colleagues, my career would be over.

Clergy-riddled Oxford was, of course, particularly conservative where such things were concerned. My erstwhile lover, Teddy Pritchard, claimed that the moral climate in London was different, and – though I knew him to be self-serving to a fault – my own experience of the capital was indeed of a somewhat more permissive culture, albeit in very particular locations.

As I followed the path taken by the furtive gownsmen, I allowed myself to contemplate Teddy briefly. Following the death of his wife from a haemorrhage after the birth of their only child, he now lived in London with his infant son and a resident nursemaid. The separation I'd enforced between us upon his marriage was no longer strictly observed, but I couldn't contemplate returning to the understanding we'd once had. Teddy's abandonment of me in favour of marriage and social status had removed stubborn scales from my eyes. I'd accepted that he would never feel for me as I did for him.

And yet I was too weak to exclude him from my life entirely.

Looking to my right, I gazed at the New College gate. The first victim – a New College man – had been displayed directly beneath the windows of the Warden's Lodgings, which were situated in the tower over the gate. Given the positioning of the other victims outside the proctors' colleges, that felt significant.

But what was the connection between the attacks, the University hierarchy and the name mentioned on the invitation attached to the Magdalen man's hood – Venatores – the Hunters?

My mind slipped back treacherously to the furtive pair I'd seen beneath the Warden's bridge.

I devoutly hoped that the Venatores' victims weren't men like me.

## Chapter 7

### *Non*

You'd think a person would be *thrilled* by the idea of having an article written about them in a London paper, wouldn't you? Or at least mildly flattered.

Not Felicia Skene.

'I don't imagine that an old woman like me could possibly be of interest to readers of a newspaper like the *Pall Mall Gazette*, Miss Vaughan.' She wasn't looking for compliments. She was stating a fact.

'You don't think they'd be interested in the daughter of a baronet sitting in prison cells, holding the hands of dying paupers?' I asked. 'A baronet's daughter who spent her childhood with French royalty and perching on Sir Walter Scott's knee telling him fairy stories? They'd be *fascinated*!'

She fixed me with a sharp grey eye. 'I can see why you make a good journalist, my dear. You understand immediately what will engage your readers. But I fear you're making me out to be far more interesting than I am.'

'No – you're making yourself out to be far *less* interesting than you are! You're becoming a local legend and I think you—'

'*No, not* her, *the work!*' Hara hissed. '*That's what's important to her.*'

'I think you,' I stumbled on, hoping she'd think I'd just paused for thought, 'or, more importantly, your work, should be known beyond Oxford.'

Felicia Skene sighed. 'I really don't think so, my dear. My position in Oxford is like that of the Martyrs' Memorial – known to everybody, interesting to nobody.'

I'd opened my mouth to contradict her when I heard a sudden tapping. It seemed to be coming from low down on the parlour door, as if somebody was lying in the narrow passageway and tapping with long nails.

'Miss Vaughan, would you be so kind as to open the door?' Miss Skene asked. 'And then step smartly backwards.'

I did as I was told and, as soon as the door was fully open, there was a flapping, and the doorway was suddenly filled with flapping red, blue and yellow. A parrot. So large that its wings seemed to fill the room. It flapped past me, landed neatly on the top rail of a high-backed chair, then turned around to face us.

'Good morning, Iain,' Miss Skene said.

'Good morning. Good morning,' the parrot mimicked.

'Iain?' I said, sounding stupid even to myself.

'I'm told that it sounds like the Gaelic word for "bird",' Miss Skene said, as her little terrier stirred at her feet.

'Does he have a Gaelic name as well?' I asked, looking at the dog.

'No. I call him Tatters. I used to give my dogs Scottish names, but I've become so thoroughly English these days that it seemed an affectation. I'm stuck with Iain, though – he's had his name a long time. And he'll likely outlive me, which is something of a worry.'

I could see her point. It wasn't everybody that was prepared to have a parrot loose about the house.

'As I was saying,' I started again, 'if more people knew about your work, then Sarah's case—'

But, before I could say anything else, the parrot piped up. 'Apple,' he said, very clearly. 'Apple, pear, blackberry.'

Obediently, his mistress got up and took an apple from the fruit bowl on the sideboard. But instead of giving it to the parrot, she sat down again, took a little ivory-handled penknife out of her pocket and began to cut the apple into quarters.

'If I don't take the core out for him, he spits pips everywhere and Jane gets annoyed,' she said, as she threw the little core segments into the fire.

There didn't seem to be anything to say to that, so I picked up where I'd left off. 'Sarah Critchley wants to clear her name and, if people know that you support her – people in London and elsewhere in the country, not just here – they might see what happened to her in a different light. But they have to know about *you* first.'

Miss Skene looked at me, her grey eyes serious. She sighed. 'Very well,' she said, rising from her chair to give the parrot his apple. 'I shall consent to your writing about my work, on one condition.'

I waited.

'If you wish to write about the work, you must observe it. You must come to the prison with me. And to church.'

'To *church*?'

'Yes, Miss Vaughan. Church. You cannot understand my work as distinct from my faith. If you wish to write about what I do, those are my terms.'

She followed my gaze to the parrot who was spitting bits of apple on the floor. 'He sucks the juice out then rejects the pulp,' she said.

'And doesn't that annoy Jane as well?' I asked.

'It doesn't bounce and go under the furniture the way the pips do.'

I stared at her. She took pains not to annoy her maid and lived the most unassuming life. A baronet's daughter who lived in a tiny house and used her comfortable income to support others. William Stead would snap her up for the *Pall Mall Gazette*. 'I agree to your terms,' I said. 'When do we start?'

'My prison visiting days are Tuesdays and Fridays, so we may commence the day after tomorrow, unless you have a prior engagement?'

As it happened, I had an algebra lecture at the AEW's rooms on Friday morning, followed by a couple of tutorials. I was just as busy the following Tuesday, but that could be changed with longer notice and a bit of goodwill. I explained the situation and Miss Skene agreed that I should come to her house bright and early on Tuesday morning.

I didn't know which was going to be worse – going into Oxford Prison, or into St Thomas's church.

## Chapter 8

*Basil*

The following morning, while I was waiting for the Magdalen undergraduate, Harcourt Ashdown, to present himself, I looked again at the invitation that had been pinned to the hood he'd been forced to wear. I'd asked Kaye if I might keep it in order to ask Ashdown whether he knew of this society.

Running my thumbnail over the engraved 'Venatores', I stared at the sigil above the word – the silhouette of a lion surmounted by a capital V. With one forepaw raised, in heraldic terms the lion was 'passant', like the royal lions of England, rather than 'rampant', like the upright lion on the Scottish royal arms.

There was no indication as to the identity of guest or host, but the quality of the card and its engraving suggested that whoever had sent it was a person of means.

A knock on the door made me jump. Odd how even something expected can be startling when one is completely absorbed in thought.

'Come!' I called.

Though almost half of all Oxford undergraduates still took their final honours in the classical languages and literature – or 'Greats' as the course was traditionally known – Magdalen had established a tradition of producing natural scientists, so I was unsurprised when I didn't recognise the young man Kaye had sent to see me.

'Good morning, sir,' he said, extending his hand. 'Harcourt Ashdown.' Taken by surprise by his easy smile, I grasped the proffered hand. 'Basil Rice.'

Had I expected a reticent, cowed individual? The need to swiftly formulate a suitable response to his cheerful self-assurance told me I had.

I waved him to a chair, and he sat, unfastening the top button of his jacket. Current fashion dictated that only the uppermost jacket button should be used, thus showing off a modish young man's waistcoat and watch chain. In Ashdown's case the chain was a gold affair that was understated but quite obviously expensive.

Over his jacket he wore the gown of a gentleman commoner, an undergraduate paying his own way at college, unsupported by scholarship or exhibition. Young men from wealthy families, like Ashdown, often regarded Oxford as a necessary step towards taking up their appointed place in the world.

Feeling the need to establish my authority, I remained standing and adopted a position in front of the fireplace like some overbearing paterfamilias. How Teddy would laugh at me.

'The Senior Proctor has asked me to speak to you in confidence,' I began. 'He's concerned that these attacks on undergraduates be nipped in the bud and, to do so, we must understand as much as we can about the circumstances in which they have arisen.'

Ashdown gave the slightest of frowns. 'I'm not sure what I can tell you that I haven't already told the Senior Proctor.'

His demeanour betrayed neither apprehension nor any kind of shame, so perhaps my suspicions as to the motive behind the hooding attacks were misplaced. Alternatively, Harcourt Ashdown might be one of those men who negotiated inconvenient questions by simply bluffing his way through.

'Perhaps you'd oblige me by telling me exactly what you remember of the attack?' I asked.

The young man crossed one elegantly trousered leg over the other and folded his hands in his lap. 'Of course. I was walking back to college from a convivial evening's dining with friends. I'd just passed St Helen's Passage on New College Lane when I heard footsteps behind me but before I could turn and see who was there, my arms were seized from behind and some kind of bag was rammed over my head. Somebody punched me in the stomach and, when I doubled over, my legs were seized.'

As he spoke, his eyes had slid away from my face, but I chose not to read too much into that; being overwhelmed in that fashion would have been frightening as well as humiliating.

'The next thing I knew, I was being manhandled into what must have been the passage itself and thrown to the ground. Then I was tied and gagged.'

He fell silent then, but his jaw muscles were tense as he recalled his ordeal. I knew St Helen's Passage. It was a narrow alleyway that led into a maze of insalubrious dwellings and workshops between New College Lane and Holywell Street.

'At what point were you taken to Magdalen and left outside the gate?' I asked.

'I can't be sure. One loses track of time when one can't see anything. But I know I was left somewhere for a period after I'd been tied up. Somewhere dark and cold.'

'Outside?'

'I had the impression that I was indoors. Though, again, with that infernal bag over my head I may have been mistaken. But I could dimly hear sounds of people coming and going.'

'Did you try to make yourself heard?'

He met my eye, briefly, then looked away again. 'It proved surprisingly difficult to produce much sound.'

I imagined that being gagged would have been a most unpleasant experience, especially as Kaye had mentioned that something had been stuffed into Ashdown's mouth to ensure his silence. In those circumstances, there would be the ever-present worry that one might suffocate.

'You told Reverend Kaye that you had no idea who attacked you,' I said, watching him carefully for any tell-tale reaction. 'I can quite understand that you might not want a senior member of your own college to know certain facts...'

I paused, giving him time to think. His eyes moved questioningly to me, waiting for me to go on.

'I'm neither a fellow at Magdalen, nor a proctor,' I continued. 'I have, however, been obliged to deal with the less savoury side of Oxford, as it relates to our undergraduates, on a couple of occasions.' I risked a small smile. 'On neither occasion was anyone subject to college discipline.'

Ashdown uncrossed and re-crossed his legs. 'Be that as it may, there's really nothing else to tell you, Mr Rice.'

I continued as if he hadn't spoken. 'My concern is not what you might have been up to, but the safety and well-being of all the

University's undergraduates. What you must understand,' I put a little more steel into my voice, 'is that if people get away with bullying and intimidation they tend to become more audacious, thinking themselves invulnerable. I wouldn't wish to see these attacks escalate to the kind of violence which might endanger life and limb.'

Ashdown uncrossed his legs once more and gazed at me. His dark-blond hair was impeccably cut and either he was very fastidious in his morning ablutions, or he went to a barber's to be shaved. I detected the faint scent of Rowland's Kalydor, a soothing lotion beloved of a particular barber on the Cornmarket.

'Mr Rice,' he said earnestly, 'I would help you if I could. Nothing would please me more than to see the proctors dragging whoever was responsible up before the Vice Chancellor, but I simply have no information to give you. I'd been out for dinner, I was walking home, I was set upon. Why they wished to display me in that fashion in front of the college gates, I have no idea.'

My eye strayed again to his watch chain. 'Were you wearing your watch, when you were attacked?'

He put up a hand to his fob pocket. 'I was.'

'That, clearly, was not taken, but was anything taken from you at all?'

'No, nothing.'

'Conversely,' I said, 'I believe you're aware that something was left on the hood that was placed over your head. An invitation to a supper party bearing the name "Venatores".' I fixed my gaze on him. 'Are you familiar with a club or society of that name, Mr Ashdown?'

Ashdown shook his head slowly. 'No, I'm afraid not.'

'Do you belong to any college or University clubs?'

'Clubs?'

'Or societies. Dining, sporting?'

His face registered bafflement though whether it was assumed or genuine I couldn't tell. 'Only the college cricket club.'

'So what happened to you isn't the result of some inter-club feud that has gone a little too far?' This was the Senior Proctor's preferred explanation.

He seemed surprised at the notion. 'Absolutely not.'

'You give me your word?'

'Give you my word?' As he repeated the question, I saw a glimpse of how Ashdown might conduct himself in his future life, standing on his dignity and forcing people he regarded as beneath him to back down lest they offend. But I was in my own rooms, a fellow of the college and he – whatever his family and pretensions – was, for now, just an undergraduate.

'Yes, Mr Ashdown, your word. This is not a joke. This kind of violence might easily be fatal, even if that is not its perpetrators' intention. I must ask you for any information you can give me, however embarrassing that might be.' I hesitated. 'And I give you my word that nothing you tell me will find its way back to the Senior Proctor. Or, indeed, anybody at your college.'

Inwardly, I sighed, knowing that – necessary as it was if Ashdown was to be persuaded to admit to dalliances with other young men – such a promise ensured that any investigation must, necessarily, be mine to undertake.

But there was to be no information. Ashdown's apparently candid blue eyes met mine once more. 'Then I give you my word, there is no feud. I have no idea who attacked me.'

A gentleman's word should be his bond. Unimpeachable.

Was Harcourt Ashdown a man of his word?

My instincts, refined through years of listening to the half-truths, evasions and downright lies of undergraduates, told me he was not.

## Chapter 9

*Non*

On Friday evening, as usual, we were expecting Basil for dinner. But for the first time in months, Tarley Askew would be there too.

Tarley and I had been introduced by Charles Dodgson, the Christ Church mathematics lecturer otherwise known as Lewis Carroll, author of *Alice's Adventures in Wonderland*. Much against Basil's better judgement, I'd involved Tarley in the Jesus College murder that Basil and I had been investigating at the time. Since then Tarley and I had been good friends and, during term time, he'd used to be as much of a regular visitor to Lily's dinner table as Basil. But, since January, he'd been in London looking after his mother who'd become very ill.

Thankfully, by the beginning of this term, she'd recovered enough to send Tarley back to Oxford but, meanwhile, we'd been writing to each other twice or three times weekly.

'*Hah! You mean Tarley wrote to* you *two or three times a week. Did you send him even* one *letter a week?*'

My sister was being annoying as usual. All right, I might not have replied to *every* letter he sent, but I'd been busy.

I had mixed feelings about seeing Tarley again. On the one hand, I'd really missed him. Good friends are hard to find, and he'd never treated me as if I was inferior because I was a woman, nor as if I'd burst into tears if he disagreed with me.

On the other hand, there were his letters. Not just the number of them, but what he'd written. As well as amusing details of everyday life in Newington Green, he'd written about matters that, face to face, we'd never really touched on.

Amongst other things, he'd told me how watching his mother suffer had affected him, and how speaking to doctors had made him reconsider the medical career he'd been planning.

*One doctor told me that unless one can put aside all personal feelings and simply view the patient as a case, an illness, one will never be a good doctor,* he'd written. *He maintained that emotions cloud judgement and prevent clear thinking. I didn't think his attitude would be common to all doctors, so I asked one or two others for their opinion, and, to my dismay, they all agreed to a greater or lesser extent. Without being utterly heartless about it, they maintained that it was necessary to keep a 'wall of reserve', as one put it, between doctor and patient. And I don't think I could, Non. Or perhaps I mean I don't think I'd want to. The whole reason for going into medicine would be to care for people, not just to see them as a collection of symptoms.*

But medicine and Mrs Askew weren't the only subjects Tarley'd confided his thoughts about. By the end of the summer, I must have known him better than anybody else alive, so I was feeling slightly uneasy about seeing him again that evening.

'Hah! It's not Tarley's letters you're worried about, it's what Basil said to you last week.'

I tried to shut my sister out, but when she was determined, she could slip around any barriers I tried to put in her way. I didn't like to imagine how annoying she'd be if she was actually still alive.

'*You didn't like hearing the truth from Basil for a change, did you?*'

I'd noticed that, since we'd come to Oxford, Hara was always finding fault with me. It was as if she thought it was her duty to take over where our mother had left off when I moved away.

'*It wasn't a question of me liking or not liking what Basil said, Hara. It was none of his business, that's all.*'

I didn't want to think about that very awkward conversation, but some of it slithered into my head anyway.

'You're being unfair to Askew,' Basil had said. 'You must know he's in love with you?'

I'd been so shocked by his bluntness that I hadn't been able to think what to say.

'If you're not interested in him romantically,' he'd barged on, 'make that clear. Don't dangle him on a string like a puppet.'

'I'm not dangling anybody! Tarley and I are friends.'

'Men and women can't be friends. Not when they feel for each other as Askew feels for you.'

I felt a sudden rush of sensation in the pit of my stomach. As if a fencing opponent had scored a direct hit. 'How do you know what he feels?' I demanded, not holding my anger back. 'Mind-reader now, are you?'

'Anybody who has eyes in their head can see, Rhiannon!' From the frustration in his voice, you'd have thought Basil had said the same thing a hundred times and I'd refused to listen every time. 'The boy wears his heart on his sleeve. The only reason you won't acknowledge it is that you don't want to have to make the decision.'

'What do you mean, *the decision*?'

'Whether you want to marry him.'

I was saved from recalling any more of the argument by a knock at the door downstairs and the sound of our maid-of-all-work, Edie, rushing up from the basement to answer it. It wasn't that she was a dutiful servant; Edie just always wanted to know who was here so that she could eavesdrop outside the sitting room if she thought she might hear something interesting. Something she could tell her friends about at Band of Hope meetings, or when she was down at the fishmonger's with the other servants.

'Good evening, Mr Askew,' I heard her say. 'It's lovely to see you again.'

In spite of my nerves, maybe it was better that Tarley'd arrived first. At least now Basil wouldn't be able to give me any more of his so-called advice.

Still, my heart was skittering in my chest like a moth's wings banging against a lamp glass as I went downstairs.

Tarley was standing there in the hallway while Edie took his college gown and hung it up for him. He seemed to have grown. Did men still grow at his age? It was his twenty-third birthday next month.

He'd had to give up rowing when he went home to look after his mother, but his shoulders seemed even broader than I remembered. Perhaps he'd been doing callisthenics to keep himself fit.

In other ways, he hadn't changed. His curly hair was still a stranger to hair oil, even if it was shorter than when I'd last seen him. He'd probably had a haircut before coming up, hoping it would last him till the end of term.

'Non!'

I couldn't read the look on his face as he saw me coming down the stairs. It certainly wasn't just straightforward pleasure to see me again.

And that was my fault, wasn't it? I'd made things unbalanced by not writing him the kind of letters he'd written to me.

'You're looking well.' I'd never said that to a living soul before and I was horrified how much it made me sound like my mother.

'You too,' Tarley said, and at least he sounded as if he meant it.

I turned to Edie. 'Can we have a pot of tea, please, Edie?' I didn't want her eavesdropping. Asking for tea would give Tarley and me five minutes' peace to get ourselves onto an even keel before Basil arrived.

But five minutes came and went, and things were still off beam. We just didn't seem to be able to settle into our old familiarity. Finally, in desperation, I told him about Sarah Critchley and what had happened to her. 'I'm planning to write an article on her case for the *Pall Mall Gazette*,' I said.

He looked at me, gravely. 'Are you sure that's a good idea?'

'What d'you mean?'

'Well,' he said, slowly. 'I suppose I don't quite see how exposure to the public gaze would benefit Miss Critchley.'

'But *she* came to *me*, wanting me to help her clear her name.'

He leaned towards me. 'But will an article for the *Pall Mall Gazette* do that, Non? Might it not have exactly the opposite effect?'

'I don't think so, no.'

He looked at me for a few seconds, as if he was waiting for me to say something else. When I kept my mouth shut, he sighed and I felt what, back home, we'd call a *ias oer*. If you were going to translate it into English, you'd probably say a 'cold chill' but the Welsh meaning includes something more, something physically disturbing. 'Just think about it, Non,' he said. 'Aren't you worried that public opinion will decide there's no smoke without fire? That she probably *did* have immoral intentions?'

'Is that what *you* think?' I snapped back.

'*That's unfair,*' Hara scolded in my head. '*Just because you hadn't thought how people might react, that's no reason to take it out on him.*'

Tarley was shaking his head. 'Of course that's not what I think. Surely you don't even have to ask that question? But you know as well as I do what some people will say when they read about what happened to her.'

'What *happened to her*, as you put it, is a *miscarriage of justice*.'

Tarley stood and went over to the fire. It was cold outside, but I didn't think he needed to warm himself. After a few moments, he asked, 'Will you name her in the article?'

In truth, it hadn't occurred to me not to. 'I'll ask her what she'd prefer,' I said, stiffly.

'And are you going to let her see the article before you send it off?'

'Of course I am.' But I'd hesitated a heartbeat too long. We both knew that showing it to Sarah Critchley first hadn't crossed my mind.

Tarley gazed at me steadily and I had to look away. 'So you don't think I should write it?' I said.

'I didn't say that.'

'Then what *are* you saying?'

'That you need to think of Miss Critchley and the effect it will have on her.'

Luckily for me, I didn't have to think of a reply to that because we both turned as the door opened and Basil came in with Albie, Lily's son, hot on his heels. I'd been so distracted that I hadn't even heard Basil's knock at the front door.

Tarley grinned. 'Albie! Good to see you! How are things at Lucy's?'

Albie, at nineteen, wasn't that much younger than Tarley but he still seemed a boy, whereas Tarley was a man. Still, he put out a hand to shake which he wouldn't have done a year ago. He'd grown up quite a lot since Tarley'd been here last and I suddenly realised that his apprenticeship as a draughtsman at the ironworks was almost over.

'Friday night dinners haven't been the same without you,' he said. Then he turned to Basil, and I could see a blush starting. 'Of course, it's always nice to see you, Mr Rice.'

'Don't worry, Albie, I'm glad to see Mr Askew back, too.'

At thirty-five, Basil had one foot in the grave as far as Albie was concerned. But he'd be used to that, dealing with undergraduates all the time.

'Actually,' Basil said, 'I'm particularly glad to see you this evening, Askew. There's something I'd like to discuss with you and Non.'

## Chapter 10

*Basil*

On the ten-minute walk to Lily's house from college, my apprehension about how Non would greet me had risen steadily. She'd clearly resented my offering her advice about being honest with Askew, and though we disagreed frequently on all manner of subjects, this particular argument had been unprecedentedly personal.

'I don't know what gives you the right to even have an opinion on how I conduct my friendships, Basil Rice!' she'd spat, her grey-green eyes feline with fury.

'Everybody has the right to speak up on behalf of their friends—'

'Oh, so Tarley's your *friend*, now, is he? Isn't that a touch irregular? A don being *friends* with an undergraduate?'

Even as my saner self knew that she was only wielding any weapon to hand in order to gain the advantage, the fearful part of me that had spent my adult life hiding what I was cowered before the implication of her words.

I forced myself to meet her eye and maintain an even tone. 'Aren't all the friendships I conduct under this roof and at your pleasure somewhat *irregular*? With you, a young unmarried woman, with Lily, a widow well below me in social status, with Albie, a young man whose path would never have crossed mine in any other circumstances? Besides, aren't you the person who's spent the last four years telling me that we shouldn't observe conventional social niceties?'

Unable to rebut the charge, and, perhaps disconcerted by the vehemence of her own reaction, Non had struck off at some other tangent at that point but equanimity had been a long time in the restoration.

A week on, would she have forgiven me for what she saw as unpardonable interference in her personal affairs? More troublingly, might she have found herself reflecting on her impulsive accusation of irregularity?

It was these nagging worries that made me decide to broach the subject of the hooding attacks. The sharing of such confidential information would remind Non of the trust I placed not only in her discretion but that of the whole family. If she was still inclined to be cross with me, I hoped she would be mollified by the gesture.

Following my conversation with Harcourt Ashdown, I'd made discreet enquiries amongst my colleagues and had discovered that most of them were unaware of the hooding attacks. The undergraduate grapevine was better informed, however, and junior common rooms were rife with speculation as to what had happened to the youths from New, Queen's and Magdalen. A theory had apparently gained ground that the hooding incidents were part of some bizarre, nocturnal, inter-collegiate challenge with participants scoring points by 'bagging' members of other colleges who were out after curfew.

'Why would they do that?' I'd asked one young man.

Sitting in my study, the essay we'd been discussing still on the sofa next to him, the gownsman had looked as if he was about to shrug, before deciding it was too casual a gesture. 'It would prove you're stealthier,' he said. '*You* didn't get caught by the proctors, but you caught the other man.'

Interestingly, JCR gossip had not included the Venatores' invitation that had been pinned to Ashdown's hood, but I remembered the boy's reference to being 'stealthy', now, as I turned to Askew.

'Askew, may I ask whether you've heard any rumours about undergraduates being found bound and hooded outside college gates?'

He turned to me, and I was struck afresh by the fact that his dark good looks were entirely untainted by arrogance or any apparent awareness of his own allure. 'As a matter of fact, my scout mentioned something along those lines this morning.'

'You've heard nothing from your peers at Corpus?'

'To tell the truth, I'm a bit out of kilter at college, just yet. Most of the chaps who came up with me took schools in the summer and have already graduated,' he said. 'So I'm left with younger men I don't know so well.'

Non was behaving as if Tarley hadn't spoken. She stared at me. 'Bound and hooded undergraduates? What's been going on?'

'That's what the Senior Proctor wants me to find out.'

'You?'

'Sidney Parker and Silas Cantwell have bestowed upon me a certain reputation,' I said, referring to the previous occasions on which I'd been required to investigate the doings of undergraduates. Non started to respond but I forestalled her. 'Even if Kaye knew about your part in resolving those cases, you're a journalist, and the University wouldn't want the *Mercury* anywhere near a potential scandal, still less the *Pall Mall Gazette*.'

'But you *do* want my help?' Non could always be trusted to put things as bluntly as possible.

'I would hardly have raised the matter if I didn't,' I said.

Non shot Askew a glance. 'Well, Tarley doesn't seem to know much, so tell us what *you* know.'

Ever alert to anything that might affect Non's academic career, Lily paused in her clearing of plates as I outlined the information I'd gleaned from the Senior Proctor and Harcourt Ashdown. 'Because of the invitation-cum-calling card pinned to Ashdown's hood, the Senior Proctor and I are working on the theory that it's a club rivalry that's gone a little too far,' I finished. 'Have you ever heard of these Venatores, Askew?'

As he shook his head, I pulled the invitation from my pocket and passed it to him. He placed it on the table between himself and Non and I was glad to see both this gesture on his part and her inclining herself slightly towards him. All evening, I'd been conscious of a coolness between them, and I had feared that I might be to blame.

'"Venatores" rather than "Hunters",' Non said. 'Is there some classical reference there that I'm missing?'

'The deity who springs immediately to mind, of course, is Artemis,' I replied.

'But undergraduates wouldn't want to associate themselves with a female figure,' Non pointed out.

I nodded. 'Pan was a hunter, as well as being the god of the wild.'

'And what about the lion?' Non asked, tapping the sigil on the invitation's obverse. 'That doesn't fit with Artemis or Pan.'

'Probably just posturing,' Askew said. 'King of the beasts and all that. Goes along with using Latin. Gives them a certain status. In their own minds, at least.'

'And this was pinned to the hood of the latest victim?' Non asked.

'Yes.'

'But there was nothing on the other hoods? Why?'

I'd asked myself the same question.

'It's an odd sort of invitation, isn't it?' Askew asked. 'No room number or RSVP address. Definitely intended for the cognoscenti who know where to go and don't need to reply.'

'Yes,' I agreed. 'It's more summons than invitation.'

'Did you ask this Harcourt Ashdown about it?' Non asked.

'I did. But he denied all knowledge of these Venatores. He also denied membership of anything but his own college cricket club.'

'Are you going to speak to the New College and Queen's boys as well?' It was Non's habit to refer to gownsmen as boys. In her mind, it cut them down to size. College fellows were wont to refer to our undergraduates as men, but sometimes their behaviour made that feel a little forced.

'I am. I've already asked the Senior Proctor to make arrangements.'

'Would you like me to make discreet enquiries at college about these Venatores?' Askew asked.

'Would you mind? Any information would be very helpful.'

'And then we just have to wait for Tuesday evening,' Non said. 'If two of the students were found on Wednesday morning,' she explained as I looked to her for clarification, 'that means they were attacked the previous evening, doesn't it?'

'Two doesn't exactly constitute a pattern,' Askew pointed out.

'It does if there have only been three events. And if you get as little out of the other two boys as you did out of Harcourt Ashdown,' she said, turning to me, 'I think you'd be well advised to go out on patrol with the proctors on Tuesday evening.'

She was right. It would be negligent not to look further into this nascent pattern. Unfortunately, however, the gleam in Non's eye told me she'd be going out on her own behalf on Tuesday evening; and, judging by the way Askew was watching her, he would insist on accompanying her.

I hoped their involvement in my investigation would mitigate any lingering feelings of resentment Non was harbouring towards me.

## Chapter 11

*Non*

At ten minutes to eight on Tuesday morning, I was standing outside the church of St Thomas the Martyr, as instructed, waiting for Felicia Skene. I didn't want to go in without her – Father Chamberlain might mistake me for a convert – so I'd arrived early.

It was a lovely autumn morning with a bit of summer warmth still in the October sun as it rose through the furious Krakatoa clouds. On days like that, Oxford was beautiful, as long as you only looked skin-deep.

But you didn't have to look very far outside the churchyard to see how shallow that beauty was. The ancient church was a little haven of peace in a parish that was known for its slums, its 'disorderly houses', its street brawls and barefoot, coughing poverty. Most of Miss Skene's prison visits were probably to people from St Thomas's.

I wondered if that's why she worshipped here – her parish church would be St Michael's, less than a minute's walk from her front door.

'Miss Vaughan!'

I turned around like a naughty schoolchild who's heard the headmaster coming. 'Good morning, Miss Skene.'

'I'm delighted to see you,' she replied in that deep, Scottish-tinged voice of hers. 'Punctuality is a very overlooked virtue but one which I prize most highly. It tends to walk hand in hand with courtesy to others, I find.'

Lily'd have laughed at that; she wasn't very taken with my manners as a rule. Said I needed to be more the captain's daughter and less of the deck hand.

'Your own parish church would be St Barnabas, I think?' she said.

I took a quick breath. I was sorry to disappoint her, but it was best to knock this church talk on the head now. 'Yes, but I rarely go. I'm afraid I'm no great lover of religion.'

'I agree,' she said, surprising me. 'It can get in the way dreadfully. But God himself is a different matter, don't you think?'

I fell into step beside her as we made our way up the path. 'To be honest, Miss Skene, I see too much suffering in the world to feel much affection for God.'

She smiled sadly. 'My dear, I fear you're guilty of a common mistake. You're confusing the state of the world – which is mankind's doing – with God's will, which can only be done by the hands he has given us.'

I felt my hackles rise. People accused me of a lot, but never generally of being confused. 'But isn't he supposed to be omnipotent?'

She cocked her head slightly. 'You surely don't believe that his being all-powerful necessitates that he should constantly be interfering in human affairs? Where would that leave our free will?'

We seemed to have tumbled down one of Lewis Carroll's rabbit holes. But, instead of a world where cats grinned enigmatically and hatters held lunatic tea parties, we were discussing theology at sunrise, barely a minute after saying good morning.

'I think,' I said, carefully, 'that there's a world of difference between God driving a coach and horses through our free will and his absenting himself from the awfulness of the world altogether.'

She stopped and turned to look at me, her grey eyes steady. 'Is there? Either God does or does not directly involve himself, surely? Otherwise when should he and when should he not? You'd very soon be accusing him of being capricious and arbitrary in his choice of circumstances in which to intervene.'

She argued like a don.

'*Cranogwen would agree with her*,' Hara pointed out.

Cranogwen – writer, poet, preacher and my friend and neighbour back home in Llangranog – was the person responsible for my being at Oxford. When my father's ship had gone down with all hands and my mother and I had been left more or less penniless, Cranogwen had stepped in and offered to pay my board and lodging at Lily's for four years. I was standing on my own two feet now, but I'd still have been teaching navigation to young sailors back in Cardiganshire if it hadn't been for Cranogwen.

'*She's probably been praying for you to meet somebody like Miss Skene*,' my sister went on. '*Somebody who can save your soul and make you into a good Christian woman.*'

The thought of Cranogwen taking time out from her speaking tours, and from editing the Welsh women's magazine she'd founded, to indulge in a bit of clandestine spiritual manipulation made me uncomfortable.

Once we were inside the church, Miss Skene curtseyed towards the altar as we made our way into the aisle. St Thomas's was a Tractarian church, so I'd been expecting Romish theology from the pulpit. But, unlike the Nonconformist churches where preachers took every opportunity to get up on their hind legs and tell people what to think, this morning's service didn't include a sermon.

It did include hymns though, even if they weren't the densely theological kind I'd grown up with. These hymns were sung in Latin, unaccompanied, in a very plain, almost haunting style.

Father Chamberlain led from the front and Miss Skene and the handful of other women at the service joined in.

Felicia Skene's voice was astonishing. It rang out like a cleanly struck bell and rose to the rafters. I stopped trying to mumble along and just listened; her voice was almost enough to make a Christian of a person, and I wondered whether singing praise to her God was the one time Felicia Skene just let rip.

'Have you known Father Chamberlain a long time?' I asked as we left the church. It had been obvious when he greeted her at the door that she and the vicar knew each other well.

'Father Chamberlain's work here is one of the reasons I moved to Oxford. My family is from Scotland, as you know, but we were living in Leamington at the time, having recently moved back from Greece. On my very first visit to Oxford, I knew it was somewhere I could make a difference.'

This was excellent background for my article. 'How long did you live in Greece?'

Miss Skene glanced at me, and I noticed a fond smile on her face. For Greece, I assumed, rather than for me. 'Almost seven years. It was a wonderful, revelatory time. It broadened my experience and my compassion for people.'

'Any people in particular?' I was making mental notes.

'Women, primarily. Everywhere, I saw how their lives were restricted, defined and dominated by the wishes and desires of men. One of the most extraordinary individuals I have ever met was a sultana in a harem in Bulgaria. We took coffee, surrounded by Georgian and Circassian slave girls, and we spoke of her life. She gave me a diamond ring in token of our perpetual sisterhood.'

I was willing to bet she didn't still have that ring. Miss Skene was famous for her generosity and unworldliness; she'd have sold it to give the money to the poor.

But I was wrong.

'I treasure that ring,' she said. 'It's a reminder of a quite extraordinary time in my life. I was travelling with a clergyman and his son, and, one day, a Mohammedan mob in the street took it into their heads to dislike our Christian looks and began stoning us. We had to flee for our lives!' She grinned delightedly, then burst out laughing as if the idea of having to run from a mob was the funniest thing she'd ever heard. Or perhaps it was the ridiculous notion of her – Miss Skene, most respectable spinster of the parish of good works – being so daring as to travel with male companions in a foreign country.

'It was a good thing I'd grown up in the countryside and spent the previous few years walking and riding,' she said. 'I just picked up my skirts and ran like the wind!'

I looked sideways at her. Her auburn hair was silvering now, and you could tell she was working hard at that upright stance, but if you looked carefully, you could still see the headstrong young woman in her.

While we were on smiling terms, I decided to switch back to theology and try and find out what she thought of the people she worked with from a religious point of view. She'd been at pains to point out that her faith was at the root of everything she did, so her views on why people ended up in the prison must come from there.

'Those references to "manifold sins and wickednesses" in the service,' I said. 'Do you think some people are born with more manifold wickedness than others? That there's such a thing as "bad blood"?'

Plenty of her kind did believe that. They saw poor people as a fundamentally criminal class who were born primed and ready to commit acts of iniquity; a class of people who'd only be dissuaded from criminality by the deterrent effects of severe punishment.

But Miss Skene gave me a sharp look. 'Does the path I have chosen suggest that I believe such a thing?' she asked. 'What a foolish waste of time it would be to try and reform people who are constitutionally predisposed to wickedness.'

'So you don't believe that people like Sarah Critchley inherit bad blood from their parents?'

'May I remind you, Miss Vaughan, that Sarah has been convicted of no crime? Bad blood or otherwise is therefore moot.'

'I beg your pardon – young women who are convicted of soliciting, then. Do you think it's just a matter of circumstance that they… fall into sin on the streets?' I couldn't persuade my tongue to say the word 'prostitute' in Miss Skene's company.

She didn't hesitate, just batted the question right back to me. 'Let me first ask you *your* opinion on the matter, Miss Vaughan?'

'I'm quite sure that girls go "on the town" because they don't know any better, or because they have no choice,' I said. 'No other means of supporting themselves.'

'And, given that you found me outside the prison to meet Miss Critchley last Thursday morning, what do you imagine my own views to be?'

I knew what she was implying, but it didn't seem that simple to me. 'There are plenty of middle-class ladies who work for the benefit of fallen women who still believe that their behaviour comes from their nature, not their circumstances.'

'Then, if your article is to be true to my own convictions, you must ask yourself in what ways my own attempts to help such unfortunate young women differ from theirs.'

As we walked past the gates of the Eagle Brewery, I breathed in the smell of malting barley and thought about her question. The answer was pretty obvious when you gave it a moment's thought: all the other middle-class women who concerned themselves with the plight of destitute and ruined women sat on committees. They didn't visit prisons or take up the cause of tramps, and they certainly didn't open their front door to people who wouldn't even be welcome at the tradesman's entrance of most middle-class homes.

'You choose to wash the feet of the poor rather than making provision for soap to be distributed,' I said. That's what the Jesus she believed in had done, wasn't it? Knelt down in the dust of Palestine and washed the feet of the poor – the act of a servant.

She nodded, smiling as if she couldn't help being delighted at the thought of the unwashed people she cared for. 'I follow the example of my Saviour,' she said. 'When he was presented with women who had fallen from grace, he showed them love and acceptance, not condemnation.'

'Let him who is without sin cast the first stone,' I said, remembering the story of the Pharisees trying to catch Jesus out by bringing a woman caught in the act of adultery to him for judgement. Only the woman, of course, not the man she was committing adultery with. The Bible didn't so much as mention him.

*Plus ça change, plus c'est la même chose,* as the French say. Humanity'd moved on the best part of two thousand years since the time of Jesus of Nazareth, but the boy Sarah Critchley'd been talking to hadn't been hauled up in front of the Vice Chancellor's court either. Only Sarah.

The undergraduate would've been asked what his intentions were, and when he'd told the proctor that he'd just been enquiring where to get ribbons for his sister, he'd have been believed. He spoke as a gentleman and a gentleman's word was taken at face value unless there was compelling evidence not to.

But Sarah, who'd been the one interrupted while she was going about her lawful business, hadn't been believed. She wasn't the one who'd started the conversation, but she'd supposedly used it for her own wicked ends.

We'd reached the gates of the prison, now, but Miss Skene carried on walking.

'Aren't we going in?' I asked.

'My visiting hours don't begin until eleven o'clock. First we'll take breakfast at my house. We can discuss what's to be done for Sarah Critchley.'

## Chapter 12

### Basil

On Tuesday morning, I rose early to breakfast in town and returned to my rooms as the clock in first quad showed a quarter past eight. My early start was occasioned by a note that had arrived from Kaye the previous afternoon.

> Magdalen College
> Tuesday 22nd October
>
> Dear Rice
> As requested, the Provost of Queen's and the Warden of New College have agreed to make the relevant young men available to you, in your rooms at Jesus, at the times stipulated. The New College man, the first victim, is Piers Haviland, the Queen's man, Augustus Vennell.
> I have also, as requested, asked Waddesworth to accommodate you on his patrol with the pro-proctors on Tuesday evening. He would be obliged if you would meet him at the Clarendon Building at five minutes to six.
> With my sincerest thanks for your assistance in this matter,
> W. Kaye.

Lincoln Waddesworth was the Junior Proctor. As Kaye had been responsible for patrols last week, Waddesworth and his team of pro-proctors and bulldogs were on duty this week. He and I weren't acquainted, and I hoped Kaye had secured his agreement before involving me in the investigation of the hooding attacks; an evening in the company of a man who resented my encroachment into what he might see as his own territory was not an inviting prospect.

I'd asked Kaye to arrange for the two young men from New College and Queen's to present themselves in my rooms at a time earlier than they would normally expect to be out and about. I'd learned my lesson from the polished Harcourt Ashdown; if I was to extract any useful information from Haviland and Vennell, I would have to get them on the back foot. If they did have anything to hide, an early interview might induce a poor night's sleep and a lower guard.

Though there was no apparent connection between the three victims, if Haviland and Vennell were hiding something, as I was quite sure Ashdown was, I didn't want to give them the opportunity to confer once I had spoken to the first of them. I had, therefore, asked Vennell to come twenty minutes after Haviland, with the intention of extending my conversation with the former until I was quite sure the latter had arrived, thus depriving them of any possibility of a conference.

—

At half past eight, a firm knock indicated that, whatever else Mr Haviland proved to be, he was at least punctual.

I invited him in, noting his rigid posture as he strode into my sitting room. In anybody but a soldier, such a stiff back betokened either a noteworthy degree of resentment, or a marked nervous tension. Or possibly both.

'Do sit down, Mr Haviland.'

Exactly as Ashdown had done, Piers Haviland unfastened the top button of his jacket as he took his seat, displaying his waistcoat and watch chain. His waistcoat was a touch flashier than his father might have been pleased with, having a distinct purple stripe through the grey, but his sober necktie was everything Papa could have wished for, as was his gold watch chain.

He didn't wait for me to open proceedings. 'I received a missive from the Senior Proctor asking me to come and see you this morning,' he said, the suggestion of a frown hooding his dark eyes, 'about the atrocity that was perpetrated against me the week before last.'

'The attack in which you were bound, gagged and hooded,' I said. 'Indeed. The Reverend Kaye has asked me to look into what happened to you and the other men who've been attacked as I have some experience in conducting investigations.' Now was not the time for self-deprecation, and if he thought my experience more extensive than it was, so much the better.

Haviland's frown did not disappear. 'Surely it's just townies having a pop at University men?'

I let a slight pause develop before responding, to remind him that he was here at my behest. 'An item left on the person of the most recent victim suggests otherwise,' I said. 'And the similarity of the attacks suggests a degree of coordination. If the attacks were planned, then so, perhaps, were the victims.'

Unlike Ashdown whose face was mobile and expressive, Haviland's countenance was mask-like, and his expression did not change.

I took out a notebook and pencil from my pocket and opened the book on my knee in an attempt to dent his rigid composure; nobody likes to think that their words are being recorded for some official purpose.

'Tell me what you remember about the attack.' Kaye had told me Haviland claimed to remember nothing.

'Very little.' One of his hands strayed towards his waistcoat pocket but, apparently thinking better of taking his watch out, he touched the spinner dangling from his fob chain then folded his hands in his lap once more. 'I was struck on the head, and that must have affected my memory.'

'What's the last thing you remember before the attack?'

His gaze slid over my shoulder to the window beyond. 'Sitting in the junior common room with a few chaps in the afternoon. I don't remember anything about the evening at all.'

I made a note of this, taking my time while he stewed.

'Have you no friends who can furnish you with information?' I asked eventually, looking up once more.

'Nobody has come forward to offer me any. Apparently I was alone when set upon.'

'Are you in the habit of being out alone in the city's streets late at night?'

His eyes met mine and this time I saw anger there. 'The fact that I was left outside my college gates after midnight doesn't mean I was out voluntarily at that hour. I may have been attacked much earlier.'

Moving my notebook to the arm of my chair, I crossed my legs, leaned back and gazed at his ramrod hostility. 'Surely if you were attacked earlier in the evening, unless you were somewhere insalubrious, somebody would have seen what was happening and come to your aid.'

'*Insalubrious*—'

I cut across his outburst. 'Is it possible that you were somewhere insalubrious that evening, Mr Haviland? Amongst people who might wish you harm?'

He curbed his rage, but his answer was terse. 'Absolutely not.'

'How well do you know Harcourt Ashdown?' I shot back.

He opened his mouth to answer, then, slightly too late to be credible, said, 'I don't know him at all. Who is he?'

'The latest man to be bound and hooded. Unlike you, he *does* remember what happened to him. He recounts being dragged into St Helen's Passage. You'll be very familiar with that particular back alley, no doubt?'

'Why should I?' Did I imagine it, or was his indignation tinged with a new wariness? My intention had been to provoke him into an unguarded response, but I had to acknowledge that there was a gratification in being so robust that did not reflect well on me.

'It abuts New College Lane,' I said, angling my head just a fraction to let him know that his wariness hadn't gone unnoticed. 'You must walk past it frequently on your way to and fro.'

Haviland's chin went up and he literally looked down his aquiline nose at me. Had the look been put into words, I could have disciplined him for insolence to a senior member of the University. 'Walking past somewhere does not imply familiarity with it.'

'Do you belong to any clubs, Mr Haviland?' I asked, hoping to throw him off balance with the non sequitur.

'Clubs?'

'University societies, sporting organisations, college clubs?'

'I belong to the Union,' he said, referring to the Oxford Union, an influential undergraduate debating society.

I turned back to my notebook. 'What's the first thing you remember on regaining your wits?'

Haviland's lip curled in a grimace of displeasure. 'Being manhandled by the pro-proctor's bulldogs. They were none too particular about how they got me to my feet.'

'Perhaps they didn't realise that you were a member of the University.' Haviland had, after all, been the first student to be found in that state. 'Were you wearing your gown?'

For the first time, he seemed less than completely assured. 'Not when I was found.'

I looked at the one he was sporting today. It had a perceptible sheen. 'Is that one new?'

'Yes.'

'Was the one you were wearing on the night in question taken from you?'

'It must have been. I wouldn't have left college without it.'

He might say that but we both knew that undergraduates sometimes discarded their gowns in order to gain entry to pubs and other places from which University rules excluded them.

'Was anything stolen from you in the attack?'

'It's possible that some money was taken from me. But since I don't remember anything about that evening, I don't know what I might have had on me.'

'They didn't take your watch or chain?' I inclined my head towards him, eyes on the garnet spinner.

His hand went to it. 'No. I'd have been furious if they had. It was a gift from my father.'

Why had he told me that? Was he implying that his father might not like to hear that young Piers had been questioned by a don who belonged to another college and had no recognised disciplinary role in the University? I had a well-founded fear of offending influential men, and Haviland's manner indicated that his father might be 'connected', as the young men had it.

A knock sounded on my outer door; Mr Vennell had also arrived punctually. I closed my notebook and rose to my feet. 'Very well, Mr Haviland, I think that's all.'

Wordlessly he stood up and turned to depart.

It would be instructive to see how he and Vennell reacted when they saw each other. If they were acquainted, I was confident that I would know.

## Chapter 13

*Non*

Miss Skene and I were at the prison far longer than I'd expected and, when we finally came back out onto the freedom of New Road just after two o'clock, I had to leave her at the gates. I was already late for my first tutorial at Somerville, so I was going to have to loosen my sails and run before the wind, as my father would have said.

If any of the ladies of the AEW committee had seen me dashing through the streets, they'd have had a fit – it definitely wasn't becoming behaviour in a young lady but, fortunately for their health, I wasn't running along streets the AEW ladies generally frequented. I scurried along Bulwarks Lane past porters and wharfmen, then threaded my way through St George's Mews onto Walton Street where I could risk running hell for leather. There were enough people there who knew me in case of trouble.

It was a relief to run, to be honest, even if I did have to hold my skirts up and tolerate my satchel bouncing on my hip. I hadn't expected the prison to affect me as much as it had.

Although the women's wing was newly built, and the cells were dry, light and well ventilated, the whole place had an oppressive atmosphere. Inmates were housed separately from one another, so the cells were small, with just enough room for a bed, a bucket and a chair to sit on while the women picked oakum.

If you didn't know any better, picking oakum sounded like delicate work – like sitting at the kitchen table picking the tops and tails out of blackcurrants – but I knew what ship's ropes were like. Just the thought of unravelling tarred rigging and pulling the fibres apart made my fingertips prickle, and watching one of the prisoners – Nellie – working away while Miss Skene spoke softly to her, it'd been obvious why picking oakum was classed as hard labour.

The front of Nellie's blue uniform dress had been red with the dust of the rope, and her fingers were the same colour. They weren't actually bleeding, but I wondered if that was because she'd been doing this so long the scabs had turned into tough scars. I couldn't see her fingernails for the dust, but I was willing to bet they were bitten short. Anything projecting more than a sixteenth of an inch would rip as she picked at the rope.

And that's what the female prisoners did all the daylight hours bar one, when they were herded into the exercise yard to walk around in silence.

Mind you, hard labour or not, in their position, I'd have been glad of the work. To be shut up in your cell twenty-three hours of every day, with nothing to do and nobody for company but yourself, would send you mad. At least doing something with your hands would free your mind to think. Once your fingers had toughened, anyway.

While Miss Skene spoke to the prisoners, I'd found myself wondering, again and again, how Sarah Critchley had coped with prison. The uniform, the solitude, the harsh attitude of the guards, the stares of the other prisoners at exercise time. She was far better educated than most prisoners, and she was used to smart clothes and the kind of well-off people who shopped at Badcock's. No wonder she'd burst into tears when she'd seen Miss Skene outside the prison gates. She'd probably been bottling them up all week.

After running half the length of Walton Street, I pulled up, panting, just before the entrance to the Radcliffe Infirmary's grounds and turned in to what locals still called Walton Manor but was now the grounds of Somerville Hall.

As I hurried along, I glanced over the wall that separated Somerville from the hospital's fever wards and laundry, and the sight of the hospital reminded me of a comment of Miss Skene's.

'*I would hesitate to say this to the Reverend Jowett,*' she'd said as we were eating toast and marmalade in her parlour, '*but the powers that the University has over the young women of the city are uncomfortably reminiscent of those granted to ports and garrison towns under the Contagious Diseases Acts.*'

Straight away, an article making that comparison had started writing itself in my head. I knew that my editor at the *Pall Mall Gazette*, William Stead, had grown up protesting against the Contagious Diseases Acts with his mother. He'd be bound to welcome an article drawing comparisons between that legislation – which was supposed to prevent the transmission of venereal diseases to soldiers and sailors – and the Vice Chancellor's court's powers over young women who were suspected of 'immoral intentions'.

I slowed as I got closer to Somerville's main building, Walton House. Best not to arrive panting. It wouldn't be ladylike.

When I'd accepted the job of tutor at Somerville, I hadn't expected to spend most of my time chaperoning the students to lectures in the boys' colleges and doing petty administrative tasks. But Madeleine Shaw Lefevre, Principal of Somerville Hall, was playing a tiptoeing game with the AEW. The association jealously guarded its territory as the overseer of teaching to female students and Miss Shaw Lefevre wouldn't openly challenge it for the right to offer tuition to her girls. On the other hand, she was determined to give the young ladies of Somerville the best possible chance of getting useful qualifications.

So, at the moment, the tiptoeing game involved assuring Mrs Bertha Johnson, the AEW's Lady Secretary, that my role was to provide additional support, on an individual basis, to supplement the lecturing I did for the AEW. The notion that I might be a tutor just like Basil and the other college fellows couldn't even be suggested – opponents of women at the University were already accusing the AEW of setting up 'facsimiles of colleges' – but Mrs Johnson agreed with Miss Shaw Lefevre that everything possible should be done to ensure that the Somerville ladies understood the subject matter of lectures.

Disguising the fact that I was a tutor to the Somerville students in all but name wasn't the way I would have played things. But then, in all probability, my way would've led to a schism between the AEW and Somerville, and that wasn't in anybody's interests. The more I got to know Miss Shaw Lefevre, the more I could see that perhaps there were benefits to not always nailing your colours to the mast and defending them with fists and feet. Sometimes it could be to a person's advantage to let a few areas of ambiguity develop here and there.

And anyway, tutoring and lecturing weren't the only strings to my bow, now. As I opened the door to Walton House, my brain was busy with the article I was going to pitch to Stead.

## Chapter 14

### Basil

As I went to meet the Junior Proctor at Clarendon House that evening, I reflected on the meeting of Piers Haviland and Augustus Vennell outside my rooms.

My years as a University lecturer meant that I was well versed in the various ways in which undergraduates who weren't acquainted reacted to each other. The guarded look. The courteous but perfunctory nod of the head. The swift and covert scrutiny designed to ascertain where each stood in the social pecking order. And, given the clandestine nature of some of my friendships, I was also attuned to the reactions of men who knew each other – sometimes intimately – but couldn't acknowledge their acquaintance in public.

It had been abundantly clear to me both that Haviland and Vennell knew each other and that they did not wish that fact to be known.

Perhaps because of their unexpected encounter, Vennell had seemed ill at ease from the moment he crossed the threshold into my rooms. He had fidgeted. He had *umm*ed and *ahh*ed. He had found it difficult to meet my eye. But, despite that, I'd got no more information from him than I had from Haviland. Only Harcourt Ashdown's account had cast any light on where and when the other attacks, so similar in their outcome, might have been carried out.

'I'm particularly interested in what happens in and around St Helen's Passage later in the evening,' I told Waddesworth when we met in the Proctors' tiny office at Clarendon House.

'Yes, so I gather,' Waddesworth said. About my own age, he was a well-built man of medium height and, like many men who took on the role of proctor, he was ambitious. The others – like Kaye – were dutiful, often religious, men who believed in the University's moral responsibility to its undergraduates.

I knew nothing to speak of about Waddesworth beyond his being a fellow at Queen's and the fact that he lectured in mathematics. And, fearing that he might resent being asked to accommodate me on his patrol, I was on my guard with him.

'So, might I suggest that we make a visit to St Helen's Passage – and the Turf Tavern – later on?' I asked. 'At, say, ten o'clock?'

'Why, just in case there's anybody loitering with a coil of rope and a hood?' Waddesworth looked up from the notes he'd been reading. 'Don't you think our mere presence would deter anybody who had a bit of undergraduate-baiting in mind?'

Despite my uneasiness at Waddesworth's lack of affability, I stood my ground. 'Two of the attacks took place late on Tuesday night, or early on Wednesday morning. And the only victim who's prepared to admit where he was attacked has named St Helen's Passage. Therefore, I'd like to know if there's anything that happens nearby on a Tuesday evening. We have no idea what these young men were doing before they were attacked, and I think it would be relevant to find out.'

'You think they may have been up to no good?'

'I suspect they're lying to us about not knowing each other, so I simply think we'd do well to gather all the information we can.'

He stared at me as if he was being forced to make a reassessment. 'Very well. We'll make our way to the Turf at ten. Meanwhile, it's business as usual. And I'll ask you, please, not to interfere in our work.'

'I'll do my best.'

However, my best proved not to be quite good enough for the Junior Proctor. For the first half an hour I contrived to look unobtrusive while Waddesworth and the bulldog patrolling with him handed out advice to undergraduates on how to wear their gowns (not slung over one shoulder or bundled into a coat pocket), and the need to hurry if they were going to be back at college in time for their dinner (when most of those accosted were clearly intending to dine in forbidden pubs). He and his bulldog, Brandon, also chose to cast a repressive shadow on street corners where the University's young men might otherwise have loitered in the hope of falling into conversation with shop girls or young women going home from the clothing factories.

However, when Waddesworth and Brandon started harassing girls who were engaged in nothing more suspicious than looking into shop windows, I felt compelled to say something.

As the most recent object of their injunction to 'move along before you get into trouble' scurried away up New Inn Hall Street, I approached the Junior Proctor. 'While I hesitate to tell you your job, Waddesworth, you do realise that we have no jurisdiction over citizens going about their lawful business?'

'The lawful business of young women isn't to accost our young men, Rice.'

'That girl wasn't accosting anybody. She was looking into the confectioner's window.'

'A girl like that can't afford sweeties. She was clearly loitering with intent to strike up a conversation with the likes of those young chaps.' He indicated a group of gownsmen walking towards New Inn Hall.

'Alternatively, perhaps she was simply daydreaming of a world in which she might afford humbugs or Fry's chocolate creams.'

Waddesworth's expression suggested that my words had not landed on fertile ground. 'It's the responsibility of the proctors to ensure that gownsmen don't go astray. If that involves removing tempting young women from their path, then so be it.'

During our brief conversation, Brandon had wandered a little further along Queen Street and had stopped a few feet away from a young woman in conversation with an undergraduate. The girl had her back to us, but it was still obvious that there was at least four feet of clear air between her and the youth who was speaking to her.

Realising the bulldog's intention and not wishing to see the girl dragged off to the cells under the Clarendon Building, I moved quickly towards the pair.

But I was too late. As I drew alongside Brandon he reached out a hand and put it on the girl's shoulder.

'Right, you little hussy,' I heard him say, 'you leave the young gentleman be, now, and come with me.'

At the same moment, Waddesworth strode past me to the undergraduate and demanded, 'Name and college, sir?'

While the boy gaped at him, the girl turned in Brandon's grip and said, 'Dad! It's me!'

The bulldog stared at her, rigid with anger. 'What're you doing talking to a college boy? You know what I've told you!'

'He thought I'd dropped a sixpence,' the girl said, 'an' ran after me. I was just sayin' thank you, that's all!'

'Is that true?' Waddesworth barked.

'Which part?' the gownsman asked with a reckless sang-froid. He might consider himself to have no case to answer where the Junior Proctor was concerned, but Brandon was visibly itching to berate him for attempting to pick up his daughter.

'Did you pick up a coin she'd dropped?'

As Waddesworth asked the question, Brandon's daughter proffered a coin. Her father's hand dropped from her arm, and I breathed a sigh of relief. It wasn't my place to interfere in a man's dealings with his family, but his attitude had felt over-zealous.

The undergraduate indicated the girl's outstretched palm. 'As you see, I did, yes—'

But Waddesworth cut off any further self-justification. 'Name and college?' he demanded.

'Smythe,' the boy said with a scowl. 'New Inn Hall.'

'Well, *Mr Smythe* –' Waddesworth clearly thought the name was false – 'Mr Brandon will accompany you back to your hall.' He turned to Brandon. 'And do ensure that they make a note of *Mr Smythe*'s entry. We wouldn't want him going astray.'

In other words, check his name with the porter.

'There was no need for that,' the girl observed to Waddesworth as her father marched the student away.

'You'd do well to keep your opinions of your betters to yourself, miss,' Waddesworth snapped, 'and take yourself home where you belong instead of engaging in conversation with undergraduates over trifles.'

'Sixpence may be a trifle to you, sir, but it takes me two hours to earn,' Miss Brandon countered with some spirit.

'Miss Brandon,' I began. The girl looked warily at me, clearly expecting more censure. 'Thank you for explaining the circumstances. I'm sure Mr Smythe will be as grateful to you for clarifying matters as you were to him for his retrieval of your sixpence.'

She bobbed her head, slightly mollified. 'You're welcome, I'm sure.' Then, cocking her head on one side, she asked, 'You're Mr Rice, aren' you? I used to see you down St Thomas's when we lived in Bookbinder's Yard.'

'I am he, yes.'

She'd obviously seen me going about my duties with the Poor Law relieving officer. I wondered whether Brandon was a recent recruit to the ranks of the bulldogs. It was a decent job and would pay for better lodgings than the family was likely to have had in down-at-heel St Thomas's.

I wondered where they lived now, and whether Miss Brandon was on a legitimate route home. But with Waddesworth standing there, I couldn't very well ask.

Instead, I ignored the Junior Proctor's glare, raised my academic cap to Miss Brandon and bade her good night, hoping that Waddesworth would come no closer to incarcerating any young women while I was in his company.

## Chapter 15

### Non

At eight o'clock Albie and I were going to walk into town to meet Tarley so we could keep an eye on things around New College Lane and St Helen's Passage.

While I waited for the clock to strike, I skimmed through the article I'd just written.

### THE MORAL DOUBLE STANDARD

*In the last two hundred years, since the Glorious Revolution effectively put paid to the doctrine of the Divine Right of Kings, the subjects of England's monarchs have assumed that they cannot legally be imprisoned unless they are found guilty of a crime.*

*However, in the United Kingdom today, there are many places in which citizens – all of them women – are being imprisoned without having committed any crime.*

*As readers of this newspaper will be aware, in ports and garrison towns throughout the land, the provisions of the Contagious Diseases Acts mean that a working-class woman suspected of prostitution – sometimes upon no more evidence than being found in the same streets as soldiers or sailors – may be taken up by the plain-clothed police officers who roam the docks and alleys specifically for this purpose, and subjected to what amounts to medical rape as she is forced to undergo an intimate examination via speculum. If she is found to be infected with a venereal disease, the unfortunate woman is imprisoned in a 'lock hospital' until such time as she has recovered or has completed her sentence – a year's imprisonment. This draconian and brutal measure supposedly maintains the fitness of our armed forces. However,* in no cases are men suspected of visiting prostitutes subjected to imprisonment without trial or forced examination of their private parts, and the work of medical men like Dr Charles Bell Taylor has called into question the effectiveness of these Acts in reducing infection of the armed forces.

Our readers may not be aware however that, in similar fashion, the proctors of the Universities of Oxford and Cambridge patrol the streets of those cities each evening to apprehend young women for the heinous crime of being caught in conversation with an undergraduate. As with the plain-clothed policemen of the Contagious Diseases Acts, these officers of University discipline assume that any working-class woman may prostitute herself at a moment's notice and that, like the poor defenceless men of the army and navy, undergraduates are powerless to protect themselves against these females' wiles. The young woman thus taken up is then marched off to the cells beneath the proctors' offices, where she is held overnight and brought before the Vice Chancellor's court the following morning. There, she is denied any legal representation and charged with no crime but having 'immoral intentions' towards the undergraduate with whom she was speaking. If the court finds the evidence of the proctors sufficiently compelling, it consigns the unfortunate young woman, quite summarily, to jail for seven or fourteen days, as a deterrent to others. In common with our brave tars and Tommy Atkinses, the undergraduate is not hauled up to be judged. All that is required of him is that he declare on his honour that he had no immoral intentions, and he is free to skip away unscathed and unslandered.

Despite the work of Mrs Josephine Butler and others, a royal commission has done nothing to bring the appalling Contagious Diseases Acts to an end and the expectation persists that women will be the gatekeepers of men's purity, without the smallest suggestion that the men concerned might accept some responsibility for their own actions. In similar vein, despite local outcry in Oxford, the University has declined to discipline its undergraduates more effectively, allowing the responsibility for their moral purity to fall entirely upon the young women and girls of the city.

> *It is clearly high time that the public made its voice more loudly heard in defence of its womenfolk and against the double standard where sexual morality is concerned.*

I was pretty sure that William Stead would approve. The article was very much in the *Pall Mall Gazette*'s own campaigning vein, and I decided that I'd send the editor this piece before I sent him the one on Miss Skene.

If they understood that some of the women Miss Skene visited in prison hadn't committed any actual crime, the more strait-laced readers of the *Pall Mall Gazette* might be less inclined to be shocked at the company she was prepared to keep in the name of her religion.

The article might also begin to build up a head of steam behind public outrage at Sarah's treatment by the Vice Chancellor's court. If enough people wrote to Stead demanding that something should be done, then maybe Tarley's objections to a story about Sarah would disappear.

Because try as I might, I couldn't get what he'd said about public opinion deciding that there was no smoke without fire out of my head.

'*Does it really matter what some people think?*' Hara asked as I reached for an envelope.

'Yes, it does! If I'm trying to clear Sarah's name, I don't want people disbelieving her whatever the evidence.'

'*So it's not because you're worried Tarley might think you're using Sarah's story to make your name?*'

I crammed the article into the envelope and pulled a letter sheet towards me to write a covering note to Stead.

'No. Tarley doesn't think that. He's just concerned about Sarah.'

Hara said nothing for several seconds. Then she huffed, '*If that's what you think, on you go then.*'

It was just the kind of thing my mother would have said.

## Chapter 16

*Basil*

Though Waddesworth had agreed that we would make our way to the Turf Tavern at ten o'clock, it was after eleven when we finally turned up Catherine Street towards New College Lane.

The bulldog, Brandon, whose attitude to me had thawed perceptibly since our encounter with his daughter, murmured, 'Don't suppose you've been to the Turf before, Mr Rice?'

'I haven't, no.'

'Just a word to the wise – they're not used to seeing college fellows come up Hell's Passage. Beg pardon, St Helen's Passage. Just don't take offence if the lads don't show quite the courtesy as you're used to.'

I nodded and, as we walked past All Souls, I lengthened my pace to draw level with the Junior Proctor.

'Waddesworth, it strikes me as significant that, of the three young men attacked, one is a member of Kaye's college while a second is a member of your own,' I said. 'I wonder, are you personally acquainted with Mr Vennell?'

Waddesworth looked at me sharply. '*Personally* acquainted?'

'Do you tutor him, for instance?'

'No. Vennell is slated for a pass degree, so he doesn't exert himself too much as far as his studies are concerned.'

Unlike honours men who were required to work more consistently if they wished to do well, passmen could get by with cramming for a few weeks before taking the less demanding exams designed for them. I found Vennell's decision not to take honours interesting. I'd noticed that all three of the young men – Ashdown, Haviland and Vennell – were gentlemen commoners; in other words, they hadn't had to take scholarship exams to support their time at Oxford. Were Haviland and

Ashdown registered for pass degrees also? And, if they were, was that relevant?

'So you've had no dealings with him at all?'

Waddesworth glanced at me. Even in the dim light of the street lamps, I could see that my questions irritated him. 'Before he was attacked, I knew nothing but his name. Obviously I've had occasion to speak to him since.'

He made to stride on past New College Lane, presumably heading for the Holywell Street entrance to the Turf, but I stopped him.

'If you don't mind,' I said, 'I'd rather go in via St Helen's Passage.'

'The Holywell Street entrance is more convenient. It's not so confoundedly narrow.'

'But the Magdalen man, Ashdown, named that as the location where he was attacked.'

'For God's sake, Rice, do you think potential attackers will be standing in the passage waiting for prey?'

I took a steadying breath. 'Of course not. I'd just prefer to be thorough. I don't know precisely what I'm looking for, so all and any information is useful.'

He made no answer but turned on his heel and proceeded to march down New College Lane, his gown ballooning around him with the force of his strides.

As Brandon and I followed, the night closed in around us somewhat. Away from Oxford's main thoroughfares, street lamps were fewer and further between.

'Mr Brandon?' The proctor's officer looked at me. 'You referred to Hell's Passage earlier rather than St Helen's?' I asked.

He gave a little chuckle. 'The council decided to call it St Helen's Passage when my father was a lad – sounds more respectable. But it was always Hell's Passage before that and most of us as were born here still know it like that.'

'Why the awful name?'

Brandon shrugged. 'The cottages up there en't much to look at, even now. Maybe they was worse once upon a time.'

As he spoke, ahead of us Waddesworth stopped abruptly at the entrance to the alleyway in question. 'Brandon, you'll have to go first. You have the lantern.'

The bulldog turned without further instruction into the narrow passage. Waddesworth followed and, taking a breath as if I was about to dive into deep water, I went in after them.

The passageway was so narrow that the full sleeves of my gown almost brushed the bricks on either side. Ahead of me, Brandon and Waddesworth turned a corner and, fearing the loss of any light, I hastened after them. After the corner, the passage widened into a lane, with cottages on the northern side. In the lamplight they looked poorly maintained, their rendering scabrous and peeling. Ash-heaps rose in dark mounds outside several doors.

Then, passing through another passage – this one, if anything, narrower than the first – we emerged into the courtyard in front of the Turf Tavern.

In one corner stood the alley for a game known locally as Bumblepuppy – a combination of skittles and bagatelle played on a long, inclined surface – and, in the other, a handcart of the kind used by dustmen, covered with a tarpaulin. A worn besom leaned against the cart, and I wondered what sort of noisome effluent it routinely swept into the drain in the middle of the courtyard.

Waddesworth looked around in distaste. 'Are we going in?' he asked.

In answer, I stepped past him and opened the door to the public bar.

The lintel being slightly lower than average, I was forced to stoop uncomfortably as I stepped over the threshold. Things weren't much better inside as the beamed ceiling offered little headroom for a man of my height.

Within three seconds of our entrance, the whole place had fallen silent. Every eye turned towards us. In our gowns and academic caps there was no disguising who Waddesworth and I were, and our presence sparked instant resentment.

I had a sudden and quite overwhelming impression that coming here had been a mistake.

## Chapter 17

*Non*

'We're not going around again, are we?' Albie complained. It was after eleven o'clock, and all law-abiding undergraduates had been behind college gates for the last two hours. The only people left on the streets were drunks, prostitutes and policemen. And proctors, of course. Mind you, we hadn't seen either Waddesworth and his little band or the pro-proctors during our circuits.

'Basil thinks the Turf is something to do with these attacks,' Albie persisted. 'So that's where we should go. But we can't, can we? Not with you dressed like that.'

He glared at me as we stood in front of the Queen's Lane coffee house. I waited for Tarley to weigh in on my side, but he said nothing.

'I couldn't exactly wear my normal clothes, could I?' I defended myself. 'I'd have attracted all sorts of attention being out at this time with two young men.'

'Well you'd attract a different sort of attention if you went into the Turf in boys' clothes,' Albie said. 'You can fool people if they're not looking too hard but as soon as you opened your mouth, which you'd be bound to do, they'd know you were female.'

I was beginning to regret letting Albie come with us. I'd only said yes because I thought he'd make us seem less eye-catching – he was the only one of us who looked like any other Oxford youth. I was too short to be anything but a young boy, and even if Tarley wasn't as tall as Basil, he was still too tall to look average. In fact, with his mop of black curls he looked slightly exotic, like one of the sailors from the Mediterranean who occasionally washed up on the docks in Cardigan.

The three of us had been alternately loitering and strolling around a circuit made up of the High Street, Catherine Street, Holywell Street and Longwall Street. Every second circuit, we'd cut along New College

Lane and come out of Queen's Lane instead of going along Holywell, but that had been our only variation.

I was wearing boots that were slightly too big for me, which made it easier to stump along like a boy, and I was keeping my hands in my pockets so that I didn't have to think what to do with them. I'd even put a cap on to try and disguise my hair.

I must admit, I enjoyed the freedom that wearing boys' clothes gave me. It wasn't just that my legs weren't tangled up in skirts, it was something about not having to defer to people. As a rule, when a woman was walking towards a man, she'd divert her path around him. It was so automatic I'd never even thought about it. But walking three abreast with Tarley and Albie, I noticed people stepping out of *our* way and I knew I'd be furious the next time I had to step aside for a man.

We agreed on one more circuit, but as the evening was drawing towards midnight and the streets were almost empty, I wondered whether we should just give up. It had been a long evening and peering into the shadows was beginning to put me on edge.

There's something about the dark. It doesn't just affect how much you can see, it changes the way you react to things. Shapes you wouldn't give a second glance to while the sun's up seem to loom at you like a threat when it's dark. In the narrowness of New College Lane with its high walls and no handy little alleyways to hide in, the darkness almost took on a life of its own – shapeshifting in the mist that was beginning to creep up from the rivers and the canal into the college lanes.

I wondered if the undergraduates we spotted here and there would manage to dodge Basil and the proctor. The gownsmen weren't as difficult to spot as they thought they were, even if they weren't wearing their gowns.

But, however many we'd seen, none of the students had been doing anything they shouldn't – apart from being out after curfew, of course. And they were probably all making their way back to college by now, anyway. According to Tarley, every college had its weak points where you could climb in after hours. I didn't ask how often he'd done that. Or what he'd been doing while he was out. It was none of my business, whatever Basil Rice thought.

It occurred to me that if a girl like Sarah Critchley was found on these college byways at this time of night, she wouldn't even need to be talking to an undergraduate – it would just be taken for granted that she'd been up to no good and she'd be carted off to the proctors' cells.

'Shall we knock off and go home?' Albie asked. Apart from a dust cart pusher making his way home late, we'd seen nobody for the last ten minutes, and I could tell Albie was disappointed. Lily's boy was no trouble, but he was still nineteen years old and young men of that age are always looking for excitement, aren't they?

'What if we cast our net a bit wider?' Tarley asked. 'Basil and the proctor will probably have chased anybody in these lanes away by now.'

'Did you have anywhere particular in mind?' I asked.

'Merton Street? Then on to Bear Lane and Blue Boar Street?'

There were plenty of colleges along the route he was suggesting. In the same way that Hertford, New College, Queen's, St Edmund Hall and Magdalen all peered over their walls at each other in this corner by Oxford's old east gate, Merton, University College, Tarley's own college Corpus Christi, Oriel and Christ Church were all jostled together inside the southern edge of the medieval city wall.

We agreed to the change of scene and crossed the High Street.

Merton Street was shadowy, half-lit and deserted. As we passed the Examination Schools and turned the sharp corner towards the colleges, the street lamps looked almost otherworldly in the dark. From this distance you could barely see the posts they stood on, so their gaslight seemed to be floating in the air.

The eastern end of the street between Merton and University College was as quiet as the grave. You'd never think that scores of students lived on either side.

We walked quietly, our strides cautious. The silence all around us seemed to demand it.

On the Merton side of the street, the pavement was dark with fallen leaves, so we kept to the other side. Your feet could easily go from under you on damp leaves and the mist was settling on everything.

I peered into the gloom ahead of us. As far as I could see, we were the only people on the street. But you could never quite tell. There might be somebody just around the slight bend in the street towards Corpus Christi, or in the shadows that gathered between street lamps and under the trees overhanging Merton's high wall.

I glanced to my right, up Logic Lane, an ancient footway through to the High Street. At this time of night, the gates at either end of the lane were locked. I wondered if it was one of the University College students' climbing-in routes but I didn't ask Tarley. It would have disturbed the silence.

Still, I glanced up at him and found him looking at me. He grinned and his teeth showed white in the dark. Walking this close to him, I could smell the Pears soap he used. I wondered if the strength of the smell meant he'd washed just before coming out this evening.

'*Of course he did,*' Hara taunted, '*he wanted to be fresh for you, didn't he?*'

Was that true? Even though he knew I'd be in trousers and trying to pass as a boy?

Albie'd pulled slightly ahead of us, and, what with that and the thoughts going round in my head, I was momentarily confused when I heard him hiss, 'Look! Over there!'

He was pointing at the Merton College gate.

Somebody was sitting in the shadows.

With a hood over his head.

## Chapter 18

*Basil*

In the Turf's public bar, not one of the eyes trained on us was friendly.

Without moving my head, I glanced furtively around but saw no Jesus College servants. If there was trouble, we could expect no help. However, it was unlikely that we would be the victims of anything more violent than hostility.

The landlord didn't stir from his post. 'You gentlemen are a bit off your beat, aren't you? There are no students here.'

I opened my mouth to say something emollient, but Waddesworth forestalled me. 'A week ago, an undergraduate was attacked in New College Lane and dragged into St Helen's Passage. We'd like to speak to any witnesses to that attack.'

The landlord looked around the smoky, low-ceilinged room, his eyebrows raised, apparently inviting anybody with any information to step forward. The patrons were surprisingly numerous for such a late hour and there was at least one game of cards being played on a table in the corner. In the past, as its name suggested, the Turf had been a gambling den, but its fortunes had changed, and it was now a semi-respectable establishment. Hidden away down the narrowest lane in Oxford, the tavern was an ideal watering hole for college servants; undergraduates were unlikely to venture here as the place was too difficult to escape from should the proctors come calling.

'Seems nobody here saw anything,' the landlord said, after a brief glance at the silent drinkers.

Waddesworth glared at him. 'A crime has been committed,' he insisted. 'Common assault. It's the duty of any citizen who knows anything to come forward.'

Not only did nobody come forward, but the looks that shot around the room made it quite clear that anybody who thought about doing so would have his peers to answer to.

'Common assault,' the landlord repeated. 'What's that then? A punch? A kick? If you ask me, some of those so-called young gentlemen could do with a clip around the ear.'

'The gentleman in question,' Waddesworth said, his lips thin, 'was hit over the head, bound and gagged. It was a serious assault which left him vulnerable to worse.'

In the half-light, I watched men avoiding each other's gaze all around the room.

Now that Waddesworth had taken the floor, all the attention was on him, so I could survey the taproom with less likelihood of causing offence. Though I'd felt the pressure of what seemed like a hundred eyes on me as we entered, in fact there were fewer than twenty men in the room; men who had nothing better to go home to, or who simply finished their working day very late, as many college servants did.

For the most part, the drinkers were decently dressed, but they were obviously not well-to-do. There was, however, one person in the room who seemed better dressed and more self-assured than the rest: a young woman standing in the corner opposite the card players, who'd been speaking to two men sitting over their pints. As we'd walked in, she, like everybody else, had fallen silent but, unlike the men around her, her attention had not been taken by Waddesworth's bluster. She was staring in my direction.

I looked behind me, assuming that Brandon must be the actual object of her gaze, but he was standing off to my right, near the door. For some reason, I had attracted this young woman's attention.

'The young man I'm referring to is not the only one who has been attacked in this way.' Now we were here, Waddesworth wasn't going to be turned away easily. 'And we're very concerned to stop these cowardly attacks before somebody's badly hurt.'

His words were received with a sustained silence. It was clear to me that we would learn nothing here.

As Waddesworth began to throw out phrases like 'aiding and abetting' and issued thinly veiled threats to 'people who might later be found to have withheld information', I moved quietly over to the young woman in the corner.

'Miss, might I ask you a question?'

She looked me in the eye as she answered, and I wondered whether she was the landlord's daughter; I wouldn't have expected such boldness from a barmaid.

'You can *ask*, Mr Rice.'

I felt a shiver of apprehension. 'You know me?'

'The tall don from Jesus College who helped a St Thomas's pieceworker escape the noose? The only college man on the workhouse union's Board of Guardians? Everybody knows you.'

The notion that, to the Oxonian on the street, I might not be an anonymous man in a cap and gown was simultaneously gratifying and disconcerting. Becoming recognisable had obvious drawbacks for somebody like me.

'What is it you want to know?' she asked.

'Is there something that happens regularly here – at the Turf – on a Tuesday evening?' I paused, then, conscious of the need to give an example, said, 'A Bumblepuppy competition, perhaps?'

She looked at me gravely. 'Are you accusing the landlord of turning a blind eye to illegal gambling, Mr Rice?'

Her eyes seemed very dark in the low light, and I wondered what colour they would be in daylight. Her face was not one to turn heads, but she seemed more self-possessed than most working-class girls. And, currently, I was fairly sure she was teasing me.

'Not at all,' I said. 'Competitions, as we all know, may be played for the satisfaction of winning, alone.'

She smiled and relented. 'Nobody much plays Bumblepuppy any more,' she said. 'Danny – the landlord – keeps the alley for a few of the older ones who have a go in the summer when it's nice out.'

'And there's nothing particular that brings people here on a Tuesday?'

She shook her head.

'Thank you for your help,' I said.

'Wasn't aware I'd given any.'

'Even the knowledge that something *doesn't* happen is still knowledge.'

'So you're looking for whoever tied your boys up,' she jerked her head towards Waddesworth without actually looking at him, 'like Mr Big Breeches said?'

I stifled a smile. 'We are, yes.'

She nodded slightly, still looking at me, as if she was weighing something up but, before she could say anything further, the door was suddenly flung open to reveal Albie Maddox, panting heavily.

My first thought was of Non and I was filled with apprehension as I crossed the taproom to the boy. However, as soon as he saw me, Albie allayed my fears. 'There's been another attack. On Merton Street. It's worse this time.'

## Chapter 19

*Non*

By the time Basil and the proctor arrived with a bulldog in tow, the boy who'd been dumped outside the Merton College gates had withdrawn into what, at home, we'd have called a *pwd* – a sullen sulk.

After Albie'd raced off to find Basil, Tarley'd taken the bloodstained hood off the boy's head and ungagged him, but we'd left him tied up. I didn't want him hammering on the Merton College gate, screaming blue murder till the porter let him in. Basil would want to talk to him.

Mind you, even if he had got inside, he'd be very easy to identify. Whoever'd attacked him had made quite sure of that. The light from the nearest lamp post barely reached him, but the damage was clear.

He hadn't been beaten. Or, at least, that wasn't where the blood was coming from. No, that came from the letters that had been carved into his face, two on either side of his mouth.

L-I-A-R.

Blood had trickled down his jaw from the bottom of each letter and the collar of his shirt was so stained that it looked black in the dim light.

The cuts to his face obviously made it painful to speak but he managed to make it clear that he wanted us to untie him. When I told him we wouldn't, he stared at me.

'You're a girl.' His lips barely moved as he spoke.

'A woman, actually.' At twenty-three, I wasn't going to let anybody call me 'girl'.

He looked up at Tarley. 'Untie me, you bloody townies!' The words were slurred and imprecise, like a drunk attempting ventriloquism.

'Is everybody at Merton as rude and ungrateful as you?' Tarley asked, very much not in a local accent.

The boy stared at him but said no more. I wondered if he knew what had been carved into his face. His attitude suggested he might.

'Do you know who did this?' Tarley asked. 'Or why?'

The boy slurred something which sounded very much like 'fuck off'.

After that he said nothing more till Basil and the Junior Proctor arrived.

As they came marching down the street, I decided that I'd do best to retreat into the shadows and watch.

Waddesworth barely took any notice as Basil introduced Tarley; he was too busy staring at the gownsman's injuries. Then he looked up, a scowl on his face. 'Why the devil have you left him tied up?'

Tarley didn't turn a hair. 'Didn't want him absconding.'

Waddesworth bent down to untie the ropes binding the boy's wrists and ankles, but they'd been pulled tight. After half a minute or so of watching him struggle, I pulled out the sailor's knife I always carried, stepped forward and made two quick cuts.

The way the proctor stared at me, you'd have thought I'd pulled out a broadsword and swung it at the boy. I said nothing and moved back into the shadows.

Waddesworth turned to the gownsman. 'I assume, since you were left here, that you're a Merton man?' he said.

The boy struggled to his feet, rubbing his wrists. 'Yes, sir,' he slurred. 'Laurence Herbert.'

'And how do you come to this sorry pass, Mr Herbert?'

Herbert took a breath and seemed to decide it was better to bear the pain and try to speak normally. 'I was set upon on my way home—'

'Where from, may I ask?' Basil interrupted.

Herbert's chin went up, but if defying Basil had crossed his mind, he thought better of it. 'From supper with a friend. In his rooms,' he added before he was accused of frequenting forbidden establishments.

'And what time were you making your way home?'

'In time for curfew.'

'At which college did this supper party take place?' Basil asked.

Laurence Herbert turned to the Junior Proctor, but if he'd expected Waddesworth to save him from Basil's questioning, he was disappointed. 'Let's hear the answer, Mr Herbert, if you please.'

If he'd been a sailor, Herbert would've sucked snot and spat it at Basil's feet; as it was he just refused to look at him.

'Trinity,' he said.

Trinity'd been the college mentioned on the summons to supper pinned to Harcourt Ashdown's hood. The Hunters' invitation. I refused to think of them as Venatores. I wouldn't give them the pretentious satisfaction.

'And your host will confirm that?' Basil asked, flatly.

In the light of the bulldog's lantern, Herbert's mutilated features were dark with fury as well as blood. 'A gentleman's word doesn't need to be confirmed.'

'Where were you attacked?' Lincoln Waddesworth was unimpressed by Herbert's little show of foot-stamping.

The boy put a hand to the cuts on one side of his face, as if his touch would stop them hurting. 'At the bottom of Queen's Lane.'

'That's an odd route to take from Trinity to Merton,' Basil said. 'Surely it would have been quicker to walk straight down the Turl, then come down Magpie Lane?'

Herbert's fingers curled into fists, as if he'd like to punch Basil. 'I was with a friend. From Teddy Hall. I walked with him.'

'Were you simply brought here after you were attacked, or were you kept elsewhere for a while?' Basil asked.

Herbert took a breath. 'That bag...' he articulated, slowly, nodding at the bloodstained hood on the ground, 'was put over my head... almost as soon... as they grabbed me.' He stopped and swallowed. I waited for him to put a hand to his face again but he didn't. Perhaps he didn't want to admit how much pain he was in. 'So I'm not... entirely sure... about where I was. But I think... they dragged me into... the churchyard... so they could tie me up.'

That would be the church just up Queen's Lane from St Edmund Hall. St Peter-in-the-East.

'What makes you think that?' Basil asked.

'Grass. Threw me down on grass. Then they tied me up.'

'Why didn't you shout for help?' Waddesworth asked. 'Your friend would still, surely, have been within earshot if you'd only just left him?'

An excellent question. I watched while Herbert decided how to answer it.

'There was... a knife... here,' he said, eventually, bringing a flattened hand up under his jaw to show where the knife had been. 'They said... if I shouted... they'd slit my throat.'

And, seeing what they'd done to his face, I couldn't blame him for believing them.

*Part 2*

## Chapter 20

*Basil*

On the morning after Herbert's discovery outside Merton, the messenger brought me a letter while I was eating my breakfast.

When I saw Teddy Pritchard's unmistakeable handwriting on the envelope, I experienced a reflex quickening of joy which I immediately battened down. Teddy was no longer a source of unalloyed delight. If I was ruthlessly honest with myself, he never had been.

> My Dearest Bas
>
> I'm determined that Mortie shall know at least one of his godfathers better than I ever knew either of mine, so as you refuse to leave Oxford during term, I shall have to bring him to see you.
>
> I thought we'd pop up next Sunday. I'll have Miss Webster with me, but we can send her off to entertain herself for a couple of hours at a tea shop.
>
> I'll telegram once I know what train we'll be on, and you can meet us at the station with a cab.
>
> Affectionately,
> Teddy

Affectionately. Damn and blast the man, he was still toying with me, still believed he could wheedle his way back into my bed. But, though a part of my sad and sorry heart would always belong to Teddy Pritchard, I had seen him for what he was, now, and I knew that I must resist. Teddy was addicted to excitement and that, for him, meant a stream of often anonymous lovers and a predilection for the kind of risky locations where such encounters might take place.

I might share his proclivities, but I did not share his enthusiasm for risk. I wished to put neither my health nor my freedom in jeopardy in the pursuit of sex.

However, in an act of weakness for which I regularly berated myself, I'd agreed to stand as godfather to his son, Morton, a relationship which, assuming no ill befell the child, would bind me to Teddy in perpetuity.

Given that he had couched this visit as a chance for me to become better acquainted with my godson, I couldn't very well refuse; and at least the child's presence would preclude any possibility of my weakening in other directions.

I scribbled a brief note in reply, then, putting thoughts of Teddy aside, I turned to a consideration of the previous evening's events. Had I been at liberty, I would have summoned Laurence Herbert to see me this morning, but, as it had been the week before, my time was already spoken for. Accordingly, I'd written a note requesting his presence in my rooms at five o'clock.

Herbert's claim that his attackers had threatened to slit his throat had alarmed me. Taken in conjunction with the mutilation of his face, it seemed a considerable escalation of violence in comparison with the first three attacks. However, as both Haviland and Vennell claimed to have no recollection of their attack, they might have been similarly threatened for all we knew.

Of course, there was always the possibility that Herbert was lying. Walking home after Askew had left us to make his way back into Corpus – something he'd done fairly frequently if his nonchalance was any guide – Non had pointed out that we only had Herbert's word that he'd been threatened, or that the threat had been in earnest.

'I mean, even if you disregard that "liar" cut into his face,' she said, 'did he come across as trustworthy to you? All that "a gentleman's word doesn't need to be confirmed" nonsense made me think he had something to hide.'

Non, having had rather a different upbringing to the one Mr Herbert had enjoyed, didn't quite appreciate the value placed on a gentleman's word, but, nevertheless, I had to concede that Herbert had seemed overly defensive.

'Tarley's going to ask some people at Corpus if they know anything about these so-called Hunters,' Non said.

'Hmmm. Fond as I am of Askew, if this society is in any way dubious, I fear he'll ask in vain. He reeks of fair play and a straight bat.'

'To us, perhaps. But don't forget, he fooled Carmichael Johnson into thinking he was a customer for dubious substances.'

She was referring to the circumstances in which Askew and I had met, and I had to admit that perhaps he had more than one face to show the world.

'Meanwhile,' Non said, 'I've been thinking about the name of the club.'

'Venatores?'

'Yes, all that Latin pretentiousness. We've been assuming that the Hunters pre-date the attacks because the initial assumption – yours and the Senior Proctor's – was that the hoodings were some kind of inter-club rivalry or feud. But what if this is something else? What if the Hunters formed their club specifically to carry out these attacks?'

'For what reason?' I asked, feeling my pulse quicken.

Non met my gaze. 'That's the question, isn't it?'

## Chapter 21

*Non*

I'd promised Basil I'd find out whether there was any gossip in town about the hooding attacks. So, on Tuesday morning, after a quick visit to the churchyard on Queen's Lane to see if there was any evidence to support Herbert's story about being taken there, I pedalled down to the High Street. I knew the person most likely to have heard something if there was anything to hear.

I left my tandem – which Lily always called the Contraption – outside the *Oxford Mercury*'s building and climbed the stairs to the offices.

'Is he in?' I asked one of the clerks, pointing my chin at the editor's door.

The man nodded. 'Want me to ask if he'll see you?'

I grinned. 'No thanks, he might say no. I'll just barge in.'

He grinned back. 'Go on then, but if there's trouble, I'll say you took no notice of me.'

I winked and walked past his desk. I'd always got on with the *Mercury*'s clerks. Unlike the staff journalists, I didn't treat them like servants.

'Morning, Mr Alconbury,' I said as I walked into his office. I had to remember to call him by his real name, because, behind his back, everybody called the editor 'Berry'. He had a very red face because of some skin condition and he was sensitive about it.

'Miss Vaughan. To what do I owe the pleasure of this *unannounced* visit?'

I took my gloves off and pulled out the chair he hadn't offered me.

'Can we have a confidential conversation?' I asked.

He narrowed his eyes at me. 'That depends…'

'There's something happening in town. To do with the undergraduates—'

'Is this going to be a farrago of hearsay and rumour, Miss Vaughan?'

I decided not to take offence. 'No. This is something I've seen with my own eyes. But it's something the University is very keen to keep quiet.'

All the Oxford papers tiptoed around anything controversial to do with the University. It didn't do to bite the hand that fed a lot of their subscribers.

'Go on.'

'You know everybody in Oxford. And everything that happens, pretty well. I just want to know if you've heard anything.'

Berry's fingers drummed on his blotter. 'Heard anything about what, exactly?'

'Undergraduates being attacked after dark. Bound hand and foot and gagged. Hoods put over their heads. Dumped outside their college gates late at night.'

He stared at me, and I stared right back. 'So... have you heard anything?' I looked at the shelf behind him. 'Are there any letters sitting up there that you've chosen not to publish because they'd embarrass the University?' The shelf held boxes of letters from readers. The ones Berry chose to print, *and* the ones he didn't.

He ignored my question. 'You say they were bound hand and foot, and hooded?'

'That's right.'

'Were their arms bound to their bodies at the elbows, so they couldn't lift their hands up?'

Basil hadn't mentioned anything like that in the case of the other boys, but now I thought about the way Laurence Herbert had been tied up, I remembered a rope around his waist, pinning his elbows to his body. 'Yes.'

'And their legs were bound at the ankles?'

'Yes. Why?'

Berry looked me in the eye. 'Because that's how they tie men up when they hang them.'

I stared at him, my mind suddenly full of images and questions. Four condemned men, ready for execution, dumped outside their colleges.

Was the binding and hooding a threat, like the knife to Herbert's throat? Were the hooding attacks a warning about what might happen next?

Berry sighed as if he was about to do something against his better judgement and stood up to take the current box of letters off the shelf.

'I received a communication the other day which may be relevant,' he said, as he started to go through the papers in the box. He had a specific way of filing readers' letters. He never kept the envelopes and he always put the letters in the box unfolded, so he could see them at a glance. Each one was gathered together with others on a similar subject with a Gem clip and a slip of paper stating what category of letter it was – labels like 'City Council', 'Elections', 'State of the Nation', 'Stone-throwing Youths', 'University', and so on.

He plucked out a sheaf of letters and held it up. I got a quick glimpse of the label. It read 'Immoral Intentions'.

After quickly scanning the letter he was interested in, he handed it to me.

> To the Editor of the Oxford Mercury
>
> Dear Sir,
>
> You probably won't see fit to print this but here goes anyway.
>
> The way young women in this town are being harassed is a disgrace. If it's not the undergraduates, it's the proctors or the bulldogs. Young women have no peace from 6 p.m. onwards when officers start their patrols and the students start prowling for innocents.
>
> Lives are being ruined and the University blames the victims, not the ones responsible for their ruin.
>
> Some of these young men are wicked. The way they ruin girls' lives, they might as well be murderers. They deserve to be hanged. And they would be if they weren't rich and protected by the University.
>
> It's about time somebody did something about it.
>
> Yours sincerely,
>
> One Who Wishes the Young Women of Oxford Well

When I looked up, Berry was watching me. 'Perhaps somebody *is* doing something about it,' he said.

# Chapter 22

### Basil

Sitting in the Board Room at the workhouse during an uncomfortable discussion on what were termed 'inappropriate friendships' that had developed between some boys at the Oxford Industrial School, I found myself forced, once again, to consider the notion that the Venatores might be hunting undergraduates who also had what they saw as 'inappropriate friendships'. Young men who, like me, were forced to lie in order to disguise their true nature.

In truth, if that was the Venatores' motive for these attacks, then they would regard the actions of their prey as something worse than inappropriate and their own response as entirely proportionate. I knew that the spectrum of public opinion on sodomy ranged from pitying tolerance (as long as its practitioners kept their distance) through mild disgust (along with a profound hope that none of the person's friends might feel such tendencies) to outright abhorrence. Opinions in the latter camp were apt to be accompanied by words like 'abomination' and 'predators', and to call for the death penalty for sodomy to be reintroduced as per the biblical stipulation. The moral purity movement which had become such a force in recent times had not helped matters, and though I knew of enough people of good conscience who saw no sin in what men like me did together, the majority of public opinion was against us.

If the Venatores were hunting sodomites, then they would find no ready opposition amongst the police, of that I was quite sure. Gangs who discovered and savagely beat men like me were not pursued. And if a man *should* happen to be charged with assault after such an attack, he had only to claim that he had been solicited for sex by the pervert he'd beaten, and he'd see the charges against him quietly dropped. The insult to a man's integrity that such an approach implied made a violent response excusable. Even, in some eyes, praiseworthy.

—

Instead of returning to college after my Board of Guardians meeting, I made a detour to Brasenose College.

The messenger's boy was sent on his errand, and within two or three minutes, I was informed that Mr Campbell would be pleased to see me in his rooms.

Though I'd known Norton Campbell since our undergraduate days when we had moved in the same clandestine circles, I'd never visited Brasenose before, and I looked around with interest as the boy led me through the first quad. The large sundial on the many-gabled northern range suggested a medieval foundation – my own college's front quad boasted a clock – and I wondered whether attitudes here reflected this longer history.

'This is Mr Campbell's set,' the boy said, extending a formal hand to invite me to knock. As I did so, he nodded at me and disappeared down the stairs.

'Rice! My dear fellow!' Campbell shook my hand. 'What brings you to my door?' He paused fractionally then asked, 'No trouble, I hope?'

He was referring, delicately, to the kind of trouble that I suspected the victims of the hooding attacks might have got themselves into.

For myself, the likelihood of my proclivities being discovered had declined markedly with Teddy's removal to London. Since then, I'd been as celibate as the University's founding priests and monks. Or, given the likely adherence to chastity of men who'd been forced to take holy orders as a means of career advancement, possibly considerably more celibate.

'No, nothing like that,' I assured him.

'Everybody's having to be a lot more cautious since the marriage ban was lifted,' he observed, raising a decanter of sherry in a wordless offer.

I nodded. 'Please.'

'Now that almost every fellow under forty has availed himself of some female to take to the altar, those of us who are left are looked upon a touch askance, don't you find?'

It was a rhetorical question; we both knew the lie of the land. And, even if we weren't looked at askance, it was becoming increasingly uncomfortable to live in college with superannuated fellows who had little enthusiasm for what they termed the 'New Oxford' with its married dons, the expectation that resident fellows should actually teach undergraduates, and an increasing emphasis on sending our young men into the world with a decent degree. The Oxford of their heyday had been a slower, lazier, less intellectually ambitious one.

'As a matter of fact,' Campbell said, eyes fixed on the sherry he was pouring, 'I'm manoeuvring my way towards marriage myself. I need the younger fellows' support if I'm ever going to be Principal, and the way to get that support is to have a wife who befriends theirs.'

I took the sherry he proffered. The glass was modern, lens-cut and had probably cost a fortune.

The sitting room was slightly smaller than mine but more stylishly furnished. I noticed a couple of pictures painted in the new, allusive French style. They were surprisingly attractive.

Campbell folded himself into one of the room's four armchairs. He was a pleasant-looking man with a ready smile and an athletic frame. He'd be highly eligible as a prospective husband.

'Do you have a bride in mind?' I asked, politely.

'Very much so. She's the sister of one of the new fellows here. Sharp, witty, and she knows University politics better than I do. I'm becoming rather fond of her.'

'And do you feel you'll make a good husband?' My mind was, inevitably, on Teddy's brief marriage. He and his late wife – who had also preferred the company of her own sex between the bedsheets – had had what he referred to as 'not so much an understanding as an explicit agreement'.

'I believe I shall make an ideal husband,' Cameron told me. 'I'll make my wife the mistress of a modern house on the Banbury Road, I'll fill it with interesting people, and I shall scarcely trouble her in the bedroom. As long as we produce an adequate number of children – I think three would be ideal – there will be no subsequent need for Mrs Campbell to endure my attentions. I imagine she'll be delighted.'

His candour made me uncomfortable, but perhaps he was right. As long as we could actually father children, perhaps men like us made ideal husbands. After all, it was accepted that many men had mistresses, so any absences from the domestic sphere as Campbell pursued alternative carnal pleasures might be discreetly ignored.

I sipped my sherry. I'd accepted the glass to lubricate the social wheels rather than because I wanted it, and it was rather sweet for my taste. 'Campbell, I don't know whether you've heard about the recent spate of attacks on undergraduates?'

He looked slightly surprised by my abrupt change of subject, but he answered readily enough. 'The chaps trussed up and hooded?'

'Yes. There was another last night. But this one had upped the ante rather.'

I told him what had happened to Laurence Herbert and explained my involvement. 'I know "liar" isn't as direct an accusation as "sod",' I concluded, 'but I wondered whether you'd heard any whispers? About whether these boys might be our sort?'

'Not a dicky bird,' Campbell said.

'Do you think it's possible?' I asked. 'Perhaps some of the social purity zealots have begun to sniff boys out?'

'I doubt it. They're more concerned with keeping undergrads away from tarts, aren't they? They're all for manly Christianity. You know, cold baths, rugger, plenty of fresh air and pre-marital celibacy.'

'Yes, you're probably right. It was just a thought. But the thing is,' I said, 'whoever's responsible, the attacks have taken a more punitive turn with Herbert's mutilation. Something needs to be done before somebody comes to real harm.'

'I suspect your Mr Herbert would feel he already *has* suffered real harm. Scarring to the face being what it is, he's going to carry that "liar" brand all his life.'

'If he's lucky, a beard will cover it.' On Laurence Herbert's long, high-cheekboned face, a beard would make him look as if he was hiding a weak chin, but that would be better than the alternative.

Campbell looked at me quizzically. 'Odd, isn't it, that you should become the University's weaseller-out of secrets?'

Though I wouldn't have characterised my role in quite that way, I had to agree. It was odd. Or, perhaps, just terrifyingly ironic. I gave what I feared was a sickly grin. 'At least while I'm doing the investigating, nobody's investigating me.'

'No, but the further we raise our heads above the parapet, the more likely we are to get them blown off. Be careful, Rice. Be very careful.'

## Chapter 23

### Non

Before leaving Berry's office, I'd asked him if he'd consider printing an article on the hooding attacks. I hadn't really thought he would, and I wasn't proved wrong.

'Not only am I loath to incur the wrath of the Vice Chancellor, Miss Vaughan, but there's also the very real possibility that, if they read about them, town youths with too much time on their hands might take it into their heads to emulate these attacks.'

It was probably just as well. William Stead had accepted my piece comparing the Vice Chancellor's court with the Contagious Diseases Acts and now he wanted more. I'd written to him suggesting an article on Miss Skene followed by a piece on Sarah's incarceration, and he'd replied by return of post asking to see both. *If they're up to the same standard as your CDA piece,* his letter had said, *perhaps we might consider a weekly column on goings-on in Oxford – Oxford Notes or something similar – where we could cover this young woman's case. Include only what you've seen or heard personally when you write about Miss Skene. First-hand experience, that's what will attract our readers' attention.*

I hadn't told him about the hooding attacks yet. I needed to have a clearer idea of who was behind them and why they'd chosen those particular victims before I put anything in front of Stead. But I knew he'd think Christmas had come early when he heard about young toffs being trussed up as if they were going to execution.

Meanwhile, I had to impress him with the two articles he wanted to see. And, as yet, my article on Miss Skene wasn't good enough.

It was the subject matter that was making it difficult. Even though I'd been writing odd pieces for the *Mercury* for more than two years, I wasn't used to writing about people. The Oxford papers only really gave details of people's lives in their obituaries, and I hadn't been trusted with any of those.

'*You should start with the parrot*,' Hara said after I'd spent ten minutes staring out of the window at the chrysanthemums in the little front garden opposite.

'The parrot?'

'*Plenty of people keep songbirds, but how many keep parrots? Especially ones that are allowed to fly about the house.*'

It was true. Iain and his antics would tell people, from the off, that Miss Skene was somebody out of the ordinary.

I could start with the parrot, move on to Tatters the terrier, then slide into Miss Skene's prison visiting by saying that the dog went with her everywhere, even into the punishment cell and the condemned cell of Oxford Prison.

'*Steady on*,' Hara said. '*Don't you think going from pets to hangings in the same sentence would be a bit shocking for readers?*'

'*I want to shock them. Or at least make them think. Miss Skene isn't your average charitable lady. That needs to be obvious from the outset.*'

So, after I'd completely redrafted my article, I made my way to Miss Skene's house to show her the result.

This time, the maid, Jane, showed me upstairs to Miss Skene's study. It was slightly bigger than the little parlour downstairs, with fewer paintings and more books. From the pile of letters on the desk under the window it looked as if Miss Skene had been up all night writing.

Tatters was with her and so was Iain. As I was shown in, the parrot stopped trying to crack the Brazil nut in his claws and cocked his head at me as if to say, 'You again'.

Miss Skene looked at the article I held out to her. 'I didn't realise that it was customary to show articles to their subjects before publication,' she said. 'I should have thought that would produce rather anodyne results.'

If I'd told her the truth, I'd have said that no article about her could possibly be anodyne, but I didn't want her to think I was buttering her up. So I just said, 'I hope not, but see what you think.'

I got more and more nervous as she read the article through once, then again, without comment.

What was she thinking? Had I offended her? Because we'd agreed that my main focus would be on her work, rather than her personally,

I'd put in short, anonymised sketches of the women we'd visited at the prison. Perhaps she didn't think that was appropriate?

But her first comment reassured me. 'Your choice of inmates to illustrate the kind of crimes these women are sent to prison for is well judged. Particularly Nellie.'

I remembered the section – and so I should, I'd rewritten it often enough.

> N____, *described in the prison register as 'twenty-three years old, married, mother of four children' was committed for stealing two pairs of trousers and two shirts from a second-hand clothes shop. She is as contrite as any magistrate could hope a period of incarceration might make her, but she resolutely refuses Miss Skene's advice that she apply to that same magistrate for a separation order which would force her feckless, drunken husband to support her and his children, and prevent him from beating her when she will not 'shift herself to work', by which he means prostitute herself or steal.*

'The question is,' I ventured, 'overall, have I captured the work you do?'

Miss Skene looked up. She didn't wear glasses to read which, at her age, probably meant that she was short-sighted, though she obviously saw me well enough across the small room.

'I believe you have,' she said. 'Though as to the depiction of me personally, I would feel happier with a few amendments. The removal of the word "extraordinary" for instance, and the word "colourful" as a description of my youth. I believe the former to be untrue, while the latter might suggest a want of morals.'

The ladies of the AEW had yet to see me blush, but I felt myself going hot now. The idea that Miss Skene thought I might have been suggesting that she lacked morals was mortifying.

After I'd finished apologising, I asked, 'If I remove "extraordinary" and replace "colourful" with "well-travelled", are you happy for me to send it to the editor of the *Pall Mall Gazette*?'

'Yes, thank you. I think Mr Stead will like it.'

'Are you acquainted?' I asked. They probably were – nobody knew more people than Felicia Skene.

'Indeed we are.' She passed the article back to me. 'Before you submit your piece on Sarah's misfortunes to Mr Stead, I should tell you that there has been a development in respect of her wish to clear her name.'

I waited.

'A barrister of my acquaintance – Mr Martin Alexis, a young man very much of your mind, Miss Vaughan – has asked me whether Sarah might consider taking her case to law and suing the University for false imprisonment.'

William Stead would be in his oils. A lawsuit against the University would be even more likely to catch the public's imagination than a simple story about Sarah's incarceration.

'How did you respond?' I asked, cautiously.

'I asked him whether he was looking for a case that would bring him to the public's attention,' she said, tartly.

Her words reminded me of what Tarley'd said about my article on Sarah's case potentially calling her reputation into question. If he'd been completely honest, would he have accused me of wanting to use her to make my name? The thought made me go cold.

'If a lawsuit were to go ahead,' I said, watching Miss Skene, who'd turned all upper-class and inscrutable, 'Mr Stead might agree to publish the details anonymously, so that Sarah wouldn't be held up for public scrutiny...'

'You overlook the fact that, unlike the Vice Chancellor's court, a civil case at the county court would be a public hearing,' Miss Skene said. 'Sarah's name would be published in the Oxford papers – and probably more widely, too, taking into consideration the interest a case like this would inevitably give rise to. Everybody would be watching to see what happened to a young woman who dared challenge the University of Oxford.'

Something clicked in my dry throat as I swallowed. 'But don't you think,' I said, 'that once the British public knows what's happening on the streets of Oxford – how the proctors harass young women – that public opinion would swing behind Sarah, and against the University? There's a lot of discontent in Oxford about the way the proctors – and the undergraduates – behave. You only have to read the letters columns in the local papers to see that.'

I had the words of the letter I'd read in Berry's office in mind:

> Some of these young men are wicked. The way they ruin girls' lives, they might as well be murderers. They deserve to be hanged. And they would be if they weren't rich and protected by the university.
> It's about time somebody did something about it.

'Sarah is very keen to clear her name,' Miss Skene conceded. 'She feels very badly done by, and she's afraid that this slur will hang over her for the rest of her life if she fails to challenge the judgement in some way.'

She reached down to stroke Tatters, who was lying on her feet, but I could see that she still had more to say.

'However, I fear that, if she were to go to law, Miss Critchley might become a cause célèbre. And I am concerned about the effect that would have on such a young and impressionable person.'

'But when you suggested to Sarah Critchley that she should write to me,' I said, eyes on Miss Skene's face for any flicker of expression that might tell me what she was thinking, 'I assume you wanted me to *do* something?'

'Indeed. What I had in mind was, perhaps, an article on the Vice Chancellor's powers and the way they are wielded against young women without education or influence. An article that, possibly, mentioned Sarah's case without using her name.'

'As it happens, I've already submitted an article to more or less that effect,' I said. 'It'll publicise the authority the Vice Chancellor's court has here – which, I'd be willing to bet, the vast majority of the British public doesn't know about and wouldn't approve of if it did. But that won't clear Sarah's name.' I hesitated. 'If that's what she wants, shouldn't we at least *talk* to her about bringing a case?'

Just then, Tatters gave a little whine, as if he was sympathising with his mistress's dilemma. Or maybe he just wanted her to start stroking him again.

Felicia Skene sighed. 'Very well. I suggest you bring Sarah here after work one evening so that we can discuss the proposal with her.' She paused. 'But, Miss Vaughan, have you considered your own position in all this?'

I didn't know what she meant and that must have been written all over my face.

'If you publish articles that make not only Miss Critchley's case but the whole issue of the Vice Chancellor's powers a matter of public debate, your life will change quite considerably.' Miss Skene gazed at me steadily. 'For instance, I fear that Miss Shaw Lefevre would consider it impossible to maintain your employment at Somerville. The blatant challenge to the University's powers that such a story would imply would mean that both she and the AEW board would, necessarily, wish to distance themselves from you.' She paused slightly. 'Are you prepared to bring that down on your own head?'

# Chapter 24

### Basil

When Non and I met at Lily's house on Friday night, we spoke of the hoodings before anything else.

'I'm afraid I have nothing to report vis-à-vis Mr Herbert,' I said, sitting down with Non and Askew for a few minutes before dinner. 'He sent a note regretting that he was *unable to leave his rooms due to the continuing effects of the attack he'd endured*. So we know no more than we did on Tuesday night.'

'As it happens,' Non said, 'we do know one more thing. Mr Herbert was lying when he told us he'd been dragged into the churchyard on Queen's Lane.'

I stared at her. 'How do you know?'

'He said he was thrown down on the grass. Well, first thing on Wednesday morning, I went up and looked over the whole churchyard. There was no trampling anywhere, nothing to suggest a struggle. Every blade of grass, dead or alive, was upright and perfect.'

'So he lied about getting dragged off?' Askew said.

'Not necessarily,' Non said. 'More likely he was just lying about where he was dragged off *to*.'

Askew frowned. 'Why?'

'To obfuscate. Maybe he didn't want to admit that he'd been taken into St Helen's Passage in case Basil made a connection with the attack on Harcourt Ashdown.'

'What kind of connection?' I asked.

Non turned to me from her contemplation of Askew. 'I have a possible answer,' she said. 'I went into the *Mercury* offices to see if Berry'd heard anything about the hooding attacks and he showed me a letter.' She took a sheet of paper out of her pocket and handed it to me.

Askew rose and came to read over my shoulder. 'This is your handwriting, Non.'

'I wrote it down when I came home.'

Askew nodded, accustomed by now – as was I – to Non's extraordinary ability to remember anything she'd read verbatim.

The final couple of paragraphs were obviously what she was referring to.

> They deserve to be hanged. And they would be if they weren't rich and protected by the University.
> It's about time somebody did something about it.

'Berry thinks perhaps somebody *is* doing something about it,' she said when I looked up.

'The Venatores? Alconbury thinks they're hunting undergraduates who try to pick up girls on the streets?'

'Berry doesn't think anything about the so-called Hunters, because I didn't mention them. He's just asking himself whether somebody's decided that enough's enough.'

Askew took the letter from me and read through it again.

'Berry said something else that was interesting as well,' Non went on. 'After he'd asked about the way the boys had been tied up, he reminded me that that's the way men are bound before they're hanged.'

Askew looked up abruptly. 'An implicit threat? "Stop what you're doing or we'll hang you"?'

'Or just the suggestion that they *deserve* to be hanged,' Non said. 'Like in the letter.'

'Wait a moment,' I said. 'We're jumping to a great number of conclusions here on little or no evidence. Non, your mind is on young women's treatment on the streets because of the Sarah Critchley case – which was presumably the spur for the well-wisher's letter too. But we've no evidence whatsoever to link these hooding attacks to undergraduates attempting to seduce young women.'

'Well, whatever their crime, I think somebody – possibly the Hunters – thinks they deserve to be punished, if not actually hanged. There's something else, too,' Non said. 'It turns out I'm not the only one with Sarah Critchley's case on my mind. A barrister friend of Miss

Skene's has suggested that Sarah should sue the University for wrongful imprisonment.'

Just then, Lily came to shoo us all into the dining room but, though our argument might have been curtailed, it had sparked a train of thought in me that might prove productive.

I was going to have to pay another visit to the Senior Proctor.

## Chapter 25

*Non*

On Saturday evening, I asked Edie to put my dinner into the warming oven and went to meet Sarah Critchley from work. I was going to take her to Miss Skene's house so that we could discuss this barrister's idea of her suing the University.

Dusk was turning to dark as I walked down Walton Street, and I watched the lamps coming on, one at a time, ahead of me, as the lamplighters moved steadily up the road with their ladders.

After a quick visit to Somerville that morning to give a couple of tutorials, I'd spent the rest of the day drafting an article on Sarah Critchley's case for the *Pall Mall Gazette*.

I was sure William Stead would support Sarah if she did decide to sue for false imprisonment. In fact, he'd probably pay her to do it. Still, exciting as that thought was, Miss Skene's warning that supporting Sarah might be an end to my academic career weighed on my mind.

I'd intended to carry on working for the AEW and Somerville until I could find backers for a new Oxford paper, but if I was involved with a false imprisonment case, I might find myself out of a job. On the other hand, if Stead's idea of an Oxford Notes column came to pass, I might be able to write a series of articles on Sarah challenging the University, and the effects of the case on the University's reputation. If that happened, I'd earn enough to cover what the AEW and Somerville were paying me and more.

'Never mind what's best for you,' my sister butted in, '*what about what's best for Sarah Critchley? What if she loses her lawsuit? Then it won't only be the Vice Chancellor's court that's decided she's a loose woman, the county court will have as well. And this time, it'll be in all the papers.*'

'The county court deciding for the University wouldn't prove anything about Sarah,' I said, '*it would just show that the system supports the powerful against* the weak. And don't you worry, if that happened, I'd be making it abundantly clear why.'

'And you think that the average newspaper reader is going to believe you rather than the verdict of a judge?' Hara scoffed. '*You can tell yourself that, if you like. We both know that this is about you trying to get backing for a new paper.*'

'You're wrong. It's about challenging the University's right to dictate to the people of Oxford.'

'*Dictate to* you, *you mean.*'

I shut her out. My sister could go and boil her head. I'd had enough of her finger-wagging.

I knew that some people called William Stead a muck-raking scandalmonger, a man who sold sensationalism, not news. But he was doing something new, something I wanted to do, too. He was uncovering the truth behind the news people were given, and confronting people with what was really going on.

And if, by throwing my hat into that ring with him, I put an end to any career I might have had as an academic – well, so be it. Stead might even prefer it if I was drummed out of the AEW in disgrace. In his eyes it would mean I'd planted both feet on the angels' side of the fence.

Nothing was likely to happen very soon, anyway, so I probably had until the end of term to hand in my notice at Somerville before Miss Shaw Lefevre could sack me.

'*What if William Stead wants the court case covered but doesn't ask you to do it? Have you thought of that?*' my sister asked, spitefully. '*There are plenty of better-known journalists that he could call on who'd be delighted to do it.*'

'He's said he'll publish my article on the Vice Chancellor's court sending Sarah to prison,' I said. '*If that's good enough, why would he ask somebody else to follow her court case?*'

Hara had no answer to that, but she'd hooked a niggling little thorn into my mind.

On New Inn Hall Street, gaggles of young men in gowns were standing about in the light of the street lamps, laughing and puffing their chests out and taking altogether too much notice of any female who walked by. I wasn't going to take any nonsense from them, so I marched down the middle of the street and ignored the whistles and catcalls that followed me. If one of them made the mistake of laying a hand on me he'd wish he hadn't. My father had taught me to defend myself before he let me set foot on his ship. He knew what sailors were like.

But I reached the bottom of New Inn Hall Street unmolested and turned left towards Hyde's clothing factory.

While I stood outside waiting for Sarah, the full darkness of night closed over the rooftops, making the street lights seem to glow more brightly. Up and down Queen Street, the bigger shops with their etched-glass windows were lit up like lanterns, their interiors glowing with golden light.

There were a few undergraduates here, too. At this hour, most of the gownsmen were in college for their dinner, but the more adventurous were dining out and hoping not to get caught anywhere they shouldn't be.

Finally, the doors to Hyde's opened and a stream of girls spilled out. I saw Sarah straight away – she was the only one not chattering to another girl. Was she being shunned, I wondered, or was she just yet to find her feet?

I went after her and called her name. When she turned, it took her a moment or two, then she smiled. 'Miss Vaughan!'

'You don't have to curtsey to me, Sarah, I'm a sailor's daughter, not a lady,' I said. 'Miss Skene would like to see us both. Have you got time to walk up with me now?'

'What does she want me for?'

'I'll explain when we get there.' Suing the University wasn't a subject to raise while we were standing in the street.

Sarah shrugged. 'All right then. But Mum'll be expecting me. I shouldn't be too long or... well... she worries. After what happened.'

I tucked her arm through mine, and she looked at me in surprise. 'Safety in numbers,' I said, thinking of the catcalling gownsmen I'd marched through.

'How are you finding the new job?' I asked as we walked.

'All right. Least I get to sit down now and then. We weren't allowed to sit down at all at Badcock's. And the hours are shorter – a bit, anyway.'

That was true. She wouldn't have finished at seven in the evening at Badcock's. Not on a Saturday when the shop was open till at least ten o'clock. But shorter hours would mean less pay, too. And all because she'd answered a question a boy had asked her as she was walking home.

In the ten minutes since I'd come down New Inn Hall Street, most of the undergraduates had disappeared to wherever it was they went until curfew, and we walked up the street unmolested. We were almost at the turning in the road which would take us to Miss Skene's house, when I heard footsteps come running up behind us and a voice, calling, 'Sarah! Sarey, is that you?'

As I whipped around, I felt Sarah pulling her arm away from me.

Coming towards us was a slim, fair-haired boy in a commoner's gown. In the light of the street lamps I could see that his suit wasn't quite the sort of thing Laurence Herbert had been wearing, and he didn't have a watch chain. He might be a student, but he wasn't a well-off one.

He came to a halt in front of Sarah and ignored me as if I was invisible. 'Sarey, I've been looking everywhere for you!' Whoever this young man was, he obviously had more than a passing acquaintance with Sarah Critchley. I turned to her, but her eyes were on him as if they'd been glued there. 'The people at Badcock's told me you didn't work there any more. They told me you'd been in prison!'

'It wasn't my fault, Gordon!' She put her hand out as if she was going to touch him, then thought better of it and pulled back. 'It was the proctors. One of your friends stopped me and I thought—'

'I've looked out for you every night after work,' he interrupted before she could explain herself any more, 'but you were never there.'

Sarah glanced at me and said, in a smaller voice. 'I'm at Hyde's now.'

Finally the boy – Gordon – looked at me, then back at Sarah as if he was waiting for an explanation.

'Sarah,' I said, 'will you introduce me to your friend?'

She looked uncomfortable and I wondered whether she was embarrassed about introducing me to him or him to me. 'Gordon, this is Miss Vaughan. She's helping me.'

'Helping? In what way?' He didn't sound very pleased with the idea.

'She's going to help me get my good name back.'

Gordon frowned, then he shook his head a little bit, and plastered a smile on his face.

Sarah looked agitated. Busy fingers had started picking at the skin around both her thumbnails. Who *was* this undergraduate and why had he been looking for her? Actually, *was* he an undergraduate? Anybody could buy a second-hand gown.

'Well, that's wonderful, Sarey,' he said. 'But how are you proposing to do that, miss?'

'Miss *Vaughan*,' I said. 'I intend to help Miss Critchley sue the Vice Chancellor for false imprisonment.' Slight poetic licence, but it seemed justified if I was going to put him in his place.

The two of them responded simultaneously.

'Go to court?' Sarah asked, wide-eyed, while Gordon shook his head vehemently. 'Oh no, I don't think that's a very good idea.'

I took hold of Sarah's arm once more and answered her question as if Gordon hadn't spoken. 'Yes, to court. Miss Skene has a barrister in mind. As long as you're agreeable.' Then, without waiting to hear whether she was agreeable or not, I turned back to the young man. 'And what gives you the right to express an opinion on this matter, Mr...?'

'Smythe. Gordon Smythe. Of New Inn Hall.'

'And he does have the right,' Sarah said. 'Because we're going to be married.'

## Chapter 26

*Basil*

Early on Saturday evening, I found myself once more in Kaye's rooms at Magdalen.

Accepting the glass of sherry he offered, I got to the point.

'Kaye, Herbert's mutilation suggests that we've entered rather different territory vis-à-vis these hoodings. I think we must accept that this is something more serious than inter-collegiate rivalry. I have a suspicion that the first three attacks may have been a warning which was not heeded, hence the mutilation. If they're allowed to continue, the attacks may escalate further.'

Kaye paused in the act of raising his glass to his lips. 'You say "allowed to continue" as if we had some say in this.'

'Perhaps we do.'

A sudden gust of squally wind rattled the windows and rain lashed against the dark glass. I shivered involuntarily. Though the walk back to Jesus wasn't long, it was far enough to get soaked if the rain continued.

'I wonder,' I said, nerving myself to present Non's theory, 'whether these attacks are, in some sense, a continuation of last year's proctorial crusade against immorality. Whether it's possible that a group of undergraduates has, as it were, picked up the baton Holland and Smith wielded against fraternisation between gownsmen and town girls.'

'Are you suggesting,' Kaye asked, cautiously, 'that undergraduates are punishing those of their fellows whom they suspect of immorality?'

'I think it's possible,' I said. 'If you consider the moral climate that's developed in the University during the last year or so, it doesn't seem so very unlikely. In addition to the proctors' campaign, you know the effect Moody and Sankey's mission had – young men swearing off all kinds of vices and committing themselves to muscular Christianity at every step and turn. And now we've got the Church of England Purity Association establishing itself in the colleges too.'

Kaye nodded. 'I gather it's practically compulsory to be a member at Keble.'

Keble College, established little more than a decade before as a less extravagant alternative for boys intending to enter the church, was still trying to establish its legitimacy amongst the more traditional colleges. As a consequence, Keble men tended to be a clannish lot, inclined to see the roistering habits of other undergraduates as evidence, if not of immorality, then definitely of a lack of moral seriousness. 'Plain living and steady reading' had been the motto of its founders and, thus far, it was largely adhered to.

'Am I right in thinking,' I asked, 'that there was a pre-existing purity society at Keble? One established before Moody and Sankey's mission?'

Kaye, apparently dissatisfied with his sherry, put down his glass. 'Yes. They rather wittily called it "Moral Intentions".'

'Does it still exist, or has it been subsumed into the Church of England group?'

'I couldn't say, my dear fellow.' Kaye stared at me, suddenly catching my drift. 'You don't suspect *them* of these atrocities? It would be incredibly hypocritical, surely, for a group dedicated to an upright life to break so many University rules?'

'Not necessarily. Presumably "moral intentions" signals a dedication to chastity and sobriety rather than an aversion to being out after curfew and chastising one's sinful peers?' I watched Kaye's troubled face as he took my words in. 'After all, pious Christians they might be, but they're still young men, and young men tend to join righteous battle rather enthusiastically on occasion, without necessarily thinking of the consequences.'

Kaye sighed. 'I suppose it's possible that some misguided zealots might have chosen a questionable path. But would they really engrave the word "liar" on a fellow undergraduate's face? It seems so... histrionic. If they suspected these fellows of immorality, why did they not just come to me – or the relevant dean?'

'Surely you're not so old that you've forgotten what it is to be in your late teens and early twenties, Kaye? Nature has suddenly given you the muscles and stamina and instincts to go out and fight. To hunt. Meanwhile, school has imposed on you a moral code which says you mustn't inform on your peers. So what choice have you but to take matters into your own hands?'

The Senior Proctor looked more unsettled by the minute. 'If that's true, Rice, what do you propose to do about it?'

I noted his use of the second person singular. Clearly, I was to be left to manage this alone. 'I propose,' I said, 'to ask the Warden of Keble for permission to address the Church of England Purity Association in his hall. If, as I suspect, "Moral Intentions" now forms a subset of the larger group, then I shall be addressing them as well.'

## Chapter 27

*Non*

Gordon Smythe – Sarah Critchley's supposed fiancé – was proving difficult to shake off.

And Sarah wasn't helping. Now that she'd declared their engagement, she didn't want her reunion with him brought to an end. She'd hooked her arm through his and they stood there like Darby and Joan.

I needed to separate them. If I left Sarah with Gordon Smythe for five minutes, he'd persuade her to drop the idea of suing the University.

But, before I took her to see Miss Skene, I wanted to know why Mr Smythe thought bringing a lawsuit was such a bad idea. If he was her fiancé, I'd have expected him to be as keen to clear her name as she was. Marrying a girl branded as no better than she should be wouldn't do his respectability any good at all.

And it wasn't just clearing her name he seemed uncertain about. Standing there, arm in arm with Sarah, Gordon Smythe looked very uncomfortable. She only had eyes for him, but his were darting everywhere. He was probably worried about being seen with us; the proctors would be out prowling now. But there'd be no trouble if he introduced Sarah to them as his fiancée, would there?

'Why wouldn't you support Sarah in suing for false imprisonment, Mr Smythe?' I asked.

His attention snapped straight back to me. 'Because the University has all the power in this city and somebody like Sarah has none. They'd make mincemeat of her, and her reputation would suffer, not benefit.' He turned away from me. 'Sarey, you mustn't do this. The University won't stand for it. They'll blacken your name just to keep their own looking whiter than white.'

She put a hand on his lapel and was about to say something, but I got in first. 'Where are you from, Mr Smythe?' There was something odd about the way he spoke.

'I believe I already told you. New Inn Hall.'

'I don't mean in Oxford. Where were you brought up?'

He took a long breath, like a man trying to be reasonable. 'Yorkshire.'

I'd heard Yorkshire accents and none of them sounded like that. 'Where exactly?'

His jaw clenched as if he was keeping angry words inside his teeth, but his voice was civil enough. 'Leeds.'

That's when I knew he was lying. One of the girls I tutored at Somerville was a doctor's daughter from Leeds and the way she spoke was entirely different.

'Ah,' I said, 'so you're an East Riding man, then?'

The test was a risk. Even if he wasn't from Leeds he might know that it was in the West Riding. But the gamble paid off: he nodded, then turned back to Sarah. 'Sarey, promise me you won't do this. If you go up against the University, it'll be in all the papers, and my parents will know what you were accused of.'

Before she could answer, I stepped in. 'Miss Critchley can't make that promise, Mr Smythe, because she hasn't discussed the case with Miss Skene and me yet. Miss Felicia Skene,' I clarified, 'granddaughter of the sixth baronet of Pitsligo.' In Oxford, it never hurt to throw in a title when you were trying to intimidate somebody. 'Miss Skene visited Sarah while she was in prison.' *Which is more than you did*, I might have added. What price his feelings for her if he'd let her languish in jail without a single visit? And if he'd managed to track her down today, why hadn't he seen her coming home on her first day at Hyde's? She'd been there a week by this point, so it seemed to me that he couldn't have tried very hard to find her.

I took Sarah's free elbow. 'Come on, Sarah, Miss Skene will be waiting.' That wasn't true, but neither she nor Gordon Smythe knew that.

'No. I want to go home,' Sarah said. 'My mum'll be worried.' She glanced at Smythe as if she was waiting for him to offer to walk her home, but I wasn't going to give him twenty minutes to bring her round to his way of thinking.

'Then I'll walk with you,' I said. 'I live on Shene Road, so it won't be out of my way.'

'Will you be at church tomorrow?' Smythe asked from behind my shoulder as I urged Sarah along.

I couldn't stop her turning around as we headed for George Street. 'I'll be there!' she called to him. 'Will you?'

'I will!' Smythe called.

'Which church is it you go to?' I asked.

'St Paul's. That's where we met.'

St Paul's church was on our way home. A Georgian building on Walton Street pretending to be a Classical temple. In Greece it would have looked lovely. In Oxford it stood out like a parrot amongst magpies. Not the closest church to New Inn Hall for any pious undergraduate. So why would Mr Smythe worship there, I wondered?

'How long have you known him?' I asked.

'Long enough for him to ask me to marry him and to give me this,' Sarah said, defiantly, and pulled out a plain silver necklace from under the neckline of her dress. Hanging from it was a gold signet ring.

'Go on, look,' she said. 'It's his. It's got his initials on. His father gave it to him when he came to Oxford.'

I looked, though I couldn't really see the engraving in the dark.

'E. G. S.,' she said as she tucked the ring away. 'Edward Gordon Smythe. I'm going to be Mrs Gordon Smythe.'

## Chapter 28

*Basil*

After leaving Kaye, I strolled up to Keble to see the Warden, Edward Talbot, and asked him whether I might speak to the Purity Association in Keble Hall the following evening. As one of the organising committee he was perfectly placed to bring the membership together and, when he'd heard me out, he readily agreed.

I had anticipated a quiet Sunday in which to plan what I would say to the gathering, but on my return from church, the porter presented me with a note from Non asking that I call in after lunch if I was free.

Accordingly, I made my way up to Shene Road, only to find Edie alone in the house.

'Mrs Maddox and Albie've gone to see Ivy and little Tommy,' she told me, omitting any mention of Lily's son-in-law, whom she detested, 'and Non's not back from her walk in that dress of hers yet.'

Edie's demeanour was such that I found it almost impossible to tell whether she disapproved of Non's walking dress or admired it excessively. Non had adapted the garment so that she could hook the hem above her ankles when necessary, and it had provoked some comment on the streets of Jericho when she'd first started wearing it out and about.

'But she said if you got here before she was back, that I should make you some tea,' Edie continued, divesting me of my coat and hat, 'and I dare say she won't be long.'

The fire in Lily's front room had been banked down when everybody went out, so I stirred it with the poker and added a few lumps of anthracite, then sat down to read a back edition of *Truth* which was lying on the arm of the sofa. The paper would be Non's. Lily and Albie confined their newspaper reading to the local rags.

I'd just started reading a gleeful account of a spat between the *Pall Mall Gazette* and *St James's Gazette* when Non returned. She popped her head around the door. 'How old is that tea?'

I consulted my watch. 'Fifteen minutes.'

She made a face and swooped in to pick up the tray. 'I'll just get Edie to make a fresh pot.'

Once she was back, she came straight to the point. 'Sarah Critchley's apparently engaged to be married,' she said, flopping down into an armchair. 'To an undergraduate.'

I tried not to show my surprise, lest I be accused of elitism. But if her use of the word 'apparently' was any indication, Non herself wasn't entirely convinced by this engagement either. 'If that's the case, why didn't he come forward when she was taken up by the proctors?' I asked.

'An excellent question,' Non said. 'I suppose, in his defence, the people who knew she'd been arrested wouldn't have known to tell him. The engagement is secret at present,' she clarified. 'At *his* request.' Her expression spoke volumes. 'That's why I asked you to come over. I want you to find out about him.'

She proceeded to tell me the little she knew, and everything she suspected, about Mr Gordon Smythe of New Inn Hall.

'And you're quite sure his name was Smythe?' I said, when she'd finished.

'Yes. Why?'

I told her about the encounter I'd witnessed on the Cornmarket between the proctor's officer, Brandon, his daughter and the young man whom she'd been speaking to. 'He gave his name as Smythe of New Inn Hall, too.'

'So I was right. There *is* something fishy about him,' Non said. 'If he's trying to pick up other girls on the street, his so-called engagement to Sarah Critchley's not worth much, is it? And,' she continued before I could speak, 'if he's not from Leeds like he says – and I'll eat my hat *and* my boots if he is – does that mean he's not really from New Inn Hall either?'

'And that's what you'd like me to find out?'

'Yes. And if he *is* a New Inn Hall boy,' she lowered her voice as we heard the door to the basement kitchen opening, 'I'd like you to talk to him. Get the measure of him. And tell him not to stand in the way of

Sarah bringing a suit against the Vice Chancellor. You're a don – that might make a difference.'

If Smythe's objection was the publicity a lawsuit would generate and his parents' likely response, I doubted very much whether anything I might say would have any influence whatsoever. Muting my voice to little more than a whisper, I said, 'You honestly expect me, a senior member of the University, to persuade him to stand aside so that a young woman can sue the Vice Chancellor and cause a national scandal?'

Non held my gaze. 'Yes. Because it's the right thing to do.' Then she raised her voice. 'Come in, Edie, I'm parched.'

—

The evening was fine, so I took my time walking up to Keble, strolling past building works at Trinity that spilled out on to the pavement, and making my way onto Parks Road.

As I turned the corner to walk under the garden wall of St John's College with its towering trees behind, I glanced across at the undergraduates milling around the entrance to Wadham College.

I could never pass Wadham without being reminded of the puerile undergraduate taunt 'Wadhamite-Sodomite' which, because of its scurrilous rhyme, had persisted for generations after whatever scandal it had originally been coined for. The accusation was deliciously transgressive to the average undergraduate and meant no more than calling a fellow student 'an absolute sod' if you disapproved of something he'd said. But to men like me, every time we heard insults of that kind, apprehension woke within us, however fleetingly.

In my mind's eye I saw the word LIAR carved bloodily into Laurence Herbert's face. Campbell might have heard nothing to alarm him, but I still feared that those responsible for the hoodings might be singling out undergraduates who had sex with other men.

The voices of the Wadham undergraduates faded as I continued along Parks Road towards a many-gabled, four-storey house on the corner of Museum Road. This was Charsley's Hall, a private establishment for undergraduates who, for various reasons, including failure to pass the required initial examinations, had chosen to receive their Oxford education outside the precincts of the colleges. As I crossed Museum Road, I noticed two young men leaving Charsley's and crossing the road. I followed them up Keble's eastern façade until they turned into the main gate. They were, presumably, destined for the meeting I would shortly be addressing.

Even in the dim light of the street lamps, Keble's polychrome brickwork stood out from the more subdued buildings around it like a sore thumb. There was a longstanding, though probably apocryphal story of a visiting French dignitary parodying Field Marshal Bosquet's comment on the Charge of the Light Brigade and pronouncing, '*C'est magnifique, mais ce n'est pas la gare?*'

I hoped it was true, because though, in its own way, Keble *was* magnificent, it did rather resemble the Midland Grand Hotel at St Pancras station.

Having explained myself to the porter, I made my way to the southwestern corner of the main quad and, entering the well-lit hall, I saw that the long tables were already crowded. Keble's undergraduates had remained in situ after their communal dinner.

Edward Talbot, who had been Warden since Keble's foundation, rose to greet me.

'Thanks for allowing me to do this, Talbot,' I said, returning his vigorous handshake.

'Not at all. If there's anything the Association can do to help in this matter you only have to ask. I'm sure I speak for all members – senior and junior – when I say that.'

'How many members do you have?' I asked.

'Well over a hundred. Which, considering our very recent foundation, is decidedly respectable, don't you think?'

I agreed politely, though actually a hundred – or even a hundred and fifty – wasn't a huge proportion of an undergraduate body of two and a half thousand. However, as Talbot indicated, it was still early days for the Church of England Purity Association.

'Does Moral Intentions still exist?' I asked.

He smiled. 'I believe they're a small but proud faction within the wider organisation.'

Given the number of undergraduates who filled the benches in the next ten minutes, I suspected that every single Purity Association member had come to hear what I had to say. If the Senior Proctor was right and my reputation as the University's investigator preceded me, then perhaps the student body had already guessed at the reason for my visit.

Talbot having introduced me, I stepped forward. 'Before I begin, gentlemen, by a show of hands, how many of you are aware of the recent attacks on undergraduates at Queen's, Magdalen, New and Merton in which the young men have been bound, gagged and hooded?'

Looks were exchanged around the hall. Hesitantly at first and then with more conviction, hands began to rise.

'What you may not be aware of,' I said, scanning the crowd for reactions as I spoke, 'is the fact that these attacks have become more sinister. The most recent attack included facial mutilation.'

It was evident from the ensuing hum of murmured comment that the majority had not been aware of this development. I looked for faces that registered less surprise than those of their peers but, in the artificial light, it was difficult to be sure of nuances of expression.

'Thus far,' I began again, bringing about an immediate hush, 'the police have not become involved. Instead, the proctors have asked me to assist with their investigations.'

I didn't add that our enquiries had, hitherto, proved fruitless. Laurence Herbert, whom I'd attempted to visit on my way home from Shene Road, had, once more, failed to make himself available. The Merton College porter had informed me that Mr Herbert had confined himself to his rooms and was refusing to see anybody. He was also, apparently, resolute in his refusal to allow his parents to be told what had happened to him. As he was of age, the Warden had little choice but to accede to his wishes.

My failure to see him notwithstanding, the letters carved into Herbert's cheeks were vivid in my mind's eye as I looked around at the youthful faces in front of me.

'As I'm speaking to young men who have espoused morality and the narrow path,' I said, 'I'll speak frankly, confident that my words won't be quoted beyond this assembly.' Then, without using his name, I outlined exactly what injuries had been inflicted on Herbert. 'Should another mutilation take place,' I said, 'and especially if the victim is yet to turn twenty-one, the University would have little choice but to involve the police. Potentially the Metropolitan CID.'

Oxford was an insufficiently large city to warrant its own Criminal Investigations Department, so the already famous Metropolitan branch would inevitably be called upon. A fact which audibly impressed – or perhaps in a few cases, dismayed – the assembled gownsmen.

'For reasons of autonomy as well as reputation, the University would prefer not to involve the police. But, if the proctors and their officers are to prevent more serious injuries, then undergraduate cooperation is vital. Not in patrolling the streets,' I hastened to add. 'What we require, gentlemen, is your moral assistance.' I paused to let them take in the implications of the adjective.

'Every man in this hall is aware that, amongst schoolboys, there is a code of honour. A code which prevents any information about a peer being shared with those in authority, however heinous the acts he has committed. But this is not school, and you are no longer schoolboys.'

Once more I paused, letting my eye alight here and there on faces in the crowd, attempting to give each young man the impression that I was speaking directly to him.

'We have little idea, as yet, who is behind these attacks, but one possibility is that gownsmen are responsible.'

I allowed the susurration generated by this statement to fill the hall for a few seconds before raising my voice to continue. 'It may be that the victims are felt to have transgressed in some way that dishonours the University. However,' my gaze scanned the hall, 'it is not for undergraduates to police their peers. If you are aware of anybody engaging in this kind of activity, I urge you in the strongest possible terms to persuade them to desist.

'However, should your persuasive powers prove unequal to the task, I ask that you speak to the proctors or myself. Providing information on this subject is not to snitch,' I said, using a word that I'd been surprised to find was as current now as it had been in my time at school, 'it's the act of a responsible man who does not wish to see violence against his peers continue and escalate. It's the act of a man who knows his responsibilities as a member of this University. And it's the act of a man who takes the Lord's injunction to love his neighbour to heart. For both the victims and the perpetrators of these attacks are our neighbours, gentlemen. And the attackers must be brought to see the error of their ways before something unforgiveable takes place.'

I saw no furtive glances being exchanged, no obvious expressions of anxiety. Every young countenance was solemn in the light of the gently hissing lamps.

'And, if you have no information to give,' I said, remembering the nature of the group I was addressing, 'I would beg you to help in another way. Please pray, gentlemen. Pray that whoever has committed these acts of violence should indeed see the error of their ways and cease forthwith.'

I had no doubt that my request for prayer would be honoured. However, whether my other pleas would find equally fertile ground seemed far less certain.

## Chapter 29

*Non*

The more I thought about Gordon Smythe, the more suspicious I was. And it wasn't just his accent. It was that ring. The signet ring he'd given Sarah Critchley to mark their supposed engagement.

'*Come on, Non,*' Hara scolded, '*he's an impoverished student and he wants to promise marriage to the girl, why wouldn't he give her his signet ring?*'

'*Why do you assume he's impoverished?*'

'*Because most of the young men at New Inn Hall are.*'

'He might have been sent down from another college,' I pointed out.

'*All right, he might, but lack of funds seems more likely, don't you think? Especially if he's been courting a girl like Sarah. Rich undergraduates wouldn't give her a second glance, would they?*'

'*If he is courting her,*' I said, '*I don't trust anything he says. Not when he's using that fake accent.*'

But I couldn't turn up at New Inn Hall and start asking questions. I just had to wait for Basil to go and make his enquiries.

And he came up trumps. On Monday afternoon, he appeared at Lily's.

'I've just come back from New Inn Hall,' he told me. 'I put on my best gown and went to talk to the porter.'

Apparently, the man had been all bluster and 'who d'you think you are?' to start with but Basil had smelled a rat.

'You'd have been amused,' he said. 'I assumed my best "don't you know I'm a senior member of the University" manner, told him I was there at the behest of the Senior Proctor – a slight untruth but pardonable in the circumstances – and insisted that he tell me whatever he knew about Smythe.'

And, when Basil had got to the bottom of the story, it had turned out that there *was* no Gordon Smythe at New Inn Hall. The young man calling himself that had paid the porter a sum that amounted to roughly a month's wages to let him in if he turned up at the gates – so much for him being an impoverished student – and to identify him as Gordon Smythe if the proctors dragged him along after curfew.

So, at half past six on Tuesday morning, I was standing opposite the house Sarah Critchley and her mother lodged in, waiting in the early grey light before sunrise for Sarah to appear.

At twenty minutes to seven, the door opened, and I crossed the road.

Sarah gasped in fright as she turned from closing the door and almost bumped into me.

'Oh, it's you,' she said when she realised who I was. For all the warmth in her voice, I might as well have been a creditor, come to collect an overdue debt.

She walked straight past me. 'I know your game,' she said as I caught her up and fell into step with her. 'You just want to use me as a stick to beat the University with because you're one of those women who want to be students and you'll do anything you can to get the University a bad name.'

'That's what Gordon told you when you saw him at church, is it?'

She glanced at me. 'I can't talk to you. It'll be bad for us if his parents find out about what happened to me.'

'Sarah,' I grabbed her arm and pulled her to a standstill. 'Listen to me. You're never going to meet his parents. He's lied to you. There *is* no Gordon Smythe at New Inn Hall.'

In the half-light, her face was pale and her eyes were huge. 'What d'you mean?'

I told her about Basil's conversation with the porter.

'You're lying!'

'It's not me who's lying to you, Sarah. It's Gordon Smythe – or whatever his real name is.'

'No.' She shook me off and started marching towards Walton Street. 'You're wrong. There must be another reason why he told me he was a student there. So his parents wouldn't find out about us, probably. But when he's twenty-one that won't matter. He can do what he likes then.'

'And when's that?'

She glanced up at me. 'Next summer.'

A conveniently long time away.

'I can find out who he really is,' I told her as we left Juxon Street and turned onto Walton Street. 'But I need your help.'

'Why should I help *you*? You want me to ruin my chances of being his wife.'

'Sarah, if I'm right – and I think you know I am – you have no chance of being that boy's wife. What's going to happen is that *you'll* be ruined—'

'What – more than I am already?'

'Yes! As things stand, a lot of people believe that you were wrongly treated by the University. If you do what Gordon wants, he'll abandon you once he's tired of you or you're pregnant and everybody'll say, "There, see, no smoke without fire, was there?"'

She carried on marching. She was still angry, but I could see doubt in her now, too.

Around us, Walton Street was waking up, shopkeepers cleaning their windows and sweeping the pavement in front of their doors.

'You know as well as I do what happens in long engagements,' I said, reminding her that I wasn't the refined lady scholar 'Gordon' had painted me as, I was a working-class girl like her. 'He'll get impatient. And you won't want to lose him.'

She looked sideways at me. She knew I was right.

Ahead of us, one of the Walton Street bakers opened his door and called 'Morning, ladies!'

Once we were past his shop, I turned to Sarah. 'I can find out who he really is,' I said again, 'if you let me have that ring.'

Her hand went to her collarbone where the ring hung on its chain under her dress. 'I can't give it to you.'

'Just lend it to me. For a day or two,' I said. 'Then you'll have it back, I promise.'

# Chapter 30

### Basil

On Tuesday morning, I was finishing my breakfast when the assistant messenger appeared at my door with a letter.

I examined the envelope. It had been postmarked in Oxford but that was the only clue as to its provenance. My name and address had been rendered in anonymising capital letters.

'Thanks, Fred,' I said. 'No response.'

I opened the envelope to find not a letter but a small, home-made booklet about the size of my palm.

I stared at the cover. It bore a single word – Venatores – and a crude, hand-drawn rendition of the lion passant sigil that had been on the invitation pinned to Harcourt Ashdown's hood.

Opening the booklet, I saw that it had been ingeniously folded from a single sheet of foolscap to make six internal pages, each bearing a list.

On the first page, under the title 'Loci Venari' – hunting sites – locations in the city centre were listed:

*Carfax*
*The High esp. covered market entrances*
*Queen Street junction with St Ebbe's*
*Cornmarket junction with Market Street*
*Covered Market*

The facing page bore the Latin heading 'Vigilate' under which were the words:

*Basket*
*Box*
*List*

*Fashion – nearly but not quite*
*Meeting eye: NB can be deceptive*

Further down the page, there was a lower subheading, 'Numquam', signifying 'never' or an absolute 'no':

*Pairs*
*Age – see rules*
*Fish*

'Vigilate': was that a sloppy attempt at a Latin rendering of 'beware'? The careless penmanship would suggest so.

Having been exposed to reams of undergraduate handwriting, I had a pretty good idea of the kind of personality that had created this book of lists. Slapdash. Not a great thinker. More concerned with spewing words onto paper for his weekly tutorial than with actually having something to say.

I turned the page to what Non referred to as the middle spread – pages four and five if the covers were accounted one and eight. Under the Latin title 'Consilium' – advice – the list read:

*Confectionery*
*Trimmings*
*The hour*
*Tram timetable*
*Particular shops*
*Handkerchief*
*Coins*

The facing page bore a shorter list under the title 'Cave' – be careful.

*Pals*
*Shopkeepers*
*Blue ribboners et al*
*Pappers*
*C's, SP/JP/Pp's, B's*

I tried to make sense of 'Pappers' as well as 'C's, SP/JP/Pp's, and B's' without success.

Hoping for inspiration, I poured myself a second cup of coffee and turned to the final two pages. This time, the heading on the left-hand page was 'Hostibus' – which I interpreted as 'to the enemy'.

*Stag deg*
*Honour etc*
*Nom et lieu de guerre*

The first was the least comprehensible. It read like a Latin contraction of the kind seen on memorial inscriptions or coins, but I couldn't imagine what it might represent. 'Stag' wasn't common at the beginning of Latin words, and I could think of few that an undergraduate might know. 'Deg' was even less common.

Page seven was almost as baffling. Under the word 'Ordinationes' – rules or regulations – several enigmatic injunctions were listed:

*Hunts must be undertaken alone*
*Confirmation required*
*Sals only – by agreement*
*No cheering – sackable*
*VI = mega kudos*

I closed the little booklet and stared at the unrevealing cover. Given that at least some of the contents seemed to be written in undergraduate slang, I decided to consult Askew.

It would have been a simple task to walk quickly down to Corpus and ask the porter to have Askew summoned to the lodge, but I didn't want to draw attention to either of us by doing such a thing. Instead, I left a message at the lodge to be delivered by Fred when convenient, and went about my morning's work.

—

'Mr Rice, I got your note.'

Askew found me in the coffee house where my note had directed him, deep in contemplation of the Venatores' little folded manual. He sat and accepted a cup of coffee.

'What did you want to speak to me about?'

He seemed slightly wary, and it occurred to me that Non might have told him about my taking her to task. If she had, I hoped Askew didn't resent my interference as much as she did; I had, after all, had his best interests at heart.

'The plot thickens on the Venatores front,' I said, sliding the foolscap booklet across the table. 'I received this odd little item in the post this morning.'

As he flicked through the pages, I said, 'I wondered if you could help me with one or two items of vocabulary?'

He returned the manual to me. 'Of course, if I can.' His initial wariness had disappeared and I felt a tension in my solar plexus ease considerably. Why is it that our bodies prepare us for physical blows when words are the only weapons likely to be wielded against us?

I turned to the page headed 'Cave'. 'This, here?' I pointed to 'Pappers'.

Slowly, Askew shook his head, thinking. 'Nothing immediately springs to mind.'

'How about "stag deg"?' I asked, turning the page and pointing to the relevant item.

'That I do know. Stout denial.' I must have looked blank. 'You know, as in "brekker" for breakfast, "rugger" for rugby football, "Pragger Wagger" for Prince of Wales?'

This was one of the most fatuous linguistic habits to be adopted by the current crop of undergraduates. It made the young men who used it sound both puerile and cretinous. But I couldn't quite see how 'stout denial' became 'stag deg'.

'Full form "staggers deggers",' Askew explained.

'Dear Lord...'

'Didn't you have college slang in your day, Mr Rice?'

'Yes, of course, but it wasn't quite so... infantile.'

Askew grinned. 'I dare say your elders thought it was.'

I was definitely getting old.

'What about "Sals"?' I asked.

'Sals and Pals,' Askew answered, finding the list headed by 'Pals' and pointing, 'what some gownsmen call town girls and boys.'

'Girls?' I queried.

'Shop girls, factory girls, domestic servants…'

'And "cheering"?'

'I've heard that from the blue blood set. I think it means blowing your own trumpet. Cheering your own success, as it were.'

'Boasting?'

He nodded over his coffee, and we stared at each other.

Askew's gaze dropped to the manual. '"Hunts must be undertaken alone",' he read from the rules page. '"Sals only".'

I knew what he was thinking, because the same thoughts were running through my mind. Stout denial. Blue bloods. Town girls. And the last line of the rules: NB – VI = mega kudos. Six equals great respect.

Askew looked up once more and I could see that he was as shocked as I. 'The Venatores,' he said, 'hunt girls.'

## Chapter 31

*Non*

Sarah had let me have the ring in the end, but that didn't mean she was going to hear a word against the boy calling himself Gordon Smythe.

'Don't you dare say anything against him! He said it would be his *honour* to stand beside me in court – but he's afraid of what his parents would say. He doesn't want to go against them.'

I didn't want to upset her so I nodded as if I could see his point of view, but it seemed a lot more likely to me that what Gordon Smythe *really* didn't want was Sarah dragging his name into court.

I needed evidence to prove that her supposed fiancé didn't actually intend to marry her. So I was going to try and find out whether the signet ring he'd given her really had been a gift from his father. If it hadn't, if it had just been a prop in the story he was telling to get what he wanted, Smythe must have bought it somewhere and the most likely place was a pawn shop.

But before I could speak to the pawn brokers of Oxford, I had to change my appearance. Miss Skene's comment, the first time we'd met, about my being both noticeable and notorious, had been a surprise and I'd realised that I'd have to take precautions if I didn't want people to recognise me as 'the female journalist'.

So I'd sent a sum of money to an address advertised in one of the London papers and, by return of post, I'd received a long blonde wig. To be honest, I was a bit squeamish about wearing another woman's hair – it felt like putting on somebody else's still-warm underclothes – but needs must.

The wig was silky and straight and a lot easier to deal with than my own hair, so, sitting in front of the mirror in my bedroom, I had it twisted up into an acceptable arrangement pretty quickly. To go with my walking dress – not hooked up, so that it looked normal as well as well-worn — I'd bought a second-hand hat which was two or three years out of fashion.

I pinned the hat neatly on the top of my head. If I'd been wearing it as me, I'd have gone for a jaunty angle, but the girl I was going to be today wouldn't want people to think she was pert.

I'd decided to stick as close to the truth as possible, so I was going to be passing myself off as the sister of a wronged woman. I'd ask each pawnbroker if they'd sold Gordon Smythe's signet ring to a young man. Then, if they didn't want to tell me, I'd break down and confess that my twin sister had become engaged to a young man who *claimed* to be a student. With my most mortified expression on my face, I'd tell them that I thought he was deceiving her just so that he could… well… you know.

Then, once I'd dried my tears, I'd show them the signet ring again, and tell them the story that Gordon Smythe had told Sarah: that it was supposedly dear to his heart because his father had given it to him.

'But I don't think his father did any such thing,' I'd practised saying in my best Oxonian accent — I wasn't bad at accents, and I could sound as English as the next person when I needed to — '*I think he bought it just so he could give it to her and spin her a yarn.*'

'*Your twin sister, is it?*' Hara said. '*So I'd be stupid enough to fall for Gordon Smythe, would I?*'

'*All right then, I won't say sister, I'll make up a cousin if you prefer. I just thought that if I said sister, it might feel more real. I might be more convincing if I was thinking about not wanting* you *to marry this liar.*'

'*Hypocrite! You wouldn't want me to get married at all!*'

'*That's not true. If you were still alive, you could do what you liked, I wouldn't stop you.*'

'*But you don't believe in marriage.*'

'*That's not true. I just don't believe in marriage for* me.'

Hara seemed to have no answer to that, so I checked my appearance in the mirror and crept downstairs.

But Lily saw me coming.

'What on earth…?'

I touched the hat. 'Don't I look right?'

'You look fine — you just don't look like… *you*. What have you done to your hair?'

'I don't want people recognising me. Miss Skene says I'm very *evident*,' I added, in case she thought I assumed that everybody knew who I was now.

Lily narrowed her eyes at me. 'What are you up to, my girl?'

'Hopefully saving somebody who's already been badly treated from worse.'

'Who?'

I sighed. Lily could be relentless, and I wanted to get on. She knew about Sarah, but the marriage proposal was news to her.

'And you think a pawnbroker's going to tell you their business, do you?' she asked when I'd explained my plan.

'I'm not going to ask them for *names*. Just whether a young man bought the ring.' I hesitated, then said, in my Oxonian accent, 'I'm going to tell them I'm her twin sister and I'm sore afraid for her.'

Lily stared at me. I could see she wanted to tell me not to do it, but I didn't need her permission.

'Right then, I'm coming with you.'

'No, Lily—'

'Yes.' She glared at me. 'Not for your benefit, miss. For that poor girl's. It'll be much more convincing if her *mother* comes and cries as well, won't it?'

## Chapter 32

*Basil*

Askew having taken his leave of me outside the coffee house, I stood for a few moments, grappling with the implications of the conclusion we'd reached.

'If the Venatores hunt young women,' Askew had said as we pored over the little foolscap pamphlet, 'then they're not the *perpetrators* of the hooding attacks, they're the victims—'

'And the invitation pinned to Ashdown's hood wasn't a calling card left by his attackers, but an accusation of membership,' I'd finished. 'Somebody's pointing the University authorities in the Venatores' direction and asking us to do something about them.'

And if the invitation identified Ashdown as a member of the Venatores, then presumably the hoods of the other victims were sufficient to identify them, too.

Aware that I'd allowed myself to be fobbed off too easily by Laurence Herbert, I made a decision and turned towards Merton College.

However, when I asked to be directed to the young man's rooms, the porter was apologetic. 'I'm afraid Mr Herbert still isn't seeing visitors at present, Mr Rice.'

'I beg your pardon,' I said, politely, 'but I seem not to have made myself clear. I don't wish to pay Mr Herbert a social call. I'm investigating the attack on him, on behalf of the Senior Proctor. I should, therefore, like to speak with him. Now, if you please.'

Having been furnished with Herbert's staircase and set number, I located his rooms and rapped smartly on his door.

My knock was answered by a young man who was not Laurence Herbert. I stated my business and was astonished when, instead of standing aside, the youth said, 'I'm afraid Herbert isn't really up to visitors, Mr Rice. Perhaps you'd be so good as to come back in a few days?'

I looked him up and down in the overbearingly donnish manner I reserved for young men who fancied that a respectful attitude to senior members of the University was beneath them. He was a slim, dark youth of slightly shorter than average stature whose balanced stance and combative gaze suggested that he might fence.

'I'm afraid I must insist,' I said. 'My business with Mr Herbert can't wait.'

For a moment, I thought he might defy me. Then he stood aside. 'Very well.'

Herbert was lying on a chaise longue beneath a window which looked out on to Merton Street.

'I'd been given to understand that you weren't receiving visitors, Mr Herbert,' I said, glancing at his gatekeeper.

'Ah, but I'm not a visitor,' the slim youth responded. 'I'm a friend. John Montague.' Belatedly, he held out a hand which, after a deliberate pause, I shook. Montague exhibited the same kind of ease as Harcourt Ashdown, the ease of a man born to glide through life on a path lubricated by wealth and influence. One of the 'blue blood set' as Askew would have put it.

'I should like to speak to Mr Herbert alone, if I may,' I said. It was an instruction, not a request, but Herbert chose to interpret it otherwise.

'No need, Mr Rice,' he said. 'Montague's been my closest friend since our first day at school. And he knows all about what happened to me. Or, I should say, he knows everything I do, which is precious little.'

I looked from one to the other. Unlike Montague, who wore a well-tailored suit, Herbert was dishevelled. Wearing neither shoes nor necktie, his braces were visible beneath his unfastened waistcoat, and he appeared not to have brushed his hair since rising from bed, despite the fact that it was mid-afternoon.

'Your wounds seem to be healing well,' I said, which was true enough, though a week's worth of wispy beard did little to hide the now-scabbed letters carved into Herbert's face.

He stared at me mutely.

'Has anything been done to find the thugs who did this?' Montague asked. He was sitting, one leg crossed languidly over the other, in an armchair at the foot of the chaise longue.

'It's very difficult to do anything substantive, Mr Montague, when Mr Herbert has been able to provide so very little information.' I turned away from him. 'Mr Herbert, I'd like you to think again about where you were taken after the hood had been put over your head. My investigations suggest that you weren't, in fact, taken to the churchyard.' I felt a moment of shame at my appropriation of Non's thoroughness, but I knew she would understand.

Herbert blinked and looked away. 'Actually, I'm almost certain I was.'

'You mentioned, I believe, that you were thrown down on the grass?'

'Yes.'

'Then it can't have been in the churchyard. The grass there was undisturbed. If you had lain there for any length of time, and especially if there had been others there, restraining you, it would have been considerably trampled.'

Disconcerted by my words, Herbert exchanged a swift glance with Montague.

'Are you sure you couldn't have been dragged into St Helen's Passage?' I asked. 'You would have been disorientated once the hood had been put over your head, added to the shock of being attacked.'

'Why should he have been taken into St Helen's Passage?' Montague asked, his expression one of no more than mild interest.

Silently, I met his eye in my best 'I'm the don, I ask the questions' manner before turning back to the invalid. 'Well, Mr Herbert? Could you have been taken to St Helen's Passage?'

Again, his eyes flicked to Montague, and I followed his gaze in time to see the smallest shake of Montague's head. If challenged, he might plausibly have protested that he thought St Helen's Passage too far from the entrance to Queen's Lane for Herbert to have been taken unseen, but I suspected that his shake of the head meant something else. *Don't tell him.*

'No,' Herbert said, suddenly more resolute. 'No, I don't believe I could.'

Now quite certain I was being lied to, I asked, 'What's the significance of the word slashed into your face, Mr Herbert? Whom did you deceive?'

Herbert's mouth opened, but no sound emerged. Instead, it was Montague who spoke, and, this time, there was a discernible edge to his voice. 'That's a rather insulting question, Mr Rice.'

I ignored him and addressed Herbert. '"Liar" is a personal accusation. It suggests that you weren't attacked at random, but for a specific reason.'

'Really, Mr Rice,' Montague remonstrated, 'you make it sound as if Herbert is guilty of something, when he's the victim.'

'I haven't asked for your opinion, Mr Montague, therefore please be courteous enough to remain silent.' I turned back to Herbert. 'As it happens, Mr Herbert, I have my doubts as to your innocence. Especially in the light of another case of undergraduate mendacity that has come to my attention. The case of a Mr Gordon Smythe who claimed, when questioned by the Junior Proctor, to be from New Inn Hall. That, in fact, was a lie, though he had bribed the porter there to say otherwise. Why would Mr Smythe do that, do you imagine?'

Given their relative seating positions, I couldn't keep my eye on both of them at the same time and I could scarcely order Herbert to sit up and Montague to take a position next to him, as if they were naughty schoolboys. The Senior Proctor wouldn't take kindly to complaints from Merton's Warden about my bullying his undergraduates.

'What does this Smythe have to do with the crime committed against Herbert?' Montague asked.

Had I answered him, I would have quoted from the little folded Venatores handbook.

From 'Loci Venari' – hunting sites – 'Cornmarket Street' where 'Smythe' had attempted to pick up Miss Brandon.

From 'consilium' – advice – 'coins' like the sixpence Smythe claimed Miss Brandon had dropped.

From 'hostibus' – to the enemy – 'nom et lieu de guerre'. Gordon Smythe of New Inn Hall was a fictitious person.

But I didn't owe Montague any explanation and I kept my gaze fixed on Laurence Herbert's ruined face. 'Are you acquainted with Gordon Smythe, Mr Herbert?'

'I've never heard of him. And why should I have? Isn't Smythe just an attempt to be something more than the plebeian Smith? My family traces its lineage to the kings of Scotland. I'd scarcely be likely to associate with a Smith.'

I let his words hang in the air for a few moments before saying, 'Given how little you or the other victims of these attacks have been willing to tell me, it seems unlikely that the perpetrators will be brought to justice. However, certain information has come into my possession recently which may be of relevance.'

I looked from one to the other. 'Are either of you gentlemen familiar with a club that calls itself the Venatores?'

## Chapter 33

*Non*

Lily and I spent an hour and a half going from one pawnbroker to another without any success. In Jericho, we were turned away by three pawnbrokers with sad shakes of the head and best wishes for our search. On the High Street the woman behind the counter told us she didn't know what our game was, but we weren't getting any information out of her. The pawnbroker on George Street said he hadn't sold a signet ring in three years; and after we'd been turned away from the shop on St Aldate's Street by a man who said he wasn't in business to stop foolish girls doing foolish things, we had to make a decision.

'Are we going down to St Thomas's or should we go over to St Clement's?' I asked. I wouldn't usually have thought to ask for Lily's advice, but her performance as a mother who was afraid her daughter had been taken in by a scoundrel had astonished me. She'd shed *actual* tears.

'If this Smythe is rich enough to bribe the porter at New Inn Hall to the tune of a month's wages,' she said, 'then I don't think he's from St Thomas's.'

That seemed like a sensible conclusion, so off we went to St Clement's.

Even though it was only a couple of hundred yards over Magdalen Bridge, the parish wasn't somewhere either Lily or I were familiar with. But, as sure as there are barnacles on a boat, we knew there would be pawnbrokers there.

We'd only walked a little way up the Headington Road into St Clement's when we saw a sign with the three golden balls on it and a shop window advertising 'money advanced on watches, books, tools, wearing apparel and any other items of value'.

In the window there were cards displaying rings, brooches, necklaces and watches. Carpenters' tools – mostly planes and chisels – were arranged along the front, and books were displayed in a little bookcase at the back. In front of the books sat a violin, a flute and a set of bagpipes.

'This looks a bit upmarket for St Clement's,' Lily murmured.

'Maybe it's having Magdalen so close by,' I said. 'Undergraduates are always getting into debt – their tailors might give them credit, but they won't get dinner on tick if they're out with their friends – and students have always got something to pawn.'

The shop's bell tinkled above our heads as we pushed the door open, and the man standing behind the counter looked up. He was middle-aged, well-dressed and, at that moment, he was busy filling out his ledger while a woman of about Lily's age twisted a purse around and around in her fingers. I wondered how often she saw the inside of a pawnshop.

Edie had once told me that, before she came to work for Lily, she'd never see her Sunday best from Monday morning to Saturday evening. First thing on Monday, her church dress and good shoes would be pawned. Then, on Saturday evening, they'd be redeemed again if the family could afford it, so that Edie could go to church and look respectable for prospective employers. And it had worked. Lily'd employed Edie straight from school after seeing her turn up in church, week after week, looking tidy and presentable.

A dumpy woman in a purple dress that didn't suit her sallow complexion bustled out of a door behind the counter. She looked us up and down. Evidently we didn't look like her usual customers because she beckoned us over to a booth that stood to one side of the counter. 'Step in here, ladies, you'll be more comfortable away from prying eyes.' She opened the door on her side of the counter, and we went into the booth from our side. The space inside had only been designed for one person, so it was quite a squeeze for both Lily and me, but we managed.

'Now, ladies,' the woman said, 'what can I do for you?'

I pulled Gordon Smythe's ring out of my pocket and put it on the counter between us. 'This ring...'

'What was you hopin' for in terms of advance for it, miss?' the woman asked. She sounded kind, but I was pretty sure she'd have halved whatever we suggested, just in case we weren't quite as able to pay the money back as we looked.

'We're not looking to pawn it,' I said, trying to sound hesitant and unsure of myself. 'We just need to know whether you sold it to somebody.'

'I know it's an odd thing to ask,' Lily said, before the woman could send us away with a flea in our collective ear, 'but it's my daughter, you see.' Her voice wavered very convincingly. 'She's got involved with this student…'

And then, as if she hadn't given the same performance half a dozen times already, the whole story spilled out with many tears and no punctuation. How she was half 'mazed' by worry for her daughter Daisy who'd taken up with a young man who promised her the moon but she was a mother and there was something about this young man and he'd given her a ring but it wasn't a proper ring it was this one but he said it was precious to him but she didn't know and she just needed to find out if he was trying to ruin her baby girl.

Honestly, nothing on the stage had ever impressed me as much as Lily's performance, and the woman on the other side of the counter went from thinking about throwing us out to hand-holding sympathy inside a minute.

'Now, now, dear, don't take on so. Let me have a look.'

She stared at Gordon Smythe's ring for several seconds before saying, 'Yes, I remember this one; and the young gentleman who brought it in an' all. Seemed like a young man of means, he did, who'd just over-extended his credit, as they say. I thought it was only a matter of his allowance coming in.' She turned the ring over in her fingers. 'Edward Sumption his name was, as I recall.' She looked up at us. 'It seemed an odd name, so it stuck in my mind.'

I was willing to bet that in her line of business you soon learned never to forget a face or a name. Pawnbrokers needed to avoid scoundrels as much as the next businessman. Probably more so.

'But it can't have been a late allowance,' the woman said, 'because he never redeemed it.' She stared at the ring as if it was a mirror to the past. 'It wasn't me that sold it, I don't think. Must have been my husband. So it's possible that Mr Sumption bought it back after the redemption period'd expired. Let me just check.' She opened the door behind her and moved two paces to the left to speak to her husband. The woman he'd been dealing with must have gone now, because neither of them kept their voices down, so Lily and I stepped out of the booth.

'No, Mr Sumption didn't come back,' her husband said. 'The young man who bought it said it'd taken his eye in the window because it had his initials.' He flicked through his ledger and located the sale. 'Here it is. June. That's when I sold it.'

Sarah'd told me that Gordon Smythe had asked her to marry him at the end of June, just before he went home for the long vacation.

This boy – whatever his real name was – had deceived Sarah Critchley twice now. He wasn't a student at New Inn Hall, and the ring hadn't been a present from his father.

He was a liar.

Just like Laurence Herbert.

## Chapter 34

*Basil*

As I walked back to college, I reviewed my conversation with Herbert and Montague. When I'd asked if either of them was familiar with the Venatores, their reactions could scarcely have been more different. Montague had regarded me with a blankness that bordered on insolence while Herbert had looked to his friend in palpable alarm.

'I've never heard of it, whatever it is,' Montague drawled. 'What does it have to do with what happened to poor Herbert?'

'What indeed?' I said. When he continued to stare at me without expression, I turned to Laurence Herbert. 'Mr Herbert, what do you have to say for yourself? Are you familiar with this society?'

'I'm in the same situation as Montague,' he said, stiffly. 'I've never heard of it.'

I looked from one to the other. 'You both deny any knowledge of a student society known as the Venatores?'

'Absolutely,' Montague said. 'Unless you've joined some secret society without telling me, Beaky?'

Herbert smiled weakly and shook his head. 'Of course not.'

'Then perhaps it doesn't actually exist?' Montague suggested. 'Where did you hear of it, Mr Rice?'

I gazed at his blandly questioning expression. 'It certainly exists,' I took the engraved invitation card from my pocket and held it up so that they could see it. 'This is an invitation to a gathering of the Venatores. As you can see,' I said, flipping the card over, 'they dignify themselves with the figure of a lion as their emblem. This was pinned to the hood placed over the head of Harcourt Ashdown of Magdalen College.'

I put the invitation back in my pocket and drew out the folded foolscap of the Venatores' manual. 'Then there is this, which I received via the Royal Mail.' I held the booklet up for their inspection, though I didn't offer it to either of them. 'It appears to be some kind of guide for members. Crudely done, as you can see. But instructive nonetheless.'

Montague leaned forward and stared at the folded foolscap. 'Surely that's the work of some schoolboy?' he said, dismissively.

'I might have reached the same conclusion, Mr Montague, were it not for the fact that the invitation clearly specifies rooms at Trinity.'

'There you are then,' Herbert said, slightly too loudly. 'It's obviously a Trinity College affair. Nothing to do with either of us.'

I turned to look at him. Montague had called him Beaky. Herbert didn't have a particularly prominent nose so, presumably, the nickname had a more obscure and possibly more obscene origin. Schoolboy humour always delighted in any opportunity to reference genitalia.

'And yet you yourself were at supper at Trinity with friends on the night you were attacked, were you not, Mr Herbert?'

The boy's eyes widened in panic. 'Yes, but... Well, I mean to say, the chaps I was with that night are—'

'There are a great number of undergraduates at Trinity, Mr Rice,' Montague cut in. 'I'm sure you're not suggesting that every one of them belongs to this society?'

I rose to my feet. It was clear that, with Montague in attendance, I would get nothing from Herbert.

Despite my standing, both the young men remained insolently seated. 'If I discover that you have misled me, gentlemen, it is not me you will answer to but the proctors and the Vice Chancellor. Better to make a clean breast of anything you know now, than to be exposed as liars later.'

Montague uncrossed his legs and sat up straight. Had he been a young man of less studied insouciance, he would have leaped to his feet. 'I know you're a fellow at another college, but I don't think it's acceptable for you to accuse us of being liars.'

'I think you'll find, if you take the trouble to recall exactly what I said, that I accused you of nothing, Mr Montague.'

*But if the cap fits...*

I summoned up my most authoritative tone. 'Perhaps I should have made it clear at the outset, as you, Mr Montague, would be unaware of my role in this investigation. I am here at the behest of the proctors, two of the most senior officers of the University. They, and I, are determined to bring an end to these outrages, and if it later comes to light' – here

I directed my attention to Herbert – 'that you were anything less than perfectly candid about what you knew of any motive for the attack on you, your injuries will not absolve you. I'll recommend that you are sent down with immediate effect.' I turned from him to include Montague in my warning. 'This is not some schoolboy jape. The violence inflicted on Mr Herbert is considerably greater than that meted out to previous victims of the hooding attacks. Whatever's happening here, it must be stopped before somebody is seriously injured. So I repeat, if you are members of the Venatores, and you know who might be responsible for these attacks, now is the time to share that knowledge.'

Both men remained silent, though Herbert swung his legs around so that he was no longer reclining but sitting on the chaise longue, his feet on the ground.

I met his eye. 'Mr Herbert?'

'I've no information to give you, Mr Rice.'

Now, walking up the Turl, I asked myself who could have sent the Venatores' manual to me. While whoever it was evidently did not wish to be identified, they *did* want me to know about the existence of the Venatores and what they might be up to.

But why?

## Chapter 35

*Non*

When Lily and I got home from the pawnbroker in St Clement's, Edie handed me a telegram. It was from William Stead.

**Send article on Critchley imprisonment by VC soonest. WS.**

When Stead said 'soonest' he didn't mean 'as soon as convenient' he meant today, or if he was feeling generous, tomorrow.

I ran upstairs, folded my article on Sarah's case together with the piece on Miss Skene which he'd showed an interest in, and wrote a covering letter which mentioned the possibility of Sarah bringing a court case against the University. Then, before I could think better of it, I scribbled,

> Meanwhile, I have discovered that Miss Critchley has been proposed marriage by an undergraduate. (Not, interestingly, the young man with whom she was in conversation when she was arrested.) I have made it my business to make enquiries into the identity and character of this young man and it's clear to me that he is practising a cruel deceit upon Miss Critchley for his own nefarious ends.

*I am*, I concluded, *in a position to send an article on this subject at your word.*

If Stead published both the articles I was sending him *and* indicated that he'd be interested in one about Sarah's supposed engagement, then an Oxford Notes column could be a *Pall Mall Gazette* feature very soon.

But if that was going to happen, I needed to start writing immediately so that I'd be ready to send the relevant article to Stead at a moment's notice. And, if my work was going to help Sarah clear her name, what I wrote would need to generate public support.

The vast majority of people are always more inclined to add their voices to an existing opinion than to be the first to speak up, so if I could show that Sarah already had supporters in Oxford, we'd be halfway to a successful campaign for her to be pardoned.

And I knew that she *did* have supporters in Oxford because, even though her appearance at the Vice Chancellor's court hadn't been reported in the papers, letters from people who were appalled at her treatment had appeared in the previous Saturday's *Mercury*.

But, if I was going to reflect public opinion in Oxford *accurately*, I needed to know whether Berry'd received other letters. And if so, how many of them were supportive of Sarah.

—

First thing the following morning, I set off for the *Mercury*'s offices, via a little detour to New Inn Hall Street East. I wanted to tell Miss Skene what Lily and I had discovered at the pawnbroker's, and I hoped to catch her after she got back from church.

When I knocked, Jane told me that her mistress was 'in conversation' in her study. 'You'd better wait in the parlour,' she said. 'I dare say she'll want to see you.'

Jane seemed to know everything that went on in Miss Skene's life and I wondered if they were friends rather than just mistress and servant. Felicia Skene was known to keep up a correspondence with the occasional ex-convict, so it didn't seem that unlikely that she'd make a friend of her housekeeper.

I hadn't been waiting long when I heard two sets of footsteps on the steep stairs and Miss Skene appeared in the parlour doorway. As I heard the front door close, I glanced out of the window and saw her guest leaving. A well-dressed man, not one of her charity cases.

'I take it Sarah hadn't mentioned Gordon Smythe to you?' I asked after I'd explained what Lily and I had been up to.

'She had not,' Miss Skene confirmed.

'Gordon, or whatever his real name is, told Sarah they had to keep the engagement a secret until he came of age.' I hesitated to say what I needed to say next. I knew Felicia Skene had seen all the degradation life could bring to a person, but she was still a lady, *and* a spinster. 'The thing is,' I said, 'as I'm sure you're aware, in the social class Sarah belongs to, long engagements often allow a certain degree of... licence when it comes to...'

'Purity on the wedding night?' Miss Skene finished, drily.

'Exactly.'

She looked at me with an expression similar to the one her parrot often gave me. Questioning. Slightly satirical. Completely without guile. 'You think he simply wanted to have his way with her?'

I almost blushed on her behalf. 'I do, yes.'

'But there are girls who would have gratified his desires without the need for a pawn shop ring.'

'True.'

'Have you considered that his affections might be genuine?'

'If they were, why would he have lied? About the ring or about his college? I also have evidence – from Mr Rice, who went out with the proctors – that he tried to pick up another girl on Cornmarket Street last week. Or at least,' I said, feeling the need to be completely honest, 'another undergraduate calling himself Gordon Smythe did.' Miss Skene didn't respond so I added, 'And, when I met Smythe with Sarah, he was obviously putting on a false accent.'

'So what do you intend to do?' Miss Skene asked, as Tatters jumped on to her lap.

'I'll tell Sarah what I've found out and see if I can persuade her to take up your barrister friend's idea about suing the University.'

Miss Skene stroked the little terrier's ears. 'As it happens, the guest I was speaking to when you arrived was the barrister in question, Martin Alexis. He has discussed the matter with William Stead and has secured his assurance that, if Sarah decides to take her case to law, the *Pall Mall Gazette* would support her in every way possible.'

Ah. So now, Stead understood that I wasn't the only one with a bee in my bonnet about the Vice Chancellor's court. That explained his telegram.

'I think perhaps it would be best to speak to Sarah sooner rather than later,' Miss Skene said. 'We don't want Mr Stead raising the possibility of a court case in print, if this young man of hers is in a position to persuade her against it.'

When I arrived at the *Mercury* offices just before half past nine, I found them busy. Thursday was the day the paper went to print, and it was always frenetic.

'This is the second visit in little over a week, Miss Vaughan,' Berry said, his eyes not leaving the copy he was marking up. 'What is it this time? Are you in need of more work? Has Somerville Hall seen fit to dispense with your services?'

I felt a thread of fear tighten inside me. If Sarah took the University to court and I stood with her, that's exactly what Miss Shaw Lefevre would do.

'Not as yet,' I grinned, as if it was a joke. 'I just wanted to ask another question about the letters you've received recently.'

He frowned. 'Ask, then. But be quick about it. I haven't got all day.'

'I know you're very careful – that you only print letters which you feel represent the opinion of a substantial proportion of the *Mercury*'s readers,' I began, trying to find the words which would get me what I wanted. 'But I'm interested in the letters you *haven't* printed. About the Sarah Critchley case.'

Suddenly I had his full attention. 'I believe I published *two* letters concerning Miss Critchley's incarceration. One condemning the court's action, the other supporting it. Why do you wish to see the rest of the correspondence?'

Berry was like a spider sitting at the centre of Oxford's web. A tiny flicker of something interesting on the very edge would alert him, and he'd be after it. Did he know how close Sarah's case was to blowing up in the University's face?

'Mr Stead has commissioned an article on Miss Critchley's treatment by the Vice Chancellor's court, and I want to be able to give the public's reaction to it.'

'*William* Stead? Of the *Pall Mall Gazette*?'

I nodded.

'Why? Surely the subject would be of little interest outside Oxford?'

I hesitated. 'If I tell you, it'll go no further?'

He gave one nod, his eyes trained on mine.

'It's been suggested that Miss Critchley should sue the Vice Chancellor for false imprisonment. She'd committed no crime, so in the law of the land, he had no right to put her in jail.'

'The Vice Chancellor has powers that sit outside the law as it applies to the rest of England.'

'That's exactly the point. *Should* he have those powers? Should University officials be able to fling people into jail willy-nilly, in this day and age? That's the question William Stead wants to put before the British public. So I'd like to know what *Mercury* readers think before I write my article.'

'So you can quote public opinion in your piece?'

'Exactly.' I watched him carefully, trying to work out which side of the fence he was on where Sarah's case was concerned. 'Did the two letters you published represent the balance of opinion, or were you sparing the University's blushes?'

Berry drummed his fingers on the stained blotter in front of him. 'I'll allow you to see the letters,' he said. 'But be aware, Miss Vaughan, you're poking a stick into a hornet's nest here.'

'What do you mean?'

He got up to take the current box of letters off the shelf. 'I mean that if you and William Stead hope to overthrow the archaic hegemony of Oxford University, then you need to think again.' Normally Berry was circumspection itself when he spoke about the University, but 'hegemony' definitely had a critical tone; like 'dictatorship'.

'The University sees itself as having given a lot of ground to the government's insistence on modernisation in recent years,' he said, as he put the box on the table. 'If this case comes to court the University will fight it tooth and nail. And not only in public. They'll be lobbying behind the scenes. Don't forget, the University has two MPs in parliament.'

The optimism I'd felt two minutes ago suddenly seemed very foolish. I'd forgotten the two MPs. In the face of that kind of influence, what chance did Sarah have?

'Still,' Berry said, 'I suppose even bringing a futile case would open the debate. So, even if Miss Critchley can't help but lose, whoever's paying her expenses – would that be Stead? – might see the game as worth the candle.'

He took a Gem-clipped sheaf of letters labelled 'Critchley Case' out of the box and handed it to me. 'Behold – the views of our letter-writing readers. You'll recognise some of the names as frequent correspondents.'

Quickly, I scanned through the letters.

'Feel free to make notes, Miss Vaughan,' Berry said.

His tone made me look up. 'Shall I take these into the main office and look at them there?'

He sat down again and picked up the copy he'd been working on when I arrived. 'If you'd be so good.'

## Chapter 36

*Basil*

Thursday morning brought a letter from Non.

Her handwriting had deteriorated since she'd learned shorthand, her impatience to put information on paper chafing at the slowness of conventional orthography. Still, I managed to decipher her headlong scrawl sufficiently to understand that the ring given to Sarah Critchley by the undergraduate calling himself Gordon Smythe had not been a cherished gift from his father as he'd claimed but had been acquired at a pawn shop in St Clement's.

I looked up from the letter. If this Smythe was a member of the Venatores, the scandal that would engulf the University when the story of the hooding attacks inevitably found its way into the press would now be magnified by the Venatores' association with Miss Critchley's imprisonment. And, if she decided to go to law to protest her incarceration – which, given Non's discoveries, must now be more likely than not – then the two cases taken together would be a gift to the editor of the *Pall Mall Gazette*. William Stead saw it as his duty to illustrate the hypocrisy of established institutions with any example they helpfully presented for the purpose.

I sighed and went to my desk. The Senior Proctor had to be informed of the latest developments.

–

As neither Kaye nor I was at leisure to meet earlier in the day, I dined with him that evening. He was considerably dismayed both by the Venatores' manual and Non's discoveries about the youth calling himself Gordon Smythe and, as I walked back to Jesus, I too found myself in low spirits. What had all our investigations discovered so far? Only evidence that heaped discredit on the victims of the hooding attacks without suggesting who might be responsible.

As I entered through the wicket gate, I was hailed by the porter, Mr Allen, who handed me a letter that had arrived in the evening post. Seeing that it was from Teddy, I put it in my pocket.

At my request, the fire in my sitting room had been banked down earlier in the evening, so the place was still reasonably warm when I entered. I hung up my gown and fell wearily into an armchair to read Teddy's letter.

It contained a suggested itinerary for Sunday's visit. Miss Webster, his son's nurse, was to take Morton to lunch with friends of hers while Teddy and I took coffee in my rooms and subsequently lunched together. We would then meet the nursemaid and her charge and take a stroll in Christ Church Meadow.

Of course, I knew perfectly well what Teddy meant by 'coffee'. Had he only had the consumption of a beverage in mind, he would have suggested one of his favourite coffee houses. No; this was a resumption of his campaign to persuade me into bed with him once more.

I put the letter aside. My determination not to submit to Teddy's blandishments, while it had remained intact during his marriage, had suffered a temporary relapse after the death of his wife. However, I'd resisted all subsequent temptations, and I did not intend to weaken now.

The truth was that both Teddy's removal to London to pursue his ambitions and his rage at my refusal to sleep with him once he was married had brought me up short. I'd been forced to reflect on the nature of our relationship and, to my considerable dismay, had come to the conclusion that my relations with Teddy had been like a drug, craved but ultimately injurious to my own well-being. I found I despised the man I'd allowed myself to become during those years, a man held in thrall. I might be soberer and sadder now, but I was more resolute too. A broader view of the world as a member of the Board of Guardians – along with my friendship with Non and the investigations we'd undertaken together – had changed me, given me a trust in my own judgement that my dealings with Teddy had never fostered.

I'd questioned my wisdom in agreeing to stand as godfather to Morton, but on the whole, I genuinely believed that I might do the boy some good. I might, at the very least, show him that it was possible to stand up to his father and live to tell the tale.

Putting Teddy's letter aside, I turned my thoughts, once more, to the Venatores and to Sarah Critchley. I was very much afraid that given 'Gordon Smythe's' deception of Miss Critchley, he might be next in line for the kind of treatment that had been meted out to Laurence Herbert.

And I had not the remotest idea how to prevent that from happening.

## Chapter 37

*Non*

On Friday afternoon, Tarley turned up early for dinner.

'There's something I'd like to talk to you about,' he said, which immediately kicked my heart into a gallop. Was he going to go back to the argument we'd had last week? Or maybe Basil was right, and he was going to make some kind of declaration.

We sat down in the sitting room and my pulse slowed slightly when he took a folded sheet of paper out of his pocket and said, 'It's this.'

I moved to sit next to him on the sofa and looked at the handbill he'd unfolded.

**PROSPECTIVE HUSBANDS**

**Daunted by the prospect of marital duties?
Ill-prepared for your wedding night?
Lacking confidence?**

**EXPERIENCED COUNSEL IS AT HAND!**

For details and terms, apply to: Dr E. Ross, care of the Turf Tavern

'Where did you find that?' I asked.

'Somebody'd pinned it up in the junior common room. Though whether for information or as a joke, I don't know. I wouldn't have thought anything of it if it hadn't been for the address.'

Not for the first time I found myself wondering what Tarley might know about such things. Would *he* be ill-prepared on his wedding night? I pushed the thought aside before Hara decided to offer an opinion.

'Somebody's playing with words.' I pointed to the name at the bottom of the handbill. 'E. Ross – Eros.'

'Greek god of carnal desire,' he said, tapping the side of his own head. 'Why didn't I spot that?'

'You're probably more used to seeing it written in Greek,' I said.

He grinned. 'That's unusually kind of you, Non.'

I was taken aback. 'What d'you mean, "unusually kind"? Aren't I *usually* kind?'

'People who are intellectually competitive are rarely also kind.'

I felt as if I'd turned two pages in a book by mistake – I wasn't quite sure how we'd got here. 'Intellectually competitive?'

He raised an eyebrow. 'Not going to deny that, are you?'

I took a breath. 'No, fair enough. But... well, I just can't see that it stops you being kind as well, that's all.'

'I'm not saying you're *never* kind. It's just that usually, if you *can* score academic points, you will.'

I shook my head. I was feeling a bit bemused.

'*Come on, Non, there's no point having a fit of the vapours. You know he's right.*'

'*Shut up, Hara.*'

'*That's what you always say when you know I'm right.*'

But she shut up anyway.

'I wondered if I'd pay him a visit,' Tarley said. 'What do you think?'

'Pay who a visit?' Half my brain was still with Hara.

'Dr Eros. Maybe this is what's been happening at the Turf on Tuesday evenings. Classes for prospective husbands.'

'Classes?' I scoffed. 'You think this so-called "doctor" sits young men in rows and lectures them? At the *Turf Tavern?*'

'*There you are,*' Hara said, '*intellectually competitive.*'

I ignored her and watched the light dawn on Tarley's face. 'You don't think Dr Ross is a man, do you?'

'I'm quite *sure* E. Ross isn't a man. Or a doctor. And I'd be willing to lay good money that her "counsel" is more practical than theoretical. Look at the phrase she uses: "experienced counsel is *at hand*".'

Tarley's complexion was definitely flushed now. I'd never seen him so embarrassed.

'Are you still keen to go, now you know what this is actually about?' I asked. 'I mean, you're right. Given where this "counsel" is being offered, it would be very helpful to find out more about this Dr Eros.'

'If you think I should, I will,' Tarley mumbled, making a proper meal of folding the handbill back up and putting it in his pocket. 'But from what you've said, isn't it just an advert for a… a prostitute?'

'You'll have to see, won't you?'

He straightened his jacket and glanced at the clock on the mantelpiece. If he was checking when Basil might come and save him from dying of mortification, he still had about twenty minutes to wait.

'Actually,' he said, in a slightly strained voice, 'while we're on the subject of favours, there's something I'd like to ask of you.'

I looked at him, my heart suddenly speeding up again. Tarley never asked me for anything. 'What?' I asked.

'*What!?*' Hara yelped. '*A nice friend you are! After all he's done for you, don't you think you should be able to just say "of course" by now?*'

'*Except he might ask me for something I don't want to give.*'

'*He's talking about a favour, Non. Asking you to marry him doesn't quite come into that category.*'

Tarley noticed my distraction. 'Your sister interrupting?' he asked.

It still gave me a little shock every time he mentioned Hara. He was the only person I'd ever told about my sister speaking to me. I nodded. 'She thinks I'm a bad friend to you.' If he thought the same, that would give him the chance to tell me.

'*Liar! You just want him to say, "that's not true, you're a wonderful friend".*'

Sometimes I could have killed my sister. Except, inconveniently, she was already dead.

'Why does she think that?' Tarley asked. My stomach clenched. Even though he knew Hara and I spoke to each other, he'd never asked me what she said before.

I was being dragged into deep water here and I had a feeling I was going to be out of my depth before I knew where I was. 'She thinks I should just say "of course" to anything you ask me to do.'

I'd expected him to grin and say 'Risky', or something like that. Instead, he just looked at me. 'Does Anghard like me?'

I swallowed, trying to stop the thud of my own pulse in my throat. 'She's never said. Now, what was this favour you wanted?'

Tarley looked as if he'd quite like to carry on the conversation about Hara, but then he took a breath and said, 'It's my mother. She'd like to meet you. I'm going up to town on Sunday to see her. Will you come with me?'

I opened my mouth, but I wasn't quite sure what words should be coming out of it.

'This is the moment where your sister would tell you to say "of course",' Tarley said. He still wasn't smiling.

'Why does your mother want to see me?'

'I don't know, Non. Why would she want to meet the person I talk about most when I tell her about Oxford? The person I wrote to every day for the best part of a year while she was unwell?'

Tarley took an ironic tone with me quite a lot, in fun, but this was more, almost sarcastic.

'*He's hurt,*' Hara said. '*This is what comes of not offering to go and see him while he was in London.*'

She was right. More than a dozen times I'd started a letter offering to come down and see Tarley and his mother, and the same number of times I'd screwed the letter up, thrown it onto the fire in my bedroom and mashed the ashes up with the poker to stop Edie reading a word when she cleaned the grate.

Why? Why hadn't I gone?

The truth was, Mrs Askew would have assumed things I didn't want her to assume if I'd visited. But I should have gone, for Tarley's sake.

'*Except that you thought he might assume those things too,*' Hara said.

'I'm sorry,' I told him. Then, when I could see that he'd taken that the wrong way, I gabbled, 'I mean, I'm sorry I didn't say yes straight away. I'd like to come and meet your mother. But the problem is, I need to be there when Sarah Critchley meets Gordon Smythe at church. I'm going to follow him to see where he goes after they part.'

I'd decided not to tell Sarah about my visit to the pawnbroker yet. I'd do that once I'd found out who Gordon Smythe really was, and the only way I could think of was to follow him back to his college.

I watched Tarley's face go from disappointment to understanding and then to resignation.

'Could we go to see your mother on a different day?'

It was a relief when Basil arrived. Even though Tarley'd agreed to me going with him another time, I could tell he was still upset with me, and I couldn't seem to remember how to speak to him normally.

Basil was very interested in Dr Eros's handbill. And, even more so, in one of the letters I'd read at the *Mercury* office. I'd made a copy from my shorthand notes when I got home because I knew Basil preferred reading to listening – he liked to be able to hold something in his hand while he was taking it in. Came of a lifetime's reading, I suppose.

He read it out loud for Tarley's benefit.

> *Dear Sir*
>
> *The fact that neither your newspaper nor any other in Oxford carried details of Miss Sarah Critchley's sham trial and subsequent deplorable incarceration illustrates two points. Firstly that, unlike normally constituted courts, the Vice Chancellor's proceedings are not open to public scrutiny. Secondly that, in common with other University conclaves which are held 'in camera', no details are vouchsafed to press or public. We are kept in the dark by a body that rules the lives of Oxford's citizens in more ways than we know. But the University needs to be aware that the people of Oxford can keep secrets too. And if its undergraduates are going to walk away scot free while our girls find themselves in jail, then we shall be forced to take action ourselves.*
>
> *Reverend Jowett, take note.*
>
> *A Concerned Citizen*

'It's easy to see why Alconbury didn't print this,' Basil said. 'It might have provoked hotheads into action.'

'*More* hotheads to *more* action, you mean.'

'Touché,' Basil said, then reached into his pocket. 'This arrived for me in the post. I've already shown it to Askew – I needed an interpreter for some of the undergraduate slang.'

I glanced at Tarley, who said nothing. It was unusual for the two of them to see each other without me and I wondered whether Basil had seen fit to discuss anything else with Tarley while he was at it.

'*You think he talked about you?*' Hara snarked. '*You think he said, "Invite her down to see your mother. Her response'll tell you what you want to know"?*'

If either of the men noticed my brief absence while my sister tormented me, they didn't react. Basil just carried on drinking his coffee while I looked at the folded booklet. Coffee was a new thing at Shene Road. Lily was a dedicated tea drinker, but I preferred coffee, so I'd bought a pot and grinder and taught Edie how to make a decent cup. 'Let's have coffee' had become the cue for Albie and Lily to leave Basil and me to it after dinner.

'Yes, I see why you'd have needed help,' I said. '"Sals" and "Pals" I know because some of the girls at Somerville use those too. C's, SP, JP, Pp's and B's I can decipher, but what about "pappers", "stag deg" and "cheering"?'

'Stag deg from the original "staggers deggers" is "staunch denial", and "cheering" is what the smart set say when they mean "boasting",' Tarley said. He sounded flat, as if all the wind had been taken out of his normally cheery sails.

I didn't need Hara to tell me that was my fault. I knew I'd let him down. But if we were going to find out who Gordon Smythe really was, the only way I could see how to do it was to follow him when he met Sarah on Sunday. It was the only time in the week when I knew the two of them would be together. He could see the logic of that, I knew, but logic obviously didn't help.

'And what do you think C's, SP, JP, etcetera are?' Basil's question dragged me back from my self-reproach.

'The C's are constables, and the rest are the proctors, et al,' I told him, trying not to sound as if I thought it was obvious.

'*Intellectually competitive*,' Hara muttered.

Tarley stared at the list. 'So SP, JP and Pp's give us Senior Proctor, Junior Proctors and pro-proctors?'

'And B's are bulldogs, yes.'

'So what about Pappers?' Basil wanted to know.

'Well, if "staunch denial" turns into "staggers deggers" – honestly, what a ridiculous-sounding phrase!' I tried a grin at Tarley but only got a sad twitch of the lips back – 'Then, applying the same rule and working backwards, "pappers" started life as a word beginning "p-a" or "p-a-p". So what do we know that has the initials PA? Or, rather,' I prompted when neither of them ventured a guess, 'more likely C of E PA?'

Basil got there first. 'The Church of England Purity Association.'

'Might be, don't you think?'

I flicked through the booklet again, looking at the places where shop girls and servants could be found, and the clues to help the Hunters spot them. Baskets, boxes and lists for the servants, and things like 'fashion – nearly but not quite' for the shop girls. That last one made me angry on behalf of the girls who had to look smart for work and were forced to spend their hard-earned wages on cheap copies of fashionable clothes. And 'meeting eye: NB can be deceptive'. Most shop girls would know better than to look an undergraduate in the eye – it just encouraged them. But not all girls who did meet their eye were 'available'. Some just knew their own worth. And some – well, mostly me, to be fair – were just looking for an excuse to kick them in the shins.

'I assume nothing has come from your visit to the Church of England Purity Association?' I asked Basil. 'Hereafter known as the Pappers.' I grinned at Tarley again. Fair play, he tried to grin back, but it was a weak effort.

'No,' Basil said, 'nothing.'

'But, seeing as they're named specifically, in there,' I pointed to the pamphlet, 'as people the Hunters need to look out for, d'you think there's any possibility that some of them have taken the law into their own hands, started hunting the Hunters?'

Basil looked troubled. 'I think it's possible that, if some members of the Association had definite evidence that some of their college mates were going out to seduce town girls, then they might feel it was better to deal with them directly rather than go to the proctors.'

I flicked the manual open at the page with 'Consilium' at the top.

*Confectionery*
*Trimmings*
*The hour*
*Tram timetable*
*Named shops*
*Handkerchief*
*Coins*

'See this,' I said, tapping the list. 'These are all things you might strike up a conversation with a girl about. Didn't you say that when Gordon

Smythe tried to pick Miss Brandon up, he claimed to be just giving her a sixpence she'd dropped?'

Basil nodded.

'And the boy Sarah Critchley was arrested for "detaining",' I said, putting all the scorn I could into the word, 'stopped her to ask where he could get some pretty ribbons. Trimmings,' I added, in case they hadn't made the connection.

Basil nodded, still looking unhappy.

'And there was no letter with this?' I asked, flicking the Hunters' book of lists. 'Nothing to tell you who sent it or why?'

'Nothing.'

'Perhaps one of the Hunters doesn't like the way the tables have been turned on them,' I said. 'Perhaps they're hoping you'll put a stop to their activities so that whoever's behind the hoodings will call their dogs off.'

'Well, if that's what they want from me,' Basil said, 'they'll have to give me a bit more information than this to work with.'

## Chapter 38

*Basil*

On Saturday morning, I was in the process of shaving when a thunderous knock on the door of my rooms almost made me slice my cheek open.

Wiping the soap from my face with a towel as I went, I opened the door.

Standing on the threshold was a man in the sober suit and bowler hat that betokened one of the proctors' bulldogs. 'Beg pardon, Mr Rice, but Reverend Kaye has asked you to come to Trinity. There's been a death.'

–

It was raining steadily so I was grateful that we didn't have far to walk. As we walked up the Turl, I learned that the body of a Trinity College undergraduate had been found less than an hour ago, bound and hooded like the others, in front of the college gates.

'The young gentleman was lying on a handcart,' the bulldog told me, 'covered in a tarpaulin.'

He led me into the Trinity porter's lodge, past the silent building works – presumably suspended as a mark of respect – and guided me to the cluster of rooms behind the main hall which comprised kitchens, buttery and other service quarters.

In a small, cramped room apparently used for storage, I found Kaye and two other men standing over a trestle table. On it lay the body of the dead man. Crates and barrels had been pushed to one side to allow the erection of the table and the space was cramped and ill-lit. There was also an unpleasantly pervasive smell of urine and faeces.

Kaye stepped forward and shook my hand. 'Thank you for coming, Rice. You know Sterne, of course?'

I nodded to Trinity's dean and to Waddesworth, who stood between me and the body. Both men were unshaven, having been roused from their beds.

'I'm told he's a Trinity man?' I said, turning my attention to the corpse.

'Yes,' Sterne said. 'Charles Gainsborough. Followed his father and his older brother here.'

'Who found him?'

'The building foreman, when he turned up for work. The body had been left on a handcart in front of the builders' workshop.'

'I see you haven't unbound him.'

As in the other hooding attacks, the unfortunate Gainsborough's hands were tied in front of him, and his feet bound at the ankles.

'Removing his bonds would make no difference to him,' Sterne said. 'He was dead when the foreman came upon him. Rigor mortis had already taken hold, as we discovered when we brought him in here. Besides, we felt the bonds might be significant.'

That was unexpectedly percipient. I would have expected a senior college official to wish to see the body tidied into a dignified state as soon as possible.

'I assume you raised the hood in order to identify him?'

Sterne nodded. 'Yes, but we brought him in with his face covered so that he shouldn't be seen and identified by his peers. An announcement will be made later.'

'May I have your permission to remove it?'

Kaye glanced at Sterne, who nodded.

I wanted not only to see the young man's face but to examine the hood itself. From where I stood, it seemed quite dissimilar to the one Herbert had been wearing. Admittedly, it had been dark in Merton Street, but I'd formed the impression that the hood Askew had removed from Herbert had been made of a stout fabric. This one appeared to be a much flimsier affair.

The three men watched as I approached the body. I wondered what exactly they expected of me.

I slipped one hand under Gainsborough's head. His neck was stiff, but I was able to raise his head sufficiently to allow me to pull the hood free. Bile rose in my throat as I saw the dead man's face. It was a gruesome sight.

'Do you recognise him, Waddesworth?' I asked, stepping back slightly so that Waddesworth could approach.

The Junior Proctor looked at the engorged face, the protruding, blackened tongue, the blood trickling from the nose. He swallowed audibly. 'Should I?'

'This was the undergraduate your bulldog, Brandon, caught speaking to his daughter on the Cornmarket. He identified himself as Gordon Smythe of New Inn Hall.'

Waddesworth looked again. 'If you say so.'

'I'm quite certain of it,' I said. If Kaye wished me to take charge of the investigation into this young man's death, then it must start with an acknowledgement that Gainsborough had been seen speaking to a young woman after dark and had, when challenged, given a false name to the Junior Proctor.

Turning away from the corpse, I moved closer to the room's one small window in order to inspect the hood more closely. It was an insubstantial affair constructed from two fine linen handkerchiefs, clumsily tacked together.

I faced the proctors. 'When you found Ashdown and Vennell outside your respective colleges, did you happen to examine the hoods they were wearing?'

Both nodded.

'Were they anything like this one?' I proffered the handkerchief hood to Kaye. 'Or were they more robust?'

'Considerably more robust,' the Senior Proctor answered. 'Made of heavy cotton, like a flour sack. In fact, it resembled a sack in miniature – it was neatly stitched.'

I wondered at his familiarity with flour sacks, but perhaps he was the fellow responsible for Magdalen's buttery.

Breathing through my mouth to exclude the excretory stench, I stepped back to the corpse. As with the hood, his bindings looked different from the ones used on Laurence Herbert.

I turned to the Senior Proctor. 'Kaye, before his bonds are removed, I should like to bring in somebody who's been assisting me in my investigations,' I said. 'Somebody with whom I've consulted on my previous investigations for the University.'

## The Hunters Club

As the daughter of a sailor, Non was well versed in the different varieties of knots. She'd be able to tell me whether or not Gainsborough was bound in the same way Herbert had been.

'Of course, my dear fellow. Whoever you feel will be of help. I'm confident that you'll ensure his discretion.'

I nodded. 'Naturally.'

Time enough to undeceive him as to the gender of my consultant when Non arrived.

## Chapter 39

*Non*

I was eating a late breakfast on Saturday when a note arrived from Basil.

> *Another hooding attack. Trinity College. This time fatal. Victim is 'Gordon Smythe'. Need your advice. If possible, please come immediately.*
> *Yours B.R.*

Typical of Basil to be so polite. If possible, indeed!

I put my coat on, picked up my satchel from the hallstand, and followed the messenger.

We reached Trinity in very few minutes, and I was shown to a corridor behind the kitchens where Basil was waiting.

'Apologies from the dean and the proctors,' he said. 'They've all gone to fulfil their usual morning duties.'

As far as I was concerned, it was just as well they weren't here. If they had been, they'd have made a fuss about me seeing the body.

Basil held his hand out to the open doorway in front of us. 'The body's in here.'

I wondered what the boy's parents would think of their son's body lying in a storeroom. But until he was cleaned up, it was the best place for him.

Basil followed me into the stinking little room. 'He was found outside the garden gates, on a handcart, covered with a tarpaulin. The works' foreman realised that the handcart had no business being there and took the canvas off to see what was under it.'

'And got a lot more than he bargained for,' I said, when I saw the corpse's face.

'It's the gownsman who was almost arrested for immoral intentions on the Cornmarket when I was out with the Junior Proctor,' Basil said. 'The one who gave his name as Gordon Smythe. Is he your Gordon Smythe, too?'

I moved closer to the trestle table. The light wasn't very good, but I took in the slim build and fair hair I remembered. How Basil had recognised him I wasn't sure. His face was very distorted. I breathed in through my mouth and looked hard at the dead features, searching beneath the unnatural colour, the protruding tongue and the bloodshot eyes where blood vessels had ruptured. Beneath those marks of death, his features were familiar enough. I might only have met Gordon Smythe once, but we'd argued for a good ten minutes.

'Yes, that's him.'

Basil nodded. 'His real name's Charles Gainsborough. Gentleman commoner of Trinity College.'

I put my hand out, then hesitated. I'd forgotten how hard it is to make yourself touch a corpse. I took a breath and wrapped my fingers around his wrist, tried to lift it. He was cold and stiff. 'The fact that rigor mortis is already well established suggests that he died some time ago,' I said. 'If he'd been left outside immediately after being killed there wouldn't have been time for it to get this far.' I cast my eye over the rope that bound his hands and feet. 'Did you tell them not to untie him?'

Basil nodded. 'I did, yes. That's why I asked you to come. His bindings seem different from Herbert's – at least as far as I can remember.'

I studied the way Gainsborough'd been tied up. 'You're right. There are three ropes here, where Herbert was tied with two – one fastened with a bowline around his waist and elbows at one end and a midshipman's hitch around his wrists at the other. The more he pulled at it, the tighter it would get round his elbows. Then his ankles were tied with a different length of rope and fastened with a reef knot. These knots,' I pointed to the ones on the dead man, 'are all reef knots – two overhand knots like the one you use to tie your shoes.'

Basil nodded.

'Also,' I said, 'it's a different type of rope. The rope used on Laurence Herbert was manila. This is jute.' I looked up at Basil. 'Whoever killed Charles Gainsborough is trying to make it look as if he's another victim of the hooding attacks.'

'But you don't think that's the case?'

'The person who tied these knots didn't tie Laurence Herbert up. That person knew his knots. Whoever was responsible for this only knew how to tie the commonest knot in the world. And with three separate lengths of rope, which is far less efficient.'

'What about the rope around his neck?' Basil asked. 'Does that tell us anything?'

I looked at the ligature that had killed Gainsborough. It had been skewed around so that the knot was at the front, like a horrible parody of a necktie.

'This is cheap jute, too.'

I took a sideways step towards Gainsborough's head and almost retched as the combined stench of the boy's voided bladder and bowels filled my head. I'd forgotten to breathe through my mouth. I swallowed hard and looked down at the dead face.

I'd seen two hanged men during a brief professional involvement with the local coroner's medical witness back home. One had been executed in Cardigan jail using the new humane drop method and the other had been a suicide who'd hanged himself in his cowshed. The two had looked very different. The convict hadn't looked much injured apart from heavy rope marks on his neck, but the one who'd hanged himself had been blue, his eyes bloodshot and his tongue swollen. The difference between having your neck broken instantaneously and being slowly strangled to death.

Whatever the noose and hood were supposed to imply, Gainsborough's injuries indicated that he'd been strangled, not hanged. I pulled the stiff body onto its side.

'He's been garrotted,' I told Basil. 'See, here and here, these indentations?' I pointed at the back of Gainsborough's neck. 'You can see the pattern of the rope's braiding as it twisted over and over on itself.'

I laid the body flat again and pointed at the ligature mark on the front of his neck which was blurred with gouges and scratches.

'He clawed at the rope,' I said. 'You can see where his nails have broken the skin.'

I looked at Gainsborough's stiff hands. Sure enough, some of his nails were torn.

'So that means...?'

'That his hands weren't tied till after he was dead.'

I bent over the dead man's face, peering at the cold, purplish skin.

'What are you doing?' Basil asked.

I didn't answer until I found what I was looking for. A mark that was almost invisible due to the amount of blood in the superficial tissues.

'See this?' I pointed to a small cut forming a neat ninety-degree angle just in front of the point of Gainsborough's jaw on the left-hand side of his face.

Basil crouched to see where I was pointing. 'He was hit with something – yes?'

'Yes. And my bet would be the edge of a square-cut signet ring. You used to box. Isn't that the best place to hit somebody if you want to knock them out?'

Basil stood up straight again. 'You're suggesting he was knocked out, then strangled?'

'From the nail marks, I'd say he was probably just stunned for a few seconds. Groggy enough for whoever killed him to get the noose over his head, put a lever under the knot and start twisting.'

Basil swallowed, staring at me. 'If he was stunned, then strangled,' he asked, eventually, 'could this have been done by a single person?'

I nodded. 'As long as they had a decent right hook.'

I looked at Gainsborough's body again. 'I don't suppose many boys at Trinity dress in a cheap suit like this. I can't swear to it because the light wasn't very good when we first met, but I suspect this is the suit he wore as Gordon Smythe.'

## Chapter 40

*Basil*

Prior to Saturday morning, though the University had been alight with gossip about the hooding attacks, no details had made their way into the newspapers. Gainsborough's death would change that. There would be an inquest – a public hearing – dashing any hope the University might have had of keeping the whole situation away from the eyes of the nation. I dreaded to think what the London papers would make of the murder of an Oxford undergraduate in such bizarre circumstances, particularly when Gainsborough's engagement to Miss Critchley came to light.

However, the inquest would not take place before Monday, and on Sunday I had Teddy's visit to navigate.

Teddy, Morton and Miss Webster were due to arrive at Oxford station just after eleven, but I'd decided that waiting on the platform would look altogether too eager, so in replying to Teddy's recent note, I'd promised to meet them outside with a cab ready.

–

Teddy and his little party emerged from the station accompanied by the friends with whom Miss Webster and little Morton were scheduled to have lunch. They proved to be an amiable couple with a small child who was now sharing my godson's enormous wicker-bodied perambulator.

Once I'd exchanged pleasantries with Miss Webster and her friends and renewed my acquaintance with Morton, who gazed at me solemnly, Teddy excused us, saying that we had some business to attend to.

I didn't contradict him when he asked the cabbie to drive us to Turl Street, but, once we'd alighted from the cab, as he made to step through the wicket gate into Jesus, I forestalled him. 'No. Let's go to Henry's.'

He looked at me quizzically. Henry's was the informal name men like us used for a coffee house near the Victoria Theatre where rooms were made available for the right clientele.

'I suppose it does have a certain nostalgic value,' he mused, grinning. 'Wasn't that where we—'

'We're not going upstairs,' I hissed, flinging a glance behind us lest any of my colleagues had emerged from college. 'We're going to talk. I've arranged to use the drawing room.'

In addition to bedrooms, Henry's offered a small ground-floor retiring room referred to rather grandiosely as the drawing room. Though it was just as private, it didn't contain a bed.

Teddy stared at me. 'Why?'

'I told you. I need to speak to you.'

'Why can't we do that in your rooms?'

The truth was that I didn't trust myself in my rooms. They held too many memories of snatched, risky encounters. I wanted a clear head.

'Let's not argue in the street, Teddy.'

As he fell into step beside me, his irritation was palpable. Teddy didn't take kindly to his plans being thwarted.

But though, previously, his petulance would have unnerved me, now I found myself impatient with it. Both his plans and my apprehension about this visit had been completely overshadowed by the brutal reality of Gainsborough's death. After a disturbed night during which I'd been unable to blot from my mind the sight of the boy's distended face, on waking I'd reread the letter Non had transcribed. Its final paragraph now seemed to imply lethal intent.

> ...*the University needs to be aware that the people of Oxford can keep secrets too. And if its undergraduates are going to walk away scot free while our girls find themselves in jail, then we shall be forced to take action ourselves.*

Was the letter writer responsible for the hooding attacks and Gainsborough's death?

And, if so, did they have anything to do with my receipt of the Venatores' manual, or had somebody unconnected with the attacks seen fit to furnish me with that?

That revolting little pamphlet with its cynical lists had disturbed me almost as much as Gainsborough's death; and now, some of my revulsion at the activities of young men who hunted shop girls and maidservants had transferred itself to Teddy. He'd always been a hunter of men for sex. During our visits to London, he'd loved nothing more than to prowl the dark and furtive corners around Covent Garden and Hyde Park while I stayed in the clubs that had ostensibly drawn us there.

For Teddy, fear was an aphrodisiac.

But as well as danger, he craved a challenge and, currently, my refusal to become his lover once more had presented him with one.

I was resolute, however. I could not allow myself to fall under his spell again.

As he stalked along beside me, the occasional, treasured words of endearment Teddy had spoken to me over the years slipped treacherously into my mind. But had those words been any more heartfelt than the ones Charles Gainsborough had whispered in Sarah Critchley's ear?

The fact that I could even ask myself the question made me despise us both.

—

Henry greeted Teddy before even acknowledging me. 'Well, well. The wanderer has returned!'

While I'd never been under the illusion that I was the only man who would miss Teddy when he abandoned Oxford for London, it was only since his departure that I'd allowed myself to wonder about the true extent of his tomcatting around the city.

'Just for the day, to see Bas, here,' Teddy said, easily.

Henry's eyes darted to me, but he maintained his professional mask.

'Could we trouble you to have some coffee sent to the drawing room, please, Henry?' I asked. 'Teddy and I have some things we need to discuss in private.'

The drawing room wasn't as big as its name implied but the furnishings wouldn't have shamed one of the new houses in North Oxford's ever-expanding middle-class suburbs.

The room's two large windows illuminated the dozens of photographs that lined the walls. Handsome youths on the cusp of manhood in 'sub fusc' for matriculation or graduation; sports teams in rowing tights and short-sleeved flannel undershirts; two cricketers in immaculate whites grinning fixedly at the camera, paused in a game of catch where both simultaneously threw a ball to the other.

I knew those cricketers. They'd come up the same year as Teddy and me and we'd inevitably gravitated to the same circles. They had found the symbolism of throwing the hard cricket balls to each other quite hilarious.

To those who knew nothing of our world, those photographs represented tableaux of University life. To us, they were charged with a hidden eroticism.

Avoiding both the high-backed sofa and the chaise longue which had been re-covered since my last visit, I took one of the upright Queen Anne chairs.

The strong smell of beeswax polish in the room sparked a paradoxical and disturbing memory of the stench of urine and excrement in the storeroom where we'd viewed Gainsborough's body yesterday. I swallowed. 'As Morton's godfather,' I began, 'I'd like to make some financial arrangements for him. As I won't have any children of my own—'

'You don't know that,' Teddy challenged. '*I* have.'

'We're different,' I said. 'I don't think I'd make any kind of husband.'

'Are you telling me you intend to live in college for the rest of your life?'

That was the obvious corollary of a failure to marry, and yet I couldn't quite imagine myself growing old amongst other men at Jesus. 'Perhaps I'll take holy orders yet,' I said, 'and go and live in a rural parish with a housekeeper to look after me.'

Teddy shook his head. 'Don't fool yourself, Bas. You'd never be able to live with the hypocrisy.'

'There'd be no hypocrisy. I'd be celibate.'

'What, and harbour not a single thought of what you'd given up? I believe your holy book is quite clear that the thought is as sinful as the act.'

'Not the *thought*. Just the *intention*. We can't always control our inclinations. The sin lies in the intention to indulge them.'

'And you genuinely persist in believing all that? After so much acceptance of Darwin and his ilk?'

'What I *believe* doesn't matter,' I said. 'What we do is *against the law*. I don't want to put my career in danger. And I don't want to be despised and rejected by people I respect – my colleagues, my family, the people amongst whom I work as a member of the Board of Guardians.'

Teddy stared at me. 'You care what *paupers* think?'

He'd always been content to view the status quo as the natural order of things, lazily choosing to believe that those who were born into poverty were somehow less able, less deserving, than those who were born to money. Before I could respond to his incredulity, a knock heralded the arrival of refreshments and I rose, gratefully, to open the door.

Unable to drop the subject, Teddy paced in agitation as I poured the coffee and passed him a cup. 'Are you telling me that to retain the good opinion of people who are nothing to you, you'd sacrifice… this?' He illustrated 'this' by moving his cup backwards and forwards between us, causing coffee to slop into the saucer.

We were back to the sticking point beyond which we'd failed to progress once before. 'But what is *this*, Teddy?' I asked, mimicking his gesture with my free hand. 'To sacrifice something, it's necessary to be in possession of it. And we don't *have* anything. We just *do* things together. *Did*,' I corrected.

He put his coffee down as if he needed his hands free if he was going to win this argument. 'What do you *want*, Bas?'

I sighed. He knew perfectly well what I wanted. He just couldn't comprehend my wanting it, still less wishing it for himself.

'Very well, if I've previously failed to make my position clear, let me be completely plain,' I said. 'I would have been prepared to risk jail and humiliation for love –' I felt a trembling in my limbs at using what was, for Teddy, a taboo word – 'but not simply for sex.'

He leaped up from the chaise longue. 'This again!'

But it wasn't *again*, it was *still*. I'd always wanted Teddy to love me, and I'd been prepared to take the risk of being part of his circle, doing as he did, running the gauntlet of gossip and rumour, in the hope that one day he'd feel for me as I did for him. Finally, when he announced his removal to London in pursuit of his career and marriage, I'd accepted that he never would.

'I'm no longer willing to take those risks,' I said. 'Because you have no interest in love, do you, Teddy?'

'*Sex* is what men like us have, Bas. Not... anything else.'

I shook my head, my eyes on him. 'Not true.' I named men whom we'd known since we were undergraduates, men who – whether married or not – maintained relationships with each other that precluded sex with any other men.

'But we're not like *them*!' he exclaimed. 'Settling for something so pedestrian, so mundane. Good God, man, they might as well be women!'

'Is that what you're afraid of? Being thought less of a man?'

'I'm not *afraid* of anything. But the thought of having a man who's basically my wife disgusts me.'

He'd never articulated it in those terms before. He'd claimed my feelings were too romantic, that I set him an impossibly high standard, but he'd never before admitted that the idea of loving me disgusted him.

'Then there's nothing more to say on the subject,' I said, taking great care to keep my voice steady. 'So let's talk about the financial arrangement I propose to make for Morton.'

## Chapter 41

*Non*

After seeing the body of Gordon Smythe – or, as I was going to have to get used to calling the lying little weasel, Charles Gainsborough – I'd written a note to Tarley explaining what had happened and asking if he'd still like me to go to Newington Green with him on Sunday.

So now, we were sitting on the train, steaming towards London.

'How did Miss Critchley take the news?' Tarley asked.

Things were still a bit stiff between us, but it looked as if he was trying to forgive me for putting my plan to follow Charles Gainsborough before meeting his mother.

'D'you mean the news that her supposed fiancé had lied to her,' I asked, 'or the news that he was dead?'

Tarley made a face at my bluntness. 'Both, I suppose.'

But I didn't want to tell him how bitterly Sarah Critchley had cried, how much she'd wept in humiliation and grief for her lost dream. If I'm honest, her reaction had shaken me more than seeing Gainsborough's strangled face.

'I think, in her heart of hearts, she'd always known that it was too good to be true.'

'*And then you came along,*' Hara butted in, '*and told her she was right.*'

'And was that more or less humiliating than being abandoned after he'd had what he wanted would've been?'

I could feel Hara smirking. '*Justifying yourself now, are you? Must be feeling guilty.*'

Tarley was watching me as if he could hear Hara, too.

'My sister putting her tuppence-worth in,' I said. 'She thinks… Well, actually, never mind what she thinks.' At this rate, it wouldn't be long before he started saying hello to Hara. 'To be honest,' I hurried on, 'Miss Skene's response was more interesting than Sarah's.'

I would've preferred to talk to Sarah as soon as I'd left Trinity, but I knew she'd be at work till the evening, so I'd gone down to New Inn Hall Street to talk to Miss Skene first.

As luck would have it, I'd arrived just as she was coming back from somewhere, her cloak wet from the rain that had been falling all morning. Jane had brought tea to us in the little front parlour, and I'd told Miss Skene what had happened to Gainsborough.

'I must confess,' she said, 'that though I have sat with more than one unfortunate before his execution, I have never seen the body after the event. You have quite the strong stomach, Miss Vaughan.'

I smiled. 'You need a strong stomach at sea.' Better to make a joke of it than to tell her I couldn't get rid of the memory of Charles Gainsborough's face. His livid purple skin and bloodshot eyes kept appearing in my mind's eye without any permission from me.

'That poor young man,' Miss Skene murmured, 'no amount of deceit justifies such violence.'

Her attitude was understandable. But she hadn't seen Charles Gainsborough standing in the street, lying to Sarah Critchley's face, calling her Sarey, pretending to be a not-very-well-off Yorkshireman who'd come to Oxford to make his fortune, a man who'd *fallen in love with her*, when all the time he was a well-to-do student from Trinity College who'd been hunting and deceiving young women so that he could tally up seductions to present to his disgusting friends.

That final entry on the list of rules in the Venatores manual was stuck in my head. *VI = mega kudos*. Six equals praise and honour.

Honour. Those vicious boys didn't know the meaning of the word.

'Miss Vaughan?'

'I'm sorry,' I said, pulling my attention back to Miss Skene, 'but, just deserts or not, Charles Gainsborough treated Sarah very badly. And I don't doubt that he'd have treated her worse still if he'd lived.'

Felicia Skene didn't bat an eyelid at what I'd just implied. 'Young men like Mr Gainsborough,' she said, eyes trained on the parrot on the back of his chair, as if he was a portal to some unpalatable truth, 'are brought up to see working-class women as creatures entirely different from themselves, incapable of refinement of emotion or intellect. And, in that way, they persuade themselves that their actions are of no great consequence, that sooner or later the girl's fate was inevitable – if not at their hands then at the hands of somebody of her own class.'

She bent down to scratch Tatters behind the ear, and I couldn't help staring at her. I knew she'd had experiences of life which probably no other British woman of her social standing had ever had, but it was still shocking to hear her speaking like that.

'I assume all this unsavoury business about the Venatores will come out at the inquest?' Miss Skene had asked.

I assumed so too. And then we'd see what other muck rose up from the bottom of the pond, wouldn't we?

Tarley listened gravely as I told him what Miss Skene had said then asked, 'Are you going to write about the inquest for the *Pall Mall Gazette*?'

'I'm waiting for a response from Stead, but I hope so. I've already got Berry to agree to me covering it for the *Mercury*.' I'd dropped in to see Berry after leaving Trinity and given him the whole story about Gainsborough and the Hunters. Once he knew that I was involved with the case already, he'd managed to put aside his reservations about ladies listening to gory details and agreed to let me write the inquest report.

'Who do *you* think murdered Charles Gainsborough?' Tarley asked. 'If you don't think it was whoever's responsible for the hooding attacks?'

I stared at him. Not one man in a hundred would sit there, waiting for a woman to tell him what she thought.

I turned around to look at the only other people in our carriage – an older couple travelling with valises and carpet bags. He was reading a newspaper and she had her nose in a women's magazine. If they were listening to us, they weren't making a show of it and, anyway, we'd been keeping our voices down.

'As I see it,' I said, 'the most likely culprit is somebody who knew what he was getting up to with town girls. Probably friends or family of one of their victims.'

Tarley nodded pensively. 'You don't think there's the possibility that one of the people who's been hunting the Venatores decided to act alone? Decided that their warnings weren't working and that more decisive action was needed?'

'Possible, of course.'

'And if it's neither of those?' Tarley asked.

'Then we're back to the coroner's fallback.'

'Which is?'

'Wilful murder by person or persons unknown.'

## Chapter 42

*Basil*

Our walk in Christ Church Meadow, suggested so that I might see more of little Morton, proved very awkward and consisted chiefly of my asking Miss Webster questions about the child while he slept resolutely in his perambulator. Eventually however, emboldened by Teddy's absenting himself from the conversation and falling back behind us, Miss Webster asked me about Miss Critchley's case, which she'd heard about from her friends at lunch.

'I had no idea that the University had such powers,' she said. 'It doesn't seem quite right, does it? The young woman not being given a proper trial, I mean.'

'You're not alone in feeling that, Miss Webster,' I said. 'In fact, I very much suspect that the University is about to find a campaign launched against its retaining such powers.' After an article had appeared in the *Pall Mall Gazette* the previous day outlining Miss Critchley's imprisonment by the Vice Chancellor's court, I feared that such a campaign was inevitable. The British public holds English common law in very high regard and anything that undermines it is liable to vocal opposition.

'How so, Mr Rice?' Miss Webster asked.

Given that Tuesday's inquest would see details of the Venatores' repugnant competition made public, it seemed petty not to indulge Miss Webster's curiosity. Without going into any salacious detail, I outlined the hooding attacks, including Charles Gainsborough's death and his engagement to Miss Critchley.

'My friends didn't mention these attacks,' she said, simultaneously horrified and slightly thrilled. 'Has there been anything about them in the papers?'

'An investigation is currently taking place,' I said. 'And, while it continues, it's better not to have too much in the press.'

From Tuesday onwards, of course, that would change. Even if no London journalists attended the inquest into Gainsborough's death, local story spotters would clip and send the Oxford press reports to their editors and the story would be in the capital's papers the following day.

'Will the poor young woman who was sent to prison have to give evidence at the hearing?' Miss Webster asked. 'I suppose she will if she was engaged to the boy who died.'

'Yes, I'm afraid she will.'

'Poor thing. As if she hasn't suffered enough.'

Miss Webster's pity for Miss Critchley made me realise, to my shame, that I'd given her little thought in all this. As we walked along the bank of the Cherwell, Miss Webster pointing the ducks out to Morton who had now awakened, I wondered what effect having to give evidence as to her own deception might have on Sarah Critchley. Would she wilt under the scorn of the undergraduate spectators at the inquest, as they scoffed at her for believing that one of their number would actually propose marriage to a shop girl?

I wondered whether Miss Critchley had truly believed in their engagement. Had Gainsborough persuaded her so thoroughly of her attractions, her superiority to all other girls, that she'd trusted in his declarations of devotion despite the difference in their stations? It was possible. She was, after all, very young.

And besides, love makes fools of us all. We want, above all things, to believe the assurances of our lovers, even when reason tells us that they are made in pursuit of ignoble ends. Reason and logic might be revered in University circles, but both are powerless in the face of passionate emotion; swept aside by the force of our desires like twigs before a flood.

Teddy, I had no doubt, would declare that Sarah's humiliation would easily be overridden by the prospect of financial compensation for her false imprisonment, that 'girls like her' would always default to money over feeling. But my experience had taught me that working people, people without money or education, did not, as a class, lack nobility of thought or feeling. Girls like Sarah Critchley might not have the vocabulary to express adequately what they felt, but like Shakespeare's Merchant of Venice, just like her betters, if pricked, Sarah would bleed, if tickled, she would laugh, if poisoned, she would die.

But the corollary that slid into place behind these thoughts was a dark one: if wronged, like the merchant himself, might she not seek revenge?

Admittedly, the notion didn't seem immediately plausible. Though I wasn't acquainted with Sarah Critchley, it seemed unlikely that an undernourished shop girl would have the physical strength to strangle a fit young man like Charles Gainsborough. And besides, if newspaper reports were to be believed, poison was the favoured method of women avenging themselves on men who had ill-used them, a less direct and visceral way of committing murder.

But there was always the possibility that Miss Critchley might have recruited a young man of her acquaintance as her accomplice. After all, just such a pair of youths had, by all accounts, tried to prevent her being taken up by Waddesworth on the Cornmarket. Was it possible that one of them was responsible for Gainsborough's murder?

## Chapter 43

*Non*

The nearer we got to London the more silent and preoccupied Tarley was. As a rule we never ran out of things to say to each other, so his quietness was putting me on edge.

I watched him from the corner of my eye as he stared out of the window.

When I'd first seen him again, in the hallway at Shene Road, I'd thought he hadn't changed at all apart from getting a bit taller and broader. But now I could see I'd been wrong. There was a seriousness about him that hadn't been there before. Or perhaps it had been there all along, and I just hadn't seen it under the chatter and laughing.

'*His mother nearly died,*' Hara reminded me. '*That would make anybody a bit more serious.*'

I suddenly felt guilty. Guilty and stupid. Tarley had told me, in his letters, how worried he was about his mother, but because she'd recovered and he'd come back to Oxford, I'd behaved as if nothing had happened. As if all we needed to do was slip back into how we used to be together.

Tarley was frowning at the countryside moving past the window. What was he thinking? Was I wrong about him forgiving me?

'*Ask him,*' Hara said.

'Tarley?' The frown disappeared and he raised his eyebrows as he turned to look at me. 'Are you still angry with me about not saying yes to coming to see your mother straight away?'

He sighed and blinked several times. 'I wasn't angry, I was... I suppose I'd just assumed...'

He'd assumed that he came higher up my list of priorities than following Sarah Critchley's treacherous sweetheart around Oxford. I didn't need Hara to tell me that.

'I'm sorry,' I said. 'I just get caught up in things.'

'Yes, I know.' The smile he gave me wasn't his usual one, something was still dampening his spirits. 'There's something I need to tell you,' he said.

My stomach turned over. Had I made a mistake coming with him today? Did he have something to say that would change things between us? Something that would force a bigger decision from me than whether I should spend Sunday going to London with him? 'Then tell me,' I said, my voice a lot calmer than my stomach.

He glanced at the other couple in the carriage and shook his head. 'Not here.' He must have guessed what I was thinking, then, because he smiled that sad little smile again. 'Don't worry, Non. It's about my mother.'

—

When we finally reached Paddington, Tarley found a 'bus which would take us to somewhere called Balls Pond Road. 'Then we can walk the last mile or so,' he said.

London omnibuses weren't very exciting. They were smaller than Oxford's trams and, on our way to Balls Pond Road, we had to stand because all the seats were taken. I was used to walking or cycling everywhere in Oxford and I was glad when we could get off.

'Newington Green's up that way,' Tarley said, pointing to a road running north. 'And it does actually have a green – the meeting house overlooks it.'

When he said 'meeting house', he meant the Unitarian chapel that he and his mother attended. I wondered if the members there had looked after Mrs Askew during her illness. That's what would have happened back in Cardiganshire if a woman had no family nearby – everybody would have rallied round to look after her. Somebody would've taken her in, others would have visited and brought gifts of nourishing food, somebody better off would have paid for the doctor to come and examine her. The way everybody knew everybody else's business – and thought they had the right to give their opinions and have them taken notice of – had driven me mad, but a community like that has its advantages.

Still, if I'd stayed there, I'd have followed the old proverb: *câr dy gymydog ond cadwa dy glawdd* – love your neighbour but tend your hedge.

As we walked away from Balls Pond Road, it was obvious that this area of London was expanding rapidly.

'Reminds me of North Oxford,' I said, looking at some of the newly built three-storey villas.

'Not quite so grand,' Tarley said. 'But I know what you mean. There's that feeling of frantic growth, isn't there?'

We walked past a pair of handsome houses covered in scaffolding. Tomorrow morning the roofers would be back but, today, everything was quiet. Miss Skene would be glad to see that even in sinful old London, people still observed the Sabbath. Well, they took the day off work at any rate.

Suddenly, Tarley started to speak. 'As you know,' he said, as if we were picking up a conversation we'd already started earlier, 'my parents met in India.'

I nodded. 'When your father was serving in the Indian Army.' He'd told me that much when we'd first met.

'Yes. But my mother wasn't one of the young women who'd been shipped out to India to find a husband. She was there already.'

I could tell that statement was supposed to tell me something, but I couldn't work out what.

'My mother isn't English,' he explained.

Before he spoke again, we'd covered another fifty yards or so. 'She's Anglo-Indian,' he said, finally. 'Her father was also an Indian Army officer, but her mother was Indian. A native.' He glanced at me quickly then fixed his eyes on the road in front of us again. 'I'm only telling you this so that you don't look at her and wonder. She's quite light-skinned. She could pass as Mediterranean.'

He'd needed to find some courage to tell me, so I needed to be careful now.

'Why did she bring you to England after your father died, if her family was still there?' I asked.

'She came because she believed I'd have a better life here.' He hesitated. 'She wanted me to meet my paternal grandmother.' He stopped, as if he wasn't sure he wanted to say anything more about that, then lurched on. 'Unfortunately, my father's delightful mother took one look at Ma and knew exactly what she was. And, therefore, what I was. And she didn't want anything to do with me. All I have from my father's family is a sum of money left in trust for me before my grandfather died. When my parentage wasn't yet known, that is,' he added, staring straight ahead.

What had that been like for his mother? Finding herself alone and rejected in a foreign country with a small child?

'Once we were here, my mother and I had no choice but to stay in England. She had nobody to appeal to at home to help us go back. Her mother had abandoned Ma at an orphanage for the daughters of Indian Army officers when she was born.'

The fact that orphanages existed specifically for officers' illegitimate half-Indian daughters told me how common relationships like that were. Presumably, there was a lack of potential British brides, which explained the young women Tarley'd referred to – the ones 'shipped out to find a husband'.

I wondered whether Tarley's grandmother had been promised marriage, like Sarah Critchley.

'Did your mother know her father?' I asked. He was being matter-of-fact, so I followed his example.

'Only from letters he wrote. Apparently, while he was still in India, he kept an eye on her and received regular reports from the orphanage. She was a bright girl and she progressed to become a teacher there. But when he resigned his commission and came back to England, the letters stopped. She never heard from him again.'

We turned into another street, this time with less prosperous-looking two-storey houses.

'Luckily for me,' he said, 'my father was cut from a different cloth. When he fell in love with my mother, he married her. Which ruined any chance he had in the army. No amount of money would have been enough for him to buy his next promotion after that. So he cut his losses. He cashed in his commission and went to work for the railway.' He glanced at me. 'And my mother, who'd been brought up to be more British than the British, suddenly found herself living amongst the demi-monde of Anglo-Indians. They all tried to maintain their Britishness – they were *half*-British, when all's said and done – but the whiter-than-white sahibs and memsa'bs didn't want them, and the native Indians didn't trust them because of their white blood.'

'Why didn't your parents come back here when they married?'

Tarley stopped in front of a house with a bright green door. 'What makes you think it would have been any better for them here?' he asked.

I looked at the door. 'Is this your mother's house?'

He nodded. 'Any questions, before we go in?'

'Yes. Why are people so stupid? It's such a lazy way to judge any person. As if the colour of your skin – or, come to that, your sex or your class – are the most important things about you instead of what's in here.' I tapped the side of my head.

'And here.' Tarley laid a hand over his heart. He looked relieved. Had he really thought this would make any difference to me? Knowing that his mother wasn't a dyed-in-the-wool middle-class Englishwoman made it *more* likely that I'd take to her, not less.

'Your mother must be a brave woman,' I said.

'Takes one to know one,' Tarley said. And this time, his real smile was back.

## Chapter 44

*Basil*

On Monday morning, I received a summons from the Vice Chancellor as I left the lecture I'd been giving.

'Has there been another attack?' I asked the messenger.

'No, sir. Not to my knowledge, anyway.'

Walking up the Turl, I couldn't suppress the slightly ludicrous thought that, if Benjamin Jowett had seen fit to stick his head out of his drawing room window and shout for me, I might have heard him from Jesus College and saved the messenger the trouble of coming for me.

But Jowett – elderly, rotund, smiling Jowett – was not a man to yell. When not lecturing, he scarcely ever raised his voice above what a colleague had once referred to as 'an amiable murmur'.

'Ah, Rice,' the Vice Chancellor said as his butler announced me at the door of Jowett's study. 'Thank you for coming so quickly.'

His courtesy was mere form. When the Vice Chancellor called, one came to heel, however mighty or occupied one might be.

Jowett picked up a newspaper from his desk and proferred it to me. 'Today's *Pall Mall Gazette*.' He tapped the open page at an article entitled 'Disgraceful Behaviour at Oxford University'.

I took the newspaper from him and began to read, my heart sinking as I detected Non's voice in the article's livid tone.

**DISGRACEFUL BEHAVIOUR AT OXFORD UNIVERSITY**

Further to our recent article concerning the unconscionably high-handed conduct of the Oxford Vice Chancellor's court in imprisoning a young woman of the city who was guilty of no crime, it has come to light that this same young woman endured yet more harm at the hands of a junior member of the same university. An undergraduate whom she had met at church, having wooed her for some weeks, proposed marriage, asking her leave to keep the engagement secret until such time as he should come of age. An unwise match for both young people, possibly, given the differences in their social stations, but hardly one to be condemned.

However, subsequent enquiries have brought to light the fact that, though his fiancée believed him to be attached to a non-collegiate hall of residence provided for the benefit of young men of scant means who wish to study at the University, he was, in fact, a member of one of the oldest and most prestigious colleges in Oxford. It has further emerged that his declarations of eternal devotion were made to the unfortunate young woman under a false name.

We await with much interest the response of the University to these revelations. If this is the conduct of young men who presume for themselves a place as the future leaders of our country, then it is hard not to conclude that Oxford University has allowed its self-satisfaction to outstrip its oversight of its undergraduates' morals.

I had barely looked up before Jowett began speaking once more. Normally the most courteous of men, he was clearly highly agitated.

'I received a telegram first thing this morning warning me of this article,' he said.

'From Stead?' I asked, thinking that the editor might have wished to give Jowett the opportunity to read the piece before Oxford started beating a path to his door.

'No. From a member of college. A former undergraduate who has our best interests at heart.'

Before I could respond, the Vice Chancellor began pacing. 'The article Stead published on Saturday on the girl being sent to prison was bad enough – but this is beyond all bearing. I am exceedingly vexed that it was my absence from Oxford that allowed this Critchley affair its genesis. When I made arrangements for the University's oversight during my visit to Manchester, I had no notion of my deputy presiding at the Vice Chancellor's court.'

'You wouldn't have sent Sarah Critchley to prison,' I said, stating it as a fact. Jowett looked at me with gratitude.

'I would not. I met with Miss Skene to discuss this whole business of undergraduate fraternisation with town girls when I took up the Vice Chancellorship. Following her advice, I would have considered the discomfort of a night in the Clarendon rooms a more than sufficient deterrent for Miss Critchley. Sending her to prison on such flimsy evidence was...'

'Unwarranted?'

'Unwise.'

I placed the newspaper on Jowett's desk and waited for him to stop pacing.

'I beg your pardon, Rice. Do sit down.'

Jowett himself remained standing. 'We cannot allow Stead to ridicule us,' he said. 'We're only just beginning to mould the University into a modern institution fit to meet the challenges which lie ahead. I doubt I shall see the twentieth century, but I should like to feel that I leave the University in good heart upon its arrival. Which includes the esteem in which it's held. This kind of thing,' he flicked a hand irritably in the direction of the newspaper, 'only makes that task so much harder.'

Finally he sat, taking the other chair which flanked the fireplace. 'The question is, how did Stead become aware of this young man's duplicity?' he asked.

Was it possible that Jowett, with his reputation for knowing everything that concerned the University, was not aware that Non had begun writing for the *Pall Mall Gazette*?

'Does Stead pay for this kind of information?' Jowett asked, when I failed to answer. 'Has he people on the lookout for stories that might damage our reputation?'

'I can't tell you, Vice Chancellor, but it would appear that the University's oversight of morality amongst the undergraduates has piqued his interest.'

Belatedly, I realised that the article hadn't mentioned Charles Gainsborough's name.

'Vice Chancellor, are you aware that the Trinity undergraduate who was found, murdered, on Saturday morning is also the man referred to in this article – Charles Gainsborough?'

Jowett had no need to answer. His horrified expression was quite sufficient.

'Whether Gainsborough truly intended to marry Miss Critchley or not,' I said, 'he gave her a ring – a signet ring – which, he told her, had been a matriculation gift from his father. The ring actually proved, on further investigation, to have been bought from a pawn shop in St Clement's. Not only that, but I myself saw Gainsborough attempting to pick up another town girl on the Cornmarket. And, when the proctor detained him, he gave his name and college as Smythe of New Inn Hall, just as he'd told Sarah Critchley.'

Jowett turned away and stared into the fire. Eventually, he spoke once more, eyes still fixed on the glowing coals. 'I was tremendously grateful when you were kind enough to agree to help the proctors in their investigations of these awful attacks on our boys. I had hoped – I think we had *all* hoped – that student high jinks had simply been allowed to get a little out of hand. But, with Gainsborough's death, that's obviously not the case. Do you have any sense of what's actually happening here, of who's responsible?'

Reluctantly, I told him about the Venatores. And when he had expressed his disgust, I handed him the little foolscap manual which I had in my pocket. I wanted him to see the full cynicism of the Venatores' campaign.

'But who would have sent this to you, Rice?' the Vice Chancellor asked when he'd looked through the folded booklet. 'And what could their motive have been?'

The same question had been occupying my mind. 'Given that it was addressed to me specifically,' I said, 'I infer that whoever sent it knows I'm investigating the attacks but doesn't wish to involve the proctors.'

That didn't narrow the field greatly; following my address to the Purity Association at Keble, well over a hundred undergraduates had that information.

Jowett handed the manual back to me. 'Have you discovered anything definitive to link these Venatores with the attacks,' he asked, 'and with Mr Gainsborough?'

I began enumerating points of evidence: 'Gainsborough was a Trinity man and the invitation to dinner was to Trinity. He attempted to pick up a young woman on the Cornmarket using one of the suggestions listed by the Venatores under "Consilium". As per the recommendation under "Hostibus", when Waddesworth challenged him, he issued a stout denial and a false name and college.'

'Thin enough, surely?'

'But evidence nonetheless, Vice Chancellor. Evidence that, I'm afraid, will have to be presented at the inquest tomorrow.'

'This?' Jowett simultaneously raised the little Venatores' manual and his voice. 'You'll present this revolting object as something you feel is relevant to his death?'

I faced down his dismay. I held Jowett in great respect, but I couldn't let his wish to maintain the University's good name stand in the way of justice. 'I see no alternative, Vice Chancellor. All evidence of Gainsborough's conduct is relevant to his death.'

'But if we aren't certain that the boy was actually a member of this club...?'

'I intend to visit Trinity before I return to Jesus, in order to confirm that Gainsborough arranged a supper party in his rooms on the night specified on the invitation. I think that will be conclusive.'

At least then we'd have positively identified one member of the Venatores.

Even if he was dead.

## Chapter 45

*Non*

I was giving a geometry lecture at the AEW building on St Giles when the door opened and one of the Association's young women looked in.

'Sorry to disturb you, Miss Vaughan, but a boy's just brought you this from Miss Felicia Skene. Apparently, she asked that you read it at once.'

I opened the note.

> *Dear Miss Vaughan*
> *Please meet me at the Police Station on the High Street at your earliest convenience. Sarah Critchley has been arrested.*
> *F.S.*

I had the Contraption with me, so I was at the police station in less than five minutes.

Inside, I found Miss Skene being waited on by policemen as if she were the Queen. The constables weren't quite walking backwards out of her presence, but it was a close-run thing.

Iain the parrot had come with her for this state visit and his exotic plumage made the police station – which was decorated as if brown was the only available colour – look even more drab than usual.

With her tall, stately bearing and the bird on her shoulder, Felicia Skene looked like the ageing ruler of some barbaric tribe.

'Miss Vaughan,' she said, handing the cup and saucer in her hand to a hovering constable, 'how good of you to come so swiftly.'

'How did you know where I'd be?'

'I didn't, of course. I simply cast my bread upon the waters in the form of three boys. One I sent to your home, one to Somerville Hall and the other to the AEW lecture rooms. Then I prayed.'

There would have been plenty of boys at her beck and call. Any shop in Oxford would have lent her a messenger for half an hour if she'd asked. Her philanthropy was legendary and virtually everybody in Oxford knew somebody she'd helped.

'What's Sarah been arrested for?' I asked.

'As it happens, since arriving here, I've learned that she has not, in fact, been arrested,' Miss Skene said. 'The sergeant assures me that she is merely required to answer some questions.'

'And what questions would those be?' I asked.

Just then, the door to the inspector's office opened and Inspector Newman emerged with two men in academic gowns. 'Miss Skene, I'm so sorry to have kept you waiting.' His eyes shifted to me. 'And Miss Vaughan, too, I see.'

The inspector and I were old acquaintances. I won't say he looked pleased to see me but at least he didn't exclude me from his conversation with Felicia Skene.

Miss Skene rose to her feet. 'You have no need to apologise, Inspector,' she said graciously. 'Good morning, Reverend Kaye, Mr Waddesworth.'

Inspector Newman held his door open. 'Please, ladies, come in.'

I followed Miss Skene and, as we went through the door, Sarah Critchley jumped up from the chair she was sitting on.

'Miss Skene!' She held out her hands and Felicia Skene took them.

'It's all right, child, we'll get to the bottom of this, fear not.'

Sarah was dressed smartly, in her shop girl clothes. She was dry-eyed but I could tell that she was agitated. When she sat down again, she started picking at the skin around her fingernails.

'Inspector,' Miss Skene began, 'perhaps you would be good enough to explain why Miss Critchley has been brought here?'

'We received an anonymous letter giving credible information about the death of Charles Gainsborough—'

'Also known as Gordon Smythe,' I said.

'I beg your pardon?' Inspector Newman said.

Hadn't the proctors told him?

I glanced at Sarah. I could see she didn't want to tell the story, so I did.

When I'd finished, the inspector looked as if he'd just been given the solution to an annoying puzzle. 'Thank you, Miss Vaughan. I'd been made aware of the supposed engagement between Miss Critchley and the deceased, but not his use of a different identity.'

No, the proctors wouldn't have wanted to talk about that. But it was all going to come out at the inquest tomorrow.

'Can you tell us what information – credible or otherwise – this anonymous letter contained, Inspector?' Miss Skene asked.

Finally, Newman looked away from me and I realised that I'd been holding my breath.

'Indeed,' he said. 'The letter claims that associates of Miss Critchley's were seen pushing a handcart along Broad Street early on Saturday morning.'

'Associates?'

'Specifically, a Mr Frank Dodds and two unnamed friends.'

'But *why*?' Sarah burst out, as if she'd asked before and been given an unsatisfactory answer. Or no answer at all. 'I *told* you, Inspector, Frank didn't *know* anything.' She turned to Miss Skene and me. 'I barely ever *see* him these days – not since me and Mum moved to Jericho. He didn't know anything *about* Gordon. I'm sorry, I mean Charles Gainsborough.'

'Just because you didn't tell him doesn't mean he didn't know, Miss Critchley,' the inspector pointed out. 'He could have followed you, seen you with the man you knew as Gordon Smythe.'

Sarah stared at him as if she couldn't think how to tell him all the reasons why that wouldn't have happened. But I could see the inspector's point. After all, Sarah had told Miss Skene and me that two lads called Frank and Alfie had tried to rescue her when Waddesworth and his bulldogs arrested her on Cornmarket Street. If this was the same Frank then he might well have been following her.

'And have you been able to interview Mr Dodds, Inspector?' Miss Skene asked.

'His address is one of the things we'd hoped to know from Miss Critchley,' Newman said, mildly enough.

'I keep *telling* you, I don't *know* Frank's address. I just used to see him about in the 'Friars. And even if I *did* know,' Sarah said, finding some spirit, 'why would I tell *you* when you want to put a noose around his neck?'

'We only want to put a noose around his neck if he's guilty of murdering Charles Gainsborough.'

'And how's he supposed to prove he didn't?' Sarah demanded.

'A man is innocent until he's proven guilty, Sarah,' Miss Skene said, 'not guilty until he's proven innocent.'

'Not when the one being accused is a working man and the one who's dead is a toff! That's not how things go, Miss Skene. Not by a long chalk it isn't.'

'May I see the letter?' I asked.

The inspector frowned. 'For what reason?'

'I'd like to see the handwriting. And the paper.'

It wasn't that I had anything to compare the handwriting with, I just knew that if I saw it, I wouldn't forget it.

Newman opened a drawer in his desk and took out a sheet of paper which had been folded into quarters.

On the outside, the address was written in a fluent, legible hand:

> For the attention of the Inspector of Police, Oxford City police force.

Inside, the message was short and to the point:

> You should be aware that Frank Dodds was seen on Broad Street early on Saturday morning pushing a barrow draped with a canvas sheet. Two other men were with him. Also, Frank Dodds is sweet on Sarah Critchley.

The note told me several things, none of which I was particularly keen to share with Inspector Newman. I passed it back to him and turned to Sarah. 'What does Frank Dodds do for a living?'

'This and that. Labouring mostly, when I knew him, but he can turn his hand to all sorts.'

'Does he own a flatbed handcart?'

She shook her head. 'I shouldn't've thought so, no.'

'How well do you know him?' I asked.

'We used to play together when we were nippers, that's all.'

'But you never walked out together?'

'No!'

'And you don't know of him being sweet on you?'

'I don't know what goes on in somebody else's head, do I? But he never said nothing – anything – to me.'

In her agitation, Sarah's grammar was slipping.

'May we take Sarah home now, Inspector?' Miss Skene asked. 'If you have no more questions for her?'

Inspector Newman sighed. 'You're free to go, Miss Critchley. But we will find Frank Dodds. And we will get to the bottom of this.'

Outside the police station, Miss Skene took Sarah off to her house for a cup of tea before escorting her back to Hyde's. If she explained to Sarah's employers that the police *hadn't* arrested her, then she might not get the sack.

'I'll come and see you soon, Sarah,' I said as we parted. I was hoping that yet another branch of officialdom picking on her might make her decide that suing the University was a good idea.

We all crossed the road together but where they went towards Carfax, I pedalled the Contraption straight up Turl Street.

I needed to see Basil.

## Chapter 46

### *Basil*

I'd barely set foot in my rooms on my return from speaking to the domestic staff at Trinity when the assistant messenger knocked on my door and showed the Senior Proctor in. I sent Fred to the kitchens for some coffee. It would never do to allow Kaye to see me making my own coffee like some penniless undergraduate, however superior the result was.

The Senior Proctor had come to apprise me of news he'd lately learned from Inspector Newman. An anonymous letter had implicated a young man in Gainsborough's death.

'I hope this will signal an end to the need for your investigations, Rice,' he said once he'd relayed the conversation he and Waddesworth had had with the inspector and Miss Critchley. 'Once this Dodds fellow has been apprehended, I'm confident that we'll see no more hooding attacks.'

I, however, couldn't help but think that the Senior Proctor's confidence was misplaced.

'I think there's something you should know, Kaye,' I said, putting to one side the unsatisfactory coffee Fred had conveyed to my door. 'I've just returned from Trinity where I was able to confirm that Charles Gainsborough was a member of the Venatores – the club that produced the revolting little manual I showed you.'

Kaye frowned. 'How were you able to do that?'

'The manciple's records indicated that it was Gainsborough who arranged the supper party referred to on the invitation pinned to Harcourt Ashdown's hood.'

'That's a bit weak, isn't it? There might have been any number of supper parties at Trinity that night.'

'Only two, actually. And the other was a small affair for three people. Gainsborough ordered three courses for seven men.'

Before Kaye could respond, Fred reappeared at my door. 'There's a Miss Vaughan in the lodge asking for you, Mr Rice.'

Non must, somehow, have got wind of Sarah Critchley's being taken to the police station.

I scribbled a quick note asking her to wait for me in the coffee room at the Golden Cross hotel, then turned back to Kaye with a word of apology. The Senior Proctor, however, seemed to have used the interruption to regroup.

'This undergraduate society notwithstanding, Rice, Inspector Newman is confident that once Frank Dodds can be detained, this whole sordid business will be at an end.'

Being slightly acquainted with Oxford's inspector of police and the unhurried, intelligent manner in which he went about his duties, I suspected that the confidence Kaye attributed to him was actually born of the Senior Proctor's own profound hope that all might now be resolved.

'I'm afraid I'm less optimistic on that score, Kaye. There are discrepancies which suggest that Gainsborough's death is not the work of the same hands as the previous attacks.'

Without mentioning Non's name, for fear of diminishing the validity of her observations in Kaye's eyes, I explained the difference in the way Herbert and Gainsborough had been tied, and the much flimsier construction of Gainsborough's hood. 'The superficial similarities in bindings and hood suggest that whoever killed Charles Gainsborough had heard how the previous victims had been trussed up and had tried, unsuccessfully, to emulate that,' I finished.

But Kaye was disinclined to have his optimism dented. 'I think you're attributing too much significance to small details, Rice. If this Dodds had associates, then it's highly *likely* that the victims weren't all bound by the same hand. As for the hood, perhaps the material used for the others had been exhausted and an alternative had to be pressed into service.'

He might be right about the bindings, but the construction of the hoods didn't differ simply in the materials used; the hood placed over Gainsborough's head had been crudely tacked together, as if by a hand completely unused to wielding needle and thread, whereas the one Tarley Askew removed from Herbert had been neatly stitched. Whoever had masterminded the hooding attacks had taken pains that each one should be identical in method and execution. If the same hand was responsible for Gainsborough's murder, why then would the perpetrator suddenly deviate from his previous meticulousness?

'I'm sorry, Kaye, but I think evidence of the Venatores' activities should be heard at the inquest. Therefore I must ask you to ensure that I am called tomorrow.'

Kaye stared at me. My insistence clearly didn't chime with my reputation as a good man to have in the University's corner when reputational damage was threatened. 'Do you seriously intend to expose Gainsborough as the kind of chap who made a sport of chasing town girls?' he asked.

'I'm afraid we can't hide it, Kaye. It's relevant information.'

The Senior Proctor shook his head. 'But the newspapers will have a field day, man! The *Pall Mall Gazette* is already out for our blood – have you seen this morning's edition?'

'If our young men have brought these attacks on themselves by their behaviour –' I held up a hand to forestall the objection I saw on his face – 'I don't in all conscience think that the evidence I've found can be withheld. Not if we truly want justice to be done.'

---

The Golden Cross hotel, set back a little from the bustle of the Cornmarket, had a very pleasant coffee room overlooking the small courtyard which the hotel occupied. I found Non making shorthand notes, a pot of coffee and two cups and saucers on the table in front of her.

'I'm sorry I had to send you away,' I said as I sat down, 'I had the Senior Proctor with me.'

'I seem to be following him around,' she said, before recounting the conversation she and Miss Skene had had with Inspector Newman.

'That anonymous note was interesting,' she said, stirring sugar into her second cup of coffee. 'Firstly, there's the paper it was written on. Foolscap. Well, actually a foolscap sheet cut in half. Most people who're in the habit of writing letters keep a stock of letter paper. And I'd say that whoever wrote that letter *was* in the habit of writing. You can tell when writing's second nature to somebody, can't you? From the way the letters are formed and how even the lines are. So why would they use foolscap?'

She was watching me as she spoke, clearly waiting for me to draw the obvious inference. 'Well, foolscap is what undergraduates use for the most part...'

'Exactly!' Non beamed in triumph. 'Which bears some thinking about, doesn't it?'

Before I could reply, she was off on a different tangent. 'Kaye must have come straight to you from meeting with the inspector, so did he have anything useful to say?' she asked.

'Nothing that you've not told me now.' I sipped my coffee. 'But he's convinced that if we catch Gainsborough's killer, we'll have resolved the hooding attacks.'

'Yes,' she scoffed, 'I'm sure he'd love to believe that. And I'm sure he'd like to believe that the killer is Frank Dodds, too. That would be so *convenient*, wouldn't it?'

'However,' I said repressively, 'we've taken *one* step forward this morning.' And I told her what I'd learned from the manciple at Trinity.

She tapped her pencil on her notes, thinking. 'So if the Hunters met in rooms at Trinity that night, does that mean Gainsborough was their leader? Or did they rotate their meetings around the members?'

'Either could be true. Though the fact that there was neither staircase nor room number on the invitation suggests the former, don't you think? As if everybody would know exactly where to go.'

'Maybe. Unless membership of the Hunters is limited to one man per college. That's the sort of stupid rule these secret societies might have, isn't it? To keep them exclusive?'

If that was the case then Non knew more about Oxford's secret undergraduate societies than I did. I indicated her notebook. 'Notes for another article?'

She glanced down as if she'd forgotten that the book was there. 'Just notes on our conversation with Inspector Newman,' she said, absently, as if she was still thinking.

Not wishing to derail her train of thought, I drained the rest of my coffee and caught the eye of a passing boy to signal for another pot.

Keeping her eyes on the table between us, Non began speaking slowly and deliberately, as if she was trying to lure out an elusive thought with her words. 'There was something Sarah Critchley said, after we'd come out of the police station. She told Miss Skene and me that she'd never have stopped to have the conversation that got her thrown into jail if the boy who'd stopped her *hadn't known Gordon*. They'd seen him about, apparently, when they were together and Gordon – or rather Charles Gainsborough – had always acknowledged him. She thought they were friends.'

Non ignored the arrival of the second pot of coffee, apparently still deep in thought.

'Would the undergraduate Sarah was arrested for detaining have been called to give evidence at the Vice Chancellor's court?' she asked, once the serving boy had moved away.

'I don't know. I'm not entirely au fait with the workings of the court, I'm afraid.'

'Could you find out his name?'

'You think he might be a member of the Venatores?'

'I'd lay money on it.'

'Well, if so, he'll probably have given a false name,' I said. '*Nom et lieu de guerre* as prescribed in the manual.'

However, it would be a simple matter for me to find out what name he'd given the proctor. It only required a visit to Kaye.

'I'll see what I can do,' I promised.

There was a slight pause then both of us spoke at once.

'There's something else—' Non said, as I asked, 'I need to know—'

We both smiled. 'You first,' Non said.

'I need to know,' I repeated, 'whether you wrote the article that appeared in the *Pall Mall Gazette* today? The one entitled "Disgraceful Behaviour at Oxford University".'

She didn't flinch. 'I did, as it happens.'

As my heart sank, I realised that I'd been trying to persuade myself that it had been Stead's own work, even if Non had provided him with the information. 'But why?' I asked.

'Because it's the truth. And people need to know.'

I sighed. 'At least you didn't say anything about Gainsborough's murder.'

'I was waiting for the inquest to do that.'

I stared across the table. 'You're going to report on the inquest for the *Pall Mall Gazette*?'

Her chin went up. 'I had a telegram this morning insisting on it.'

'Non, are you not familiar with the phrase "hoist with your own petard"?'

Though she was clearly trying to appear nonchalant, I could see her pulse beating in her slim throat and she was slightly flushed. 'How's that relevant here?'

'Your contracts with Somerville and the AEW won't be worth the paper they're written on once the board finds out that you're systematically attempting to bring the reputation of the University into disrepute.'

She leaned forward, both her hands clenched in small, fierce fists. 'I think you'll find that it's members of the University that are doing that. All I'm doing is reporting on it.'

I stared at her in frustration. 'There are members of the Hebdomadal Council who are just *itching* for an excuse to bring an end to the University's flirtation with female education. Are you seriously willing to put that at risk?'

'Articles in the *Pall Mall Gazette* are written anonymously.'

I had the sudden urge to bang the table. 'Don't be so naive! Unless you've sworn Stead to secrecy, it'll get out. Then *boom*! The bomb you've been priming to blow up the University's reputation goes off in your own face!'

She stared at me. 'Who are you trying to protect?' she asked. 'Me or the University?'

'You!'

I said it without a moment's hesitation, and I was slightly surprised to find that it was true. 'I don't want to see you burning bridges between yourself and the AEW. I know journalism is your current focus, but I'd hate to see you denying yourself any possibility of a future academic career.'

Her response was entirely unexpected. She sighed, unclenched one of her fists and reached for my hand. 'Thank you, Basil.' She released my hand again with a small squeeze. 'But this isn't about me. All right, I know what you're going to say, and perhaps it is a bit,' she admitted. 'It'll put me in Stead's good books at the very least. But the main thing is, Stead has given me an opportunity I might never have again to change things for girls like Sarah Critchley. Shouldn't I do that?' Her eyes were fixed on mine, and I felt the usual discomfort at such prolonged contact. 'I'm not well-connected like women who try to bring about change politically. I'm just a girl from Cardiganshire. I don't have influential friends who have the ear of government. All I have is an inquisitive mind, a pig-headed determination and words.'

She reached down to the leather satchel she always carried and pulled out an envelope which she placed on the table between us. It was addressed to 'Mrs A. H. Johnson, Secretary to the Association for the Promotion of Higher Education of Women in Oxford'.

'It's my resignation,' she said. 'I'll hand it in at the end of term or when Sarah Critchley's case goes to court, whichever is sooner. Or, if they get wind of what I'm up to and haul me in without warning, I'll just whip this out and be done with it. I won't let the AEW be embarrassed by me.'

'And that's it? You'll just sever all ties?'

'For now, yes. But things will change. They always do. And then we'll see.' Non slipped the letter back into her satchel. 'Right, my turn.' She drained her coffee cup and put it to one side. 'Tarley found a very odd advertisement for classes for "prospective husbands" in the Corpus JCR the other day. Classes to make men more confident on their wedding night. Run by a Dr E. Ross.' She waited for me to see the pun, then continued. 'And guess where the advertisement asked these nervous bridegrooms to apply?'

Initially, I shook my head, unwilling to guess. Then, when I saw a smile pulling at her lips, I exclaimed, 'No! Not the Turf Tavern?'

She nodded, grinning. 'And Tarley's going there this afternoon.'

## Chapter 47

*Non*

Basil wasn't the first person to ask me whether I was determined to cut my ties with Somerville and concentrate on journalism. Mrs Askew had asked me the same thing on Sunday.

While I waited for Tarley to come and see me after his consultation with Dr Eros, I found my mind wandering back – not exactly for the first time – to his mother.

If I hadn't known Mrs Askew's parentage, I might have assumed that she was Italian or Spanish, just like Tarley'd suggested. Her complexion wasn't much darker than his own and, if I'd expected her to sound Indian, I was very much mistaken. She had the cut-glass accent of her teachers at the orphanage school. They'd been determined to make ladies out of all their girls and, in every respect but her colouring, Mrs Askew was the perfect English gentlewoman.

Or so I thought until we began discussing Sarah Critchley's case. Most middle-class ladies would have shied away from commenting on the charges against Sarah, but Mrs Askew was made of sterner stuff. Living amongst the rump of Radicalism in Newington Green had probably done that.

'It seems to me,' she'd said, 'that this whole business of the proctors detaining young women isn't so much to preserve the morals of the University's young men as to keep them from forming alliances with women of lower class.' She looked at me over her roast beef. 'It's exactly the way the British behave in India. The races are kept apart at all costs so that the purity of the British nation isn't tainted by native blood.'

And the British couldn't allow themselves to be tainted, could they, because if their blood, their culture, their *civilisation* wasn't superior, then what right did they have to be lording it over Indians in the first place?

'Yes, you're right,' I said. 'If the boys at Oxford were allowed to fraternise with town girls – marry them even – then it would be an implicit acknowledgement that undergraduates aren't superior to city folk. And the University can't have that, because if the young men at the colleges are no better than Oxford town people, why does the University have what's basically a separate jurisdiction inside the city?'

'And the ladies of your association for female education?' Mrs Askew asked. 'What's their view on this?'

I glanced at Tarley who was watching us like a nervous young father whose firstborn is taking its first steps.

'I'm afraid the AEW worry that the willingness of town girls to associate with undergraduates will make it harder for women students to be accepted,' I said. 'Because if college boys are used to fraternising with young women, won't they prefer to do it with those of their own class? And the middle classes can't have unchaperoned fraternisation. Especially not if it's going to put the young women off their academic stride.'

'What about Miss Critchley? Do the ladies support her wish to clear her name?'

'I wish they did. But the ladies of the AEW feel that the more we challenge the University's authority, the more the men who rule us will say that our behaviour shows we're unfit to enter what they think of as the male sphere.'

Mrs Askew nodded, her eyes still on me. 'And yet you're encouraging her to pursue a lawsuit?'

I sighed. 'Sometimes,' I said, carefully, 'you have to take your eyes off what the lady secretary of the AEW calls "the long game" and look at the injustice that's right in front of you. And not just look at it but do something about it. Sarah Critchley's been unfairly saddled with a reputation she doesn't deserve. That needs to be remedied.'

Mrs Askew nodded, slowly. 'I admire your determination to uphold this young woman's cause,' she said. 'But I'd be worried that exposing her to so much scrutiny can only do her harm, even if her suit is justified and the court finds for her. Won't she always be "the girl who went to court against the University"?'

'And would that be a bad thing?' Tarley asked.

'It might make her stand out in her own community in a way which makes it hard for her to continue to be accepted,' his mother said. 'And any young man might think twice about marrying a girl who's prepared to fight one of the most powerful institutions in the land. Most men want a quiet life, and that wouldn't generally include a wife who has ideas some might consider to be above her station.'

Tarley laughed. 'So says the woman who left everything she'd ever known to throw in her lot with a British army officer who was committing professional suicide by marrying her!'

'But, my dear, I can't tell you the extent to which your father and I were the exception rather than the rule! Most people marry for convenience, to establish a home and family, not from the kind of love your father and I felt for each other.'

'The stuff of legends and romances,' I said, to try and throw off the uncomfortable feeling that had taken hold of me.

'Indeed,' Mrs Askew said, drily. 'But neither legends nor romances tell the reader what happens to the lovers after their marriage. Rejection and ostracism isn't generally included in stories of love.'

'But it was in yours?'

I could almost feel Tarley holding his breath.

'Sadly, yes. When we had each other – and Tarley, of course,' she said, with a fond smile at her son, 'it didn't seem to matter much. But after my husband died, I had nobody to turn to, nobody to support me.' Her eyes met mine and neither of us looked away. 'My concern would be that a young woman who challenges the University would find herself removed from her own community by her actions.'

Something told me we weren't talking about Sarah Critchley any more.

If I supported Sarah's case, I would cut myself off from the female academic community, at least for the foreseeable future. But Sarah deserved to have her name cleared and the Vice Chancellor's court needed to be held up for public scrutiny.

'*And you want to write for Stead,*' Hara pointed out.

Which was true, but what I wanted even more was a newspaper that would print the kind of things the *Pall Mall Gazette* printed, but just for Oxford. If I could find the backers I needed, I'd call it *The Oxford Mirror*. I'd hold a mirror up to the city, and the University wouldn't like what it saw reflected there.

'Actually,' I said, giving Mrs Askew a little grin, 'knowing the people where Sarah grew up – who aren't necessarily the respectable poor, if you know what I mean – they'll cheer Sarah to the rafters if she wins, then they'll try to borrow money from her. And if she loses they'll say it was bound to happen, with the University being what it is, and rally round.'

Tarley's mother had clasped her hands in her lap at that point, as if she was signalling an end to the discussion. 'Well,' she said. 'I only hope you're right. Having experienced the effects of being ostracised, I wouldn't wish it on anybody.'

—

Fair play to Tarley, he waited till we were halfway back to Balls Pond Road before he raised the subject of his mother.

'You and Ma seemed to hit it off,' he suggested.

'We did,' I agreed. 'By which I mean we actually did hit it off, we didn't just seem to.'

He grinned. 'I wish you'd met her before. I know she probably seems perfectly fine to you, but compared to how she was before her illness she's a shadow of her former self. She barely ever sat down before she was ill. She had such energy.'

I'd assumed that because Tarley'd come back to Oxford, his mother must be fully recovered. But he was obviously still worried about her. 'What do the doctors say?' I asked. 'Will she make a full recovery?'

He sighed. 'They can't say, because they don't really know what was wrong with her in the first place. I think, for all the pills and potions and sea bathing at Margate, it was time and rest that got her to where she is now. She's desperate to get back to work but I don't know if it's a good idea.'

'What, because it'll overtax her delicate female constitution?'

He turned sharply to look at me and stumbled over a raised paving stone. I grabbed at his arm to steady him, and our eyes met as he straightened up. 'That's not fair, Non,' he said, quietly. 'You know I don't think that women are weaker than men. But any human being can have their constitution damaged, and the kind of demanding work Ma does for the charity might set her recovery back.'

I think we both realised I was still holding on to him at the same moment but, as I let go, he took my arm and threaded it through his.

'May I walk you to the 'bus, Miss Vaughan?' he asked, a little grin on his face to let me know I was forgiven.

As long as we'd known each other, we'd always walked side by side, like equals, and I didn't want that to change. But I did want to apologise for accusing him of thinking women were constitutionally feeble, and for not saying yes straight away when he asked me if I'd come and meet his mother, so I left my arm where it was. 'Yes, Mr Askew,' I said, 'you may.'

With our arms entwined, it took me a while to adjust my stride so that we walked smoothly. To start with, we joggled up and down against each other, but once we'd got that sorted, the sensation of being so physically close to him was disorientating. I found it difficult to think of anything but the heat of his arm coming through the cloth of his coat, and the smell of Pears soap from his warm skin. Then, beneath that clean, comforting smell, I noticed the sour trace of fear-sweat. Had Tarley been so worried about me meeting his mother that it had made him sweat? And, if he had, had he been worried about her reaction to me or mine to her?

'*Both, probably,*' Hara said.

And that was the only answer I was going to get. I couldn't ask Tarley, because he might have felt the need to tell me why it was so important to him that we should get on.

Which would probably have led to declarations I wasn't ready to hear.

I turned my mind away from that intimate walk, got up to put some more coal on the fire and tried to get back to the tutorial I was planning. But, try as I might, I couldn't seem to put Tarley out of my mind.

How was he getting on with Dr Eros?

The so-called doctor had replied to his request for an appointment with a note asking him to come to the Turf Tavern at two o'clock today, so he'd have been there half an hour already. I tried not to think about what they might be doing. Tarley'd been very clear that he was just going to *talk* to her.

'*Why do you care?*' Hara asked, a sly edge to her voice.

I had no answer for that.

# Chapter 48

### *Basil*

Having parted from me barely an hour before, Kaye was clearly surprised to see me when I knocked at the door of his rooms.

'I won't keep you,' I said as he closed the door behind me, 'I just require one thing.'

He looked at me enquiringly.

'The name and college of the undergraduate in the Sarah Critchley case.'

Kaye's expression changed from polite attention to acute discomfort. 'Ah.' He removed the spectacles he wore for reading and proceeded to polish their lenses with his handkerchief. 'I'm afraid that won't be possible.'

'Why on earth not?' After our rather fraught conversation earlier about my wish to bring Gainsborough's membership of the Venatores into evidence at the inquest, did Kaye now wish to dispense with my services?

The Senior Proctor put down his spectacles. 'It's rather embarrassing, I'm afraid. Inspector Newman wished to speak to him about the youths who attempted to intervene when Waddesworth and his bulldog took Sarah Critchley into custody. So, following my visit to you at Jesus, I made my way to Charsley's Hall to see the young man concerned and ask him to make himself available to the police.'

Kaye seemed about to repeat his spectacle-cleaning but, thinking better of it, withdrew the hand he'd extended and continued.

'The young man had identified himself as Anthony Farmer, but when I spoke to William Charsley, he informed me that he had no such person enrolled at his hall.'

First Smythe, now Farmer. First New Inn Hall, now Charsley's. *Nom et lieu de guerre.*

'I assume,' I said, 'that Charsley's porter had been bribed to accept this Farmer as one of their own if he was brought in by you or the bulldogs?'

'That seems likely, yes,' Kaye admitted, 'though the man wouldn't confess to it. He claimed that he'd confused the boy with another undergraduate of a similar name. It's ridiculous, of course, but Charsley wasn't prepared to sack him on that basis. At least not in front of me.'

I sighed. 'So we have no idea who this young man actually is?'

'Regrettably, no. Nor even whether he's actually an undergraduate.'

'I think you'll find he's both an undergraduate *and* a member of the Venatores.' Ignoring the Senior Proctor's grimace, I asked, 'Was it you or Waddesworth who arrested Sarah Critchley?'

'Waddesworth.'

'So he'd know the boy if he saw him again?'

'I'm afraid I couldn't say, Rice. You'd have to ask him.'

—

When I was shown into Waddesworth's rooms at Queen's I found them palatial, with separate rooms for entertaining, dining and studying. I wondered whether he'd sought a larger set when he'd become Junior Proctor. Having stepped onto the next rung of the advancement ladder, he might see better accommodation as an investment in his reputation.

My own rooms bore no comparison to the splendid Queen Anne architecture of Waddesworth's, but as I hardly ever entertained, few people had occasion to form an opinion of my living arrangements.

Teddy was an exception, and his response to the previous year's redecoration of my rooms sprang to mind. 'You're maturing, Bas,' he'd said, on the one occasion when I'd weakened and welcomed him into my bed after his wife's death. 'These are now the rooms of a man who knows himself. Knows what he likes,' he added with a lascivious look.

'Glad you approve.'

Teddy arched an eyebrow. 'Did I say I approved?'

That was Teddy: give with one hand, take away with the other.

I'd heard nothing from him since his visit with his son and Miss Webster. In spite of my being Morton's godfather, I feared he might now cut off all communication with me.

When I asked Waddesworth about the pseudonymous Anthony Farmer, the Junior Proctor shook his head. 'I have only a vague recollection of him. I've no great memory for faces and, besides, it was dark.'

'So you wouldn't know him again if you saw him?' I asked.

'I shouldn't be confident of doing so, no.'

We lapsed into silence, and both resorted to the sherry he'd poured for us.

'There is, of course, one person who's likely to be able to identify the boy,' I said. 'Miss Critchley herself. But unless he has some very definitive identifying feature, any description she might give would be next to useless unless we already have somebody in mind. Therefore, likely candidates will need to be put before her.'

'And how do you propose to do that?'

I temporised, sure that Waddesworth wouldn't approve of the suggestion I was about to make. First, I explained that I'd now discovered conclusive evidence that Gainsborough had hosted the Venatores supper party after which Harcourt Ashdown had been captured, bound and hooded.

'We know, therefore,' I went on, 'that Gainsborough was a member of the Venatores. If, as I strongly suspect, Vennell, Haviland, Ashdown and Herbert are also members, then we have the identities of five of the seven men who dined in Gainsborough's rooms at Trinity three weeks ago, making one of them highly likely to be Miss Critchley's interlocutor. So I propose that we require the four undergraduates who have been victims of hooding to attend Gainsborough's inquest as potential witnesses.' I paused, but Waddesworth did not respond.

'Miss Critchley will be asked to give evidence as Gainsborough's fiancée,' I continued, 'and I propose that, after she's done so, she be discreetly asked whether the undergraduate who approached her is amongst those we suspect of being Venatores. Without identifying him to anybody else, of course.'

'I beg your pardon, Rice. Am I to understand that you'd take the word of a *shop girl*?' Waddesworth could scarcely have been more dismissive if I'd suggested taking the word of a tram horse. 'You're proposing to rely on a young woman who, if the information we were given is true, was always very free with her favours.'

'What do you mean, "the information we were given"?'

A look of slight unease briefly occupied the Junior Proctor's inexpressive features. 'Earlier that week – the week of her arrest – an anonymous letter arrived at Clarendon House, purporting to be written on behalf of, and I quote, "all beleaguered undergraduates", and stating that a particular young woman was regularly making a nuisance of herself on New Inn Hall Street and the Cornmarket.'

I had a sinking feeling. 'The nuisance being?'

'Soliciting. Specifically gownsmen.' I waited. 'A description was given, along with the times when she appeared.'

'So you lay in wait and took her up?'

'I make no apology for it. Sarah Critchley was behaving exactly as specified, attempting to detain an undergraduate.'

'An undergraduate who gave a false name and college.'

'A fact of which,' Waddesworth glowered, 'we were unaware at the time.'

'This accusation notwithstanding,' I said, 'in the light of Gainsborough's death, these young men may be in danger, so we must act on even the least reliable evidence. Will you please ensure that Ashdown, Haviland, Vennell and Herbert are at the inquest tomorrow, as well as Miss Critchley?'

Waddesworth acquiesced with ill grace and, in answer to my question as to which of the University coroners was tasked with taking the inquest, he informed me that Dr Darbishire would preside.

'In that case,' I said, 'I shall pay him a visit now.'

## Chapter 49

### Non

The clock struck four, and there was still no sign of Tarley. I'd expected him here before now and I couldn't settle to the work I was supposed to be doing. If I did manage to put Tarley and Dr Eros out of my mind for a minute, in would pop what Basil had said earlier about blowing myself up, which made me feel very uncomfortable because neither the AEW nor the University's Hebdomadal Council were going to like my article on the inquest any better than the one I'd written on Charles Gainsborough's outrageous behaviour. Because, as well as reporting on what actually happened, I planned to give some commentary on the whole notion of University inquests.

For instance, I was willing to bet that not one *Pall Mall Gazette* reader in a hundred knew that the University appointed its own coroners. Or that those coroners only had to look into one or two deaths every year, compared with the one, solitary city coroner who conducted at least one inquest a week.

If *Gazette* readers chose to interpret those facts as suggesting that the University fostered incompetence – or let's be charitable and say inexperience – for its own ends, then I wasn't going to stop them. At the very least, appointing University members to the two posts meant that everything was kept in-house, so the circulation of distasteful or damaging information could be limited.

To settle my thoughts, I started jotting down notes for the following day's hearing under the journalist's basic headings – *what, where, when, who, why, how*. Anything I could write ahead of time would speed the process of sending the report to Stead. I knew he'd want to publish it on the day after the inquest if he possibly could, and with the mail being sorted on the train ready for distribution in London, we might just make it.

*Point 1:* I wrote. *What?*

I could write that brief paragraph already. *Inquest into the death of Trinity College undergraduate Charles Gainsborough, also fraudulently known as Gordon Smythe.* I might save the second half of that sentence for Stead. Berry wouldn't print it, even if the fraud was a plain fact. Still, it would come out later in the report.

*Point 2: Where?*

It was traditional that University inquests were held in the college the deceased had belonged to unless there were good reasons against. In this case, with the need to provide space for the kind of crowd a murder would draw, the hearing would probably be held in Trinity's hall. I wondered if the college president would try to keep the public out. Technically, because an inquest was a public hearing, he wasn't allowed to do that, but in practice, the head of an Oxford college could do pretty well what he liked.

But if citizens were excluded, either explicitly or implicitly, that would be something to report in my *Pall Mall Gazette* article, though definitely not in the copy I'd write for Berry. I'd have to be very careful not to say anything in the *Mercury* that might upset the University authorities. Facts and quotations only, that's what Berry would want. No commentary, especially of the critical variety.

*Point 3: When?*

I'd have to record the date and time when Gainsborough's body was found and, for the ten-dozenth time, I wondered whether it was significant that his body had been left outside the Trinity gates first thing in the morning, when the other victims had been dumped in the small hours. Fair enough, the intention might have been to humiliate the live victims by having them sitting there for hours, but it still felt like a significant difference.

*Point 4: Who?*

There were going to be a lot of *who*'s, so I added some subheadings:

*4a. Presiding Coroner:*

As yet, I didn't know which of the University's coroners would be sitting. If the powers that be wanted a doctor, they'd nominate Samuel Darbishire, who was a physician at the Radcliffe Infirmary.

On the other hand, seeing as a lawsuit from Sarah Critchley might be in the offing, the University might prefer to keep things tight on the legal side. In which case they'd go for Frederick Morrell, Solicitor to the University.

For Morrell's sake, I hoped it would be Dr Darbishire. A medical man would be better able to cope with the state of Gainsborough's engorged face at the viewing of the body.

*4b. Jury members:*

The men on the jury would all be members of the University, of course. Fellows from Trinity and other colleges, possibly the odd head of house if Trinity's president was owed any favours.

I wondered whether Benjamin Jowett would attend. The Vice Chancellor didn't necessarily turn up at inquests, but Jowett might want to be at this one to see just how damaging to the University's reputation the evidence was.

*Point 5: How?*

The doctor who'd carried out the post-mortem examination – whoever he was – would testify as to exactly how Gainsborough'd died. Which was slowly and painfully, with ample time to know exactly what was happening to him. Of course, the doctor probably wouldn't say that. He'd stick to less emotive facts about compression of the carotid arteries and lack of blood flow to the brain, damage to the trachea and compromised oxygen supply.

But it seemed to me that exactly how Gainsborough'd been killed was very significant. Garrotting was so personal. Killer and victim were bound together by the ligature which one twisted tighter and tighter around the other's throat. It wasn't an act of sudden, uncontrollable violence. You didn't just snap and kill somebody by garrotting them. You arrived with a noose and something to twist it tight with in your pockets.

Of course, there was other information to go under *how* as well. How Gainsborough'd been lured to wherever he was killed. How his body'd been transported to Trinity.

Did the police know the answers to those questions?

We'd find out tomorrow.

But it was one final *how* that was occupying my mind while I waited for Tarley to knock on the door. If an undergraduate *had* written the note to Inspector Newman on that half-sheet of foolscap, how had he known Frank Dodds's name? Or even that Frank Dodds existed?

My eyes strayed back to the clock. What was taking so long?

'I think you know the answer to that perfectly well,' Hara said.

I pushed the images conjured up by her snide little comment right out of my mind. Tarley'd gone to talk to Dr Eros, nothing more.

'*But what if he decides that the best way to win her confidence is to accept the services she's actually offering before he starts asking questions?*' Hara goaded me. '*I mean, why should she tell him anything about what does or doesn't go on at the Turf on Tuesday evenings – or any other evening, for that matter?*'

In truth, it was probably a coincidence that two of the hooded gownsmen had been found in the early hours of Wednesday morning. Probably nothing went on at the Turf Tavern. More than likely, Dr Eros wouldn't have any information to give Tarley. The fact that she gave the Turf as her 'apply to' address was probably just a coincidence. But still… the cottages in the little court at the end of St Helen's Passage might be home to any kind of ungodly goings-on.

'*You think members of the Venatores would go there?*' Hara scoffed. '*Not exactly competitive, is it? Picking up a girl in a place like that would be like catching a fish in a trough. And they're certainly not going to have meetings there.*'

No, they weren't. But Harcourt Ashdown had been dragged into that little alley and Laurence Herbert almost certainly had been, too. Maybe they all had.

But if they had, why – apart from Ashdown – would they all try and hide the fact? Had they been threatened, warned not to mention it? Or were they ashamed of what had happened to them there? Perhaps being tied and hooded like condemned men wasn't the worst that had happened to them?

Just then, I heard a knock at the door and my heart jumped in my chest. Tarley was here.

## Chapter 50

### Basil

Having spoken to Dr Darbishire and ensured that he was furnished with all the relevant facts as to Charles Gainsborough's amorous activities, I left the Radcliffe Infirmary to take up the tattered remnants of my day.

By half past four, however, I could no longer concentrate on the mundane. Hoping that Askew might have some relevant news from his foray into the world of marital preparation, I walked up to Lily's house and found him already ensconced with Non.

To my relief, as I gingerly tested the emotional temperature of the room, I detected none of the unease that had existed between Non and Askew the previous Friday. I devoutly hoped that, if my forthright advice to Non had been the cause of their strained relations, all was now resolved. Forcing unsolicited advice concerning matters of the heart on Non had, on painful reflection, been unwise, and I had resolved to interfere no more.

'So?' I asked. 'What news from the Turf Tavern?'

Non grinned at Askew. 'Shall I tell him or shall you?'

Askew, who was almost unshockable where Non was concerned, managed to respond as if the notion of listening to her relay the details of what he'd learned wasn't utterly horrifying, while at the same time very definitely taking the helm. 'I'll tell him. Better it comes from the horse's mouth.

'As Non suspected,' he began, 'Dr Ross is a young woman. I was shown into what the publican called her "consulting room—"'

'I beg your pardon, Askew,' I interrupted, 'but did the young woman see you alone, or with a male companion?'

'Alone.'

It was hardly surprising that a young woman engaged in work like this would reject the notion of a chaperone, but even if Dr Eros felt she had no reputation to protect, seeing young men alone suggested a lack of regard for her own physical safety.

'Was the room at the Turf?' I asked.

'Yes. A small sitting room, rather nice actually, with modern furniture and rugs, even a small bookcase with a little vase of dried flowers on it. And a day bed in the corner,' he added, attempting nonchalance.

Evidently Dr Ross was a young woman of some subtlety. Taking nervous young men who'd come for 'experienced counsel' into a bedroom would do nothing to alleviate their anxiety. But a day bed could be pressed into service – or not – as needed.

'Dr Ross is relatively young,' Askew continued, 'twenty-four or - five I should say, and nicely spoken, though she still has the trace of an Oxfordshire accent. She seems educated, a little refined. As if she'd once had a different kind of life.'

There were several kinds of employment that might result in the semi-refined demeanour Askew described. Being engaged as an assistant in a high-class milliner's or ladies' outfitters, teaching at a girls' school, or a position as a lady's maid sprang immediately to mind. However, to have exchanged such desirable employment for days spent offering the kind of advice unthought of by a respectable woman, something must have brought this young woman into disgrace.

'Her manner's very pleasant,' Askew said, as if he was giving evidence. 'She asked me a little about myself – what subject I was taking schools in and so forth – and wanted to know whether I really was a prospective husband or simply curious.'

I glanced once more at Non, who turned to meet my eye then immediately looked away again, as if she was afraid of what her expression might reveal.

'What did you say to that rather presumptuous question?' I asked.

He grinned uncomfortably. 'I fudged it. Asked her whether all men weren't prospective husbands. I could tell she wasn't impressed but she didn't comment, just produced two books – *Aristotle's Masterpiece* and *Every Woman's Book* – and asked if I'd seen either of them before. I told her that the *Masterpiece* had been passed around at school, but that most of the boys hadn't looked beyond the naked woman at the front.'

'And the other?' I asked.

'I was given a copy of the Carlile by a member of our congregation when I came up to Oxford,' Askew said without further explanation.

I remembered very vividly my headmaster's rage when he'd discovered a copy of Richard Carlile's *Every Woman's Book or What is Love?* in a boy's possession. He'd called the whole upper school together to castigate what he considered to be the author's heretical statement that a marriage should be dissolved if the parties' desire for each other waned, and new attachments formed. And he'd almost foamed at the mouth at what he described as Carlile's 'promotion of promiscuity and harmful information that would destroy our society', by which I assumed he meant the contraceptive advice contained in the book.

When Askew didn't continue with his account, I realised that he was looking to me for another question. 'So did Dr Ross enlighten you on husbandly duties, as advertised in the handbill?' I asked, attempting to emulate his sang-froid.

A flush bloomed on Askew's cheek. 'Yes. She did.'

'And did she offer...' I glanced at Non who would despise my reticence. 'Did she suggest that you should put theory into practice?' I managed.

Askew's blush became more pronounced. A young woman offering to reveal her most intimate parts to him and engage in sexual acts was not something that even a broad-minded young man like Askew would find it easy to speak about.

'She did,' he said, tersely. 'I declined. By that point, I felt that I'd learned all I needed to know about the services she offered. *But*,' he said, with slightly more force, 'I did ask her whether she'd heard rumours about the hoodings, and her answer was interesting. She told me that she'd seen you in the Turf, Mr Rice, looking for information about Tuesday evenings. Then she said, "But I think he'll find he's looking at this whole thing from the wrong end. Sometimes, it's the so-called victims you need to investigate."'

'Was Dr Ross a young woman of medium height and slight build with mid-brown hair and hazel eyes?' I asked.

'Yes. Though that description doesn't do her justice.' He took a moment, then elaborated. 'There was something poised, collected, about her, as if she knew her ground and was prepared to stand on it if need be.'

I nodded. 'Yes. We spoke briefly when the Junior Proctor and I went to the Turf.'

Before I could say anything further there was a knock and Edie put her head around the sitting room door.

Her eyes firmly trained on Non, she asked, 'Can I have a word with you, Miss Non?' Her gaze shot to Tarley then immediately glanced off again as if he was made of glass. 'It's about the young woman at the Turf.'

## Chapter 51

### *Non*

It wasn't a shock that Edie'd been eavesdropping, but her knocking like that was a surprise.

'I'm sorry for listening at the door,' she said, when I joined her in the hallway, 'but everybody's been talking about poor Sarah Critchley and when I knew you were taking an interest, I couldn't help it. The woman you're talking about – the one who goes by Dr Ross? I know her. Her real name's Cat Hammond.'

I stared at Edie. 'How do you know her?'

'She's Jericho born and bred, like me. I know her family.'

'Go on.'

Edie's eyes flicked to the sitting room door. She was worried Basil and Tarley would hear what she had to say.

'Let's go and sit in the kitchen,' I said. Lily was out taking tea with one of her church friends; she wouldn't disturb us.

'Right,' I said, when we were both sitting at the kitchen table where the makings of dumplings were waiting to be mixed, 'tell me about this Cat Hammond.'

Edie couldn't look at me. Her fingers were busy collecting a little spill of flour on the table into a tidy pile and straightening the edges. Now it had come to it, she didn't seem to know where to start.

'You said she was from Jericho, so let's start there. Who are her parents?'

'John and Agnes Hammond – he's a wharfman on the canal. They're good souls, John and Aggie. Cat was the only child they had who lived beyond four years old and they wanted a decent life for her, see? They made sure she went to school, and she was good at her lessons. Quick. When she was twelve, one of the ladies at St Barnabas's said she'd take her on as a scullery maid. See if she could take to service.

And if she could, she'd get her trained up. Even for a lady's maid if she gave satisfaction. Then Cat'd have opportunities.'

Edie rolled that last word around her mouth like a sweet, ripe strawberry. *Opportunities*. These days, it was difficult for girls to get taken on to be trained for domestic service. People wanted their servants already competent, to have experience. They didn't want some Jericho brat learning on their fine china and good linen if they could help it. Cat Hammond had been lucky.

'And did the lady from St Barnabas's stick to her word?'

'She did, yes. Like I said, Cat was quick – by the time she was sixteen, she was all trained up to be a lady's maid.'

'And what did she do then?' That would have been the moment for Cat Hammond to capitalise on the opportunities Edie'd mentioned.

'She went to some lady in a big house up Headington way. I heard the family had another house in London as well, but I don't know if that was true – maybe they just stayed there sometimes.'

Edie's eyes had been opened to the ways of the middle classes – or the lower middle classes at least – by working for Lily, but she still couldn't quite imagine that people who lived somewhere as familiar as Headington could possibly be well off enough to keep two establishments. She was still fiddling with the little pile of flour, pushing it into a square shape, then cutting it in half to make two triangles.

'So she went to this lady in Headington. Then what?'

'There was a son—'

Of course there was.

'—her mistress's son. Came home from school for the summer about a twelvemonth after Cat went there. Waiting to go to the University, he was.'

And he'd had nothing better to do than harass his parents' female servants.

'My sisters reckoned he'd had his eye on Cat from the off,' Edie said. 'They knew her better than me – Cat and our Hild were in the same class in school. But Cat could see what he was after, and she tried to keep out of his way. Still, everybody reckoned it was him when she was chucked out with no character and a baby on the way.'

It was pointless asking whether Cat had complained that she'd been forced. Even if the family had believed her, they'd still have sided with the son. It wasn't convenient to believe that you'd raised a rapist. Far easier to tell yourself that he was only a lad, easily led on by a worldly-wise servant with her eye on money or presents.

I watched Edie chopping her flour. She had something more to say, I could tell, but she wasn't sure how to broach it. 'When you say everybody reckoned it was the son,' I said, 'did you actually mean *everybody*?'

'Well...' Edie wet her lips and glanced at the basement door as if she thought Basil and Tarley might have tiptoed down the passage to listen at the keyhole.

'Yes?'

'I did hear some gossip...'

'About the baby's father?'

Edie nodded.

'Well, come on then, out with it. Don't worry, I won't tell anybody I had it from you if it comes to that.'

She licked her lips again. 'The son swore blind it wasn't him. Said he'd seen Cat with one of the University men. You know.' She dropped her voice till she was almost whispering. 'One of the *dons*.'

'*Seen* her with him...?'

Edie flushed. 'Not like that. Just out and about. Lady's maids are always coming and going on little errands, aren't they?'

And, if a maid knew in advance when her mistress would want something collected, she might send a note to her lover and ask her mistress for an extra half an hour to run some errands of her own. If she had a tolerant mistress, that wouldn't be too hard to arrange.

'What do you think, Edie?' I asked. She might not be very educated, but Edie had an uncanny knack for separating the nuggets of truth from general gossip.

'Dunno, really,' she said. 'Don't really know her, do I? But Nellie and Hild – that's my sisters – they reckoned Cat would've kneed the boy in the... *down there*... if he'd tried anything. She was never one to take no nonsense, Cat. That's what they reckoned anyway.'

'That's really helpful, Edie,' I said. 'Thank you.' There was no point saying 'but you shouldn't have been listening at the door', because it wouldn't stop her. It was like telling a cat not to lap up spilled milk.

I started to get up, then stopped. 'What happened to Cat's baby?' I asked.

'She's four now. Lives with Cat's ma and pa. They wouldn't have nothing to do with her to start with, but they couldn't keep it up. Not with their only grandchild.'

'Does Cat live with her parents, too?'

'Not her. She used to live off Hell's Passage, but now she's gone up in the world. Moved up to Bath Place with them nobby lot as works for the colleges and thinks they're better than everybody else.'

College domestics had a habit of lording it over other working-class people. They might only be servants, but they were *college* servants and, as far as they were concerned, that put them a cut above.

But I was very interested to hear where Cat lived. Bath Place was behind the Turf Tavern, at the northern end of the warren between Holywell Street and New College Lane. And at the southern end was St Helen's Passage, where Harcourt Ashdown had been taken after he'd been grabbed and hooded.

'And how exactly has she gone up in the world?' I asked. 'With an illegitimate child and no character references?'

Edie wouldn't meet my eye. 'That'd be because of her lessons, wouldn't it?'

'How do you know about that?' I asked.

Edie was back to making shapes with her little pile of flour.

'Like I said, I know her family and I know some of the girls that used to be friendly with her. They're my sisters' friends really but, you know...'

I did know. Five or six years was a huge gap when you were little, but now that Edie was nineteen and her sisters in their mid-twenties, the gap had closed. Now, she could talk to their friends – the unmarried ones at least – and be accepted as an equal.

'One of the girls I know reckons Cat told her that most men haven't got a clue. I mean –' she stared at the flour – 'they haven't got a clue about... you know... the girls'... *down there.*' She tilted her head to flick a glance at her lap. 'And I suppose she should know after what happened to her. You know, getting broken into.'

I'd never heard the phrase before, but it wasn't hard to understand. It was honest about the violence of rape, instead of hiding it behind hypocritical middle-class euphemisms. People like Cat Hammond's employers would refer to girls being 'seduced', to a man 'having his way' with her, or 'sowing his wild oats'. Or, worst of all, brushing violence off with 'boys will be boys'.

'Some men go to the girls on the town to find out what to do,' she said. 'You know, to...'

'Find out how to please their wife?' I asked. Tarley wasn't the only one who'd read *Every Woman's Book*.

Edie's nose almost touched the table as she nodded.

'But going with prostitutes is a risk, isn't it?' I said. A risk to their own health and the health of their wives, present or future.

' 'Zac'ly,' Edie said, rubbing her fingers through the flour so it was a mess again and starting on a circle. 'Cat reckoned a lot of men would be keen for somethin' a bit...'

'Less risky?'

' 'Zac'ly,' Edie muttered, again. 'And it'd be better for her too. Doin' lessons'd be better than goin' on the town, I mean.'

I thought of Tarley in Cat Hammond's nicely decorated sitting room with its day bed sitting discreetly in the corner like an afterthought. I wondered if he really had stopped at the theory.

'How long has Cat Hammond been doing this?' I shifted on the hard kitchen chair and wished I could get the thought of Tarley with the 'poised' Dr Eros out of my head.

'Since not long after her nipper was born.'

I swallowed. Took a breath. Tried to gather my thoughts. If Cat Hammond's little girl was four years old, her consultations had been going on for some time. 'Is what she does common knowledge?' I asked. 'I mean, do you only know because your sisters are friends with Cat's sisters, or...?'

'I don't know if only common people know about it,' Edie said, misinterpreting the phrase, 'but it's not a secret.'

'And is she the only one who does this?'

Edie chewed at her lip. 'I dunno...'

'Perhaps not?'

Edie's eyes moved up to my face, then quickly away again. 'I know girls go to her, when... you know...'

When they'd been broken into.

I got to my feet. 'Thanks, Edie. I think this might be important.'

I wasn't sure how exactly, but the fact that Cat Hammond lived in Bath Place – a minute's walk from St Helen's Passage and New College Lane – must be significant.

## Chapter 52

### Basil

On Tuesday morning, I arrived at Trinity in plenty of time for the inquest. I wanted to satisfy myself that Waddesworth had done as I'd asked and ensured that Sarah Critchley and the putative members of the Venatores had been required to attend.

In the hall, I found Waddesworth and Kaye in conversation with Darbishire and the Vice Chancellor. Jowett looked perturbed and I wondered whether the University coroner was proving more interested in airing the truth than he was in sparing the University's blushes.

Greetings having been dispensed with, Waddesworth was quick to address me. 'As requested, the four undergraduates have been asked to attend and to sit in the front row.' He turned to Darbishire. 'I assume Rice has apprised you of his theory that there's a group of undergraduates preying on young women in the town?'

It was obvious that Waddesworth wished to ally himself with the doctor while distancing himself from me. He might have been more guarded if he'd realised that my work for the Board of Guardians meant that Darbishire and I knew each other quite well.

'Indeed. Rice was good enough to send me a written summary of the facts in this case, as revealed by his investigations,' Darbishire said, with a small but noticeable emphasis on my own name. As coroner, he might have expected the proctors, as de facto coroners' officers in this case, to have done him the courtesy of presenting all the evidence that we'd gathered about Charles Gainsborough's death. It seemed to me that Kaye and Waddesworth had been unprepared for the disreputable facts uncovered by my investigations and were floundering somewhat as a consequence.

As the hall filled, Non and Askew arrived, seating themselves a few rows behind Ashdown, Vennell, Haviland and Herbert, who had taken up their appointed places directly beneath the coroner's gaze. Non, I noticed, didn't sit with the other journalists who already occupied a table at the back of the hall. Mercifully, only members of the Oxford press seemed to be represented, though the fact that Non's thoughts on the inquest would appear in the *Pall Mall Gazette* made that less comforting than it might have been.

As undergraduates and fellows began filing into the hall, along with a smattering of the ungowned public, Trinity's head of house made his entrance, accompanied by a man and a youth in mourning dress. Gainsborough's father and brother, I assumed.

Felicia Skene slipped in just as the jury were taking their seats, accompanied by a young woman whom I presumed to be Sarah Critchley, and a tall, dark man in his late twenties who squired them both to their seats. This must be the barrister who wished to sue the Vice Chancellor for false imprisonment. No doubt he would be interested to see how Sarah Critchley fared when giving evidence.

I watched his gaze sweep around the hall before coming to rest on the dais. Flanking the coroner, the proctors sat on one side, the President and the Vice Chancellor on the other. Seeing them through the barrister's evaluating eyes, their formal academic dress and air of unassailable superiority must seem hollow at best, fraudulent at worst.

Whatever this man's background, if Felicia Skene endorsed his presence at Sarah Critchley's side, he must be a man of integrity. Miss Skene wouldn't encourage a mere adventurer to propose such a lawsuit. The stakes were too high for all concerned.

Once the jury had been seated at right angles to the High Table, opposite the chair where witnesses would sit, Darbishire called for order in the packed hall and proceeded with his inquest.

The first witnesses were two Trinity undergraduates who gave evidence as to Gainsborough's amiable and charming character and his unchanged demeanour in the days before he died.

As I listened to their bland testimony, I considered the one aspect of Gainsborough's behaviour that still perplexed me. If, as the foolscap manual suggested, the seduction of as many young women as possible was the Venatores' goal, with six winning particular accolades, then the dead man's dogged pursuit of Sarah Critchley over many months seemed an odd strategy. It was so time-consuming.

Was it possible that we'd made an error in assuming that 'VI' in the manual's '*NB – VI = mega kudos*' represented the Latin number six? The use of Latin in the titles of each page and, indeed, in the name Venatores itself, had caused both Askew and me to jump to that conclusion, but perhaps we'd been wrong, and it was another of the Venatores' cryptic references.

Next, the building foreman testified as to the discovery of Gainsborough's body on the handcart outside the college gates; then Darbishire himself gave a brief overview of the state of the body as he'd observed it when called upon to certify death.

'From the progress of rigor mortis,' he began, 'I estimated that Mr Gainsborough had been dead between six and fourteen hours, putting the time of death sometime between late afternoon and the early hours.'

He then went through more or less the same physical details that Non had – though he failed to mention the right-angled cut on Gainsborough's jaw – and concluded that he had died by strangulation with a garrotte.

'It seems,' Darbishire continued, 'that Mr Gainsborough's death may be connected with the so-called hooding attacks that have plagued us since the beginning of term. Therefore, to understand as much as we may about his death, we must consider these attacks and what might have provoked them.'

Then, having touched on my role in the investigation, Darbishire called me to give evidence.

As I rose to take the witness seat, I'd never been more conscious of my divided loyalties; to the University and its reputation on one hand, and to the people of Oxford whom I'd promised to serve on the other.

I knew how mortified the Vice Chancellor would be to hear the Venatores' manual read out in public, but I had little choice. Without revealing the pamphlet's detailed advice on how to pick up town girls, Miss Critchley's evidence would not give the jury an adequate understanding of Gainsborough's character. I was all too aware that her experiences at the dead man's hands might be seen as a motive for murder, but I hoped that, by now, the inspector might have found Frank Dodds and established an alibi for the young man.

I scanned the room as I took my seat on the dais but there were very few men in the room who weren't gowned, and none were wearing working men's clothes. Had Dodds been located? And, if so, had he been called to give evidence?

## Chapter 53

*Non*

Even though I was taking verbatim notes for my inquest reports, I couldn't keep my whole attention on Basil's evidence. I'd heard it all before and, as I took down what he was saying in shorthand, my mind kept sliding away to something that had happened just before the inquest started.

When Miss Skene and a man I didn't recognise had walked Sarah Critchley into the hall, before I could move, Tarley had jumped up and gone to greet her.

How did he know Felicia Skene?

I'd followed him over and, after Miss Skene had introduced him to Sarah Critchley, she'd presented us both to the tall, dark man sitting with them.

'This is Mr Martin Alexis. Mr Alexis is taking an interest in Sarah's imprisonment by the Vice Chancellor's court.'

So, this was the barrister who wanted Sarah to sue the University. He looked like an up-and-coming type. A well-cut suit with a waistcoat that fell just the right side of flashy. A nicely understated gold watch chain. Recently cut hair and a shave so clean his face almost shone. When he shook my hand he had a firm grip, not the limp fish one that men normally gave women. If they bothered to shake their hand at all.

Dr Darbishire had called the hall to order just then, and as we walked back to our seats I'd asked Tarley how he knew Miss Skene.

'I'll tell you later,' he said, his eyes on the University coroner.

'*I don't know why you're making such a mystery of it,*' Hara said. '*Tarley's obviously one of Miss Skene's young men. Her undergraduate acolytes.*'

Felicia Skene might have a calling to work amongst the poor, but that didn't mean she didn't associate with anybody else. Just as she never turned a beggar away, she never closed her door to an undergraduate – or even a don – in need of a listening ear.

'*That's probably how she knows Martin Alexis too,*' Hara pointed out.

But I wasn't particularly interested in Mr Alexis. My mind was taken up with why Tarley might have gone to Miss Skene for advice.

'*He'll have gone to ask her what to do about you, won't he?*' Hara said, casually, as if she was filing her nails while she spoke. I wondered if she would have bothered with fashionable beauty aids like that if she'd lived. But then, we disagreed over most things, so she'd probably have been one of the first people to buy a nail file when they came onto the market, just to annoy me.

'What d'you mean, to know what to do about me?'

'*He might think she'd have some insight into whether you're ever going to want to marry or whether you'll insist on staying independent.*'

'And why should she?'

'*Because,*' Hara said with that exaggerated patience she used on me sometimes, as if I was a *twpsyn*, '*she's cut from the same cloth, isn't she? Married to her work instead of a man, because what man would stand for some of the things she gets up to?*'

It made me uncomfortable, thinking that Tarley might have spoken to Miss Skene about me. Very uncomfortable. Why couldn't he just speak to his mother?

'*She wouldn't understand in the way Miss Skene would,*' Hara said, still filing. '*Miss Skene's a much safer bet.*'

Miss Skene who was 'married to her work'. Was that what Hara thought I wanted? Come to that, *was* it what I wanted?

'Members of the jury will, of course, make up their own minds on this matter,' I heard Basil say. 'Particularly once Miss Critchley has given her evidence. But, in my opinion, it's clear that Charles Gainsborough was a member of the Venatores.'

Poor Sarah would be mortified. Everybody in this hall would hear that her relationship with Gordon Smythe had just been part of a cruel game.

I glanced at Benjamin Jowett. I could see how much Basil reading the lists in the Hunters' manual had upset him. But, instead of seeing the Hunters for what they were – the inevitable consequence of the way upper-class young men were taught to see working-class girls –

he'd probably be telling himself that in a barrel of over two thousand undergraduates, there had to be a few bad apples.

After Basil stepped down, Lincoln Waddesworth took the witness chair and testified that he'd caught a young man, whom he now knew to be Charles Gainsborough, 'engaged in animated conversation with a young woman on Cornmarket Street' and had asked for his name and college.

'He gave it as Gordon Smythe,' Waddesworth said, 'of New Inn Hall.'

'A false name and identity, as prescribed in the material Mr Rice quoted from,' the coroner clarified. '*Nom et lieu de guerre?*'

'Indeed.'

Dr Darbishire then asked Waddesworth to describe how the victims of the hooding attacks had been tied up and whether he agreed with Mr Rice that the bindings and hood had been different in Mr Gainsborough's case.

Waddesworth shot a glance at Basil.

'It seemed to me that they were broadly the same,' he said, stiffly.

'Broadly but not exactly?'

'Perhaps.'

'Mr Rice has stated that the knots used were different. Would you agree?'

*The coroner,* I scribbled in shorthand, *not to be fobbed off with superficial similarities, persisted.*

'I would have thought a knot was a knot and therefore of no significance as long as it achieved the desired effect,' Waddesworth huffed. 'However, I hadn't looked too closely at how the other victims had been bound. I'd been more interested in releasing them.'

'And the hood?' the coroner said, patiently. 'Mr Rice has told this hearing that the one placed over Gainsborough's head was less substantial, being formed of two linen handkerchiefs rather than an actual bag in a stout cotton fabric.'

'Correct,' Waddesworth bit off the end of the word as if he couldn't get his mouth shut fast enough.

'And the needlework on Gainsborough's hood?' Dr Darbishire asked.

'Was, *apparently*, different. Less accomplished.'

Hah! Waddesworth might as well have said 'but I couldn't be bothered to look because a hood's a hood, isn't it?'

Next, Sarah Critchley was called. I recorded the details of her dress for the *Pall Mall Gazette* – brown and yellow check, high neck, close-fitting sleeves. Berry would never print that kind of detail, but the description would show William Stead's readers that Sarah wasn't some drudge in tatters; she dressed just like them, even if the fabric of her dress was cotton instead of silk. She'd even worn the small bustle she'd have had for Badcock's but which I was pretty sure she wouldn't wear to Hyde's factory.

As she walked towards the High Table, one of the gownsmen started hissing, and the sound was quickly taken up by other undergraduates, along with some scattered booing.

But the coroner wasn't going to stand for that kind of behaviour. He was on his feet and glaring in five seconds flat, along with Trinity's president. 'How dare you, gentlemen? How dare you treat this witness and my inquest with such disrespect?'

Sarah, who'd faltered when she heard the hissing, looked relieved. She straightened her back and marched the rest of the way to the witness chair.

And, however hostile the undergraduates were, the coroner's attitude to Sarah while he heard her evidence was nothing but respectful. In spite of the reputation the proctors and the sender of that anonymous letter had tried to give her, Dr Darbishire spoke to Sarah Critchley as if she were a lady. And unless the jury had a prejudice against girls like her knitted into their bones, they must have felt some sympathy with her, too.

While I transcribed Sarah's testimony, I kept half an eye on Charles Gainsborough's father and brother. At least, I assumed that's who the ungowned man and school-aged boy sitting ten feet away from the witness chair were. Sarah's testimony must have made them very uncomfortable, but outwardly they didn't turn a hair. Not as far as I could tell from the half-profiles I could see from where Tarley and I were sitting.

I found it interesting that Gainsborough's mother wasn't here. Of course, she might be dead, but it seemed far more likely to me that this was the kind of family where the father dealt with everything important, leaving his wife to instruct the housekeeper, twiddle her thumbs and go quietly mad with boredom. What was Gainsborough senior's attitude to their female servants, I wondered. Had young

Charles begun his conquests of working-class girls in his own home, like the boy who'd supposedly raped Dr Eros when she was a lady's maid?

Then, suddenly, Sarah's testimony pulled my full attention back to her.

'Something in those rules that Mr Rice read made me think, Mr Darbishire. It was when he read out *Hunts must be undertaken alone* and *Confirmation required*', she said. 'I realised then that men from that club must have been watching us all the time.' She hesitated, then added, 'For the confirmation.'

*Miss Critchley was visibly mortified*, I wrote. She'd be recalling moments she and 'Gordon Smythe' had shared; moments she'd thought were private. She'd assured me that they'd never 'gone as far as we might have done' but she and I both knew that, once Smythe had given her his ring, she had less reason not to give in to him. It was a binding contract, asking a girl to marry you. Jilting her could have left him open to a lawsuit for breach of promise.

At least, that's what Sarah would have thought. But Charles Gainsborough would have been confident that, if Sarah'd tried to raise a case, nobody would have taken her word over his.

'The thing is, Dr Darbishire,' Sarah said, 'we'd always see the same few young men when we were walking out together. They all knew Gordon – I beg your pardon, Charles Gainsborough – because they'd always raise their caps and smile, and sometimes they'd pass the time of day, like friends. They must've been watching us, mustn't they? *Observing.*'

And laughing at her. Because she was just a 'Sal' to them. Just as they were laughing at the whole working class with the '*noms de guerre*' they'd used: Smith, Farmer.

'Did you ever broach the subject of these young men with Mr Gainsborough?' the coroner asked.

'Once. But he brushed it off. Said Oxford was a small town and of course we'd run into the same chaps from time to time.' She took a breath, and her chin went up. 'But it's not that small, is it? And there are thousands of undergraduates, so I should've been more suspicious about seeing the same faces over and over again, shouldn't I?'

*Miss Critchley took the blame as women are schooled to do*, I wrote, thinking of my copy for the *Pall Mall Gazette*, *judging herself deficient in self-preservation, rather than her lover deficient in morals.*

Interestingly, Dr Darbishire agreed with me. 'Please don't assume any portion of the blame for Mr Gainsborough's actions, Miss Critchley, nor those of his friends. You could hardly be expected to harbour such suspicions. They would have suggested something quite egregious.'

Egregious. Exactly. I underlined the word to remind me to make some comment on Dr Darbishire's response. Berry probably wouldn't print it, but Stead would. I could already see the words in the clear, well-spaced typeface of the *Pall Mall Gazette*. *Even the University's own coroner clearly felt enormous sympathy with Gainsborough's victim.* If that didn't recruit a few hundred supporters to Sarah's cause, I didn't know what would.

The final part of her testimony was Gainsborough's failure to turn up at the Vice Chancellor's court and defend her. 'I was sure he'd be there,' she said. 'Sure he'd tell them that it was a mistake, that I'd only spoken to the boy because I'd often seen him when we were walking out together, and it was plain they knew each other!'

I glanced across at Gainsborough's father, but his face was like stone, and the younger brother looked to be cut from the same block.

Sarah left the witness chair, and I jumped when I heard my own name.

I shoved my notebook into Tarley's hands. 'Make notes,' I said. 'Please.'

## Chapter 54

*Basil*

As Non stepped onto the dais I saw Waddesworth staring intently at her. Did he recognise her as the boy who'd stood guard with Askew over a trussed-up Laurence Herbert in Merton Street? If he did, both she and I might find ourselves being asked difficult questions.

'Miss Vaughan,' Darbishire began, 'can you tell us how you became acquainted with Miss Critchley?'

'She asked for my help to clear her name after she was thrown into Oxford jail by the Vice Chancellor's court. A miscarriage of justice which, I hope, is now clear to all,' Non replied, training her gaze on the proctors.

Darbishire nodded. 'Miss Critchley told you, I believe, that Mr Gainsborough had proposed marriage to her. Did you doubt the sincerity of his proposal?'

'I did. When I saw the two of them together, it was obvious that he was putting on an act.'

'And I believe it was that suspicion that led to your decision to find out whether the signet ring given by Mr Gainsborough to Miss Critchley had, in fact, been a gift from his father, as he claimed, or whether, as you suspected, he'd acquired it with the express purpose of giving it to her?'

Darbishire was clearly keen to keep things tight and factual and Non had little to do but agree.

She was then asked to give an account of her conversation with the pawnbroker in St Clement's, which she did with admirable succinctness.

The coroner finished taking his notes and looked up. 'Thank you, Miss Vaughan. Do you have any other relevant information to give this inquest?'

Non glanced at the seats immediately in front of the jury where the suspected Venatores sat, and I braced myself for whatever she might be about to say. But when she turned to Darbishire, she seemed to have dismissed the young men from her mind.

'I noticed, when you described the injuries Gainsborough'd sustained,' she said, 'that you didn't mention the mark on his jaw.' She paused for a moment. 'So I thought it would be worth mentioning in case anybody present knew of any way in which Charles Gainsborough might have come by that injury. It seemed as fresh to me as the rope marks, but it might have been caused in the hours before his death by something quite unconnected.'

Had Darbishire been wearing a pair of spectacles, he would have removed them in order to see Non more clearly as he stared at her. 'Am I to understand, Miss Vaughan, that you had sight of Mr Gainsborough's body?'

Non didn't flinch. 'Mr Rice asked me to give an opinion on the knots used to tie him. He knows very little about knots, whereas I'm acquainted with many different varieties. And as I was one of the people who came upon Mr Herbert lying outside the gates of Merton College, I was able to give an opinion as to the knots' similarity or lack thereof.'

I suppressed a groan of exasperation. Non seemed determined to scupper her own academic career. The AEW couldn't help becoming aware of her involvement in the investigation, now. And whereas being asked to give an opinion might be seen as pardonable, going out onto the streets after dark looking for hooding victims would not. Especially as she'd been unchaperoned and dressed as a boy at the time.

'I see. Thank you, Miss Vaughan.'

I was profoundly grateful that the coroner didn't ask how she came to be outside Merton College at midnight. But then, he would be well aware that any answer she might give would be unlikely to bolster the credibility of her evidence as far as the jury was concerned.

Darbishire turned from Non to address the spectators in the body of the hall. 'May I ask if there is anybody present who might be able to account for a small contusion on the point of Mr Gainsborough's left jaw?'

His precise location of the injury indicated that Darbishire had, indeed, taken note of it. I wondered why he hadn't mentioned it. In the end, I supposed, the injury added nothing to the verdict, though it would be of use to the police to know that one person might have killed Gainsborough alone, rather than the deed requiring several people to subdue him.'

There being no response from the spectators, the coroner thanked Non and called Inspector Newman to give evidence.

'Inspector, I believe your men have discovered some information that may be pertinent?'

Newman got straight to the point. 'The morning of the body's discovery was miserably wet and, before sunrise, only two cabbies had taken up their positions on Broad Street. Neither apparently observed anything suspicious but one did notice a man parking a handbarrow covered in tarpaulin in front of the Trinity College garden gates. The man then attempted to open the builders' workshop associated with the college's current construction works and, when he proved unable to do so, he left.'

'Are we to understand that there is access to the workshop from Broad Street as well as from within the college?' Darbishire asked.

'That's correct. The arrangement ensures that workmen aren't constantly traipsing in and out through the lodge and across to the works. The cabbie thought no more of it, assuming that the man was simply making a delivery which nobody was there to receive. However, we believe that this man, whoever he was, brought Gainsborough's body through the city, parked it at the workshop's gates and made a pretence of attempting to enter the workshop, just for show, before simply walking away.'

I thought of that early morning, driving rain keeping the cabbies away and the eyes of any early passers-by on the pavement lest they step in a puddle. The conditions had very much favoured the murderer, but even so, such an audacious act in broad daylight suggested a recklessness that bordered on madness.

Or the arrogance of someone who felt himself to be invulnerable.

With no further witnesses to call, Dr Darbishire asked the jury to retire and consider their verdict. As they trooped ceremoniously down the hall to sequester themselves in the room made available for the purpose, the coroner brought the chattering spectators to order once more.

'If I may, ladies and gentlemen,' he said in a quelling voice. 'If there are, in this hall, any members of the society we've heard so much about – the Venatores – then I would urge you, gentlemen, in the strongest terms, to desist from your reprehensible activities. Not only does such a determined and apparently competitive pursuit of young women fall very far short of the standards your University requires and bring its name into disrepute, such cynical immorality is injurious to your growth into men of honour.' He paused and looked around at faces transfixed by his words. 'I hope it goes without saying that any undergraduate caught engaging in the kind of duplicitous and dishonourable behaviour Charles Gainsborough was guilty of will be sent down with immediate effect.'

This brought definitive nods from Jowett and the two proctors as well as Trinity's president.

In the front row, Mr Gainsborough senior's back remained ramrod straight and his son did not so much as turn his head to look at his father.

As the spectators resumed their conversations, I approached Felicia Skene and her companions.

Once I'd paid my compliments to Miss Skene and had been introduced to both Sarah Critchley and the tall, dark barrister, Martin Alexis, I addressed Miss Critchley. 'May I offer you my sincere condolences on your loss, Miss Critchley? Whatever Mr Gainsborough was, I know you were very fond of him, and all this must have come as an enormous shock.'

Her surprise indicated just how little respect Sarah Critchley was used to receiving from men of my class. No wonder Gainsborough had been able to sweep her off her feet. 'Thank you, Mr Rice. It *has* been a shock. All of it.'

'Might I ask you a favour? Something related, I'm afraid, to your painful ordeal at the hands of the proctors?'

Sarah Critchley looked at me steadily. 'You can ask,' she said, guardedly. 'But I don't know that I shall be able to say yes.'

'Of course.' I allowed a brief pause to develop before continuing. 'I should like you, if possible, to tell me whether the undergraduate you were speaking to when you were arrested by the proctors is here.'

She stared at me, eyes wide with sudden alarm. Poor girl. Not only had she been obliged to parade her own humiliation in front of disparaging strangers, I was now raking up the actions of the would-be seducer whose attentions had landed her in jail.

'I'm sorry to ask, Miss Critchley, but have you seen him? Is he here?'

She turned to Miss Skene, who nodded her encouragement, then faced me once more, drawing in a breath that lifted her chin. 'Yes. He's here.'

'Would you mind coming to show me?'

'No! If he sees me coming to the front, he'll know it's me who's told you. I can do it from here – tell you where he is and what he's wearing.'

'Very well.'

'He's right at the front. With the others we used to see when we were walking out. The ones who were there for *confirmation*.'

Unhurriedly, I turned to where Haviland, Vennell, Ashdown and Herbert stood. Despite not having been specifically requested to attend, John Montague, Laurence Herbert's overprotective friend, had seated himself next to Herbert on the very end of the row and was now standing with him, apparently engaged in desultory conversation. I'd barely recognised Herbert when he and Montague had entered the hall as he was wearing a false beard that pretended a much fuller growth than nature had yet bestowed.

From the sporadic attention I'd paid the Venatores during the hearing, scarcely a word seemed to have passed between them. They had made a show of introducing themselves to each other as they took their seats, but had otherwise continued their pretence of being unacquainted.

'Do you mean the young men standing on the left-hand side at the front of the hall?' I asked.

'Yes,' Miss Critchley confirmed. 'That's them. The one who got me put in prison is the very slim dark one talking to the man next to him.'

John Montague. Otherwise known, when the occasion demanded, as Anthony Farmer of Charsley's Hall. Given his close friendship with Herbert, it came as no great surprise that he was also a Venator.

'They were all staring at me as I gave my evidence,' Miss Critchley said. 'It was horrible.'

Noticing our gaze, John Montague looked up at Miss Critchley and me, and the suggestion of a frown formed on his face. Slightly discomfited, I returned Miss Critchley to Miss Skene's side and found myself drawn into a discussion on the jury's verdict.

'It can't conceivably be anything but wilful murder by person or persons unknown,' Alexis said.

He had a direct and intense way of looking at a person and I felt the power of his attention as we spoke. It was like stepping out from the shadows into the full glare of the sun; a physical sensation on my skin.

When the door opened to signal the jury's return, I excused myself and he held out his hand. 'Good to make your acquaintance, Rice. I hope to renew it again soon.'

I put my hand in his and his eyes held me in their gaze as his warm, dry fingers gripped mine for a second or two longer than was warranted.

As I made my way between the long tables of gownsmen to the dais, I felt light-headed. What had just happened had been utterly unexpected. But actually, I remonstrated with myself, *had* anything actually happened? Might Alexis not just be the kind of chap who shook hands more vehemently than others?

No. In my suddenly unsteady heart of hearts, I knew that a message had been sent. Martin Alexis was a man like me. And he wanted to further our acquaintance.

Immediately, self-defensiveness sprang up. Had anybody else noticed our prolonged handshake, the exclusivity of our gaze? It seemed unlikely; both had been fleeting. But Miss Skene had long been alert to who and what I was. Was she, even now, regretting that she'd brought Alexis here today?

Once the jury had delivered the verdict Alexis had predicted, and Darbishire had concluded his final remarks, I approached the proctors.

'Miss Critchley has just identified the undergraduate who passed himself off to Waddesworth as Farmer of Charsley's Hall,' I told them, keeping my voice low. 'His name is John Montague and, given his conduct, as well as his appearance here today, I think we can be sure that he is a member of the Venatores.'

Kaye glanced at Waddesworth, but the Junior Proctor kept his eyes firmly on me. 'What do you expect us to do with that information, Rice?' he asked, his back to the spectators. His tone, though abrupt, was at least pitched at a confidential volume.

'Isn't giving the proctors a false name and college a rusticatable offence?' I asked.

'And if we accuse him and he denies it – claims mistaken identity?' Waddesworth's tone was combative. 'I've already told you I couldn't positively identify him – it would be his word against the girl's.'

'The bulldog who escorted him to Charsley's would surely be able to recognise him after spending longer in his company?' I objected.

'And would we take the word of a bulldog over that of an undergraduate?' Waddesworth hissed.

I wondered why Kaye didn't intervene. Despite the fact that Waddesworth had been the arresting officer, the decision as to whether to pursue Montague rested with the Senior Proctor.

'Well, I must leave the decision to you, as proctors,' I said, 'but I should warn you – a barrister is currently trying to persuade Miss Critchley to sue the University for false imprisonment, so Mr Montague's membership of the Venatores may soon be determined by a far more public hearing than an inquest.'

*Part 3*

*Potential article for* Pall Mall Gazette, *final draft.*

## HOBSON'S CHOICE FOR WOMEN

*Miss Sarah Critchley's recent incarceration by the Vice Chancellor's court of Oxford University illustrates the sad fact that young women will throw themselves into advantageous marriages even when those unions seem destined to end unhappily. For even Miss Critchley must have foreseen that, in being bound to a young man far above her not only in education but in social status, she would doom herself to a life in which she was perpetually looked down upon by the wives of her husband's friends, and, in all likelihood, once her initial attractions had faded, her husband himself.*

*Of course, if her union had been the result of genuine attraction, as she believed, Miss Critchley would scarcely be the first young woman to have made this particular bad bargain, nor her groom the only moonstruck young man. However, his choice as to whether to marry would have been a free one. Hers would not.*

*Her supposed suitor presented himself as an undergraduate of no independent means, the son of a tradesman, but even without a private income, once he had completed his degree, such a young man would be able to look forward to a future in which he earned enough for a decent house, a servant or two, and a standard of living befitting his status.*

*Like all her sex, Sarah Critchley finds herself in a far less advantageous position. Though she works sixty hours a week in a well-respected Oxford establishment, even when her wages are added to those of her mother, with whom she lives, the two women* are forced to share a single room in a boarding house, and neither has any hope of better employment.

Shop work is the most lucrative a working-class girl with nothing more than an elementary education can aspire to, but, as she earns half what her male peers earn, she receives scant reward for all her endeavours and must spend what little free time she has searching for a husband who can raise her out of penury and desperation.

Of course, it will be argued that males must be paid more than females; as the heads of households, they have families to support. But being the head of a household is hardly confined to those of the male gender. Widows are left with the sole care of their offspring. Children whose parents die in epidemics or of the diseases so rife in the poorer areas of our cities often find themselves the unwilling heads of their own households, desperately turning their hand to whatever they may in order to keep their siblings out of the workhouse. Many a girl, left thus to care for her brothers and sisters, will look to matrimony as the only moral solution to her family's predicament. A man, be he young or old, cruel or kind, will put a roof over her head and those of her siblings.

When he marries, a working man is gifted a housekeeper, a bedmate and an easy life. His wife is gifted drudgery, endless pregnancies and, all too often, physical violence which is ascribed to her failure to be a sufficiently obedient wife.

And are unmarried middle-class women any better off? They, too, are paid less than their male peers. If, that is, they can overcome the many obstacles society puts in the way of suitable potential employment. And, if they do succeed in securing a job, their reward for their determination is a pittance, a mean room in lodgings and a life of quiet, albeit independent, desperation.

Small wonder most middle-class women, too, marry. Without a private income, it is the only route to a comfortable life.

## Chapter 55

*Non*

'What are you working on?' Tarley asked, nodding at the article I was amending as he sat down opposite me.

He'd sent me a note that morning asking if we could meet in the Queen's Lane coffee house to talk about Charles Gainsborough. I'd come straight from chaperoning two Somerville students to a lecture, so I'd been there twenty minutes already.

'Something I've written on spec for Stead,' I said. 'The idea was going round and round in my head last night after writing the inquest reports. I just couldn't stop thinking that if Sarah Critchley hadn't been desperate for a better life for herself and her mother, she'd never have persuaded herself to trust Charles Gainsborough.'

'May I see?'

It was on the tip of my tongue to tell him it wasn't ready yet, but the last time I'd said 'yes but not yet' to him – over the visit to his mother – I'd hurt him. So I passed it over. 'You'll have to excuse the scrawl at the end, I've only just added that.'

As he started reading, I reached out for the coffee pot to pour him a cup and realised that my hand was shaking.

'*You shouldn't be letting him read it,*' Hara said. '*Not yet. You'll probably cut half of it. Or William Stead would.*'

In the dark, silent hours, with everybody else in Lily's house asleep, the words had flowed from my pen onto the page so quickly I'd had to start writing in shorthand. I'd transcribed the piece first thing in the morning and brought it with me to redraft while I was waiting for Tarley. It was only when I'd been sitting there, drinking coffee, that I'd added the final two paragraphs. Reading the article through, I'd realised that what I'd written about girls like Sarah applied to most middle-class girls, too – matrimony was the only way to leave the family home and have some kind of independent adult life that didn't leave you starving in a garret.

But now, seeing the article through Tarley's eyes, I regretted including those extra thoughts.

Finally, he looked up. He'd been staring at the piece so long he must have read it two or three times. 'Is this what you really think of marriage?' he asked, quietly. 'That it's a necessary evil – something women enter into for want of any other choice?'

I pulled the article towards me and avoided his eye. 'How can it not be, when women are either kept out of employment altogether or paid half as much as men?' I bent down to slip the folded sheets into my satchel, so I didn't have to look at him. 'How *can* women make a free choice about whether to marry,' I asked, 'if it's their only means of having any kind of respectability and status?'

He shook his head. 'But marriage doesn't have to *be* like that. It could be a union of equals.'

Finally, I looked him in the eye. 'Could it?'

'Of course, as long as both parties wanted that!'

'But how, when *society's* so unequal? When control is always in male hands?' My cup rattled in the saucer as I picked it up.

I could feel him staring at me. 'You're afraid of a man trying to control you?'

'That's what marriage *is*,' I said, looking up. 'A way of keeping women under men's control. It's in the actual words of the marriage service – *'who giveth this woman to be married to this man?'* – a woman's father *gives* her to the husband. From one man's control to another.'

'Or from one man's *care* to another—'

'Why must we be *cared* for? We're not children. And we're not fragile! And there's that other thing in the marriage service, isn't there – another inequality. The woman has to promise to *obey* her husband.'

'It's a form of words, Non – it's not binding on a couple to behave in that way—'

'But it's the *law*, isn't it? Women are *supposed* to obey their husbands and if they don't, they can be beaten, or, in middle-class circles, carted off to an asylum—'

I knew I'd gone too far by the look on Tarley's face. I added more sugar to my coffee so that I could watch myself stirring it.

'I would never—'

'The article isn't about *you*. Or me. It's about the society we live in.'

'Then let's talk about—'

He stopped abruptly and we both looked up as the coffee house door banged open. A gaggle of chattering gownsmen came swaggering in. One of them bumped our table as he went past. 'This place is going downhill faster than Dr Nolan's comments on Abbot's essays,' he said, looking at me.

His friends brayed like donkeys, which was about the level of their intelligence judging by their sense of humour.

Tarley glared at them then turned back to me. But, instead of picking up where he left off, he raised his cup and drained it. 'D'you think Stead will print it – your article?' I could tell he was making an effort to sound matter-of-fact. Continuing the marriage discussion was out of the question with the idiots at the next table close enough to hear.

'I hope so,' I said. My voice felt tight, as if it was trapped in my throat. 'It's very relevant to Sarah's case.'

'What's that dreadful noise?' one of the donkeys brayed. 'Oh, it's a woman trying to express an opinion.'

In any other circumstances, I'd have given him an opinion he wouldn't forget in a hurry, but just at the moment, I was glad of the distraction.

'*You could have just told him you didn't want to marry him,*' Hara said. '*You didn't have to let him read that article. What would Basil think? What would* Lily *think?*'

I knew what Lily'd think. She'd think I'd been cruel.

'*It's not that I don't want to marry* him,' I told Hara. '*If marriage was what he thinks it could be – a union of equals – then it would be different. But that's not how things are, is it? There's no place for that kind of equal marriage. All his friends would think he was mad if he tried it, and he'd end up agreeing. And then where would we be?*'

Tarley cleared his throat and poured himself another cup of coffee. 'It was interesting meeting Martin Alexis yesterday. Is Miss Critchley definitely going to sue, do you think?'

I shut the door on Hara's comments and pulled myself together. 'I hope so. I think she could count on a lot of public support after everything that came out at the inquest. And with Stead's backing in the *Gazette*, the University wouldn't be able to write her off as a gold digger.' I realised I was gabbling and stopped speaking.

Tarley sipped at his coffee and glared at the undergraduates, who'd started taking a personal interest in him.

'What college are you from, sir?' one of them wanted to know. 'Do the proctors know you're fraternising?'

'They're schoolboys,' I said. 'Take no notice, it only encourages them.'

He put his cup down and kept his eyes on me. 'I can see the benefits to Alexis in prosecuting the University,' he murmured, keeping his voice down, which seemed like a rebuke because I'd been speaking normally. 'He'd make his name with a case like this, win or lose. But I can't honestly see that the possibility of clearing her name would be worth all the criticism and judgement Miss Critchley would have to face. Not to mention the fact that her name might *not* be cleared. She might not win.'

'Speak up!' one wag called. 'We can't hear you making love to her.'

Tarley gritted his teeth.

I decided to change the subject. 'I heard that Frank Dodds has come forward,' I said. 'With an alibi. So it definitely wasn't him who killed Gainsborough. Not that I ever thought it was.'

'Frank Dodds being the man accused of barrowing something about the streets in the early hours on the morning of Gainsborough's murder?' Tarley asked. 'The one who was supposed to be sweet on Miss Critchley?' He was still keeping his voice low, but it sounded more normal now, and I wondered how often he did that – pretended everything was fine between us.

'Yes, him. And he couldn't have been barrowing anything around the streets, because he was on the malting floor at the Lion Brewery. I got a note from Miss Skene yesterday evening. Apparently, Frank Dodds turned up at the police station yesterday afternoon. Brought the man he works with to confirm his whereabouts, too.'

'That settles that, then.'

'So it would seem.' I said. 'But I've been wondering – if it *was* the Hunters who sent the anonymous letter, how did they know Frank Dodds's name? And I think I've worked it out.'

I'd looked forward to telling Tarley, but working it out didn't seem so important, now. Not with him sitting there like a kicked puppy. Still, he was waiting, so on I went.

'Sarah Critchley said that when the two lads tried to stop the proctor taking her away, the bulldog recognised them and warned them off *by name*. So, assuming that there would've been a Hunter there loitering as an observer, he'd have heard, wouldn't he?'

I glanced at the braying undergraduates. They'd got fed up with not being able to get a rise out of Tarley and piped down. Now they were just muttering and tittering amongst themselves, like eight-year-olds laughing at fart jokes.

Tarley leaned towards me and I felt my heart beat faster. But when he spoke, I realised he just didn't want the buffoons to hear. 'Coincidentally, anonymous letters were what I wanted to talk to you about. I've been thinking about the one that was sent to the proctors complaining about Sarah Critchley.'

'What about it?'

'D'you think one of the Venatores might've sent it? As a way of getting her thrown into jail and out of Gainsborough's reach?'

'Why would they want to do that?'

'He'd been courting her – or apparently courting her – for months. Maybe they worried that he was really getting attached to her. Think about it – we know that he'd been walking out with her so much that she'd started recognising the other Venatores. She could identify them. That could have been a potential threat. Maybe one of them thought it was time to put an end to his pursuit of her and that seemed the best way.'

I considered what he'd said. The theory certainly fitted with what we knew.

'And if Sarah was a threat to them,' he said, 'then maybe the Venatores thought Gainsborough was, too.'

## Chapter 56

*Basil*

I put aside the copy of the *Pall Mall Gazette* I'd risen early to acquire and sighed. Non's inquest report had denigrated the University and its junior members to exactly the degree I'd expected. She'd pulled no punches in her outrage at Gainsborough's activities, and though she'd acknowledged the complimentary things said about him by the dean and his peers, when set alongside his pursuit of Sarah Critchley and other young women, their encomia rang as hollow as Non had known they would.

Jowett would be beside himself, distressed both by the boy's activities and their exposure, and deeply wounded on behalf of the institution to which he'd devoted his life. As I had had it in mind to pay him a visit this week, anyway, I decided that now might be the moment, before the tutorials I was due to give later.

—

I found the Vice Chancellor in the subdued mood I'd anticipated.

'Are we really as parochial as this makes us sound?' he asked as he waved the *Pall Mall Gazette* at me. But it was not Non's inquest report that I saw on the page in question, but Stead's leader.

'*No doubt*,' Jowett read, sliding his spectacles up his nose, '*the Hebdomadal Council congratulates itself on retaining powers known nowhere else in the land save at its fraternal twin, Cambridge. However, those excluded from the marbled halls of academe see the Vice Chancellor's court for what it is, an academic star chamber, completely outwith the common law of these islands. A medieval institution that has no place in modern Britain.*'

'The tone is uncomplimentary, certainly,' I acknowledged. 'But unfortunately, nothing in either the leader or the inquest report is untrue.' I hesitated. 'In answer to your question, Vice Chancellor, I fear that perhaps we *are* parochial. Those of us who came here as callow youths and have never left are apt to take our special status so much for granted that sometimes we fail to understand how those outside the University see us.'

'You're very generous, Rice, but you shouldn't include yourself in such a collective lack of understanding,' Jowett replied. 'I'm well aware that your seat on the Board of Guardians has given you a perspective that many of us lack.'

'All of us are guilty of blinkered vision to some extent. It's hard not to be when one is part of an institution as all-encompassing as the University.'

Home, employer, focus of future ambitions and proxy family, each of Oxford's two dozen colleges was its own little world, ruled by the ordinances of the University.

However, as both Jowett and I were aware, at the government's insistence those ordinances had changed profoundly in the last twenty-five years, and Oxford was no longer the place the young Benjamin Jowett had found when he came up as an undergraduate. But it was those very changes that made some members of the University determined to cling to the powers and traditions that remained.

I wondered what Martin Alexis made of it all. Recalling his parting words, I felt again the warm dryness of his hand.

Jowett interrupted my reverie. 'I suppose there's no point my writing to Stead and appealing to his better nature?'

'I suspect that asking him to desist would rather add fuel to the fire,' I replied, accepting the glass of sherry which the Vice Chancellor had poured for me in lieu of the coffee I should have preferred. 'However, you may wish to take control of a situation which, otherwise, might result in far worse than that.' I inclined my head at the newspaper.

'And this situation would be...?'

'A potential lawsuit against the University.'

Once I'd explained Martin Alexis's proposal and Felicia Skene's support of it, Jowett stared at me in horror. 'But Martin Alexis is a Balliol man. He took Greats in—' He calculated quickly. 'It must have been seventy-three.'

Alexis, then, was a few years older than I had taken him for – he'd come up only a year after I'd graduated and been appointed a fellow at Jesus.

'I don't think his acting for Miss Critchley should necessarily be seen as disloyalty on his part,' I suggested, quietly. 'You're seen as the great moderniser in Oxford, Vice Chancellor. Alexis may well feel he's following in your footsteps.'

'But to challenge the University in court...'

'Could that not be seen as an attempt to help you in your efforts at reform?' I suggested. 'After all, you didn't preside over the court that incarcerated Miss Critchley. Alexis might well imagine that you'd like to see the anachronism of the Vice Chancellor's court abolished.'

I wasn't simply trying to make Jowett feel better. I wanted him to take what I was about to say seriously. And, perhaps, I wanted both of us to think well of Martin Alexis.

'Anachronism?' Jowett repeated. 'Is that your word, or one you would put in Alexis's mouth?'

'Both. I do believe it's an anachronism – one that might be used as a stick to beat the University with if we don't take action. The accusation that the court is an "academic star chamber" is likely to be the least damaging thing said about it if an action goes to trial. Imagine what the *Manchester Guardian* would have to say about Miss Critchley's summary incarceration.'

It was slightly terrifying to conjure up the field day that liberal newspaper would have in reporting on a lawsuit brought by a shop girl against one of the two great universities of the Empire.

'And how, specifically, do you feel we should take control of this situation, Rice?'

'I think a public apology and a sum of money to compensate Miss Critchley might be appropriate.'

'Wouldn't a public apology bring almost as much publicity as a lawsuit? It would, after all, imply that – had she gone to law – her case might have carried the day.'

As it happened, I hadn't for a moment expected that Jowett would agree to issue a public apology. But I'd learned from Non that, in what she called 'horse trading', one should always ask for more than one thought reasonable, in order to allow one's partner in the bargain to drive the metaphorical price down and feel that they had the better end of the deal.

'A private apology, then,' I conceded. 'But I do feel that it should be accompanied by financial compensation.'

Jowett sighed. He might be an idealist, but he was no fool. He knew that an injustice had been done and that the University would be wise to make amends.

'Very well. But it must be a private arrangement. I do not wish this to be the subject of popular gossip.'

'Would you like me to arrange a meeting with Mr Alexis to discuss the matter?' I asked, the blood rushing in my veins at the thought of encountering Alexis again.

'I think we'd do better to ask Miss Skene to broker this arrangement,' Jowett said, causing my spirits to plummet unreasonably. 'Might you be good enough to ask her to facilitate a meeting with the young woman concerned?'

I nodded. That was wise. Sarah Critchley would feel secure in any decision reached with Miss Skene at her side.

'And perhaps you'd be kind enough to attend with me, Rice?'

'Certainly. And there's one more person who should be there, I think.' Jowett waited for me to elucidate. 'Waddesworth. He, of all people, owes Miss Critchley an apology.'

## Chapter 57

*Non*

Even though Tarley's idea that the Hunters might have been responsible for Gainsborough's murder didn't ring true to me, their cynical treatment of Sarah Critchley and other girls meant that they deserved to be thrown out of the University in disgrace. But that couldn't happen until we'd identified them all. I didn't want to leave a single member of the pack out there, bitter at his friends' being sent down and hell bent on revenge.

After Basil's visit to the domestic staff at Trinity we knew that Charles Gainsborough had hosted a supper party for seven men. Six of them we'd already identified – Gainsborough himself, the four who'd been bound and hooded, plus Laurence Herbert's friend, John Montague. Which left one. If we could identify all the Hunters then we could bypass the proctors – who, as far as I could see, were only interested in taking the word of undergraduates at face value – and go straight to the Vice Chancellor. But we had to find the seventh Hunter.

And I thought I knew how to find him.

If Edie was right, and Cat Hammond was helping ruined girls, there was a good chance that she'd know all about the Hunters and what they were up to, even if she didn't know they were a club. Which meant that she'd know some poor girl who'd be able to identify the seventh man, just as Sarah had identified Montague.

So, when I'd finished my afternoon duties at Somerville, I decided to visit Miss Hammond.

I had a feeling she wouldn't see me if she knew I was a journalist, so in case she'd heard about the *Mercury*'s red-headed female scribbler, I put my blonde wig on again. But this time, instead of the pert little hat I'd worn to the pawnbrokers, I wore a battered, ten-year-old straw hat with sad silk flowers and an equally sad and ancient shawl. I'd got them both from a second-hand clothes shop in Jericho. I needed to look down-at-heel and a bit desperate.

I was used to being stared at as I went about the city. Even when I wasn't riding the Contraption, my short hair and lack of a hat made me quite noticeable. So, as I walked down from Jericho in my blonde wig and poor woman's clothes, it felt odd to be mostly ignored. Some people frowned as if they were trying to place me, but most eyes just slid past.

It was also strange not having my satchel bumping against my hip as I walked. To be honest, it was more difficult pretending to be a different kind of woman than it was pretending to be a boy. Swaggering about the streets with my hands in my pockets with Tarley and Albie had been easy compared to trying to be this downtrodden, hat-wearing girl. I kept forgetting not to look men in the eye and I missed the freedom that riding the Contraption gave me. I didn't have to step out of anybody's way when I was on the tandem, and I didn't have to walk behind slowcoaches either.

Still, you can get used to anything if you try, and by the time I reached Holywell Street, I'd got used to the naked feeling of not having my satchel on my shoulder and I was managing to walk hunched over, my arms crossed over my chest, holding on to my shawl.

Bath Place, which, according to Edie, was where Cat Hammond lived, was immediately opposite the Music Room on Holywell Street. Despite its grand-sounding name, Bath Place was a run-down little medieval alleyway in what had once been the ditch outside the city wall.

I walked through the narrow passage into a jumble of higgledy-piggledy brick and timber houses which were slowly shedding their ancient lime plaster onto the cobbles beneath. Shutters were open on all the cottages, and I walked slowly, hoping that one of the doors would open as I went past so that I could ask where Cat Hammond lived. When none did, I turned into an even narrower passage that led to the Turf Tavern.

Before I went into the taproom, I peered cautiously through the long, low bay window that jutted out into the courtyard where the pub stood. But I couldn't see much. It was gloomy inside.

I touched my hat to make sure it was still pinned tightly to my wig and opened the door.

The place was almost deserted. Out of the corner of my eye, I saw three middle-aged men sitting at a table, their pint mugs in front of them, but they seemed to be the only patrons. I pulled my shawl a bit tighter around me for their benefit and moved towards the bar.

From under my lowered eyelashes, I saw the landlord raise his head as I came towards him and, when I glanced up, I saw him looking me up and down.

'Help you?' he grunted.

I lowered my eyes again. 'I need to speak to Cat Hammond,' I said, in a small voice. 'I know she lives in Bath Place, but I don't know which house. Can you help me?'

When he didn't reply, I glanced up again trying not to look him in the eye. If I'd had to guess, I'd have put him somewhere between forty and fifty; the right time of life to have a daughter my age. So, hopefully, he'd want to help a girl in trouble. And I had a pretty good idea that any girl coming into his pub wringing her hands, speaking in a defeated voice and wanting Cat Hammond would be in trouble.

'Knows you, does she?' he asked.

I shook my head, eyes on the floor, as if I couldn't look at him for shame.

'All right. Wait there a tick.'

He slipped out from behind the bar and disappeared through a dark-painted door that was almost invisible in the gloom.

When he'd gone, I raised my head cautiously and looked about. The taproom was low-ceilinged and dark, but it was pretty large by the standards of Oxford pubs, and he obviously kept the place spick and span. The lamps were clean and burned bright, and the bar and tables were varnished and clean.

I supposed the Turf's patrons would expect a certain standard. College servants weren't rich, but they were decently paid and accustomed to well-kept surroundings.

A few moments later, the landlord reappeared. 'Cat's through here.'

'Through here' turned out to mean a room at the end of a narrow corridor with a very uneven floor.

'She said to go on in,' the publican encouraged me. And he stood there, watching me make my hesitant way towards the door. I took little steps, still a bit hunched over, as if I was trying to make myself smaller, less noticeable.

When I reached the door, I turned the handle slowly and walked in.

The room was very much as Tarley'd described it, down to the vase of dried flowers on the bookcase and the day bed in the corner. But there was one thing he hadn't mentioned. The birds. There were pictures of birds everywhere.

Most of them were species I didn't recognise, and some were so colourful that they didn't look real. They looked like the kind of birds a child would paint if they were given a set of watercolours and told to make up birds for a fairy story.

The woman who'd stood as I came in – Cat Hammond, presumably – saw me staring at them. 'They're birds of paradise,' she said. 'Pretty, aren't they?'

She wasn't what I'd expected. Tarley's description of her – in her twenties, well spoken – hadn't mentioned her physical appearance – and I hadn't asked in case he wondered why I wanted to know.

I'd assumed she'd be pretty, but she wasn't particularly. She was an ordinary-looking woman who knew how to make the best of what she had.

Her brown hair was swept up into a complicated kind of arrangement and the severe, dark dress she wore – silk, if I wasn't mistaken – showed off her alabaster complexion.

But ordinary looking or not, the way she held herself meant that Cat Hammond would never be overlooked or fade into the background. Mrs Johnson and the ladies of the AEW wouldn't have blinked if she'd sat alongside them in one of their drawing rooms. Being a lady's maid had taught her a lot more than how to be a good servant. Or perhaps, being her parents' only child, she'd been brought up to have a good opinion of herself.

I looked back at the birds again and answered her question. 'They're extraordinary.'

Then I did something I hadn't intended to do. I unpinned my hat, took off the wig and shook my own hair free. 'D'you mind if I sit down?' I asked. 'I need to talk to you.'

Cat Hammond's eyes widened for half a second, but that was all the reaction I got.

'Did you come on your bicycle?' she asked as I sat down on a chair upholstered in gold velvet.

So, she knew who I was. 'It's a tricycle, actually,' I said, 'but no, I walked.'

She looked at me, her head cocked ever so slightly. 'Why did you bother with the disguise if you were just going to take it off the moment you got here?'

'I wasn't going to. I was going to pretend to be a ruined girl who needed help.'

She almost smiled. 'What changed your mind?'

'I could see straight away that you're a woman who'd prefer straight talking. Dr Eros.'

She smiled properly then. And it transformed her – she sparkled when she smiled. 'You'd be amazed how many people don't spot the name,' she said. 'Including the students, who really should.'

I smiled back. 'They really should, yes.'

An image of Tarley shaking his head at his own slowness when I'd pointed out the pun came to my mind and I suddenly felt uncomfortable, imagining him here, sitting in this room with Cat Hammond.

'If we're going to talk,' she said, 'would you like some tea?'

When I said yes, she swung a trivet over the coals in the grate and filled a little kettle with water from a jug on a side table.

Then, still standing, she looked down at me. 'So what brings you here?'

I put thoughts of her asking Tarley that question firmly out of my head. 'I think you know that, Miss Hammond.'

'Humour me. It wouldn't do to go jumping to conclusions.'

I wondered how men reacted to her. What Tarley'd thought of her self-possession, the way she looked you boldly in the eye.

'*You're jealous!*'

I slammed the door on my sister.

'Very well then,' I said, 'I've come to give you some advice and to ask a question.'

She waited, which impressed me. It had taken me years to learn when to speak up and when to keep quiet. Actually, Lily would've said I was still learning.

'If you don't want to be accused of Charles Gainsborough's murder,' I said, 'you'd do well to draw a line under your hooding and binding activities. Others might feel differently – the Venatores in particular – but I wouldn't want to see you hang.'

## Chapter 58

### Basil

As I still had an hour or so before I needed to return to college, immediately upon leaving Jowett I made for Felicia Skene's house. It seemed best to enlist her help in brokering the Vice Chancellor's offer of compensation to Miss Critchley as soon as possible.

As I strode down George Street, I remembered the first time I'd approached Miss Skene's house as a nervous undergraduate. I'd been pointed in her direction by a lecturer who'd obviously seen in me the same desires he felt himself. One day in my second term, I'd been attending one of his lectures and I must have seemed particularly preoccupied, because he'd taken me aside as the other students left. 'I know young men are encouraged to take their troubles onto the rugby field or the river and exhaust them there,' he'd said, kindly, 'but, sometimes, wise counsel does more to settle a troubled mind than an exhausted body. Should you feel the need, Miss Felicia Skene is a friend to many and doesn't sit in judgement.'

He'd gone on to tell me about Miss Skene's work and, without ever referring to the turmoil I might be feeling, had assured me that she was 'quite unshockable'.

And so it had proved. Given her devotion to the church, I'd assumed that her unshockability wouldn't extend to matters amorous, but that couldn't have been further from the truth.

'In case it is of relevance, Mr Rice,' she'd suggested when I'd failed, yet again, to reveal the real reason for my repeated visits, 'when giving advice on matters pertaining to particular friendships, as in all things, I follow the master.'

I recalled, now, not only the look of clear-eyed acceptance she had directed at me as she spoke, but the feeling both of enormous relief that she had broached the subject for me and terror as to what she might say.

'Christ,' she continued, 'had much to say about love, was damning of divorce, equally damning of hypocrisy and had absolutely nothing to say about whom it was appropriate to love. Indeed, he had a particular friend amongst the disciples whom, we are told, he loved more than the others.'

She'd smiled then, a smile that was like a warm hand of benediction on the crown of my head. 'It is not love that we must fear, Mr Rice, but licentiousness, using others for our own gratification. That is always to be condemned.'

Miss Skene would thoroughly have disapproved of Teddy's promiscuous activities, but she saw my love for him as something that might make me noble.

But I hadn't been able to love Teddy nobly. I couldn't live in his circle, go with him to London, visit the clubs and continue to be the one he might – if I was lucky – love above all others, without indulging in what Miss Skene would have termed licentiousness.

I'd known that must mean that Teddy was bad for me, that my soul was being corrupted by what I did to stay in his good graces. But I hadn't been able to help myself.

And that meant that I'd stopped going to see Felicia Skene after a while. I simply hadn't, any longer, been able to look her in the eye.

More recently, of course, circumstances had changed. My work amongst the poor had brought me into regular contact with Miss Skene once more and, having distanced myself from Teddy and his circle, I was able to look the lady squarely in the eye again. Little by little over the last twelve months or so, we had been finding our way into a genuine friendship that I believe we both found sustaining.

I pulled up in front of her house but, as I put my hand to the door handle, it was pulled out of my hand as the door swung inwards. Felicia Skene appeared on the threshold, and I stepped back smartly, lest she walk into me.

'Miss Skene – good morning!'

'Good morning, Mr Rice,' she said, as if it was no surprise at all to see me on her doorstep. 'How very nice to see you.'

'Thank you, yes, I just… I'm sorry, you're on your way out. May I call again later?'

'I'm on my way to the prison,' she said. 'Perhaps you might accompany me?'

She took the arm I offered, and we made our way down New Inn Hall Street. Miss Skene walked everywhere, absolutely refusing to board a tram as she objected most stridently to the company's bar on dogs in their vehicles.

'I'm actually here on behalf of the Vice Chancellor,' I began.

'Ah. Has Reverend Jowett, perhaps, got wind of the fact that Miss Sarah Critchley is considering bringing a suit against the Vice Chancellor's court for false imprisonment?' The grin that accompanied her words was wicked. Felicia Skene delighted in being able to surprise her friends, but I should have known that she would guess the reason for my visit. After all, her attendance at Gainsborough's inquest meant that she was aware of my investigations into the Venatores and my consequent interest in Miss Critchley's plight.

'Quite so,' I said with a rueful smile, and, as we walked past the graveyard of St Peter-le-Bailey, the now vanished church which had once stood at the bottom of New Inn Hall Street, I outlined Jowett's proposal for reparations. 'Would you be so good as to broach the subject with her?' I concluded. 'I know the Vice Chancellor would be most grateful.'

If she'd been a different woman, I might have worried that, as the person who'd introduced Miss Critchley to Martin Alexis, Miss Skene might be less than wholehearted in conveying news of Jowett's offer. But Felicia Skene would do what was right, not what was convenient.

'Of course. But I can make no promises as to her response.' She paused. 'Miss Critchley will, of course, wish to know the kind of sum envisaged.'

Jowett and I had discussed this, and I named a figure that would enable Miss Critchley and her mother to buy a modest property and become landladies if they had a mind to do so.

'Very well,' Miss Skene responded. She paused, then said, 'I hope you will not take it amiss if I ask Mr Alexis to be present at our meeting with Reverend Jowett?'

Hoping that none of my reaction to Alexis's name had communicated itself to Miss Skene via the arm which she held, I replied, blandly, 'No, of course not. I'm sure Reverend Jowett would be delighted to see him. He is, after all, a Balliol man.'

She turned to me and, addressing me by my Christian name, which she had not done since I was an undergraduate, she said, 'Be careful, Basil. You have a great capacity for love. I would not wish it to be your downfall.'

## Chapter 59

### *Non*

Cat Hammond didn't flinch at my suggestion that she was responsible for the hooding attacks. She just carried on making the tea.

'And what makes you think I'm responsible?' she asked with no more surprise in her voice than if she'd been asking whether I preferred my tea weak or strong.

'I realised that a woman had to be involved when I saw Laurence Herbert sitting outside Merton with "liar" cut into his face,' I said. 'A man would never do that to another man. But I only realised that it had to be you, specifically, when Edie Bishop told me that you were Dr Eros and that you helped girls who came to you.'

I paused to see if she'd say anything, but she was keeping her powder dry.

'And,' I went on, 'there's more than one way to help girls than to give them work with prospective husbands, isn't there?'

She looked up at that. 'Edie Bishop. Is that Nellie and Hilda's little sister – from Cranham Street?'

'Yes. She's my landlady's maid-of-all-work.'

'So she may be, but if she's going about suggesting that I give husband education work to other girls, she's wrong. There's only one Dr Eros.' She looked me in the eye. 'Who else knows you suspect me?'

'Nobody.' I hadn't wanted to tell Basil and Tarley that I believed a woman was involved, not until I was sure myself. 'But even if the girls who come to you for help aren't part of your Dr Eros business,' I said, 'you do *something* for them, don't you?'

She sat down lightly on the end of the chaise longue, like a wren coming to rest on a twig. 'What I do for them is pass on the skills I learned in my previous life. I teach them how to be good servants. Just scullery maids or maids-of-all-work for most, but if a girl's got more about her, I'll teach her to be a parlourmaid or even a lady's maid.'

'But what use is that without references?'

She looked at me with a half-smile.

Of course. It was obvious when you thought about it. 'You write references for them.'

'Dr E. Ross sounds very respectable, don't you think?'

It did. And as long as the girls were going to Witney or Abingdon or somewhere outside Oxford for work, nobody was going to know that Bath Place wasn't a respectable, middle-class address.

'Why don't you set up classes for older girls in one of the schools?' I asked. 'The city's crying out for well-trained servants.'

'What school would let somebody like me in?' she asked.

'You could always write yourself a reference. Or ask Miss Skene to help you.'

She shook her head. 'The likes of Miss Skene would think I'd lead the girls astray.'

The kettle boiled and Cat Hammond poured water into a little teapot.

'She wouldn't, you know,' I said. 'Felicia Skene is the least judgemental person I've ever met. But what if you took your own premises and just started a school?'

'I'd still need somebody respectable to back me, put money up. And then I'd be beholden to them. This way, *I* decide what I do and how I do it.' She put a patchwork tea cosy over the pot, then looked up. 'And anyway, don't you think I'm doing a public service to the future wives of Oxford by training their husbands?'

When I didn't reply, she said, 'Look, if you think it's demeaning, let me tell you, Miss Vaughan, it's a lot less demeaning than what some wives have to put up with. Besides, I make damn sure it's worth my while. I'm not offering a sixpenny knee-trembler up Hell's Passage. I'm offering anatomical advice with practical demonstrations. Only men with two guineas in their pockets need apply.'

Two guineas. No wonder she could offer to train girls up to do domestic work. She wouldn't need many consultations a week to live handsomely.

But I wasn't here to talk about her income or how she came by it.

'How long have you been watching them?' I asked. 'The so-called Hunters. The Venatores.'

She gazed at me, equal to equal. 'Once we knew who they were, it was easy enough to keep an eye on them. Men like that never notice working people. Not unless they're young and pretty.'

I noted that 'we'. So, she had collaborators.

'What gave you the idea to truss them up as if they were going to be hanged?' I asked.

She snuffed a humourless kind of laugh. 'It was a warning.'

'Desist, or worse will happen?'

'Yes. And that's what I whispered in their ears when I put the hoods over their heads.' Her eyes gleamed with tamped-down rage. 'But I'd never have done worse.'

'I don't think Laurence Herbert would agree.'

'What – a few cuts where his beard'll hide them? Compared to what he did, that's nothing.'

'He'll have them lifelong,' I said, playing devil's advocate.

'Yes, and he'll probably live to a ripe, debauched old age. But the girl he *seduced*,' she filled the word with all the contempt it could hold, 'will have no life at all. When she knew she had his child in her belly she drowned herself in the river.'

I remembered that death. The girl had drowned at Iffley Lock at the end of the previous term, in early June. I hadn't reported on the inquest, but I remembered the report Berry'd printed in the *Mercury*, including the sad little statement that the girl's drowning had taken two lives – hers and her unborn child's. The knowledge that Laurence Herbert had just cast this young woman aside when her condition made her inconvenient to him filled me with all the cold rage Cat must have felt when she put the knife to his degenerate face.

'Her name was Louise,' Cat Hammond said. 'Louise Mander.'

'You knew her?'

Cat shook her head. 'No. But it matters that she had a name. That she was a real person with a family and a life ahead of her. Not just a corpse dragged out of the river.'

'Had Laurence Herbert promised her marriage?' I asked, trying to keep my voice steady, thinking about the kind of life Louise Mander might have imagined as his wife.

'From what I've been told, he'd promised her the *world*.'

I didn't ask how Cat Hammond knew about Louise Mander or that Laurence Herbert was the man responsible for her condition. Those weren't the important questions here.

'You must've been shocked when Charles Gainsborough turned up dead?'

Cat went over to the room's only window – a little north-facing four-pane – and raised the sash to reach for a jug on the sill, covered with a bead-hung cloth.

'Shocked but not sorry,' she said, lowering the sash on the cold air that had come trickling in over the windowsill. 'I knew he was one of them. I'd seen him at it. Picking girls up. I've seen them all at it. They're not the only ones who can watch and *confirm*.'

'How did you find out about them?'

'One of the men who drinks here. A servant at Trinity. A year or so ago, he found that little home-made book Basil Rice read from at the inquest and brought it to me. Took me a while to understand the Latin. I got the words translated one at a time. Didn't want to give anybody the whole list in case they started asking questions.'

I admired her cool intelligence. 'But why would this college servant bring the manual to you?' I asked.

'You know what it's like. Word gets about. You can't stop it. And I wouldn't want to. I want girls to know I'm here to help.'

'And that's why you sent the manual to Mr Rice – because you thought it would help?'

She didn't reply straight away, took her time as if she was sifting through exactly what she wanted to tell me. 'I'd heard good things about your Mr Rice. I hoped he wouldn't turn a blind eye once he'd seen those lists and knew what they were doing.'

'But you didn't give him a name, or even a college.'

'The man who brought that little Venatores book to me has a job to keep – I wasn't going to put that in danger. Besides, Mr Rice has a reputation for sniffing things out.'

A reputation he mostly owed to me, but I let that go. 'Do you know who killed Charles Gainsborough?' I asked, looking right at her.

She didn't look away. 'No. But it wasn't me. Or Frank Dodds.'

So she knew about the accusation against Mr Dodds. 'Do you know him?' I asked.

She nodded. Just one dip of the head.

'Did he help you with the hoodings?' I asked. 'You couldn't've overpowered those boys by yourself.'

Cat Hammond just gazed at me. Her grey eyes were clear and bright, and it struck me that Miss Skene's must have looked just as bright and intelligent when she was a young woman. They'd get on, Cat Hammond and Felicia Skene, whatever Cat thought.

'Look,' I said, 'I've got no interest in taking anything you tell me to the police or the magistrates. As far as I'm concerned, those boys deserved all they got and worse.'

'Good. Because if you did go to the police, I'd deny that this conversation ever took place,' Cat said. 'Danny Palmer – the landlord – will swear that I was working for him on any evening I ask him to.'

'I'm sure he will. But whoever killed Gainsborough has made things riskier for you, now. You need to stop before you get caught. Basil Rice knows who the Venatores are. He'll put a stop to their activities.'

'And the proctors and their bulldogs? What about *their* activities?' The way she spat the word 'proctors' sparked a startling idea. Edie'd said that her mistress's son – the boy who adamantly denied seducing Cat – had seen her with a don.

'Waddesworth?' I said, cautiously. Of the two proctors, he was the younger and by far the better-looking.

Cat Hammond's eyes widened. Just a fraction, but enough to tell me I was right.

'Lincoln Waddesworth is your little girl's father?'

## Chapter 60

### Basil

Later that afternoon, I was preparing a cup of pre-prandial coffee and ruminating on Miss Skene's slightly concerning advice, when Fred skipped up to my room with a note. I recognised Non's handwriting on the folded notebook sheet immediately.

> *Dear Basil*
> *Just been to visit Cat Hammond (Dr Eros) and learned some very interesting and relevant facts. Come to Shene Road for supper and I shall reveal all.*
> *Non*

It was typical of Non not to include what she'd learned in the note. She didn't trust college messengers not to read communications left at the lodge and, instead of taking the obvious precaution of carrying a packet of sealing wafers in her satchel, she chose to leave gnomic communications like this one.

I made a mental note to call in to one of the butcher's shops in the Covered Market on my way to Jericho and order a joint of beef to be delivered to Shene Road. Non was forever inviting me to dinner ad hoc and I didn't like to impose on Lily's hospitality without offering something in return.

—

When I arrived at Lily's house, I found Askew also in attendance, though whether he, too, was there to hear Non's revelations or because he'd been invited to dine anyway wasn't made clear. He was, however, as astonished as I at what Non had discovered.

'But what on earth made you suspect Cat Hammond in the first place?' I asked. The notion of a former lady's maid in the role of nocturnal attacker seemed outlandish.

'I knew from what Edie'd told me that Miss Hammond helped girls in trouble, so it seemed logical that she might've heard about the Hunters and their methods from some of the girls who'd come to her, even if they wouldn't have had a name to put to them. And I'd suspected that a woman might be involved from the moment I saw Laurence Herbert's face. Men don't do that kind of thing to each other.'

I yielded to her greater worldly wisdom. Non's experiences on board ship and in various ports gave her a far greater insight into knife-wielding men than I. Indeed, she was no stranger to wielding a knife herself.

'Then,' she continued, 'as soon as I met her, I realised that she's a woman who doesn't just let things happen to her. She takes control.'

The words 'pot' and 'kettle' sprang to mind, and I raised my eyebrows at Askew who stifled a smile.

'So you just came straight out with it and accused her of the hooding attacks?' I asked.

'I didn't *accuse* her of anything,' Non corrected. 'I just advised her to stop if she didn't want to be suspected of Charles Gainsborough's murder.'

'And will she stop?' I asked.

Non tucked her feet up under her in the armchair, evidently finding her slippers unequal to the task of keeping her warm in the draught that came under the door. 'Yes. She's no fool. She knows that whoever killed Gainsborough deliberately implicated whoever was responsible for the hoodings. She won't want to risk getting caught now.'

'And if the Venatores continue their vile competition?' I asked.

'Surely they won't, now they know we're on to them?' Askew objected. 'They'd be mad to keep it up. Especially after Dr Darbishire's warning at the inquest.'

'Let's hope you're right.'

'What about Waddesworth?' Askew asked. 'Has she wreaked some kind of revenge on him too?'

Non shook her head. 'She wouldn't talk about him. Absolutely refused.'

I wondered whether Miss Hammond's hunting of the Venatores wasn't, in fact, some kind of vengeance for what she'd suffered at Waddesworth's hands. If she couldn't avenge herself on him for his abandonment of her and her child, then she could at least humiliate young men who were behaving in the same way.

Now I understood Waddesworth's reluctance to go to the Turf Tavern when I'd accompanied him on his patrol. He hadn't wanted to be confronted by Miss Hammond.

'Was she directly involved in the hoodings?' Askew asked. 'Or has somebody else been carrying out the attacks at her behest?'

'Unless another woman carved "liar" into Laurence Herbert's face,' Non said, 'then yes, I think she's been directly involved. Edie told me that Cat Hammond's father is a wharfman,' she added. 'She could've learned to tie knots from him.'

'If she led the attacks,' Askew said, 'perhaps that's one of the reasons the Venatores didn't want to talk about what had happened to them. It would've been humiliating enough to admit they'd been bested by townies, but so much worse if those townies had been under a woman's command.'

'Perhaps that was part of it,' Non conceded, 'but there was also the small matter of whatever Cat Hammond whispered in their ears as she put the hoods over their heads. She wouldn't tell me exactly what she said, but I'd imagine she threatened worse to come if they transgressed again or told anybody what had happened to them.' She paused, and I had the impression that she was weighing up whether to say what was in her mind. Eventually, she said, 'I think Frank Dodds might've been involved. In the hoodings, I mean, not Gainsborough's death. I think that anonymous note implicating him was revenge.'

As it happened, I'd been wondering about Frank Dodds myself. 'Given his attempt to intervene in Miss Critchley's arrest,' I said, 'I assume he's one of the young men Miss Hammond had recruited to keep an eye on the Venatores?'

Non nodded, slowly. In front of her, a cup of coffee was going cold which showed how distracted she was by our conversation. She'd become a positive coffee addict.

'So does that mean that one or more of these putative watchmen murdered Charles Gainsborough?' Askew asked. 'With or without Miss Hammond's knowledge?'

'It would have to be without,' Non said, turning to him. 'She was adamant that she had nothing to do with Gainsborough's murder, and I believed her.'

'It was the foreman at Trinity's new building who found Gainsborough's body,' Askew said. 'Is there any suspicion that he might already have known the body was there and arrived early so that he could raise the alarm?'

'I gather Inspector Newman had the same thought. But the man was able to give a satisfactory account of his movements.'

Non rose to close the curtains. The lamplighters had already been out as I'd walked up to Shene Road and now it was fully dark.

'Might we just review Askew's suggestion that one of Miss Hammond's watchmen might be responsible for Gainsborough's murder?' I asked. 'I'm willing to accept your conviction that Miss Hammond knew nothing about it, but shouldn't she at least be asked to identify these young men so that they can be questioned by the police?'

'Cat would never give them up,' Non said. 'She made it very clear to me that if I went to the police, she'd deny our conversation had ever taken place.'

'Which I can understand if we're talking about the hooding attacks,' I countered, 'but surely she wouldn't want to protect a murderer?'

Non looked at me steadily. 'She might not have strangled Charles Gainsborough herself, but I'm pretty sure she thinks he got his just deserts.'

I was about to respond when the door opened. 'If you three can tear yourselves away from discussions of murder and similar unpleasantness,' Lily said, 'dinner's ready.'

## Chapter 61

*Non*

We were all in the front room after dinner, listening to Albie telling us how people were boycotting the University parks because the new laboratories that were being built there were going to perform experiments on animals, when there was a knock on the front door.

'Who can that be at this time of night?' Lily asked.

Actually, it wasn't even half past eight, but it had been dark for three hours and it felt later.

I got up to go and answer the door, but Lily waved me back down to wait for Edie. She was probably out in the passage, anyway, listening to us.

Sure enough, we heard the door open after a very short run of footsteps and an unmistakeable voice said, 'Good evening. Might I speak to Miss Vaughan, please? My name is Miss Skene.'

Edie showed Felicia Skene in, and I introduced her to Lily and Albie. She already knew the men, of course, and when I saw the obvious fondness Tarley had for her I couldn't help wondering about his visits to the little house on New Inn Hall Street.

'I'm so sorry to intrude on your evening, Mrs Maddox,' Miss Skene said, 'but I've come on a matter of some urgency.'

'You're very welcome, Miss Skene. I've never heard Non speak so highly of anybody as she does of you, so it's very nice to make your acquaintance.'

Felicia Skene smiled as if she'd been complimented by royalty, then turned to Basil and me. 'I won't beat about the bush. I'm very concerned about Sarah Critchley. I went to meet her after work to speak to her about the matter we discussed earlier, Mr Rice. However, she did not emerge with her colleagues at the end of their shift, and on enquiry, I was told that she hadn't presented herself for work today. I made straight for her home, only to find her mother anxiously awaiting her return. Mrs Critchley informed me that her daughter had left this morning as usual. Evidently, something happened between Cranham Street and Hyde's to prevent her arriving at the manufactory.'

Lily and Albie, who knew no more than the bare bones of Sarah Critchley's case, didn't immediately see the danger she might be in. But Basil, Tarley and I knew enough to feel the same anxiety that had brought Miss Skene straight from Cranham Street to Lily's house.

'John Montague,' I said, putting aside questions of what Felicia Skene and Basil had been talking about that involved Sarah Critchley. 'He was the one who got her thrown into jail, so he wouldn't want to be called as a witness if she takes her case to court. And, after he spotted you speaking to her at the inquest, he knows she's identified him.'

'But he couldn't know about her intention to go to law, surely?' Basil asked. 'It's hardly common knowledge.'

I swallowed. 'Gainsborough knew,' I said.

'Sarah Critchley told him?' Basil asked. 'I didn't think she'd been so decided before he died.'

I took a deep breath. 'It wasn't Sarah. It was me. Charles Gainsborough accosted Sarah and me on the street on the day that Miss Skene told me about Martin Alexis's suggestion.'

I'd just wanted to wipe that complacent 'everything's fine now your Gordon's here' look off his self-satisfied face. But now my need to slap him down had put Sarah in danger.

Basil looked just as troubled as I felt, but he didn't ask how I could have been so stupid. 'If Gainsborough told the other Venatores,' he said, 'that might give them a motive for his murder.'

'You think he would've implicated them?' Tarley asked.

Basil shook his head. 'He wouldn't have needed to. The Venatores already knew that Miss Hammond had identified them because of whatever she whispered in their ears as she hooded them. And because of the invitation pinned to Ashdown's hood. They might have reasoned that, without Gainsborough, Miss Critchley's case might never come to court.'

'Well, if the other Venatores *did* murder Gainsborough,' Tarley said, 'then Miss Critchley is in mortal danger. How are we going to find her?'

'I'll go and see the Senior Proctor,' Basil said. 'Or, if Kaye's on patrol, Waddesworth. We'll round up the Venatores and take them to the police station. If they're involved in Miss Critchley's disappearance, I dare say it will be easy enough to find out.'

'We still don't know the identity of the seventh Hunter at that Trinity supper,' I said, my heart thudding in my chest and my hands trembling. 'And we need them *all* if we're going to find her.' I was desperate to get out there, desperate to do whatever I could to find Sarah before it was too late. 'If you and the proctors round up the rest of the Hunters, I'll go and see Cat Hammond. She and whoever she's got working for her have been watching them for months. If anybody knows who the seventh man is, she will.'

## Chapter 62

### *Basil*

Having calculated which of the proctorial teams would be on duty, I realised with a sinking heart that I would have to enlist Waddesworth's help. Given what I'd learned from Non about his treatment of Cat Hammond, I wasn't sure I could be civil towards him. That a man whose conduct was so absolutely reprehensible should feel qualified to uphold discipline and morality amongst our undergraduates was breathtakingly hypocritical.

Having slipped into Queen's with barely two minutes to spare before the curfew bell rang out around the city, I made my way to Waddesworth's room and knocked.

The Junior Proctor opened the door in his waistcoat and shirtsleeves. I braced myself. 'Waddesworth, I need you to don your proctor's robe and come with me. Miss Sarah Critchley is missing.'

Waddesworth didn't move. 'And how exactly do you imagine that her whereabouts are the business of the proctors?'

I felt my hackles rise. 'I've learned, this evening, that Gainsborough was aware of Miss Critchley's intention to sue the Vice Chancellor's court for false imprisonment.' He attempted to interrupt but I spoke over him. 'It seems inevitable that he would have apprised his fellow Venatores of the threat, and it may be that, as a result, they chose to silence him before he could be forced to give evidence that might compromise them. If that *is* the case, then Miss Critchley's disappearance, early this morning, suggests that she may be in mortal danger.'

Waddesworth stared at me, brows drawn together. 'You're suggesting that these Venatores *killed* one of their own? You've picked up too many penny dreadfuls in the homes of your paupers, Rice.'

I wasn't going to stand there and be insulted by a man like him. 'If you won't come with me, I'll find Kaye, or failing that, appeal to the

Vice Chancellor to intercede with the city police. I'm not prepared to allow another murder if it's within my power to prevent it.'

For a second or two, I thought he might just call my bluff. But perhaps he saw that I wasn't bluffing.

'Come in,' he instructed. 'Wait there.' I stood in his sitting room while he disappeared to dress. A minute or so later he reappeared suited, shod and gowned.

'Very well, what do you propose?' he asked, his tone a fraction south of sneering.

On my hurried march down from Jericho I'd sketched the outline of a plan in my mind. 'That we visit all known members of the Venatores, ask them what they know about the disappearance of Miss Critchley, and escort them to the police station to be interrogated.'

'The police station?' Waddesworth stared at me. 'What are you thinking of, man? These are members of the University. Kaye and I are the disciplinary officers in this case, not the city police.'

'Don't be a fool, Waddesworth! You and Kaye aren't qualified to deal with this kind of situation. One murder has already been committed – are you prepared to see another?'

'The city police have no jurisdiction—'

I snapped. Every second might be closer to Sarah Critchley's losing her life, and Waddesworth was arguing about protocol. 'I understand that you may feel some sympathy with these boys, Waddesworth, given your treatment of Miss Hammond and your failure to acknowledge your own child—'

Waddesworth lurched towards me, his face livid, and threw a clumsy punch. Learning to box at school had buried instincts deep within me and, as I dodged his fist, I balled my own and launched it at his midriff with all the considerable force of my disgust at his behaviour.

As he doubled over, I grabbed him by the lapels and hauled him upright. 'If you won't help me, I'll arrest these boys myself in the name of the Vice Chancellor. Now, will you do your duty and come with me, or must I go alone?'

Waddesworth pulled himself free and glared at me with loathing as he struggled for breath.

'Have it your way,' he croaked. 'But when we're… hauled up before the Heb… I shall tell them… you claimed Jowett's authority.'

I ignored this schoolboy threat and stared him down. 'We believe there are seven Venatores. We know the identities of five, Gainsborough was a sixth. We can arrest Augustus Vennell before we leave Queen's and take him to the police station en route to Merton. With Herbert in custody, we arrest Haviland and Ashdown. I'm sure one of them can be persuaded to tell us where Montague lives.'

Though I'd met him in Herbert's rooms, I didn't know whether Montague was also a Merton man. Non had suggested that the Venatores might have a 'one member per college' rule and, given that none of the members we'd identified thus far shared a college, I was inclined to think she was right.

—

We marched into Augustus Vennell's room without knocking, to find him entertaining friends. He assumed an outraged reaction for his companions' benefit, but his fear was palpable.

Waddesworth dismissed the revellers and, as soon as the door closed behind them, folded his arms and looked at me. I was clearly to take the initiative and, if necessary, the blame.

'We know you're a member of the Venatores, Mr Vennell. What we don't know,' I said, over his protestations, 'is whether you have anything to do with the disappearance of Miss Sarah Critchley. If you do, it would be very much in your interests to tell us now, before we take you to the police station.'

Vennell ceased his denials and stared at me as if I'd just uttered a profanity. 'The police?' He looked at Waddesworth, clearly expecting him to contradict me.

'A young woman has disappeared,' I said. 'A young woman who had it in her power to do considerable damage to the reputations of anybody associated with your sordid little club. The game is up for you, I'm afraid. Your career at Oxford is over. The best you can do, now, is to tell us what you know and mitigate the consequences of your actions as far as you may.'

Vennell's sleek good looks were somewhat dishevelled and evidence that he and his companions had been drinking stood in the bottles and glasses scattered around the room. So much the better. Inebriation would make it more difficult for him to lie to us.

'Do you know where Sarah Critchley is?' I demanded.

Vennell's eyes shifted from me to the Junior Proctor and back again. He was visibly sobering up, the shock of our entry and the starkness of my warning acting like a plunge into icy water.

'No – I...'

'But you do know who she is?' I demanded.

'Of course. We all saw her at the inquest. Heard her tell those lies about poor Gainsborough. She's got her eyes on a lot of money, hasn't she?' He turned to Waddesworth. 'Are you going to let him insult me like this, Mr Waddesworth? Accuse a gentleman of your own college of associating with a prostitute?'

It was clear that Augustus Vennell was used to getting through life using the tactics outlined in the Venatores' manual. Stout denial. Appeal to a gentleman's honour.

'Do you know where Sarah Critchley is, or what has happened to her?' I demanded. 'Yes or no?'

Vennell raised his chin. 'No.'

And that was all we got out of him. He resorted to silence and would give us no answer as to where we might find John Montague.

We took him up the High to the police station, where I wrote a note to the inspector and asked that it be conveyed to his home immediately. Leaving Vennell in a cell under the watchful eye of a slightly bemused sergeant, we set off for Merton and Laurence Herbert.

Like his co-conspirator, Herbert denied any knowledge of what had happened to Miss Critchley but unlike Vennell, he didn't have the presence of mind to deny being a member of the Venatores. For that reason, I immediately pressed him on where we might find John Montague.

'Montague?' he said, uneasily, his fingertips straying to the scabs on his cheek. 'What's he got to do with this? He wasn't attacked.'

'No. But he was the man whom Sarah Critchley was caught speaking to on the evening she was arrested, and he's also a member of the Venatores,' I said, watching his eyes darting around, looking for a way out of the bind he found himself in. 'You'd do better to tell us,' I warned. 'If Miss Critchley comes to harm because we wasted time trying to find Montague, the court will try you as an accessory.'

Herbert cracked. 'Worcester,' he said. 'Montague's a Worcester man.'

'And the other member?' I demanded. 'We know there are seven of you. Gainsborough's dead, you and Vennell are in custody, we shall shortly apprehend Ashdown, Haviland and Montague. Who's the other?'

Vennell seemed surprised that we knew so much. 'Seven?' he said, sounding genuinely confused.

'Yes. We know about Gainsborough's supper party on the night Ashdown was attacked. There were seven men there. So who's the seventh?'

But this, evidently, was a question too far. Given enough time, Vennell knew we had the means by which to find out which college John Montague belonged to but giving up men as yet unsuspected was a betrayal he was not prepared to commit.

Once we'd deposited him at the police station, I faced something of a dilemma. Should we make our way to Worcester and attempt to apprehend Montague first, or leave him till last, having swept up Ashdown and Haviland from Magdalen and New College respectively?

The presence of Vennell and Herbert in their colleges at curfew suggested one of two scenarios. Either Miss Critchley was being detained by one or two individuals, or she'd been seized and killed, allowing all the Venatores to be back in college where they should be. Montague, as the member who stood to lose most by her testimony seemed the most likely kidnapper, but of the three colleges, Worcester was much the furthest away. And, if Miss Critchley was being held, possibly to be murdered later, then time was of the essence. If Montague had seized her, we needed the other members of the Venatores to tell us where he might be keeping her.

'Right, Magdalen, then New,' I said. 'We can leave Ashdown in the care of the New College porter while we arrest his friend, then take them both down to the police station. Then we'll go to Worcester.'

## Chapter 63

*Non*

When we left Lily's, I suggested that Tarley should come with me. We were minutes away from the University curfew and he'd get back to college more quickly on the Contraption than if he ran. And, to be honest, I needed his company. The thought of what the Hunters might do to Sarah – and the fact that it was my fault – was making me feel physically sick.

We rode down Walton Street with Tarley behind me, standing on the cranks. The warmth of his hands on my shoulders as he kept his balance brought back memories of dancing with him at a ball the previous year – one hand holding mine, the other lightly on the small of my back as we moved together around the dance floor.

'*How can you think about dancing when Sarah Critchley's in mortal danger?*' Hara snapped.

I shivered and felt a cold sweat on the back of my neck.

We passed Worcester College and I turned the steering handles hard to take us round onto Beaumont Street with its tall Georgian houses. These were the kind of homes Cat Hammond might have worked in as a lady's maid if fate hadn't taken her to Headington.

St Giles was almost deserted as we cycled past the rearing spire of the Martyrs' Memorial and the dark, looming bulk of St Mary Magdalen Church, and on to Broad Street. Was Sarah Critchley being kept somewhere in the dark? Or was she already dead? Had my need to wipe the smile off Charles Gainsborough's lying face signed her death warrant?

I pulled across the road and stopped at the end of Turl Street. If Tarley ran down to the High Street and then cut down Alfred Street, he'd be at Corpus in two or three minutes. My watch showed nine o'clock but the clock at Christ Church ran on sun time, so the curfew bell wouldn't start ringing for five minutes yet.

Tarley climbed down from the Contraption, and as he took his hands away, my shoulders felt bare and cold.

'It doesn't feel right,' he said, 'going back to college when we don't know what's happening.'

'There's nothing you can do.' That came out more abruptly than I'd intended. I took a breath and started again. 'Basil's gone for the Hunters we already know about and, hopefully, Cat Hammond will be able to give us the last name—'

'But what if Miss Hammond has information about where Sarah Critchley might be?'

It was a good point. If the Hunters had killed Gainsborough, I'd be foolish to go up against them on my own.

I shivered. 'All right, come to Bath Place with me. You can wait outside while I speak to Cat Hammond.'

## Chapter 64

*Basil*

Though Harcourt Ashdown had been every bit as shocked and outraged as his fellow Venatores at being arrested, he'd been considerably less cowed.

'Mr Waddesworth, Mr Rice, let me repeat – I am not a member of the club you're investigating,' he had stated firmly, 'therefore I can't answer your questions.'

I could only hope that Piers Haviland would prove an easier nut to crack.

When we arrived at New College to take Haviland into custody, we found the college gates firmly closed. Before I could take action, Waddesworth thudded his fist on the wicket. 'Open in the name of the proctors!' Following our interruption of Vennell's little soirée, he'd obviously decided that ceding the initiative to me didn't become a proctor, and on entering the other men's rooms he'd immediately seized control.

We heard bolts being withdrawn and the wicket gate swung open.

'What is it, Mr Waddesworth?' the porter asked.

'We need to speak with Piers Haviland,' Waddesworth said. 'Be so good as to take us to his rooms, please.'

Carrying his lamp so that both his way and ours were lit, the porter guided us through the college and up a staircase in the new buildings on Holywell Street.

However, bang on Haviland's door as he might, the porter could elicit no response and, on gaining entry to the set, we found it cold and dark.

Using the porter's lamp, Waddesworth and I searched the well-furnished study-cum-sitting room and Haviland's bedroom to no avail. The rooms were empty.

Jesus College undergraduates were not, on the whole, the sons of rich men, and most bought the furniture in their rooms from their predecessors. Haviland, however, had furnished his rooms from scratch. Every stick of furniture was in the latest style and bore few signs of wear.

Waddesworth turned to the porter, who was loitering around the set's outer door as if he was afraid to sully Haviland's rugs with his plebeian feet. 'Do you know where Mr Haviland might be?' he asked. 'Has he any particular friends in college?'

'I couldn't say, sir.'

Couldn't, or wouldn't? We knew that the Venatores had bribed the porters at both New Inn Hall and Charsley's. Perhaps the porters at their own colleges had been given similar inducements to keep their activities quiet if the proctors came asking.

'We're investigating the murder of a Trinity College undergraduate and the disappearance of a young woman,' I said, holding up the lamp to illuminate both my face and his reaction. 'So, if it's been made worth your while to say nothing about Mr Haviland's associates, you might wish to reconsider. The law takes a very dim view of people who withhold evidence.'

The porter's face took on a closed, resentful look. 'You've no call to speak to me like that, sir. I've told you nothing but the truth. Mr Haviland seems on good terms with everybody, but I've never noticed him being particularly friendly with any other gentleman in college.'

Once more I was thrown back on Non's surmise that the Venatores might confine themselves to one member per college. How did they know each other, these depraved young men? Montague and Herbert had been at school together – had they all been schoolmates?

There was nothing further to be achieved here, but as Waddesworth and I moved towards the door, we heard footsteps coming up the staircase and I drew the Junior Proctor back into the room, leaving the porter standing on the threshold.

'Quaid,' a voice said, 'what are you doing?'

'Evening, Mr Haviland, sir,' the porter replied. 'Mr Waddesworth wanted a word.'

'So you saw fit to let him into my room when I wasn't here?'

Waddesworth took the lamp from me and stepped forward. 'Mr Quaid was acting under my instructions.' He dismissed the porter and indicated that Haviland should step into his own rooms.

'Where have you been?' I demanded.

For a moment, I thought the boy would tell me it was none of my business; his face wore that mask of arrogant resentfulness that I'd seen on our previous meeting. But, probably aware that appearing too defensive would increase our suspicions, he composed himself. 'One of the chaps at dinner invited a few of us for a post-prandial glass in his rooms.'

I stepped up to his side and took a deep breath through my nose. 'You smell of cold air, Mr Haviland. You've been outside for some time.'

He looked at me without a flicker of concern. 'I took a turn around the garden before coming back.'

'In the pitch dark?'

He smiled tightly. 'Young eyes, Mr Rice.'

'The name and staircase number of your friend?' I asked.

Haviland held my eye for a full three seconds, and I felt the intensity of his restrained fury before he turned to address Waddesworth. However, the Junior Proctor forestalled him. 'Answer Mr Rice's question, if you please.'

Haviland stared at him, then gave a small shrug. 'Anderson,' he said, in a tone that almost achieved nonchalance. 'Main quad, staircase three.'

'Would you speak to Mr Anderson, please, Waddesworth?' I asked. 'He'll be obliged to answer questions from you and time is of the essence.'

Without a word, Waddesworth turned on his heel and left, taking the lantern with him. Haviland closed the door and, in the sudden dark, took a box of matches from a little table immediately inside the door and proceeded to ignore me while he lit the room's lamps and candles.

As he applied a taper to the final candles on the mantelpiece, I decided that I'd indulged his silence long enough.

'Three of your fellow Venatores have already been taken into police custody,' I said. Shock flashed over his features before he realised that I was watching his reflection in the mirror.

'You mentioned that society when we first met,' he said, his voice apparently untroubled and his hand steady. 'I'm afraid I'm no wiser about it now than I was then. Why have these men been taken into custody?'

'Miss Sarah Critchley is missing. We think one of you – if not all of you – know where she is.'

Haviland extinguished the taper, removed his gown and hung it on the back of the door. It was a defiant gesture. It announced that, while others might have been weak enough to allow themselves to be taken into custody, Piers Haviland would remain where he was.

I had the sudden, very distinct impression that this was a performance. Or, more accurately, a game. One that, perhaps, the Venatores had been playing ever since they came up to Oxford.

Heavy footfalls sounded on the staircase and, seconds later, a panting Waddesworth reappeared.

'Mr Anderson proved to be absent from his rooms,' he said, his eyes on Haviland. 'So wherever you were, you weren't with him.'

'Perhaps he also went for a stroll?' Haviland suggested, sitting down in a leather-upholstered armchair next to the cold grate. 'It can be dreadfully annoying, being in all evening after nine. Men like us are used to coming and going in London. It's irksome to be treated like children and ushered to bed.'

'Nobody has been in that room for at least an hour. The lamps were cold and the candles hard.'

Haviland's response was not marked, but I had the impression that he was surprised at Waddesworth's thoroughness.

'Kindly get up and put your gown on,' I said. 'You'll accompany us to the police station. Unless, that is, you wish to tell us where Sarah Critchley is?'

Haviland didn't stir from his chair. 'You can't hand me over to the police, I'm a member of the University.'

Waddesworth strode to his side, seized his arm and yanked him bodily from the chair. 'You're under a common misapprehension, Mr Haviland. The proctors may deal with all disciplinary matters relating to undergraduates, but murder and kidnap go far beyond disciplinary offences. Murder is a capital offence.'

Haviland shook him off, his anger now very apparent. 'You should think very carefully before doing this, Mr Waddesworth...'

Striding past Haviland, I unhooked his gown from the back of the door and threw it at him. 'Do as the Junior Proctor says. Put it on.'

'You'll regret this.' Haviland's voice was hard. 'My father has the ear of Members of the Cabinet.'

'Then he'll be all the more embarrassed,' I said, 'when his son is thrown out of the University and tried for murder.'

## Chapter 65

*Non*

Tarley and I didn't have time to waste, so I just knocked on the first door in Bath Place, asked which house belonged to Cat Hammond and went straight there.

'Miss Vaughan,' she said, when she saw me on her doorstep. She looked past me and raised her eyebrows. 'And Mr Askew, too.'

'We need your help,' I said. 'It's urgent. Sarah Critchley's missing.'

Without speaking, Cat turned and pushed her front door open so that we could see into the little front room. A small figure was sitting, hunched in on herself, on the sofa in the corner. Her arms folded, Sarah Critchley's hands were gripping her elbows as if she was trying to hold her body together.

I was relieved to see her alive, but something was very obviously wrong. I looked at Cat for an explanation. She invited me in with a tilt of her head that didn't include Tarley.

'I'll wait outside,' he said.

'No, go back to college. I'll see you tomorrow.' Whatever had happened to Sarah, he wasn't going to help matters by being there.

He hesitated. 'Shouldn't I find Rice and tell him?'

'No. I don't want anything to stop him rounding up the Hunters. I'll go to the police station later. Hopefully they'll have all of them under arrest by then.'

Tarley nodded once, then left.

'What happened?' I asked Cat.

She closed the door and looked over her shoulder at Sarah. 'She's still terrified,' she said, under her breath. 'She thought he was going to kill her, but she managed to get away.'

'Who? Who took her?'

Cat shook her head. 'I don't know. She's only been here a matter of minutes.'

Much as I wanted to know who was responsible for whatever had happened to Sarah, I could see that now wasn't the time for questions. 'Shall I go and fetch her mother?'

Cat raised her eyebrows. 'Do you know where they live?'

'I do.'

—

All the way to Cranham Street, Sarah's hunched silence was in my mind.

Cat might not know who'd taken her, who'd hurt her and terrorised her, but I was sure.

Montague.

It must have been.

He knew she'd identified him at the inquest. Tarley and I had watched Basil approach her, knowing what he was going to ask. And there'd been a moment when Montague had turned and seen them staring at him.

So, from then on, John Montague had known two things. Firstly that Sarah was intending to sue the Vice Chancellor's court for false imprisonment. And secondly, that his false name wasn't going to protect him now. He would, inevitably, be called to give evidence in support of her lawsuit.

Montague could call Sarah Critchley's word into question all he liked; he could deny being a member of the Venatores till he was blue in the face; but when the court proceedings were published in the *Pall Mall Gazette*, mud would stick. And John Montague knew that.

Between us, Basil and I had put a target on Sarah's back.

'*Don't blame Basil,*' Hara snapped. '*He didn't know you'd been stupid enough to tell Gainsborough about the court case.*'

I didn't try and defend myself. We both knew she was right.

The Critchleys' landlady looked worried when she saw a stranger standing on her doorstep.

'Can I speak to Mrs Critchley, please?' I asked before she could say anything.

'Is it about Sarah?'

I nodded. 'We've found her. She's safe.' I wasn't actually sure about that. But she was alive, at least.

Sarah's mother, who'd come down the passage after the landlady, almost collapsed with relief. She clutched at the door jamb. 'Thank you, miss! Where is she? Did the proctors take her again? I told her not to think about going against the University in court. I told her they wouldn't stand for it—'

'No,' I interrupted. 'This is nothing to do with the proctors. Sarah's with a friend. But she needs you.' I waited while Mrs Critchley looked at me in confusion, taking in what I'd said.

'What friend?'

I glanced at the landlady, who was all ears. 'She can introduce herself when we get there. Can you come with me, now?'

Sarah's mother ducked back into the house for a shawl which she wrapped around her shoulders.

As I put my hands on the Contraption, she said, 'I'm not going on that thing!'

'No,' I said. 'I'll push it. But I can't leave it here. I need it with me.'

In boys' clothes, I'd back myself in a running race against any man. But in a dress I was at a disadvantage. The Contraption evened things up.

All the way down Cranham Street and on to Walton Street, Mrs Critchley was silent. It wasn't until we passed the monumental buildings of the University Press that she asked, 'What happened to my Sarah today?'

I sighed. She'd been bound to ask, and from the sound of her voice she was pretty sure she wasn't going to like the answer. 'I don't exactly know,' I said.

'I *told* her no good would come of people like us going against the University,' she said, again. 'And, to tell you the truth, miss, I never really saw any good coming of her walking out with that Gordon Smythe either. But she wouldn't be told. She'd just say, "You don't know him, Mum. He's different. You'll see."' She sighed. 'That's my Sarah all over, that is. Always been the same. Even when she was a little girl, you could never keep her down. She was like one of those jack-in-a-boxes – always springing up, whatever happened. I don't know where she gets it from. I'm not like that and neither was her poor dad, God rest him.'

Would that jack-in-a-box spirit survive? Would Sarah be strong enough to go through everything a court case would put in her path? Or would whatever horrors Montague had subjected her to make sure that she kept quiet?

If she did, it would be nobody's fault but mine.

## Chapter 66

*Basil*

When our foray to Worcester College in search of John Montague revealed only another set of cold and unoccupied rooms, Waddesworth and I returned to the police station. There we looked on as Inspector Newman interrogated the four members of the Venatores whom we had managed to apprehend.

We'd hoped that, by separating them, one of the group would break ranks. But, it seemed, we'd hoped in vain. Despite the application of such pressure as Newman felt able to bring to bear on young men whose families had influence enough to see him removed from office, they all maintained the same line: they were not members of a club, they barely knew each other, they didn't, therefore, know the whereabouts of John Montague and they had nothing to do with the disappearance of Miss Critchley.

'You can't possibly have any evidence against me,' Harcourt Ashdown maintained. 'And I fear it reflects very badly on you, Junior Proctor, that you would assent to my arrest on nothing more than the word of a girl who is a known prostitute.'

'But we have evidence, Mr Ashdown,' I said. 'We have the invitation which was pinned to the hood placed over your head. An invitation to a Venatores dinner at Trinity on the evening of your attack. On that very same evening, Charles Gainsborough of Trinity College ordered a supper party for seven in his rooms.'

'Bully for Gainsborough. Perhaps being a member of this club is what got him killed. But it's nothing to do with me.'

I ignored him. 'We have identified five other members by dint of each being an observer of Gainsborough's amorous activities with Miss Sarah Critchley, as per the rule in the Venatores' manual that conquests must be observed. Four of those men, including you, Mr Ashdown, were hooded and dumped outside their colleges, suggesting that somebody other than the proctors and I were aware of your activities.'

Ashdown showed not a flicker of unease. 'I'm becoming tired of repeating myself, Mr Rice. I am *not a member of this club*.'

Ashdown was returned to the cells where the presence of a constable in the corridor outside the bolted doors would prevent any exchange of information between the Venatores, and Inspector Newman invited Waddesworth and me into his office.

'With a bit of luck,' he said, 'a night in the cells will loosen their tongues.'

Waddesworth looked uncomfortable. 'I'm not sure that's wise. We have no actual evidence of wrongdoing. It's all hearsay. And these young men have powerful families. I think we should consult the Senior Proctor and the Vice Chancellor.'

'Please feel free to inform Reverend Kaye and Reverend Jowett if that's what you think is best, Mr Waddesworth,' Newman said, 'but their opinion won't change my mind.'

Waddesworth made no further comment but took his leave, presumably to wait until Kaye returned from his patrol to report to him.

Inspector Newman eased himself into a chair, indicating that I should do likewise, and proceeded to fill his pipe.

'Even with the four we've got in custody,' he said after a minute or so, 'I'm still concerned for Miss Critchley. If you're right, Mr Rice, there are still two members of this club out there – Montague and the seventh man who was at that Trinity dinner.'

I nodded, and was about to speak when I heard Non's voice in the outer office. With a glance at the inspector, who nodded his permission, I rose to open the door to her.

'Good,' she said, without preamble, 'you're still here. I've found Sarah Critchley. She's at Cat Hammond's house.'

'What on earth is she doing there?'

'She went there after she'd escaped from the room Montague had locked her in.' Non's voice was tight.

'So it *was* Montague who took her?' the inspector asked.

Non turned to him. 'Yes. He was waiting for her on George Street as she went to work. He said he wanted to talk to her, that he was sorry for not coming forward when she was hauled up in front of the Vice Chancellor's court. Gave her some cock-and-bull story about wanting to make it up to her, said he'd give evidence in court if she went ahead with her case against the University.'

Having observed Montague at close quarters in Herbert's room, I could imagine just how convincing he'd been. But, surely, after all Gainsborough's deceptions, and after everything she'd heard at the inquest, Miss Critchley hadn't been persuaded to believe him?

'She heard him out,' Non continued, 'then said she had to get to work and started to walk away. That was when one of the others came out of the woodwork. Piers Haviland, from her description. He must have been watching, waiting for some signal from Montague. She couldn't run from them and before she could even cry out, they'd hustled her into a building on Sewy's Lane.'

Sewy's Lane was an ancient, narrow little thoroughfare where a smithy and various other indeterminate industrial buildings were located, and which gave access to a labyrinth of yards, mercantile premises and houses between New Inn Hall Street and the Cornmarket.

'She was terrified, but she didn't dare shout for help because Montague told her that with two gentlemen present and one whore – that was the word he used – no one was going to take notice of the whore.'

I swallowed, repelled both by Montague's words and by what I feared Non was going to tell me next.

'Did they—' I faltered before bracing myself. Non wouldn't be impressed by pusillanimity, nor Miss Critchley helped. 'Was she violated?'

Non's face was hard. 'Yes.' She paused and I saw her swallow. Perhaps she, too, had had the urge to vomit.

'They locked her in the room by herself afterwards, and, eventually, she managed to escape.'

I couldn't look at Non. Could hardly bear the shame of being a man, of possessing the same anatomy as Miss Critchley's rapists.

'What—' My mouth was so dry that my voice caught in my throat, and I had to work up some saliva before I could continue. 'What was their aim in taking her? Not just to...' I couldn't say the word, but Non had no such compunctions.

'The rape was a warning. It was made very clear to her that if she tried to go to the police, it would happen again,' she said, her eyes cold. 'And if she pursued her suit against the Vice Chancellor's court, the consequences would be the same.' She swallowed. 'They told her they could take her off the streets whenever they liked and that nobody would stop them.' Non's fury moved from me to Newman. 'And they're right, aren't they? Nobody'd believe her if she went to the police. Not when she's been in prison for soliciting.'

She was right. Sarah Critchley could expect no justice. Without corroboration, no jury would convict undergraduates of such a thing. Even with corroboration, it was unlikely. Sarah's reputation had been ruined by her conviction in the Vice Chancellor's court, and her credibility with it.

'The only way we can get justice for her,' Non concluded, 'is by finding evidence that the Venatores conspired to murder Charles Gainsborough.'

'And how do you propose to go about that, Miss Vaughan?' Newman asked.

'I don't know. But we have to find out who the seventh man at that Hunters' dinner was.'

## Chapter 67

*Non*

It was late when I left the police station, but I had to speak to Cat Hammond again. By the time I'd got Mrs Critchley down to Bath Place, Cat had managed to persuade Sarah to tell her what had happened, and as I'd listened to her explaining it all, quietly, to Mrs Critchley I knew that wasn't the time to start asking Cat about the seventh member of the Hunters, so I'd left them to it.

But now that most of the other Hunters were in custody, I was worried that Montague and the seventh man might hide or destroy crucial evidence. And, if I'm honest, I didn't want to give that anonymous member the chance to get away scot free. I wanted him in the cells with the rest of them.

So I climbed onto the Contraption and cycled back to Cat's house.

The night seemed darker now. The ragged clouds that had flitted across the sky all evening, playing now you see them, now you don't with the stars, had slowed and piled up as midnight fell, blotting out moon and starlight.

I chained the Contraption up and slipped from the gaslight of Holywell Street into the shadowy little alleyway that led to Bath Place.

As I moved carefully down the cobbled alley, waiting for my eyes to adjust to the lack of street lights, I heard the sound of a door opening.

I ducked quickly into the shadow of a protruding gable end and peered around it. A small patch of light spilled from an open door. Two figures were leaving Cat Hammond's house. Cat herself, holding a candle lamp, and the dark shape of a man behind her.

Without speaking, they walked away from me, towards the Turf.

After a few seconds, I followed them. Though Cat's lamp led me on like the glow of a corpse candle, there was a pool of darkness between us and I couldn't see where I was putting my feet, so I had to go carefully.

As I passed Cat's house, I saw a faint glow around the shutters. Sarah and her mother were still in there. I wasn't surprised. Sarah'd been in no state to walk home.

The light ahead disappeared as Cat and her companion turned a corner and Bath Place was instantly sunk into darkness. A sound behind me made me whip round, ready to kick and punch. But a hand covered my mouth.

'It's me,' a man's voice murmured in my ear.

Tarley. Not somebody I had to fight off. But my heart hadn't got that message yet. It was pumping fit to drown a fire.

He took his hand away. 'Who were you following?' he asked, softly.

'Cat Hammond. And a man.' I was glad to see him. With Tarley here, I was on an equal footing with Cat and her unidentified companion. 'I have to talk to her,' I said.

He didn't hesitate. 'Off we go, then.'

We slunk down Bath Place, our hands out in front of us lest we bump into anything.

It's not easy to walk quietly when everything around you is still and silent and you're effectively blind. Distances feel much greater when you can't see to judge them. It seemed to take whole minutes to get to the corner where Cat's lamp had disappeared, though in reality it must only have been a few seconds. The noise our boots made on the damp, gritty cobbles seemed bound to give us away, but when we caught sight of Cat's lamp again up ahead, neither she nor her companion turned around. Left and right they turned, and we found ourselves in one of the courtyards that belonged to the Turf Tavern. Light from the unshuttered windows spilled out and Tarley and I shrank back into the shadows.

Basil had seen Cat Hammond in the Turf – was that where she and the man were going? No. They ignored the tavern and carried on through to the next courtyard. The one that led to St Helen's Passage.

As the light from Cat's lamp disappeared down the tiny alleyway out of the courtyard and into St Helen's Passage, I pulled Tarley back slightly. They'd hear us for certain if we followed too closely.

Cautiously, we stuck our heads around the corner where the passage widened into a narrow court. Cat and her companion were just disappearing through a doorway.

My instinct was to follow them. Reason told me to wait.

Tarley was so close behind me that I could feel the condensation of his breath on my neck. He was breathing quickly. I wondered if his heart was thumping against his ribs, like mine.

The place where we were standing stank, as if all the men who drank in the Turf emptied their beer-filled bladders here before heading home. I started breathing through my mouth but stopped when the smell seemed to settle on my tongue.

'Before the light disappeared,' Tarley murmured in my ear, 'I saw something in the corner. Something covered in tarpaulin.'

'Show me.'

He reached for my hand and, blindly, we shuffled as quietly as we could towards whatever it was he'd seen. Fortunately for us, the tarpaulin wasn't tied down, just draped, and Tarley heaved it up so that we could try and feel what was there.

But feeling was unnecessary. With the tarpaulin off there was the unmistakeable smell of coal ash and cinders.

'It's a dust cart,' I said.

Most of Oxford's dust carts were horse-drawn and clopped about the streets from morning to night, but a few small ones like this were trundled around the city's little courts and yards by hand.

Just then, the door that had closed behind Cat Hammond opened again.

We ducked down quickly behind the dust cart.

I peered through the shafts. In the light of Cat's lamp, I could see that the man at her side had something over his shoulder. As they came closer and the flickering lamplight was stronger, that something resolved itself into the shape of a man, dangling boots roped together at the ankles.

Cat's companion looked up, like a dog scenting a kill. 'Who pulled the canvas off?'

Cat moved forward with the lamp. It was a matter of seconds till she saw us, so I stood up.

'Who have you got here, Cat?' I asked, marching around so I could see the face of the unconscious man.

I don't know why, but it was a shock to see that he was hooded.

Before Cat could stop me, I whipped the bloodstained hood off. Underneath was a battered and mutilated face. In the light of Cat's lamp, I could see blood dripping from savage knife cuts sliced into his face.

'John Montague?' I asked. To be honest, it was a guess. Somebody'd made a bit of a mess of him and, for all I could see, it might as well be our unknown seventh man.

Cat held her lamp up. 'I underestimated you. Should have known better, shouldn't I?'

She obviously thought I'd been hanging about, keeping watch, after I'd left Mrs Critchley at her house. I wasn't going to tell her otherwise. It would be all to the good if she thought I knew more than I did.

'The business about Sarah escaping and running to you,' I said. 'That was all nonsense, wasn't it? You found her and rescued her. And gave this one a hiding in the process.'

Cat didn't reply.

'How did you find her? Apart from us and her mother, nobody knew she'd even been taken.'

The man moved restlessly at her side. 'We jus' gonna stand 'ere natterin', or what?'

Cat angled her head in the direction of the cart. 'Stick him in there. He must be getting heavy.'

' 'S'not that. It's just—'

She silenced him with a hand on his arm. 'It's all right, Frank. I'll sort this. I know Miss Vaughan. She's not going to turn us in.' She looked at me. 'Are you?'

Two could play at will-I-answer-or-will-I-not and I watched Frank – presumably Frank Dodds – pull the tarpaulin back over the cart, dump an unresponsive Montague none too gently onto it, then fold the canvas over him.

'Is he dead?' I asked.

Cat shook her head. 'No. But he's not going to look very pretty for a while.'

'Not ever,' I corrected. 'Not with RAPIST cut into his face.'

This time, the word had been sliced into the flesh where a beard would never cover it. John Montague would have to wear stage make-up for the rest of his life.

'You don't think he deserves it?' Cat asked, in a voice which defied me to say no.

'Did I say that?'

Everybody in that stinking little courtyard knew that this was the only justice Sarah Critchley was ever likely to get for what had happened to her. 'I assume you're going to dump him outside Worcester?'

Cat gave a single nod. 'Nobody thinks twice about a man pushing a dust cart home at the end of a long day.'

All the hooded men bar one had been found by the proctors at the end of their evening's rounds, so the dust cart was probably what had transported all of them. The exception was Charles Gainsborough, whose body hadn't been found till first light.

'Did you kill Gainsborough?' I asked.

'What would you do if I said yes?' Cat asked.

'Cat!' Frank Dodds protested.

She motioned him to be quiet. At my side, Tarley was silent, but I could feel the tension coming off him.

'That might be less easy to turn a blind eye to,' I said. 'Humiliating the Hunters, marking them for life, even – I can let that go. An eye for an eye. But killing somebody—'

'Louise Mander's dead because of them,' she spat. 'Laurence Herbert was responsible for that just as surely as if he'd held her under the water himself.'

I nodded. 'I won't argue with that. So I'll ask you again. Did you kill Charles Gainsborough? You or one of the men you've got spying for you?'

She laughed then, and it was the most unexpected sound in that rank little courtyard. 'You're a fine one to talk about men spying for you when Mr Askew runs around doing your bidding.' She gave me a half-smile, the kind of smile she might have given me if we'd just been two women, alone. 'You should marry him, Rhiannon,' she said. 'You'll never find a better, truer man, and a woman like you is going to need a man. By yourself, you'll never be taken seriously. You'll just be another unregulated woman.'

She couldn't have floored me more if she'd stepped forward and punched me on the nose.

'But to answer your question, no, we didn't kill Charles Gainsborough.' She sucked in a deep breath. 'Right. Are you going to let us get on? It's late.'

'On one condition.'

She waited.

'That you tell me who the seventh member of the Venatores is.'

She cocked her head at me. 'There is no seventh member – there are only six.'

'But there were seven men at the supper party at Trinity. The one whose invitation you pinned to Ashdown's hood.'

Her eyes caught the lamp's light as she looked at me. 'The seventh man wasn't a member of the Venatores. He's got nothing to do with this.'

'Then who was he?'

She glanced at Frank Dodds. 'It's a long story, and we've got things to see to,' she said. 'Come and see me tomorrow afternoon. We can have tea.'

## Chapter 68

*Basil*

The Jesus College porter was scandalised when he found Non banging on the gates after midnight.

'Can you come and speak to her, Mr Rice?' he said. 'She seems quite agitated.'

I doubted the accuracy of that description, but nevertheless I donned my cap and followed him. I'd still been up and dressed when he knocked, having found myself absolutely unequal to the notion of simply going to bed after the events and revelations of the evening. I had wrapped myself in my gown, seated myself before my cold hearth, and drunk sherry. Intrusive thoughts of Miss Critchley's ordeal had required an anaesthetic – or, more accurately, something to induce amnesia.

When I reached the lodge, Non was standing next to her tricycle outside the wicket gate.

'There's been another hooding,' she said. 'Montague.'

–

Non had roused the Worcester College porter to ensure that the unconscious Montague would be removed from his slumped position in front of the gates and receive medical attention.

'Not that he deserves it,' she said, as we made our way to Magdalen to rouse the Senior Proctor, 'but at least if the doctor comes to him, he won't be able to abscond.'

'You were convinced there'd be no more hoodings after you'd spoken to Miss Hammond,' I replied. 'Does this mean you were wrong, that she wasn't responsible?'

Non stopped in her tracks and stared at me. 'After what happened to Sarah wouldn't *you* have wanted to punish Montague?'

I would, of course. However, if his victim had been a relative of mine, I would have had recourse to the law. Miss Critchley and Miss Hammond would believe that they did not. Not when the men responsible were so far above them in status.

'Montague's lucky that you had to pass Worcester on your way home,' I said. 'He might have come to even more harm if you hadn't found him.'

Non gave a snort that indicated how little she cared about Montague's coming to harm. 'It was the people who taught him a lesson I was concerned about, not him. Wouldn't want them to have a death on their conscience.'

As we passed the entrance to Queen's Lane a question emerged in my alcohol-befuddled brain. 'If Cat Hammond and whoever is working with her didn't kill Montague after what he did to Miss Critchley, then it seems unlikely that they killed Gainsborough either, doesn't it?'

'I agree. Which makes it far more likely that the Hunters did. Or one of them at least.'

As we reached Magdalen's gate, Non climbed onto her tricycle. 'Best if I leave this to you. I'll see you tomorrow. Come for breakfast.'

–

Though the Worcester College porter was displeased by the appearance of yet more nocturnal visitors to college he couldn't refuse admission to the proctors. 'I didn't expect anybody more tonight,' he said as he admitted us. 'The doctor's with Mr Montague now. So's the dean.'

I followed Kaye – and Waddesworth, whom we'd collected at Queen's – through the gates. I felt curiously bereft without Non at my side, though she'd been wise to absent herself. Worcester's dean and Provost wouldn't welcome the presence of anybody but University men in the discussions that would now be necessary.

'You trust me to fight Miss Critchley's corner?' I'd asked as Non turned the Contraption around, very aware of how often my divided loyalties had prevented me from doing as she would do.

Non had looked at me quizzically. 'Of course.'

Two words had scarcely ever meant more to me, and I followed the proctors, determined to do battle if I must.

We found Worcester's Provost, William Inge, in conference with the dean, who'd just returned from Montague's rooms. Inge was fully dressed and gowned, not only out of deference to the seriousness of the situation but also to the temperature in his study. The grate was cold and the embers grey. Worcester's head of house was not a career academic and didn't sit late into the evening at his books. He'd only been appointed two years before and was still finding his feet as far as University politics was concerned. I had no doubt that, until tonight, he'd thanked providence that none of his own undergraduates had been victims of the hooding attacks, with all the speculation that entailed.

'We hadn't anticipated a visit from you until tomorrow, gentlemen,' he said as we were shown into his study. 'Mr Montague is hardly in a fit state to furnish you with any information about what happened to him.'

'Unfortunately, Inge,' Kaye said, 'we're not here to discuss the attack on Montague but his own alleged assault on a young woman.'

At that point, the Senior Proctor turned to me and indicated that I should take the floor. As I leaned forward to begin, I caught a glimpse of a photographic portrait of a young man in the BA gown and hood. Of course, Inge had sons – and daughters, too. How much more shocking would that make what I had to tell him?

I gave the Provost a brief outline of my investigation into the hoodings before progressing to Gainsborough's murder and the events of this evening, couching my account in the least offensive language possible while ensuring that the Provost remained in no doubt as to the atrocity that had been committed against Miss Critchley. As he listened, Inge seemed to withdraw into himself. He was a thin, ascetic-looking man, the flesh of whose high-cheekboned face seemed to sag into his long, dark beard. He moved his head from side to side in sorrow and confusion as I concluded my account.

'These Venatores,' he said, 'why has nobody stopped them? If you knew about them, Kaye, why were they allowed to persist in this bestial, amoral fashion?'

'Every man whom we suspected of being a member was approached,' I replied, in our collective defence, 'but our evidence was either circumstantial or based on the word of a person no court would take seriously when weighed against apparently upstanding young men.'

'Do you propose to take Montague to be interrogated by the police inspector?' the dean asked.

'We'll consult Inspector Newman and follow his advice,' I said, looking from Kaye to Waddesworth lest they demur. 'In the meantime, we would like to speak to Montague now, please.'

'I'm afraid that's quite impossible,' the dean said. 'The doctor has administered a sedative. He's barely conscious.'

I sighed in frustration. 'Very well, we will return first thing in the morning. Montague will, doubtless, appeal to his family to come and take him home at the earliest possible opportunity. However, I must ask that he not be allowed to leave the college until Inspector Newman has had the opportunity to interrogate him. Also, that nothing should be removed from his rooms until the proctors and I have searched them tomorrow.'

'Search his rooms?' the dean asked, his distress at all he'd been obliged to listen to emerging as tetchiness. 'What on earth for?'

'Any evidence that can connect him with the murder of Charles Gainsborough,' I said. 'We shall be searching all the Venatores' rooms before they are released from custody.'

## Chapter 69

*Non*

First thing the following morning, the cocky young Jesus College messenger turned up at my door, with a note from Basil.

> *Dear Non,*
> *I'm afraid I'm unable to come for breakfast as I'm searching Venatores' rooms, then summoned to see Jowett. I'll come to Shene Road, when possible, later today.*
> *B.R.*

'Not like Mr Rice to use us for private messages,' the boy said, grinning as I read the note.

I gave him a look which had brought cockier lads than him to heel. 'For your information, this is *University* business. But I'm sure it'll interest Mr Rice to know that you speak ill of senior members when you're officially representing Jesus College.'

'Oh, now, steady on, miss! I didn't mean anything by it.'

I glared at him. 'Yes, you did. You were after gossip. That's not something Mr Chambers would approve of, is it?'

At the mention of the senior Jesus College messenger, he looked panicked. 'I'm sorry, miss, truly. I forgot myself, is all. Comes of seeing a pretty face – turned my head, it did.'

'And now you're flirting on duty. Shame on you.'

I knew he'd write me off as a shrew, but I didn't care. His attitude was too much like the Hunters' for comfort.

'Wait there,' I said, 'while I write a reply.'

I shut the door on him and went up to my room where I scribbled a quick note telling Basil that I'd be in the Golden Cross hotel taking coffee from two o'clock and he could find me there if he was free. 'If not,' I wrote, 'come for supper.'

When I opened the door, Mr Cocky was standing exactly where I'd left him. I gave him the note, which I'd sealed, and sent him on his way.

While I waited for Basil at the Golden Cross, I could make a start on writing up the first instalment of a series Stead was keen to publish on the hunt for the Venatores.

—

Three hours later I was cycling to the AEW's rooms on St Giles to give a lecture.

I wondered whether Basil and the proctors had found anything incriminating in the Hunters' rooms. Whatever Cat said, seeing Frank Dodds pushing a handcart with a body in it last night had made me wonder whether he had been responsible for Gainsborough's death after all.

'*Frank Dodds doesn't wear a signet ring,*' Hara pointed out.

I thought of his hands, gripping John Montague's legs at the knee as the rapist lay unconscious over his shoulder. '*True.*'

'*And anyway, Frank Dodds is vouched for, isn't he? By the other brewery worker.*'

He was. But it wasn't what I'd call a watertight alibi. Maybe the man who'd vouched for him had a daughter who'd been picked up by one of the Hunters. That might persuade the most honest of men to lie if he thought the guilty were getting their just deserts.

But all thoughts of Frank Dodds went out of my mind as I ran up the stairs at the AEW's rooms straight into Mrs Bertha Johnson, Lady Secretary to the AEW board. She'd obviously been waiting for me.

'Miss Vaughan, good morning. Perhaps you'd be good enough to step into the office for a few moments? There's something we need to discuss.'

*Something we need to discuss?* That didn't sound encouraging. But as usual Mrs Johnson's well-bred face was giving nothing away.

'I'm scheduled to give a lecture in five minutes,' I said.

'This takes precedence, I'm afraid.'

I followed her up a further flight of stairs to the modest room which did duty as an office. Mrs Johnson ushered me in, and I sat down in front of the small desk. There wasn't any other furniture, but the floorboards were covered in an old, but still beautiful, carpet and the walls had been hung with Oxford prints and photographs of the first students at Somerville and Lady Margaret Hall.

Mrs Johnson sat behind the desk, her back straight, her hands quiet in her lap. 'Miss Vaughan, the board has been informed that you were recently observed on the streets after dark, unchaperoned, in the company of two young men. Not only that, but you were dressed in male attire. Is this, in fact, the case, or has somebody been mistaken?'

Waddesworth. It had to be him who'd told the board. He'd seen me in boys' clothes at Merton, and then he'd heard me give evidence at the inquest that I'd been one of the people who found Laurence Herbert. I might as well have taken out an advertisement in the *Oxford Journal* that said 'Non Vaughan goes out at night dressed in boys' clothes'.

'Yes,' I admitted, 'both those things are true. Though, to be fair to me, one of the young men is a cousin of mine.' Which was true, up to a point. Lily was my second cousin once removed, so I wasn't sure exactly what kind of cousin that made Albie, but we were definitely related.

'And the other young man?'

'He's been helping Mr Rice in his investigations into the hooding attacks.' That was true as well, but the look I got from Bertha Johnson told me she suspected it wasn't the *whole* truth.

'Your testimony at Charles Gainsborough's inquest indicated that you had seen his body,' she said. 'Is that also the case?' I could tell she was finding this difficult. The thought of a young lady – and that was how she'd think of me, however I thought of myself – voluntarily examining the corpse of a brutally murdered man would be deeply shocking to somebody like Mrs Johnson. It occurred to me just to take out my resignation letter there and then and save her a lot of discomfort, but I restrained myself. Part of me wanted to see what she'd do with the information she thought it was her duty to extract from me.

'Mr Rice wanted my opinion on the knots used to bind Charles Gainsborough,' I said. 'He suspected that they weren't the same as those that had been used on the other hooded men. As you know, I have sailing experience and I'm well acquainted with various kinds of knot. I was able to tell him that he was right – the knots used to tie Laurence Herbert and Charles Gainsborough were completely different.'

'But how did you become involved in this unsavoury business in the first place, Miss Vaughan?'

'My involvement began,' I said, carefully, 'when Miss Felicia Skene advised Sarah Critchley – the young woman wrongly imprisoned by the Vice Chancellor's court – to enlist my help in righting that particular miscarriage of justice.'

Felicia Skene's name acted like magic. The frostiness in the room went down by almost a season's worth.

'Miss Skene involved you?'

'In Miss Critchley's bid to clear her name, yes. The circumstances of her arrest subsequently proved to be inextricably linked to the hooding attacks.' I hesitated. 'It may sound self-aggrandising, but I don't believe that link would have been made without me. Miss Critchley was able to provide me with information that the proctors would simply never have learned.'

Bertha Johnson gazed at me, eyes very blue in her unmistakeably English-looking face. 'You really are a most singular young woman, Miss Vaughan.'

I spied judgement lurking behind what might have been a compliment, like a pickpocket waiting behind his smiling decoy.

'I've had experiences that other women at Oxford haven't,' I said. Then, perhaps unwisely, I couldn't help adding, 'If we allowed women out of the domestic sphere a little more, I believe many of our sisters would show how remarkable they could be.'

Mrs Johnson inflated her lungs as far as the rigid stays of her corset would allow and held her breath for a few seconds before sighing quietly. 'Perhaps. But I'm not entirely sure that I should like our young ladies to aspire to quite your own degree of sang-froid, Miss Vaughan. In those charged with the upbringing of our children, I believe finer sensibilities are essential.'

I blinked. Of course, I'd heard the 'men have their sphere and women theirs, therefore they are equal but different' argument often enough; I'd just never expected to hear it from one of the AEW, even one who was the mother of young sons.

'That's certainly a widely held view,' I said. 'But would you really rather I hadn't given evidence to Dr Darbishire?'

'Speaking for myself, rather than the AEW, I should have preferred that the information you had to offer had been delivered by Mr Rice.

Being made privy to the distressing testimony that is inevitable at an inquest into violent death can surely only coarsen one's feelings?'

'I'm afraid I don't agree,' I said, reining myself in hard. 'And neither, I suspect, would Miss Skene. She's a witness to the most distressing sights and speech day in, day out, but you couldn't hope to meet a more perfect lady.'

Mrs Johnson reached out to straighten the pen box above the blotter in front of her. She must be agitated. Women like her didn't normally fiddle with things because it would draw eyes to them. 'Felicia Skene is acknowledged as a genuine saint of our times,' she said. 'But one cannot generalise from such a very particular person. I believe the sensibilities of most ladies would be significantly eroded by listening to such distressing facts. More to the point, that is what our detractors believe. They will observe you, roaming the streets in male attire, unchaperoned, viewing bodies and giving testimony as to unedifying circumstances without turning a hair, and they will conclude that you are—'

She stopped abruptly, evidently unwilling to say the word. I helped her out. 'A freak?'

Mrs Johnson took another audible breath. The poor woman really was in a bad way. 'They will maintain that you represent an inevitable consequence of female education. They will look at you, Miss Vaughan, and draw their own conclusions about the results of an entirely unsupervised course of study. One without a wise, guiding hand.'

'By which you mean a male hand?'

'As things stand, only men have the kind of education to which we aspire.'

'Sadly,' I shot back, 'education does not equate to wisdom. Or morality. I advance the so-called Venatores as evidence to support that.'

Outside, a squally wind had blown up and was throwing handfuls of tiny raindrops against the window. The Contraption's saddle would be soaked.

'Speaking of that extremely unpleasant society,' Mrs Johnson adjusted the pen box again, 'I gather that Mr Sinclair Gainsborough found the details revealed at the inquest into his son's death profoundly upsetting.' She looked up at me. 'He was extremely glad that he had forbidden his wife from attending.'

Forbidden. Yes, he'd looked like the kind of man who'd go about forbidding things.

'Mr Gainsborough confessed to my husband that he would rather be publicly flogged than endure such a thing a second time.'

It took me a second to get beyond what she'd actually said to the implication. 'You're acquainted with the Gainsboroughs?' I asked, cautiously.

Bertha Johnson blinked. I'd asked a personal question and she wasn't sure whether she was obliged to answer. 'We moved in the same circles when they lived in Headington,' she said.

'Headington?' I was as surprised as I sounded. 'Their address was given as Abingdon at the inquest.' I'd written it down, ready to tell the *Mercury*'s readers that Gainsborough's bereaved parents, Mr and Mrs Sinclair Gainsborough, lived at Boar Hill Lodge, Abingdon.

'They moved out to Abingdon a few years ago,' Mrs Johnson said. 'There had, I seem to recall, been some unpleasantness with a servant.'

I leaped to my feet. 'Mrs Johnson, I'll be forever grateful for the opportunities the AEW has offered me. However I fear that, over the next few weeks, I shall be following a course which the University will deplore, and I wouldn't want to tarnish the reputation either of the AEW or Somerville.' I took the letter out of my satchel and offered it to her. 'This is my resignation – I'm happy to give my last few lectures this term if you wish, but meanwhile, you can tell anybody who questions my impending actions that I'm no longer employed by the Association. And now, if you'll excuse me, there's someone I must see urgently.'

## Chapter 70

*Basil*

Having learned of the attack on Montague, Inspector Newman agreed to continue to detain the members of the Venatores at the police station.

'Since we don't yet know the identity of the second man involved in Sarah Critchley's kidnap and rape,' he said, 'I can argue, if challenged, that they are all here for their own protection while we make our enquiries.'

'Excellent,' I replied. 'If we find evidence that links any of them either to Gainsborough's death or to Miss Critchley's kidnap and rape, then you'll have them to hand.'

The inspector stood to see the proctors and me out. 'It will suit both our purposes,' he said, 'to make a search of the location where Miss Critchley was held. While you search college rooms, my officers will go to Sewy's Lane. They should be able to identify the building concerned and I'll obtain the necessary warrants.'

At my suggestion, Kaye, Waddesworth and I made for Montague's rooms at Worcester College first. The boy might already have contrived to have a telegram sent to his father, and I wished, if possible, to avoid an encounter with Montague senior until we had all the facts.

However, when we arrived, we found Montague still in bed, debilitated both by his ordeal and the effects of the opiate he had been given.

Ordered to rise and dress by the Senior Proctor, he made no objection when Kaye announced our intention of searching his rooms, and as the proctors and I went about our search, Montague simply looked on, his livid, ruined face impassive.

He held himself carefully, as if movement caused him pain. As well as the savage cuts to his cheeks, both his eyes were blackened and partially swollen shut.

I wondered if he'd yet seen his face in a mirror. Despite the doctor's ministrations, it was evident that the lacerations had been deep. Each letter had been carefully executed and the process had, I suspected, been designed to inflict the maximum degree of pain as well as permanent and obvious scarring.

'Do you know who did this to you, Mr Montague?' I asked as Kaye sorted through his writing box and Waddesworth removed the contents of a large carpet bag.

Montague didn't reply. He simply stared at me, his insolence another expression of the arrogance I'd previously observed in him.

'Are you afraid that, if you name your attackers, they'll accuse you of much worse crimes?' I asked.

Montague's only response was to fold his arms and look away.

'No matter,' I said. 'Once this is done, you'll be taken into custody to join your fellow Venatores. They'll already have been told that we intend to search their rooms and that we will examine the place off Sewy's Lane for evidence of Sarah Critchley's incarceration and rape.'

His Adam's apple bobbed up and down as he swallowed. Had he expected Miss Critchley not to name her attackers or the site of her ordeal? If so, he had woefully underestimated her.

'What else might we find there, Mr Montague?' I asked. 'Evidence that connects you to the murder of Charles Gainsborough? If that's the case, then I would guess that the other Venatores will be falling over themselves to be the first to give the police the information they need to convict the murderer, lest they be tried as an accomplice.'

Until now, the Venatores had been united in their adherence to staunch denial, but we'd previously had nothing to put before them except questions that were easily batted aside. However, if our searches uncovered hard evidence, their response might be very different. Defying the police and the proctors was one thing; putting your head in a communal noose was quite another.

'I have something,' Kaye said, turning from the desk. Waddesworth strode from the bedroom to his side, and I joined them.

Kaye was holding a silk square in dusky pink which – from the obvious creases – had been folded into quarters. Now opened and laid flat on Kaye's palm, we saw that the fabric had been wrapped around a paper of needles and a small skein of silk thread.

'Is this the thread you used to make the hood for Gainsborough?' Kaye asked. 'The one you put on his head after you killed him?'

Montague stared, unmoved, at Kaye. 'Those are a present for my sister.' Though he spoke stiffly, he did not demonstrate as much discomfort on speaking as Herbert had. I wondered whether the doctor had left further doses of morphine or laudanum to ease the pain from his wounds. Or perhaps Montague was simply more determined not to acknowledge his pain than Herbert.

'Would that be the same sister for whom you were supposedly buying ribbons when you tried to pick up Sarah Critchley?' I asked, not attempting to hide my contempt.

He turned to me, his eyes cold. 'The ribbons were for my little sister, Elise. My embroidering sister, Daphne, is nineteen.'

Montague obviously saw that I didn't believe him. 'Ask any lady,' he said, turning away from me, 'and she'll tell you. That's an unbroken skein of embroidery silk.'

'Then why was it hidden in the concealed compartment under the pen drawer?' Kaye asked.

Montague regarded him with all the disdain his ravaged face was capable of. 'Hardly concealed if a casual search revealed it, Senior Proctor.'

Something about his words made me wonder whether there was more to be found here. I stepped forward and drew the writing box towards me. Taking out each drawer in succession, I searched for a release mechanism and eventually found one in the roof of a tiny compartment intended for stamps. With a well-oiled click, the lid of the box proved to be hinged along its long edge. I raised it to reveal several shallow compartments.

In one lay a key.

I held it up to the proctors. 'I'd be very surprised if this wasn't the key to a building on Sewy's Lane.'

—

Rather than the proctors and I conducting each of the remaining four searches together, we agreed to divide them between us and regroup at the police station once they were complete. Waddesworth naturally took Vennell's rooms at Queen's, and Kaye Ashdown's at Magdalen while I agreed to search Haviland's set at New College and Herbert's at Merton.

Efficient though our division of labour was, however, our searches proved fruitless. We hoped for better luck at the rooms Newman's constables had identified as the Venatores' haunt in Sewy's Lane.

We were an official-looking little party as we made our way through the busyness of a working day; the constable in possession of the search warrant at our head creating a path through the crowds, the two proctors marching side by side behind him, while I formed the rearguard.

As I followed Kaye and Waddesworth stride for stride, I wondered whether they felt any sense of responsibility for what had happened to Sarah Critchley. It was difficult not to feel that, had they taken a more punitive attitude towards undergraduates caught fraternising with young women, this awful chain of events could have been prevented.

Undergraduates heading to lectures stared at us as we marched up New Inn Hall Street and turned right, into Sewy's Lane, without breaking stride.

A man in working clothes was standing outside one of the ramshackle properties which lined the lane. The render on the timber-framed building was patchy and the walls bulged in places. Though every building in Oxford bar the very newly constructed was, to some degree, soot-blackened, the state of the Venatores' premises suggested that they hadn't been whitewashed in decades. Nevertheless, the building's position in the centre of Oxford would make it sought after and I didn't imagine the rent had been cheap.

Nevertheless, it would have been priceless to the Venatores. Situated between New Inn Hall Street and the Cornmarket, it was in the dead centre of their hunting ground.

'Orright, Arthur?' the loitering man greeted the constable. 'Been stood 'ere all the while, just like you said. I'n't nobody come in or out.'

'And you're sure this is the one the young man rented?'

'Seen any one of a pack of 'em comin' in an' out often enough, 'en't I?'

The constable nodded. 'Good enough. I got a warrant.'

'Don't s'pose you'll need it. Landlord i'n't never 'ere. Just takes 'is money once a quarter and that's 'im done.'

The constable turned to the Senior Proctor. 'Right then, sir. Want to try that key you've got?'

We all watched as Kaye applied key to lock. The door opened easily, and we followed him inside.

## Chapter 71

### *Non*

Less than five minutes after leaving Mrs Johnson at AEW building I was in Bath Place. I jumped off the Contraption outside Cat's house and banged on the door.

It was only at the third time of asking that I got an answer and then it was from behind me.

'Where's the fire?' Cat Hammond asked, coming up Bath Place towards me.

I spun round. 'I need to talk to you.'

'I thought I'd invited you to tea this afternoon.' She stepped past me to open her front door.

'This isn't a social call. We're not middle-class ladies taking tea. I *need to talk to you.*'

She looked at me, eyebrows raised. 'You'd better come in then.'

I followed her into the little house.

'Why didn't you tell me that Charles Gainsborough was the son of the house where you worked as a lady's maid?' I asked.

Cat took off the little hat she was wearing, stuck the hatpin through it and put it on the sideboard. 'What makes you think that's the case?'

I could see she was playing for time, trying to think. 'The family used to live in Headington,' I said, instead of answering her question, 'and then they moved to Abingdon after the scandal over your pregnancy and everybody suspecting that Charles was the father.' I watched her tidy her hair and re-pin it. 'Did Charles's parents believe he was the father?' I asked. 'Is that why they moved?'

'The little bastard would've been the father if he'd had his way,' she flashed back. 'Luckily for me, I grew up having to fend off bargees and wharfmen. I know how to grab a man's balls and squeeze so that he can't move, don't you worry.'

Her tone and her accent had both dropped a couple of social classes and I could hear just how she'd have sounded when she warned Charles Gainsborough off.

'So why should I save him from judgement?' she demanded. 'He'd fully intended what everybody suspected.'

'But he hated you for not exonerating him.'

'He didn't hate me half as much as he hated Lincoln Waddesworth. He accused Waddesworth in front of his parents and Waddesworth flatly denied it.'

'You were there?'

'No, I'd been thrown out by then. The housemaid told me. She was listening outside the door. All the female servants hated Charles.'

So that's where the rumour about a don being involved with Cat had come from.

I waited for her to ask me to sit down. The little front room was shabbier than her room at the Turf. But then, she didn't invite clients into her house, so it didn't need to impress. All available funds went on reassuring the well-off men who came to see her that they were in safe, respectable hands.

Well, they wouldn't feel so safe if they knew what those hands had done to Laurence Herbert and John Montague, would they?

'As you're here,' Cat said, 'may I offer you a cup of tea?' The nicely spoken lady's maid was back.

I'd had nothing to drink since breakfast and I was parched from pedalling here at a rate of knots. 'Yes, please.'

There was no fire in the grate, so I followed Cat through into the kitchen.

A little, well-blacked stove stood against one wall. Cat opened the door to the fire box and threw some more coal in from the scuttle, then moved the kettle onto the hot plate.

'I was going to get cakes in for this afternoon,' Cat said, 'from that fancy bakery on Cornmarket Street. But you'll have to do without now.'

'I'm not fancy,' I said.

'What are you then? Apart from too silly to see what's good for you?'

She looked at me in just the way that I imagined Hara looking at me sometimes. 'I'm not here to discuss Tarley Askew,' I said. 'You made your views on him very plain last night, so there's nothing more to be said on that score.'

I pulled an upright chair out from under the table and sat down.

'You know why I'm here,' I said. 'If there's no seventh member of the Venatores, who was with them that night in Gainsborough's rooms at Trinity?'

## Chapter 72

*Basil*

I don't know what I'd been expecting when we followed Kaye into the ill-kept little building. I supposed the exterior had suggested damp walls, bare floorboards and general neglect. Instead we found, if not grandeur and luxury, then a passable facsimile of it in miniature.

We stepped into a tiny lobby decorated in chinoiserie-style wallpaper and furnished with a mirrored coatstand and umbrella holder.

Kaye opened the inner door into a room that was hidden from prying eyes behind closely fitting shutters, which he proceeded to unfasten. As light was admitted, we saw that the same wallpaper had been employed here; long-tailed birds sat on slender branches whose sparse foliage and blossoms meandered over a golden yellow background. But these images were the only delicate thing before us. The room was crowded with furniture that was far too large for such a confined space. To navigate around it, visitors were forced to sidle between the glass-fronted display cabinets that lined the walls, two large sofas and several occasional tables bearing lacquerware vases and jugs. So little floor space remained that it was difficult to discern the pattern on the overlarge rug whose fringed edges rose up the walls at either side of the room.

The overall effect suggested that somebody had simply bought the entire contents of a room at a house auction and had it delivered here. The cabinets were variously filled with small stuffed animals, porcelain statuettes and ancient musical instruments, an eccentric eclecticism wholly at odds with the character of the youths who comprised the Venatores.

'Not exactly what I was expecting,' I remarked, feeling the need to say something.

'What were you expecting?' Waddesworth snapped irascibly. 'Whitewashed walls and a bed? Bars at the window?'

Despite his scorn, the exactness of his description suggested that precisely such a scene had filled his own imagination prior to our gaining entry to the Hunters' lair.

I looked at the fireplace. The grate hadn't been cleaned nor the fire re-laid after it had last been lit. Evidently nobody was regularly employed to look after this place. Clearly, the Venatores wouldn't want anybody to know of its existence, lest gossip get about, but I couldn't imagine any of them on their knees raking out embers and laying fresh kindling. Indeed, I shouldn't have been able to make much of a fist of lighting a fire myself.

Kaye squeezed between the back of a sofa and one of the display cabinets to reach the door in the corner of the room. But, instead of opening it, he simply stood and stared.

I followed his gaze and felt a shock of revulsion run through me. Bolts had been fitted to the top and bottom of the door, effectively making the room beyond into a potential prison. However, care had been taken to ensure that the bolts weren't immediately visible. They'd been painted the same colour as the door.

'They'd hardly be noticeable by lamplight,' I said. 'Especially if your attention was on the person who'd brought you here with promises of goodness knows what.'

Without making any reply, Kaye opened the door and Waddesworth and I followed him into a bedroom. I opened the shutters and, in the dim light provided by the grimy window, we saw that here, too, the furniture had been designed for a much larger room. Almost the entire floor space was taken up by a high, brass-framed bed.

The only other item of furniture was a nightstand which stood in one corner, a small lamp and several smeared glasses on its stained surface.

The bed was in disarray. A damasked silk bedspread lay askew over the rails at its foot while a blanket and top sheet had been yanked aside and trailed drunkenly on the floor, clinging to one corner of the bed by the portion tucked under the feather mattress. The bottom sheet was twisted where bodies had lain and was stained, amongst other things, with livid spots and smears of blood.

If an artist had been asked to paint the aftermath of debauchery, he would have been required to change nothing.

I turned away, unable to bear the images summoned up by that bloodstained bed. My exit to the sitting room being blocked by Waddesworth and the constable, I opened the other door in the bedroom and found myself in a windowless closet that seemed to be doing duty as a dressing room. Occupying the whole of the short wall facing the door stood a wardrobe fronted by a full-length mirror. This caught the weak daylight from the bedroom and showed two chests of drawers standing opposite each other on either side of the closet.

Behind me, I heard Kaye instructing the constable to be so good as to light a lamp and, once he had done so, the proctors joined me.

There was just room for me to examine the contents of the wardrobe while Kaye and Waddesworth addressed themselves to the chests of drawers.

Six jackets hung from hooks, the corresponding waistcoats and trousers folded beneath them. I opened the wide drawer at the base of the wardrobe to find men's boots and shoes suitable for all weathers.

'They must have raided the second-hand shops of Oxford,' Kaye remarked as he slid a drawer closed. 'There are enough shirts here to last a month.'

'I don't suppose they wanted to have to wash them,' I said.

Kaye opened another drawer. 'Gowns,' he said, removing one and shaking it out. 'Elderly. All commoners'.'

'There are no scholars or exhibitioners at the halls,' I pointed out. 'And if they were passing themselves off as impoverished students, then second-hand would be more convincing. The girls they were trying to seduce would know new from used at a glance.'

I was about to close the boot drawer when I spotted a battered carpet bag stuffed into a corner.

Taking it out I saw that its fabric was worn in places, and one of the handles had been clumsily replaced with a folded strip of canvas. From its capacious interior I pulled out a set of heavy boots, much worn, a patched and sweat-stained shirt, a suit of clothes that was inferior even to the ones in the wardrobe and a battered cap of the type worn by the city's labourers. Even in the poor light, it was obvious that the jacket was threadbare and patched while the dusty trousers, when I held them up, bagged badly at the knee.

These were the clothes of a manual worker. Or, in this case, somebody who wished to pass as such.

'Here's something Inspector Newman will find interesting,' Kaye said, examining a document which he'd placed on the top of the chest of drawers. 'It's a contract between the building's owner and one Anthony John Farmer, who gives his address as Charsley's Hall.'

Farmer was the alias Montague had used when Waddesworth had arrested Sarah Critchley for detaining him. Finally, we had something concrete.

As I stuffed the workman's clothes back into the bag, Waddesworth spoke.

'Look at this.'

Kaye and I both turned from our respective tasks and Waddesworth held out a square of fine linen – a gentleman's handkerchief – folded into quarters exactly as the silk square in Montague's writing box had been. Here, too, the fabric had been used to enclose something.

'I found it in there,' Waddesworth indicated the open drawer, 'under a pile of socks.'

He put the handkerchief on the top of the chest of drawers and unfolded it.

It contained a reel of white cotton, a needle thrust through the threads.

## Chapter 73

*Non*

'Who was it, Cat? Who was the Hunters' guest?'
She looked me in the eye for a full five seconds. Then she said, 'Lincoln Waddesworth.'
'*Waddesworth?*'
'Yes.'
'How do you know?'
'You know I had people watching them. The Venatores.' She paused for a moment. 'The evening of Gainsborough's supper party, they saw all of them go into Trinity.'
'And they saw Waddesworth as well?'
Cat nodded. 'The window to the porters' lodge is right at the side of the pavement. One of my boys was waiting there, so he could tip the others the wink when they came out again.'
Of course. Later that night they'd hooded Harcourt Ashdown. They must have followed him from Trinity.
'Anyway, standing nearby, he heard Waddesworth telling the porter that he had business with Mr Gainsborough. The porter tried to put him off, told him Gainsborough was entertaining, but Waddesworth said he'd just have to make time for him.'
'All right, but he might not have been going to the supper party,' I objected. 'Maybe he *did* have business with Gainsborough. Maybe he'd found out about what he was up to with Sarah Critchley.'
'He was there for over an hour,' Cat said.
Waddesworth. The fact that he'd been there that evening brought everything else we knew into a different kind of focus.
'So,' I said, thinking as I spoke, 'Charles Gainsborough hated Waddesworth because he wouldn't admit that he was your daughter's

father, and everybody was left thinking Charles was responsible. D'you think he might've been blackmailing Waddesworth?'

Cat turned away from me to warm the teapot. 'I'd be surprised if he *wasn't*. It would've paid them – the Venatores – to have a proctor in their pocket, wouldn't it?'

'But if Waddesworth was being blackmailed,' I said, 'that would give him a compelling motive for murder. Any rumours about immoral behaviour would have brought his term as proctor to a very swift end and he'd probably have lost his college fellowship as well.'

Cat took the cups into the scullery and came back with milk in them. 'God knows, I've got no reason to defend Lincoln Waddesworth,' she said, 'but *murder?*'

'Who then?' I asked. 'One of the Hunters?'

'Why would *they* kill Charles Gainsborough?'

'So that he couldn't be called to give evidence if Sarah took the University to court for false imprisonment. There's a barrister Miss Skene knows who's ready and waiting for her to do that.'

Something that should have occurred to me long before this suddenly jostled its way to the front of my mind. 'Why didn't you ever bind and hood Charles Gainsborough?'

Cat passed me a cup of tea and sat down at the table with me. 'Because we never saw him coming out of Sewy's Lane. He was the only one who never took a girl there. Or rather, we never caught him.' She looked pensive. 'If I hadn't known him of old, I might've thought he was genuine about Sarah.'

'*Genuine?* He lied to her about *everything*, Cat. His name, where he was from, his family, his accent, his college, even where that ring he gave her came from.'

'I know.' She took a sip of her still-scalding tea. 'But Sarah refuses to believe that it was all a lie, and she's nobody's fool. What if he lied to her to begin with, just like they all do, but then he really did fall in love with her, but didn't know how to tell her who he really was?'

'Oh, come on, Cat—'

'Then how d'you explain him not going after any other girls?'

'He did! Basil Rice saw him talking to a girl on the Cornmarket, using one of the Hunters' tricks to pick her up.'

Cat paused. 'Maybe he did that for the other members' benefit. So as not to make them suspicious.'

She'd sowed a seed of doubt in my mind, now and she could see it. In the weak afternoon light coming in from the window behind her, she looked at me narrowly.

'If you think they might've killed Charles because he was a threat to them – because of him having to give evidence,' she said, slowly, 'then Sarah was even more of a threat. She was the one who'd bring the case. So why didn't they kill her when they had the chance?'

## Chapter 74

### Basil

Before the proctors and I returned to the police station, I sent the constable to canvass Oxford's haberdashers to see whether any remembered a young man – gowned or otherwise – buying needles and thread recently. I was sure it would be an uncommon enough occurrence to have been remarked upon, especially if the purchaser had been gowned.

'If anybody does remember a man buying those items,' I said, 'please ask if they can recall any distinguishing features – height, build, colour of hair or eyes, et cetera.'

Once Waddesworth had discovered the needles and thread, I'd looked more closely at the workman's clothes, holding them up against myself and Kaye to estimate size.

The likeliest candidate for Gainsborough's murder must be whoever had dressed himself in these clothes in order to leave the handcart bearing the boy's body in front of Trinity College. However, none of the Venatores differed in height from their fellows by more than two or three inches, so the clothes might have been worn by any without attracting more than a passing glance. A labourer's choice of clothes was often dictated by price rather than excellence of fit.

The constable having marched off to begin his enquiries amongst Oxford's haberdashers, Kaye, Waddesworth and I made our slightly subdued way back to the High Street.

I was sure that none of us would be able to prevent our mind's eye dwelling on that dishevelled bed, the bolts on the door. How many other young women had been held prisoner there, to be released in the knowledge that nobody would believe them if they accused gownsmen of rape?

Having listened to our disturbing discoveries, Inspector Newman nodded thoughtfully. 'One or two of your young toffs did find it difficult to retain his composure when I told them that you were about to search their little bolt-hole,' he said. 'I also broke the news – to each individually – that John Montague had been attacked and badly beaten. Herbert was the only one who enquired as to the nature of Montague's injuries, so I may, possibly, have left the others with the impression that his life might be in danger.'

Kaye and Waddesworth stared at him, uncomprehending.

'If Montague were to die,' I explained, 'he'd have no further hold on them. Suggesting that his life is in danger gives them notice that now is the time to break ranks. Montague can, potentially, be blamed for everything.'

'And *has* any of them broken ranks?' Waddesworth asked.

Newman stood. 'Augustus Vennell has requested pen and paper and is writing a confession of his part in the Venatores' activities as we speak.'

'What, exactly, is he confessing to?' I asked.

'He's adamant that he knows nothing about Gainsborough's death nor the attack on Miss Critchley. Nevertheless, I'm hoping his account will be instructive.'

While we waited for Vennell to complete his confession, I suggested that we confront John Montague with the needles and thread from the drawer at Sewy's Lane.

Accordingly, Newman had Montague brought up from the cells into the small, poorly lit room where the other interrogations had taken place. With its barred window, cold linoleum floor and flaking, distempered walls it was barely any more welcoming than the cells.

Newman deferred to Kaye, who began by outlining our search of the rooms on Sewy's Lane, sparing Montague none of our horror at what we had discovered.

'It will be no surprise to you, I suspect,' he concluded, 'that we found this in one of the drawers in the dressing room.' He placed the folded linen cloth on the table between Montague and himself.

The boy glanced at it momentarily then looked him in the eye. 'A handkerchief,' he said, baldly.

'Unfold it,' Kaye instructed.

Montague did as he was instructed, disclosing the needle and cotton.

He looked up coolly at Kaye, his bruised and mutilated face greasy with some kind of salve. 'I assume, from your excitement at the discovery of embroidery needles and silk in my rooms earlier, that you consider this to be evidence that I murdered Gainsborough and tacked a hood together in order to put it over his head?'

I wondered at his composure. The scars on his face were livid and must be causing him a great deal of pain, yet he spoke as if he hadn't a care in the world. Pehaps the salve had analgesic properties.

'If that's not the case,' Kaye replied, 'perhaps you'd like to give another explanation.'

Montague sat back in his chair. 'I don't believe it's an accused man's job to offer alternatives to erroneous assumptions, Senior Proctor, so I will merely make two small points. Firstly, I have never seen this handkerchief before. You've already searched my rooms with a fine-toothed comb, and you will have found no trace of a linen handkerchief. All mine are silk. Secondly, if I wished to have sewing done, I would pay a woman to do it.' He glared at each of us in turn. 'Let me make something perfectly clear. I did not kill Charles Gainsborough. Therefore, try as you may, you will find absolutely no evidence to prove that I did.'

He stared implacably at Kaye, and I thought what a formidable politician he might have made if he hadn't chosen the path of violent debauchery.

'Now, gentlemen, I intend to say nothing further until my father gets here.'

His lack of any kind of consternation was troubling. Either he felt neither remorse nor guilt or he was innocent of Gainsborough's murder.

I looked at his fingers, interlaced loosely in his lap.

None bore a signet ring, and we'd found no ring of any kind in our search of his rooms.

'Unfortunately for you, Mr Montague,' Inspector Newman said, 'Charles Gainsborough's death is not the only crime you're suspected of. There's also the abduction and rape of Sarah Critchley.'

The boy met his eye without turning a hair. 'As with the other case, you have no *evidence*.'

'On the contrary. We have the contract between you, under your Anthony Farmer alias, and the building's owner. Moreover, we have

Miss Critchley's evidence that you took her there against her will and forced yourself on her. She is quite prepared to testify against you.'

I wondered whether that was, in fact, the case, but I held my tongue.

Montague grunted a mirthless laugh. 'A shop girl who was sent to prison for soliciting? There isn't a jury in the land that would believe I forced her. So unless you have eyewitnesses of a more respectable kind, I suggest that you take great care what you accuse me of, Inspector.'

His arrogance was breathtaking, and though I suspect even Waddesworth would quite happily have added to his injuries at that moment, with scrupulous attention to the law, Inspector Newman ordered that he be taken back to the cells.

As the proctors and I prepared to take our leave, the front door of the station opened, and Non walked in.

If she was surprised to see the proctors and me there, she gave no indication of it. Instead, she addressed herself to Newman.

'Inspector, might I have a private word with you and Mr Rice, please?'

## Chapter 75

*Non*

The proctors weren't best pleased at being kicked out of Newman's office, but I couldn't very well tell Basil and the inspector what I knew about Waddesworth and Gainsborough with Lincoln Waddesworth sitting there. And, quite frankly, I wasn't going to shed bitter tears about them being offended. If they hadn't let their lying undergraduates get away with abusing the young women of the city, we wouldn't be where we were.

'I've discovered that there was no seventh member of the Venatores,' I said, using the Hunters' pompous Latin for Newman's benefit. 'The seventh man at the supper party at Trinity was Lincoln Waddesworth.'

'Waddesworth?' Basil was incredulous. 'What on earth was *he* doing there?'

'Gainsborough was blackmailing him.' That was the short answer. The longer one took a little while because, as far as I knew, Inspector Newman hadn't heard of Cat Hammond until that point. So I had to try and make sure that he thought she had no more involvement than a) being the maid Charles Gainsborough'd been suspected of seducing, and b) being the friend Sarah Critchley'd run to when she'd supposedly escaped. The inspector wasn't a fool, and I suspect he knew there was more to it, but he didn't ask any questions. Not for now, at any rate.

Once I'd finished, Basil told me what he and the proctors had discovered in their searches.

'So the Hunters would go to Sewy's Lane, change into less expensive clothes, then go out after young women?' I asked. 'And, if they could, they'd take them back there?'

Basil looked away. 'Yes.' It wasn't like Basil to be curt. I wondered just how horrible what they'd found in those rooms was.

'And this handkerchief with the needles and thread,' I said. 'You're convinced they belong to John Montague?'

'The handkerchief was folded around the needle and thread in exactly the same way as the silk one in his writing box. It's too much of a coincidence, surely?'

'It's not necessarily a coincidence at all,' I said. 'It just proves that somebody'd seen the way Montague'd wrapped his present for his sister. His bosom pal Herbert could easily have seen that.'

Basil shot a glance at the inspector as if he was looking for moral support, but Inspector Newman was looking at me, thoughtfully.

'And ask yourself,' I said, 'why would Montague keep such an incriminating piece of evidence in one of the drawers at Sewy's Lane? Just in case he decided to garrotte another one of the Hunters? Unless we think he was planning a murderous spree, I think finding that needle and thread is a bit convenient.'

I waited for them to catch up but neither of them did.

'Did you say it was Lincoln Waddesworth who found them?' I prompted.

Basil hesitated, as if he'd finally seen what I was getting at. 'Yes, but—'

'Did you actually see him open the drawer, spot the handkerchief bundle and take it out?' I asked.

Basil took a moment to recall the scene. 'No,' he said, quietly. 'Both Kaye and I had our backs to him.'

'So Waddesworth could have taken the handkerchief with the needle and thread out of his own pocket then drawn your attention to it?'

Basil's face had that tense, troubled look that meant he didn't like something I'd said but couldn't actually find a way to disagree with it.

'Did he go back to his college at all after you'd searched Montague's rooms?' I asked.

'Yes,' Basil admitted. 'To go through Augustus Vennell's set.'

'So he could easily have picked up the needle and thread then. Does Waddesworth wear a signet ring on the fourth finger of his right hand?' I asked.

Inspector Newman stood up. 'Let's see, shall we?'

But, when he put his head round the door to ask the proctors to come back in, he was told that they'd left. I was all for going after

Waddesworth and arresting him, but the inspector shied away from the thought like a horse from a warble fly.

'We'd do better to await the results of my officer's visits to the haberdashers,' he said. 'With luck, that might give us a clearer idea of who that needle and thread belonged to.'

I thought that was a mistake and said so, but my opinion didn't carry much weight with Inspector Newman so, instead, we read Augustus Vennell's statement.

His account of the Hunters' activities contained a lot more self-justification than revelation but it did clear a few things up. As I'd suspected, the Hunters were schoolmates who'd come up to Oxford at the same time. Because every one of them was registered for a pass degree they'd never had much work to do, so they'd decided to make life more interesting by having a bet for a hundred pounds as to who could seduce the most town girls. And, to make things 'fair' and put them all 'on the same footing', they'd come up with the rules and tips we'd seen in the foolscap manual. Apparently Laurence Herbert had produced an identical manual for each of the Hunters, so that none of them could conveniently 'forget' what they'd agreed.

As far as the hoodings went, according to Vennell, when he'd been snatched off the street, a voice in his ear had warned him that if he tried to report his attackers or give details of where he'd been taken, all his sordid activities would be passed on to the Queen's College authorities. *The voice,* Vennell's statement said, *was female and well-educated.*

The same thing had happened to each of the Hunters, and they'd been convinced that a lady was somehow involved, which must've scared them witless. I could imagine the questions that had gone around in their toffee-nosed heads. Who was she? Did she know their fathers? What would happen to them now?

*We thought we had no choice but to keep quiet,* Vennell's scrawl bleated, *but I regret it bitterly now. If we'd called her bluff, Gainsborough might still be alive.*

Interestingly, he claimed that, on the night Charles Gainsborough'd been murdered, all the other Hunters had been at a supper party in his rooms at Queen's.

*We knew something must be up when Gainsborough didn't arrive,* his statement said. *But we thought his turn had come — that they'd just do to him what they'd done to the rest of us. We didn't know they were going to kill him.*

In theory, that meant that, unless he was lying and that version of events had been agreed in advance, the Hunters provided alibis for each other. Or rather, they would have done, if there hadn't been just enough latitude in Dr Darbishire's estimated time of death for Gainsborough to have been murdered before they met at Queen's.

Once we'd read Vennell's statement, it was time to start interviewing him and his friends. But the inspector was adamant that he wasn't going to let me be a part of the interrogations.

'I'm afraid I can't allow you to sit in on these interviews, Miss Vaughan. We simply won't get anything out of the young men if you're present.'

I put up a token resistance but, as it happened, I was happy to leave the station and let him and Basil get on with it.

I had plans of my own.

## Chapter 76

### Basil

Vennell was questioned first.

Inspector Newman picked up his statement and began reading aloud. '*...we thought they'd just do to him what they'd done to the rest of us. We didn't know they were going to kill him.*' Just to be clear, who did you think was responsible for Gainsborough's murder?'

'The scum who attacked us, who cut Herbert's face.'

Newman nodded pensively, running his eye down the pages in front of him. 'You say that, quote, "*Gainsborough's blackmail of the Junior Proctor wasn't simply a way of protecting the Venatores, he hated Waddesworth with a passion because Waddesworth had refused to clear his name over the pregnancy of his mother's maid. Gainsborough took every opportunity to parade in front of Waddesworth with Sals on his arm and lie to his face about who he was and which college he was from.*"' He gazed at Vennell impassively. 'It didn't occur to you that Mr Waddesworth might have become tired of being blackmailed by Gainsborough?'

It took the boy a few seconds to realise what Newman was implying, but when he did, he appeared genuinely shocked. 'Waddesworth? He's the Junior Proctor, for God's sake!'

'But also a flawed man,' the inspector pointed out. 'Which was why Charles Gainsborough was able to blackmail him in the first place.'

'Are you sure Mr Waddesworth wasn't at your meeting on the night Gainsborough died?' I asked.

'No. He was only at the meeting at Trinity because Gainsborough wanted to dress him down in front of the rest of us for arresting his Sal and having her thrown into jail.'

'Dress him down?' Newman reclaimed control. 'What exactly did he say? As close as you can remember.'

Vennell hesitated, glancing at me. 'He was furious. Said that if Waddesworth ever arrested a girl he was working on again, the Hebdomadal Council would get a letter telling them that he had impregnated Mrs Gainsborough's lady's maid then abandoned her and the child.'

But instead of being brought to heel by this ultimatum, Waddesworth had played with fire by almost arresting Gainsborough when he'd flaunted his attempt to pick up Brandon's daughter.

'And how did Mr Waddesworth take this threat?' I asked, recalling the look Charles Gainsborough had directed at Waddesworth as the Junior Proctor stood, toe to toe with him on the Cornmarket, demanding that he give his name and college. At the time, I had thought it was simple arrogance on Gainsborough's part; now I saw it as incredulity that Waddesworth would dare provoke him.

'I thought he was going to punch Gainsborough,' Vennell said. 'He told him in no uncertain terms that he'd brought the girl's arrest on himself by his behaviour in encouraging her. He also said that the proctors' office had received a letter of complaint about the girl and her activities. The Senior Proctor had seen it and insisted that he – Waddesworth – do something as he was the proctor on duty that week.'

'It's been suggested,' I said, 'that John Montague wrote that letter of complaint precisely in order to have Miss Critchley arrested. Do you think that's true?'

'It's plausible, I suppose,' Vennell said. 'Gainsborough'd become obsessed with her, and Montague was worried that she'd end up causing trouble for us.'

'You say he was obsessed. Miss Critchley claims something a little more romantic – that they were engaged,' I reminded him.

'Which is obviously preposterous!'

'And yet,' I said, 'he walked out with her for months.'

Vennell made a derisory sound. 'He claimed he hadn't invested all that time in a VI not to take her virginity from her. None of us believed him.'

'A VI,' Inspector Newman said. 'What does that mean?'

I recalled the line in the foolscap manual: *vi = mega kudos*.

'Virgo Intacta,' Ashdown said. 'Any Sals were a point, but a VI was ten.'

I rose and left the room. Had I remained, I fear I might have wrought violence on Vennell. His casual reference to the deflowering of young women for sport made me angrier than I think I had ever been.

I had been sitting in the inspector's office, attempting to master my rage and revulsion, for possibly a quarter of an hour when Newman entered the room in the company of the constable who'd come with us to Sewy's Lane. He had now completed his canvassing of haberdasheries.

'It was the third shop I went into,' he said. 'Lady there remembered a gentleman in a gown buying needles and a reel of white cotton. But not an undergraduate. Somebody older. Medium height but stocky, she said. And wearing one of those gowns that are like an overcoat.'

I felt a cold weight settle in the pit of my stomach. The proctors' gowns were particularly weighty and had velvet facings. I hadn't wanted to give credence to Non's suspicion, but it seemed that her instincts had been right.

'She asked him if he was running an errand for his wife and he said he was.'

'When was this, did you get a definite date?' Inspector Newman asked.

'Ten days or a fortnight or so ago was as close as she could remember.'

Waddesworth had bought that needle and thread not as a favour to his wife, because he wasn't married, but because he planned to make a hood for Charles Gainsborough. Then he'd killed him. Not on the spur of the moment, enraged at some further provocation from his blackmailer, but with malice aforethought.

Lincoln Waddesworth was a cold-blooded murderer.

## Chapter 77

*Non*

I could understand why Inspector Newman didn't want to arrest Lincoln Waddesworth immediately. He was a senior member of the University – if I was wrong, there'd be hell to pay.

But I didn't think I *was* wrong. And I knew Waddesworth would have the wind up now. His little misdirection trick with the needle and cotton had backfired on him. He wouldn't have anticipated Basil sending the constable to track down whatever gownsman had bought them.

The Junior Proctor might not be the most noticeable man in Oxford, but if he'd made the mistake of popping into a haberdasher's while he was wearing his proctor's gown, he'd have been conspicuous enough to be memorable. And I didn't think he'd have left his gown at home. It was obvious that Waddesworth enjoyed the power being a proctor gave him. He wouldn't want to walk the streets of the city anonymously when he could walk about with all that black bombazine billowing.

The constable might come back empty-handed from his haberdashers' tour, but I didn't think Waddesworth would take that risk.

I thought he'd cut his losses and run – now while he still could. And the thought of him getting away, on top of what I knew the Hunters were going to get away with, just because of who they were, boiled my blood.

So, I pedalled quickly down to Corpus Christi College, parked the tricycle next to the college gates, and pulled out the soft felt hat that I kept in my satchel for emergencies. It was a second-hand relic of a passing fashion amongst the undergraduates and, even if it made me look a bit eccentric, any hat was more respectable than none.

As well as the hat, I put my best middle-class English voice on for the porter.

'Excuse me, but it's very urgent that I speak to Mr Tarley Askew.' The man opened his mouth to tell me why that wasn't going to be possible, but I barged on. 'I have an urgent message for him about my aunt, *Mrs* Askew,' I said. 'I'm Mr Askew's cousin, Evelyn.'

Everybody in the college would know that Tarley'd spent months away from Oxford looking after his mother and the man's attitude to me turned on a sixpence. Before I could say another word, he'd turned on his heel, whistled up the messenger's boy who went trotting across the quad, and disappeared up a staircase.

'He'll just be a tick, miss,' the porter said. 'You wait there.'

And the next thing I knew, Tarley was shooting out of one of the staircases and coming towards me full pelt. He skidded to a halt when he saw who was standing there under the felt hat.

'Non!'

I grabbed his arm and pulled him towards the gate. 'Your mother's fine. I'm sorry – that was the only way I could think of that would persuade them to get a message to you straight away.'

He took a deep breath and let it out in a rush. 'Don't ever do that to me again.'

'I hoped the messenger would tell you the nonsense about me being your cousin, so you'd know something wasn't right.'

Tarley shook his head. 'There was no mention of a cousin. Only that a young woman was in the lodge with urgent news of my mother.'

'I'm sorry.'

'Why did you need me so urgently?'

I started pushing the Contraption along Merton Street. 'I think the police have made a mistake and Charles Gainsborough's murderer may be about to try and escape. Come on, we need to hurry. I'll explain on the way.'

—

The Queen's Lane coffee house wasn't busy, and I managed to sit at the table in the window.

There were two options if you wanted to leave Queen's College. Either you marched out of the front gate, past the porter's lodge, in full view of everybody coming and going, or you left quietly via the back gate onto Queen's Lane.

I didn't think Lincoln Waddesworth would want to draw attention to himself by leaving via the main gate. Not when he'd be carrying luggage.

So, assuming that he'd use the little gate next to the library, he'd either come quietly down Queen's Lane onto the High Street, or he'd walk up onto New College Lane and make his way to Broad Street.

Which is why Tarley was loitering on the corner where Holywell Street ran into Broad Street, and I was sitting in the coffee house.

I'd told Tarley that I thought Waddesworth would go for the taxi rank on Broad Street and that he'd be able to stop the proctor more easily than I would. But I'd lied. Tarley fought like a gentleman. He'd get knocked down in five seconds flat by a man who was fleeing for his life.

With the odds stacked against me, I wasn't going to bother fighting fair. And I had absolutely no intention of letting Lincoln Waddesworth get away.

I was pretty sure the Junior Proctor would come down onto the High Street rather than go up to Broad Street, purely because he'd prefer to avoid St Helen's Passage. Fair enough, Cat Hammond would mostly leave Bath Place via Holywell Street, but if she wanted a tram, she'd come through the Turf and out onto New College Lane via the passage. And Waddesworth wouldn't want to risk meeting her.

So I was sitting where I'd easily see him coming out of Queen's Lane.

My second cup of coffee was going cold in front of me when I spotted him. Shoulders hunched, carpet bag in hand, tall hat on his head instead of his academic cap, Waddesworth was striding up towards the taxi cabs waiting on the High Street. He'd be banking on there being one free before he drew level with the Queen's gates where he might be seen, and I'd made it easy for him by persuading one of the cabbies to turn his cab around so that he was facing up the High Street in the direction of the railway station.

I grabbed my satchel and followed Waddesworth up the street. The Contraption would have to stay where it was.

A quick trot and I was only a couple of strides behind him.

'Going somewhere, Mr Waddesworth?'

If I hadn't known he was guilty before, the look on his face when he whipped around would have given him away. I felt a savage triumph when I saw his shock and fear.

But I'll say this for Lincoln Waddesworth: he adapted quickly – by the time he answered me he'd altered his expression to something that was almost convincing as regret. 'I've been called away, I'm afraid. A family matter. But Kaye and Rice are more than capable of dealing with the Venatores.'

He was being too polite. Waddesworth despised me and my interference in the case. If he hadn't been trying to hide his need to escape, he'd have told me to mind my own business.

'The Venatores are guilty of terrible things,' I said, remembering Sarah Critchley's hunched figure on Cat Hammond's sofa. 'And I'd see them all rot in jail if it was up to me. But they didn't kill Charles Gainsborough. You did.'

He tried a disbelieving smile. 'I beg your pardon? I'm afraid all this sleuthing has gone to your head Miss… Vaughan, was it? Now, if you don't mind, I'm in rather a hurry.'

He turned and stepped up, as I'd anticipated, to the only taxi whose horse was facing westwards.

'I can't let you do that,' I said. Then I called up to the cabbie, 'This man is wanted by the police, you can't take his fare!'

The cabbie looked down and sneered very convincingly. 'Going back to his wife, is he, miss? Shouldn't have believed him, should you?'

'Park End Street station,' Waddesworth said as he climbed in.

The cabbie called 'Hup now' to his horse and the cab began to move off. But if Waddesworth thought he was getting away that easily, he had another think coming. I lifted my skirts, grabbed the side of the cab and hopped up next to him.

'What the devil—'

'Don't worry, Mr Waddesworth,' I said as the cabbie manoeuvred across the road, 'I won't inconvenience you for long.'

'I won't stand for this,' he blustered. But the horse was trotting by now so if Waddesworth had any idea of jumping down, he thought better of it.

We'd gone about three hundred yards up the High Street when the horse slowed and stopped. The cab lurched slightly as the driver jumped down.

'Cabbie? Where are you going?' Waddesworth demanded.

But the man didn't reply, and as he disappeared down the little lane to the police station's door, Mr Junior Proctor realised what was happening. He reached down for his bag but before he could move another muscle, I whipped my hand out of my pocket and leaned across him. 'I wouldn't, if I were you,' I said. 'This is extremely sharp.'

I gave him half a second's glance at my sailor's knife, then held it to his throat where he could feel its sting. 'If you move, your momentum could cause a nasty accident.'

Could he feel my hand shaking? If he could, so much the better.

With luck, the cabbie would be out with a constable or two inside a minute. But that depended on him getting my note to the inspector immediately.

And Waddesworth wasn't going to wait.

With a nerve I hadn't expected, he grabbed my arm and wrenched it away. But as he tried to swing himself down out of the hansom, I brought my knife hand around. An absolute fury towards him and all the men who thought women were there for the taking ran flaming through me and I stabbed him deep in the thigh.

He yelled in pain, and I wrenched the blade back, shearing at the muscle as I pulled it out. He thrashed his arm back against me, catching me on my shoulder and chest, but my blood was up and I didn't feel any pain. And I still had the knife. Before he could move again, I bent down and slashed at his right bootlaces. He'd have a job running with one of his boots falling off and his thigh muscle sliced open.

Waddesworth half fell out of the cab and started stumbling up the High Street, dragging his right leg.

I clicked the blade back into the handle and jumped down out of the cab. I don't know where he thought he was going. He couldn't exactly hide the fact that his trousers had been slashed and that he was bleeding profusely. Soon, somebody'd be bound to fetch the beat bobby from Carfax.

But the bobby wasn't needed. Waddesworth hadn't even got as far as the end of the High Street before two constables came running up behind me.

'There!' I shouted, pointing.

Lincoln Waddesworth's flight was over.

*Part 4*

## Chapter 78

*Non*

A week after Waddesworth's arrest, I went to Miss Skene's house to escort her and Sarah Critchley to Balliol for a meeting with Benjamin Jowett.

Jane showed me into the little front room where Sarah and Miss Skene were sitting at the table under the window. Before they could greet me, the parrot ruffled his feathers and flapped his huge wings. 'Good morning!' he screeched. 'Good morning!'

Sarah laughed, which I was glad to see. I hadn't seen her since the night Cat Hammond and Frank Dodds had rescued her from Sewy's Lane, and even though Miss Skene had arranged everything, I'd been worried that Sarah wouldn't want to go through with meeting the Vice Chancellor. I should have known better. Sarah Critchley was a young woman with a lot of backbone.

Still, what had happened to her would mark her for the rest of her life, and I'd always feel my share of the guilt for that. But together, we were going to make sure the University paid for the Hunters' crimes.

I watched her take an apple quarter from the table between her and Miss Skene and get up to offer it to Iain.

The parrot leaned forward and took the apple delicately in his beak before transferring it to a claw and biting chunks out of it.

Sarah watched him eating. Then, without turning her head, she said, 'There's going to be no more nonsense about Frank Dodds killing Gordon – I mean Charles Gainsborough – is there?'

I shook my head. 'No. They've got all the evidence a jury'll need to convict Lincoln Waddesworth.'

'Good. Because I wouldn't be here if it wasn't for Frank. He'd come to watch me home safely from Hyde's that day and when I didn't come out with the others, he went to look for me.'

And because he'd been one of the men watching the Hunters for Cat Hammond, he'd known exactly where to look.

'I imagine the Vice Chancellor was deeply shocked when he heard that the Junior Proctor had been arrested for murder,' Miss Skene observed, neatly steering Sarah away from what had happened to her in Sewy's Lane.

'Very much so,' I said. 'And even more at his cold-blooded planning of the whole thing.'

Lincoln Waddesworth had refused to cooperate after being arrested. He'd stayed stubbornly silent throughout his time in the police cells, presumably hoping that the police didn't have enough evidence to convince the magistrates. But that hope had proved false, and he was now in Oxford jail awaiting the decision of a grand jury as to whether or not he should be committed to trial for murder.

Grand juries didn't have the best reputation when it came to sending the upper classes to trial, but in this case, Inspector Newman was hopeful. He'd established what he thought was a likely sequence of events which began with Waddesworth luring Gainsborough to a meeting in the Sewy's Lane rooms before killing him there and stealing his key to the place. Prior to the murder, he must have stolen a handcart from somewhere and left it outside the Venatores' den. Nobody would have thought twice about seeing a handcart in a place like that.

Then, just before sunrise, dressed in the workmen's clothes Basil had found in the wardrobe, if Newman was right, Waddesworth had loaded Gainsborough's body onto the handcart and taken it up to Trinity where he'd parked it in front of the workshop. The cabbie'd watched him going through the pretence of knocking on the workshop door when he'd known perfectly well that there'd be nobody there. Then, after getting no answer, Waddesworth had walked off, cool as you like, back to Sewy's Lane to change into his normal clothes.

He'd taken a huge risk in leaving Gainsborough's body outside Trinity, but he must have thought it was the only way he could implicate whoever was behind the hoodings. And, if he hadn't tried to incriminate John Montague with the needle and cotton he'd used to make Gainsborough's hood, he might just have got away with it. But once he'd seen the conclusion Kaye and Basil had jumped to when they saw the needle and embroidery silk in Montague's writing box, the temptation to give them what they were looking for had proved too much for him. After going through the motions of searching Vennell's set at Queen's, he must have nipped back to his own rooms to retrieve the needle and thread.

Sarah Critchley picked up another apple quarter and gave it to the parrot. 'Are you sure the Vice Chancellor is going to offer me money, Miss Vaughan?' she said, eyes on the bird. I knew why she wasn't looking at me. She didn't want me to see her face if I disappointed her.

'Yes. Quite a lot of money, in fact.'

'He's told you that?'

'He's told Mr Rice, which is better than telling me.'

'Good, because I've got plans. With Cat Hammond.'

I sat down in the third chair under the window. 'Oh yes?'

'Me and Cat—' she glanced at Miss Skene and grinned, '*Cat and I* are going to start a training school for servants. Girls. They won't have to pay. The people who employ them will pay us. We'll be an *employment agency* – that's right, isn't it, Miss Skene?'

Felicia Skene smiled that youthful smile of hers. 'A training establishment for domestic servants is very much needed in Oxford. I'm forever hearing that a decent maid can't be found for love nor money. And it's only right that some good should come of the terrible things that have happened to you, my dear.'

So, Cat Hammond was moving on from husband-training and writing false references to something more respectable. She was good at turning disasters into opportunities.

Iain spat out some sucked-dry apple pulp and squawked, 'Blackberries and apples.'

'You haven't finished that yet,' Miss Skene scolded, 'you're a greedy bird.'

But Sarah gave him another piece then sat down again opposite Miss Skene. In the small room, their knees almost touched. 'And they're all gone, now?' she asked.

'The Hunters?' I nodded. 'Yes. Gone in disgrace. Though not half as much disgrace as if you'd pressed charges.'

Sarah looked down at the hands clasped in her lap and said nothing. We both knew there would've been no point in her accusing them. Not with the reputation the Vice Chancellor's court had given her.

'Reverend Jowett was talking about offering you compensation even before what happened at Sewy's Lane,' I told her. 'All this has forced him to see the truth – that it's not the undergraduates that need protecting from young women, it's the other way round.'

'Is he going to do away with the court, then? And the cells under the Clarendon Building?'

'I'm not sure that's his decision to make,' I said. 'But I don't suppose either the court or the cells are going to see much use in future. Not for young women, at any rate.'

I hoped to play a part in that. I'd written the articles Stead had commissioned on the Hunters and their vicious campaign, and the first in the series was due to go to press in two days' time.

'How did Miss Shaw Lefevre take your resignation from your post at Somerville?' Miss Skene asked.

I smiled. 'She was very gracious about it. Said she hoped that when the circumstances for women in the University were more favourable, that I might reconsider.'

'And might you?'

'Who knows what the future holds, Miss Skene? Apart from the next five minutes.' I stood up. 'That holds our departure for Balliol if we don't want to be late.'

# Chapter 79

### Basil

The Vice Chancellor had asked that both the Senior Proctor and I be present when he spoke to Miss Critchley. I had no idea whether he'd invited me as an acknowledgement of the part I had played in discovering Waddesworth's crimes, or because he fondly imagined that I might have some influence with Non, but whatever the reason, I was glad to attend. Jowett had been deeply affected by the discovery of Waddesworth's crimes and required the support of those who knew and sympathised with him.

When I arrived at Balliol at the appointed time, however, I found not only Kaye in attendance but Martin Alexis, whom I had expected to arrive with Miss Critchley's party.

I hoped that if either Jowett or the Senior Proctor noticed my reaction to seeing him, they put it down to astonishment at being confronted with the lawyer who had, potentially, been preparing to go into battle against the University.

Alexis put out his hand. 'Good to see you again, Rice.'

Again, I was held in that intense gaze, my hand embraced by the warmth and strength of his. 'I was expecting you to escort the ladies,' I said, aiming for a sardonic grin. In which effort, I fear, I failed lamentably.

He looked slightly discomfited. 'Ah, yes, well... Reverend Jowett asked me to meet with him last week to discuss this whole affair,' he said. 'As a Balliol man, I couldn't refuse.'

'Alexis has been most helpful,' the Vice Chancellor piped up. 'Particularly in terms of the University's insistence on certain conditions to our offer.'

'I think,' Alexis smiled, 'if those terms are agreed upon, you should, as we discussed, err on the side of generosity. There is nothing like the prospect of a comfortable life to nullify the desire for retribution.'

Spoken like a lawyer. What, I wondered, would Alexis himself forgo to ensure a comfortable life?

As we waited for Miss Critchley and her entourage, I watched the barrister chatting convivially with Kaye and Jowett. He seemed entirely at ease, and I wondered about his background.

During a brief lull in the conversation I asked, 'Was being a barrister always on the cards for you, Mr Alexis? A family profession, perhaps?'

He put back his dark head and laughed in genuine amusement. 'My father would kiss you on both cheeks if he heard you say that! He's a Greek barber,' he grinned. 'He fled to this country from Crete after one of their periodic uprisings against the Ottomans.'

'Mr Alexis gained an open scholarship,' Jowett informed me with all the pride of a surrogate parent. 'Which, fourteen or fifteen years ago, was no mean feat for a grammar school boy.'

Alexis was both clever and ambitious, then. I might have said the same of Teddy, though he hadn't had to work his way up from a grammar school.

'Please, Master,' Alexis said, using the title by which he would have known Jowett during his time at Balliol, 'that was all a long time ago. At my age, I can't continue to trade on my luck as a youth. Besides, we have something to discuss before the ladies arrive.'

I looked at him quizzically, but though he briefly acknowledged my gaze, his attention was focused on Jowett, waiting for his response.

'Yes,' the Vice Chancellor said, somewhat reluctantly, 'Miss Vaughan.'

'What about her?' I asked when he seemed at a loss as to how to proceed.

'I had lunch with some of the members of the AEW board yesterday,' he said. 'And they informed me that Miss Vaughan has resigned both her AEW lectureship and her tutorial role at Somerville. It seems she told Mrs Johnson that she found herself obliged to follow a course of action the University would deplore, and that she wished to avoid causing any embarrassment to the AEW.' The Vice Chancellor fixed his mild gaze on me. 'Do you know what that course of action is, Rice?'

I drew in a cautious breath. 'Miss Vaughan doesn't make me privy to all her activities, Vice Chancellor.'

Jowett was no fool. He knew I'd swerved his question. Nevertheless, he wasn't obliged to pursue the point as Alexis took it up.

'You may not know, Rice, but I believe I may.' He turned to Jowett. 'I gather that Miss Vaughan has begun writing articles for the *Pall Mall Gazette*, and I assume that it was she who wrote the recent, highly colourful account of the inquest into Charles Gainsborough's death. If so, then I believe she may intend to write something similar on the activities of the Venatores.'

I stared at him. Non had told me, after Waddesworth's arrest, that she'd resigned her teaching posts, and I'd assumed that the article on Gainsborough's inquest had been the reason.

Alexis sighed. 'That being the case,' he said, 'we must prevent Miss Vaughan from making an Aunt Sally of the University for every liberal progressive in the country to throw his missiles at.'

## Chapter 80

*Non*

When Miss Skene, Sarah and I were shown into the Vice Chancellor's drawing room, Basil was looking decidedly shifty.

No, that's not fair. Not shifty. Uncomfortable. Something was going on. And what was the barrister, Martin Alexis, doing there?

The pleasantries took a while, and so did the apologies from Jowett and the Senior Proctor to Sarah, who responded with a lot more grace than they had any right to expect. Then, after refreshments had been distributed, Jowett got down to business.

'Miss Critchley, the University, as represented by the Hebdomadal Council, wishes to make you an offer of compensation for the ordeals to which you have been subjected. Though the University was, as I hope you realise, completely unaware of the activities of this group of vicious young men, nevertheless we accept that their conduct fell far short of what we would expect.'

'Not just the undergraduates,' Sarah corrected. 'The proctors too. Or the Junior Proctor, at any rate.'

Benjamin Jowett looked like a man who's been trying to pretend that he hasn't got dog turd on his shoes and has just had it pointed out to him by his hostess. 'Indeed,' he said. 'Yes. Indeed. A circumstance for which I cannot adequately express my horror.'

'It's for that reason,' Kaye took up the reins, 'that we would like to offer you an *ex gratia* sum of a thousand pounds.'

In truth, a thousand was more than we'd thought they'd offer. But it was still less than Sarah needed.

'That's very gracious of you, Vice Chancellor,' I said, 'but I'm afraid that a thousand pounds is insufficient.'

Jowett stared at me. He couldn't believe that somebody like Sarah wasn't biting his hand off at the elbow. A thousand pounds represented more than ten times what she and her mother, together, could earn in a year. But her plans with Cat Hammond would need considerable investment.

'Miss Critchley wasn't subjected to some petty inconvenience, the consequences of which she can shrug off and continue her life as before,' I pointed out. 'The combined effects of her imprisonment and the appalling attack on her by your undergraduates have destroyed her reputation and materially altered the entire course of her life. If we were simply dealing with her false imprisonment, then a thousand pounds might be reasonable, but considering the other injuries done to her, we feel that *two* thousand pounds is the least you might offer.'

'I must confess,' Kaye said, looking to the other men for support, 'I hadn't anticipated haggling.'

'And Miss Critchley hadn't anticipated being arrested and imprisoned for committing no crime,' I told him. 'Nor being taken from the streets and used more vilely than I can express.' I glared at him, and he looked away. 'This isn't *haggling*, gentlemen, this is a polite request for the justice Miss Critchley has been denied by the certain knowledge that the courts would side with her abusers. We expect better from the University.'

I glanced at Sarah, who was sitting next to me. She was trembling.

Miss Skene spoke into the uncomfortable silence. 'It might be of interest to you, Vice Chancellor, that Miss Critchley intends to use this sum for the good of others as well as her own future well-being and that of her widowed mother. With my help, she intends to establish a training school for young women to fit them for domestic service.'

Jowett blinked. 'I see. That's extremely laudable, Miss Critchley. And, if I may say so, it shows a very Christian spirit.'

'Miss Critchley is a faithful worshipper at St Paul's,' Miss Skene said. And if the Vice Chancellor felt that as a gentle rebuke, then so he should. He was still judging Sarah as if she was a common streetwalker and her incarceration had been justified.

'In that case,' he said, 'the University will accede to your request.'

I turned to Sarah. 'Is that acceptable to you, Sarah? I know we've talked about it, but this is the time to decide.'

'What would I have to do for the money?' Sarah asked. 'You're not just going to give me two thousand pounds and let me walk away, are you?'

Before we'd left New Inn Hall Street East, Miss Skene had advised Sarah that the University might want to specify conditions.

'In fact, our offer comes with very few caveats,' Jowett said.

But very few wasn't none. 'Perhaps you'd be good enough to outline them?' I suggested.

Jowett cleared his throat but proceeded to say nothing and the Senior Proctor stepped in. 'Miss Critchley would be asked to agree not to disclose the making of this *ex gratia* payment. It must remain between you and the University.'

'And, furthermore,' Mr Alexis added, with a glance at Basil that told me there'd been an argument about this, 'everybody connected to you, Miss Critchley, including your family, friends and persons in this room, must agree neither to disclose nor discuss the events which resulted in this payment.'

Straight away I saw where that was directed. The 'persons in this room' meant me, and not disclosing or discussing those events meant that Stead wouldn't be able to publish my articles about the Hunters.

'Now wait a minute—' I began.

'I beg your pardon, Miss Vaughan, just one moment,' Jowett said. He turned away from me and directed his benevolent great-uncle attention back to Sarah. 'I'm afraid there can be nothing in the newspapers, Miss Critchley, however discreet,' he said, sounding firm and, at the same time, sympathetic. 'If the University is to make such an unprecedented payment, it must be on the understanding that neither the payment, nor the wrong committed, would be publicly discussed.'

Damn them. They were silencing me as efficiently as if they'd bound, gagged and hooded me.

Sarah's expression was pleading with me to tell her what to do. I'd promised her that she'd have her revenge, even if it was in the newspapers rather than in court. But I'd also seen how her spine straightened when spoke about the plans she and Cat Hammond had.

I looked Jowett in the eye. 'Very well,' I said. 'If Sarah agrees to your terms, then so be it.'

# *Epilogue*

### *Non*

'Stead wasn't surprised, then?' Tarley asked after I'd repeated my conversation with the *Pall Mall Gazette*'s editor pretty well word for word.

'No. He said he'd half expected something like that from the University,' I said as I watched London slipping by outside the carriage window. 'And, much as he'd have liked to print the articles on the Hunters, he couldn't run them at Sarah's expense.'

'So are you still going to be writing for him?'

'If I can find stories good enough, yes. And Oxford being Oxford, that shouldn't be too hard.'

I could still feel Stead's piercing blue eyes on me as he said, '*There are stories there, Miss Vaughan – you know it and I know it. Stories that do not show the University or the men who presume to run it in a favourable light. Sniff them out! The whole place is a microcosm of the establishment – it needs root and branch reform!*'

'But,' I admitted, 'I don't know how much time I'm going to have to write for Stead.'

Tarley frowned. 'What do you mean? Has somebody else asked you to write for them?'

I turned to look at him. There was only one other person in our carriage, and he was fast asleep, his newspaper on his lap. 'Actually, it looks as if I'm going to be able start my own paper.'

He gaped at me. And well he might. 'Non! Why didn't you tell me this before? You let me prattle on all the way down to London and you never said a word!'

'It's just the germ of an idea at the moment,' I said.

'But who's come up with the money?'

I grinned. 'Sarah Critchley.'

The idea had come from Miss Skene. 'Miss Critchley and her friend will do very nicely with a thousand pounds,' she'd said. 'It will enable them to buy premises instead of rent, which gives them security, and to equip the training establishment. Once that's done, it can support itself, leaving Sarah with money to invest. So I suggest that you begin looking for other journalists. And meanwhile,' she'd said with that sparkling smile of hers, 'I have one or two men of influence, including Martin Alexis, who are also interested in supporting your venture.'

I wasn't sure about men of influence supporting me. I had a nasty feeling they'd try to use their influence to manipulate me. But when I told Tarley that, he thought I was being unfair.

'Look at the AEW board – men and women working together. Not all men are to be mistrusted, Non.'

He looked at me with those deep-brown eyes of his.

'No,' I said, 'fair enough.'

He carried on looking at me. 'If you're going to be the editor of a newspaper,' he said, 'then I think we should get married.'

You hear of people's mouths falling open in surprise, but I'd never felt it happen to me before. He couldn't have surprised me more if he'd said he thought we should go to the moon. 'What?' I croaked.

'Sorry, that wasn't a very romantic proposal. But then I'm not sure you'd thank me for one of those.' I didn't reply so he carried on. 'I know you don't want to get married. I know you think it's unequal and risky and all those things you said in your article. But think about it, Non. If you're going to run a newspaper, you'll need to be seen as respectable, stable, not as a law unto yourself, which is how your critics see you now. There's no point protesting,' he said when I drew breath to object. 'You know that's how other people – *some* other people – see you. If you have a husband, people will take you more seriously.' I started to argue, but he shook his head. 'I know it's not fair, but it's how the world is. You can't fight everybody, all the time, Non. If you want to be taken seriously, you have to play by at least some of society's rules. And this one might not be such a bad one to pick.'

He looked at me. I didn't know what to say.

'If you're really worried that, with my fearsome legal powers as a husband, I'll pack you off to a mental asylum,' he said, 'then we can *say* we're married, live together as man and wife, but not actually go through with the ceremony, so you'd still legally be your own woman.'

He looked at me. Didn't touch me or try to influence me in any way.

'So what do you think?'

# Historical Note

### Organisations

In the late nineteenth century, the medieval Vice Chancellor's court (abolished for all but university disciplinary offences in 1977) still sat in judgement on Oxford citizens who had offended against members of the University. As shown in the novel, the hearings were held 'in camera', evidence was not given on oath, and the defendant was not represented by a lawyer.

Sarah Critchley's prospective lawsuit against the University was inspired by events in 1892, when 17-year old Daisy Hopkins sued a Cambridge pro-proctor for false imprisonment. Daisy, like Sarah, had been drawn into conversation by an undergraduate, seized by the pro-proctor and, after a freezing night in the cells, summarily committed to jail.

However, unlike most girls, she wasn't taking that lying down. Her family sought legal advice, a writ of habeas corpus was granted by the Lord Chief Justice's court less than a week after her arrest and she was released from prison, her barrister having argued that 'the girl had been committed to gaol for an offence unknown to any law' to whit 'walking with an undergraduate'.

Daisy subsequently instructed her solicitor to start an action against the arresting officer, claiming damages of £1000. The case was eventually heard at Ipswich before a packed crowd. The presiding judge found against Daisy, having been persuaded by extremely prejudicial evidence, and stated that, 'If damages were to be given in this case, the control of the University at present would be swept away and Cambridge would be inundated by prostitutes, whom this very knowledge of it kept from the town, and immorality would spring up.'

The Venatores, however, are entirely my own invention, though events in 2020 at Durham University suggest that the impulse of upper-class young men to seduce working-class girls competitively has not died out. [See Josh Halliday's article in the *Guardian* on Wednesday 23 September 2020.]

The Church of England Purity Association was a real organisation, and the crusade against undergraduates fraternising with town girls actually took place, led by proctors Holland and Smith between 1882 and 1883, in the wake of the Christian mission in the city by American evangelists Dwight L. Moody and Ira D. Sankey. 'Moral Intentions' on the other hand, is my own invention, based on the fact that, as Basil states in the book, the term 'immoral intentions' was the code used by the proctors to indicate an undergraduate's intention to seduce a town girl or seek out a prostitute for sex.

### People

To misquote Voltaire's line about God, if Felicia Skene hadn't existed, I would have had to invent her. Miss Skene is someone who deserves to be far better known and I've tried to do my bit to spread her fame in *The Hunters Club*. To the best of my ability, I've represented her as her friend and biographer, Edith Rickards, drew her in *Felicia Skene of Oxford* which, if a tad hagiographic, paints a picture of a remarkable woman.

In the novel, I've given Miss Skene a particular stance on homosexuality which might be slightly surprising to readers given her obvious piety. However, this is based on Felicia Skene's long friendship with Frances Power Cobbe, the writer, philosopher and social reformer who lived with her partner, the Welsh sculptor Mary Lloyd, for almost forty years until Lloyd's death in 1896.

As in previous books, Benjamin Jowett was the real life Master of Balliol and Vice Chancellor of the University from 1882.

Rev William Inge was, as in the book, the Provost of Worcester from 1881 until his death in 1903. However, without endless time spent in archives which I decided would be better spent actually writing the novel, I was unable to find out the name of the Dean of Trinity in 1883, so I simply named him Sterne.

The names of the proctors for the academic year 1883–4 would have been easier to find but as these men were to be main characters I didn't want to misrepresent them (particularly the egregious Waddesworth, obviously), so Kaye and Waddesworth are entirely fictional characters.

## Places

The street in which Felicia Skene's house stands, proudly sporting its blue plaque, is now called St Michael's Street but until 1899 it was known, as in the book, as New Inn Hall Street East.

In 1883, the main entrance to New College was not on Holywell Street, as it is today, because that frontage was still in the throes of construction, but was via the original entrance on New College Lane.

As indicated in the novel, the alleyway now known as St Helen's Passage had previously been known as Hell's Passage – or, in a 1772 survey, simply 'Hell'!

The Turf Tavern is one of Oxford's hidden gems and is ensconced in the middle of what was once 'Hell'. A rambling building, it's now the haunt of tourists and undergraduates but in 1883, as indicated in the novel, it was very much the resort of college servants.

Sewy's Lane, the thoroughfare's name for centuries, has now been converted to the more picturesque sounding 'Shoe Lane'. At the time of the novel, it ran from New Inn Hall Street, via the Clarendon Hotel complex, to Cornmarket Street, but is now a non-thoroughfare. The earlier name is thought to be that of a thirteenth-century mayor of Oxford, Thomas de Sowy.

St Peter-in-the-East church, where Laurence Herbert claimed to have been taken when he was bagged, was then a parish church but is now St Edmund Hall's library. I've played a bit fast and loose with gates and entrances here, as Basil needs to be able to see into the churchyard from Queen's Lane. However, there is an obviously blocked archway in the wall so I'm assuming that was originally an entrance to the church. I beg historians of Oxford to forgive me if I'm wrong!

Basil refers to 'Catherine Street' which was the name given, at that point, to what is now Catte Street. Running from the High Street to Broad Street, it was originally called 'Cat Street', but the council renamed it in the nineteenth century (temporarily, as it turned out) to sound less medieval.

## Other Notes

In the narrative, Non uses the phrase 'in his oils' to illustrate just how pleased William Stead is going to be. It's a phrase my Welsh mother used to use and, when I investigated, I found the expression listed and explained in the *Talk Tidy* glossary by John Edwards. The original Welsh expression is 'Yn ei hwyliau' which, via English mutations like 'in his hwyls' ('happily in his element' or 'in high spirits') became 'in his oils'.

The curfew bell still rings out from Christ Church College every evening during term time at five past nine, Oxford 'sun time' in the days before standardised 'railway time' across the whole of the UK. Nowadays – if it's noticed at all – the curfew bell is seen as a quaint anachronism by undergraduates rather than the signal to scurry back to college lest they be 'gated'.

## *Acknowledgements*

Novels are a marathon not a sprint and marathon runners depend on support to get them through. Nobody could have a better support than my partner, Edwina. Without her there would be no books. Full stop. Thank you, my love, for making all this possible, in so many ways.

My books and I also get great support from my publisher, Canelo, who really believe in Non and Basil's adventures and have worked with me in so many ways. Thanks to my commissioning editor, Craig Lye for being a steadfast support; to my development editor – himself a great writer – Russel D McLean, for always getting what I'm trying to do and helping me do it; to the eagle-eyed Jenny Page, who copyedited *The Hunters Club* and spotted some of my besetting sins; and to all the sales and marketing team for their enthusiasm and support.

Thanks also, for support and encouragement about this book and all my writing, to my agent, Francesca Riccardi at the Kate Nash Literary Agency. I'm looking forward to all that's yet to come, Fran!

I know it's axiomatic that you shouldn't judge a book by its cover but we all know we do. I love the look Sarah Whittaker has designed for the Oxford Mysteries series and this cover is absolutely brilliant.

I have so many friends who are supportive of my work. All the members of the Border Belles who cheerlead for me and spread the word; and my stalwart fellow writers in the MNW group and Welsh crime writers' cooperative, Crime Cymru – thank you all, so much. Particular thanks go to Chris Lloyd, my partner in historical crime and fellow-panellist at so many events – thank you for being such a great 'in conversation' partner, Chris; and to Gail Williams for being on the end of the phone and checking in when I've gone a bit quiet. And huge thanks to Alison Stuttart for all the emotional and practical support you've provided in this last year. You're amazing.

Writers are nothing and nobody without those who bring our books to readers – bookshop owners, librarians and festival organisers. It's an absolute joy to work with so many dedicated book professionals and I look forward to working with you all again in publicising *The Hunters Club*. Particular thanks are due to Jools Golden at Maesteg Library and Rebecca Hollebron at Gloucester Library for their infectious enthusiasm for my books and warm-hearted welcome; and to Emma Corfield-Walters at UK Bookshop of the Year, Book-ish in Crickhowell, for not only supporting my own books but for allowing me the opportunity to interview some of my favourite and most-admired writers – I've learned so much every time.

Finally, thank to those without whom my books would never see the light of day – you, my readers. Thank you for buying my books, for borrowing my books from libraries, for listening to them on audio and for reviewing, recommending and writing to me about them. Every time I hear from somebody who has read one of my novels, either via email, on social media or at an in-person event, it means so much to me and reminds me why I do what I do. Thank you for all your support and encouragement and for loving Non and Basil. I look forward to hearing what you think about *The Hunters Club*.

Do you love crime fiction and are always on the lookout for brilliant authors?

Canelo Crime is home to some of the most exciting novels around. Thousands of readers are already enjoying our compulsive stories. Are you ready to find your new favourite writer?

Find out more and sign up to our newsletter at canelocrime.com